ROAD KILL

ROAD KILL

Hanna Jameson

HEAD of ZEUS

Typeset by Adrian McLaughlin

Printed and bound in Great Britain by
CPI Group (UK) Ltd, Croydon CR0 4YY

Head of Zeus Ltd
Clerkenwell House
45–47 Clerkenwell Green
London EC1R 0HT

WWW.HEADOFZEUS.COM

For C & C, S, and Marianne

'Faith, one was told, could move mountains,
and here was faith – faith in the spittle that healed
the blind man and the voice that raised the dead.
The evening star was out: it hung low down over
the edge of the plateau: it looked as if it was
within reach: and a small hot wind stirred. The
priest found himself watching the child for some
movement. When none came, it was as if God had
missed an opportunity. The woman sat down, and
taking a lump of sugar from her bundle began
to eat, and the child lay quietly at the foot of the
cross. Why, after all, should we expect God to
punish the innocent with more life?'

—GRAHAM GREENE, *The Power And The Glory*

PROLOGUE

Daisy

If I'd felt the ripples of the implosion to come the following morning, I'd have got so much more hammered that night.

'Does that even work?' I asked, as Noel wrapped his MDMA in a Rizla and washed it down with a gulp of vodka and coke.

It was his last vodka and coke before AA in the morning. He'd insisted on a last hurrah, a final big one, the ultimate in apocalyptic benders before a new life of attempted sobriety. Noel celebrated anything if it meant an excuse to get trashed, even the end of his own alcoholism.

Attempted sobriety.

I put a lot of emphasis on that word. Attempted. According to Ronnie, Noel had tried to do this at least three times before. He was being quietly pessimistic about the endeavour, but had still come out to get wasted.

It wasn't a particularly special night. I only remembered this one because it was the last time any of us were actually happy together. It was an illusion of calm, of harmony, before everything started to go so spectacularly to shit.

It was an illusion of calm, of harmony, after *she* had left.

'It gets into your bloodstream faster,' Noel said, sitting on the toilet lid and holding open the sachet.

I licked my finger, took a load of white powder onto it and sucked it off. I sipped my Southern Comfort and lemonade but the acidic tang remained stuck to my tongue and the roof of my mouth.

'I don't think so, not through the paper. It's not gonna be faster than just eating it.' I sucked at my finger again.

'Well, you can do more this way.'

'How about I'll do it my way and you do it yours? The *wrong* way. Yours is the wrong way, by the way.'

Everything was moving as we sat chatting in the Ladies, as if we were on a train. Music pounded through the walls. Outside there was a queue but neither of us gave a shit.

I guessed we had about twenty minutes before we starting buzzing off our tits, for the second time that night in my case. I'd taken some before coming out.

Noel put the sachet back in his wallet.

'Are you nervous about tomorrow?' I asked, leaning against the side of the cubicle and stretching my bare legs across the space. I was careful not to lean on my left arm. It still hurt sometimes and even when it didn't I slung it across me like it was deadweight, not part of me, out of habit.

'I've done it all before, haven't I?' He smiled. 'I'm a pro.'

'Yeah, but like... if you've done all this before, don't you just tell the same stories over and over again?'

'Every alcoholic has the same stories. We're all so fucking boring, Daisy, and we all go on as if our alcoholism is special.' He sniffed, half-heartedly looking for tobacco. 'Also, everyone in the world is an alcoholic, right, so everyone has the same story. Why are you an alcoholic, eh?'

I blinked a couple of times, hard. 'I'm not.'

'Yeah, you are. You're drunk all the fucking time. You're drunk at work! We don't give a shit, but admit it.' He raised his eyebrows at me. 'And even when you're not drunk, you're high.'

It bothered me. I was unsure why.

'You're just drunk,' I retorted.

'*You're* drunk.'

I shrugged.

'I mean, look out there.' He gestured at the cubicle door, presumably at the flailing contents of the eighties night happening outside our paradise of drug-taking calm. 'Look at those animals. All anyone does is drink. It's because life is so fucking empty, you know.'

'Jesus, give it a rest. I can't wait for your Mandy to kick in.'

'But it's true! God, just shut up for a moment, will you?'

'Fuck you,' I snapped, but waited for him to speak again.

'We're all alcoholics, love.'

Why, Captain Mansplain?'

I got tired of standing and swiped his hand off his knees to sit across his lap.

'Because that's how we all kill ourselves. I mean, think about it. Nature has created us, right, this super species that's so fucking hell-bent on progress we're gonna fuck up the planet. We're like a virus. This is how nature makes sure we all get wiped out, after a while.'

'Oi!' Someone knocked and said, 'Some of us are waiting for a piss out here!'

'Oh, piss me a river!' I shouted back, banging my fist against the door.

'So,' Noel continued, unfazed, 'that's what this all is. Nothing can kill us any more. So nature's insurance is to hardwire us to kill ourselves. We all drink, we take drugs, people who aren't taking drugs are eating shit food, we're pumping chemicals into everything, we fuck up our hearts, our stomachs, our livers, we kill each other, we hold poor people down by the necks and arse-fuck them into dying en masse because they haven't got money to fucking eat, we gas each other, we blow each other up, we fire tonnes, fucking *tonnes*, of radioactive shit into the atmosphere, into the sea, we throw all our rubbish into landfills, we're drilling into the *actual* planet looking for oil to power things we can't sustain, we're *fracking* and all that shit, we're bringing tsunamis and earthquakes, hurricanes and drought and... stuff... all on ourselves. We all want to die so fucking badly it's almost funny, right?'

I'd put my drink on the floor and started rolling myself a cigarette midway through his rant, but I stopped. 'Hilarious.'

'Yeah.' He shook his head, took another gulp of vodka and coke and looked at it. 'Actually, I think I'll have one more of these. I know it's technically past midnight, but it's not tomorrow until you go to sleep really.'

There was a commotion outside, sounds of women complaining, and then Ronnie's booming voice. 'Hey! Noel, *you cunt*, where are you?'

'We're in here!' I yelled, resuming rolling my cigarette.

'You aren't shagging, are you?'

'No! God, we're just doing Mandy, chill out.'

'Well, come out, you wankers! They're playing fucking *Toto*!'

'Man, you're all so old,' I muttered, sniggering.

Ronnie was told to fuck off out of the toilets by at least three women and I assumed he did as he was told because we didn't hear any more from him. I wobbled on Noel's lap and knocked tobacco onto the floor. There was a black smudge on my thigh, probably from where I'd leant against the wall in the smoking area. I licked my finger again, which still tasted of the Mandy, and rubbed it.

'Fuck.' It seemed too soon, but I was sure I could feel my jaw starting to lock. It was probably because of the hit I'd taken before going out, drug upon drug hitting my system. 'I need another drink, I'm gonna come up in a minute and I want to be dancing to something.'

'I am so ready.' He downed the rest of his drink and put the glass down to clap his hands.

'Did you text Mark?'

'Yeah, he said he's gonna come later. Ron's so out of it he won't care.'

'So... wait a second.' It was hard to coordinate my thoughts. 'If everyone's killing each other and you feel so bad about it, why are you selling everyone drugs? Why aren't you off in... Ethiopia building a school with a load of gap year students?'

Noel shrugged. 'Got to make a living?'

I got off his lap and unlocked the door.

'Also, you're wrong,' Noel said from behind me. 'I don't actually feel that bad about it.'

When I woke up the next morning the gunshot wound, the horrible disfiguring scar fucking up my shoulder, was stiff and inflamed.

I moved out of my boyfriend's flat within a week. *Ex*-boyfriend, as he had come to be known within days.

Ronnie flew to Philadelphia with a hangover, to meet his little brother out of prison.

I had this funny feeling that he wouldn't come back.

In a way, he didn't.

Noel did make it to AA in the morning, I noted. But it was the last time he made it for a while.

CHAPTER ONE

Ronnie

'James Madison? Who the fuck would wanna go on a bender with Madison?' I finished my second whisky of the night, chuckling. 'He was a weird little nerd.'

'He was the only president who fought a war without curtailing the civil liberties of the American people,' Carey said, bleary-eyed but coherent.

Fucking lawyers. They were built to argue, even when they were so wasted they could barely lean their elbow upon the bar-top without it slipping off.

Some old nineties rock was playing. I didn't know if there was a jukebox here or whether Eli, behind the bar, was picking the tunes. The Phillies were being thrashed on a muted TV screen to our upper-right but I couldn't tell who they were being thrashed by because I didn't give a shit about baseball.

'Bollocks, he introduced conscription,' I said.

'No, only at the end, but Congress denounced it. It failed.'

'Well, he tried.'

'His entire presidency – hell, his entire ideology – was focused on the avoidance of war.'

'And what's so great about that?' I indicated for Eli, languidly polishing glasses, to bring us another round of drinks, and pushed Carey's further towards him. 'War is necessary sometimes. He was also a slave owner; I'd like to see you try and justify that old chestnut.'

'They were all slave owners, Ronnie.'

I saw him cast his eyes about the joint – looking for any people of colour, no doubt – but we were the only ones left, and had been for a while. The dregs of a quiet Wednesday night, far removed enough from Philadelphia's city centre to find some peace.

'Who would you want to go for a drink with anyway?' Carey asked, eyes sliding down towards his drink and lowering his face to the rim of the glass, having lost the coordination or the willpower to lift it.

'Andrew Jackson.'

'Bull*shit*.'

I spread my hands. 'I like Jackson, he was a nutcase.'

'I mean, Madison was a slave owner but it was Jackson who passed the Indian Removal Act.'

'Should've known you'd be anti-expansionist, you fat bastard.' I reached out and poked him in the kidney, trying to pinch an inch or so of flab. But Carey wasn't fat.

He was sensitive though, and swiped me away with an expression of genuine hurt.

Our next round of drinks arrived. I gave Eli a nod and he moved away. He was a tall and antagonistic-looking man with big eyes, high cheekbones and slicked-back hair that hovered between black and grey. Waistcoats had never been my bag but he carried his off with apathy.

'He used more vetoes in his first term of office than all the previous presidents combined,' I said, realizing I was struggling with my words and returning my new glass of whisky to the bar. 'I like a guy who knows he's boss.'

'He was a douche.'

'He was more of a socialist than your fucking Madison. Peoples' President and all that.'

'I'm not a socialist, I'm a capitalist who gives a shit.'

'Carey,' at that point I grasped his shoulder, 'no. Just no.'

It was almost sad, to be this oblivious. He'd had been my brother's defence lawyer, had known our family for years, and all that time I had despised him. It had taken root as an irrational baseless hate that originates in the head. I hated the way his face was begging to be classic frat-boy attractive but wasn't. The features hung together wrong; lips too thin, eyes too far apart. I also hated that he was blond. I'd never trusted a blond man; not a grown adult.

But the more I'd got to know about Carey recently, the more the hate had sunk right into the soul, hammered into my being with confirmation after confirmation. It was like sinking into a luxurious bath of vindication.

Carey liked me, of course, but his approval wasn't worth a damn. He was a lawyer; he liked everyone who paid him and had the potential to pay him more.

'I suppose you believe in *trickle-down* economics and all that,' I said.

Over my shoulder, I watched Eli shut the venue doors, lock and bolt them. It was just after two in the morning and I didn't want Carey to realize how late it was and make a dash home. It was a school night for him after all.

'Yeah,' he replied, with inexplicable smugness. 'It's not a matter of believing in it. It's a *fact* that it works.'

'You live in one of the most unequal societies in the world and you think it needs more millionaires. Really?'

'The problem here isn't inequality, it's' – another cursory glance around the bar to check that no one could overhear us, and failing to notice there was no one else – 'it's drugs. It's the ghettos.'

'And that's not a product of your fucked-up economics?'

'No, it's a product of social decay. *Moral* decay, Ron.'

Christ, he made me sound liberal. I forgot sometimes that being a Conservative in the UK put you on the far left of the spectrum over here. All the cosmopolitan and affluent American cities, like the one we were in, were full to spewing with arseholes like Carey, whose idea of politics was little more than a masquerade for racism.

'You're talking about blacks?' I said, helpfully.

'*African-American*, geez.' But he shrugged. 'I'm talking about ghettoes. No one's employed, all in social housing or in… slums. That's where the problems are.'

I had to lean back. 'Ghettoes were created by your *war on drugs* in the first place. It was fucking made up by Reagan, when drug use was at an all-time low, to criminalize African-Americans because you lot couldn't hack desegregation.'

Carey's expression melted into distaste. 'I never had you down as a conspiracy theorist.'

'Just saying. Convenient, isn't it? You criminalize a generation of African-Americans through biased stop-and-searches, give them records for smoking half a joint before they're old enough to drink, and then they *can't* work, can they? The whole damn system is against you and there's nothing you can do about it. Apart from sell substandard smack to people who can't afford fucking curtains.'

There was a tense silence. One of Carey's eyes was twitching.

He laughed, when it became too uncomfortable to do anything else, and clapped me on the shoulder a little too hard. Eyeing up the second whisky, he glanced at his watch, and as he did so I glanced at Eli.

Eli had stopped pretending to clean glasses.

'You know, you're funny. You're a funny guy, just like your brother.'

My smile was mirthless. 'Eamonn's not funny, he just loves puns way too much.'

'So the big day is tomorrow?'

'Yep.'

'You must be stoked. It's great, man. It's really great that he's coming home.' He picked up the whisky gallantly and drank some. 'I'm sorry he even had to be away this long. The law, you know... The law. I devoted my life to the thing but it can be a real bitch. If it weren't for that blood spatter, man... I mean, *you* know I think it was planted evidence – in the majority of the CCTV footage he didn't even touch the guy.'

'I know.'

'No, really. You never stop learning about the new and fucked-up ways the opposition can screw you over.'

'No, Carey.' I caught his eyes. 'I *know*.'

That sobered him up. His first look was to Eli, who was leaning against the liquor shelves with his arms folded and a small smile on his face. His second look went to the doors, one of which had been propped open the last time he had checked. His third look was to me.

'Ronnie...' He spread his hands, palms up. 'I don't like what you're trying to say. What are you trying to say?'

'I'm saying that I *know*.'

'You know *what*?'

'I *know* that you swung the case.'

'I swung the... I swung the... What?' Scoffing, desperately. 'You're *insane*.'

'There's always a money trail, you know that, right, Carey? Dad followed it all the way back to Borselle and his *planted* evidence. You're a lawyer, how could you not know that?'

He made to lunge at me but I grabbed him around the neck, finding the collar of his shirt and slamming him backwards over the bar.

Eli was ready to step in if I needed assistance, but I didn't. Carey was soft; built for desks. I was barely breaking a sweat.

'No! No! … No! No!'

'Maybe that's what you should have said before Borselle paid you off, eh? Just. Say. *No*.'

Growling, snarling, '*No! Ron!* … *No!*'

I took a knife out of my pocket – he hadn't bothered searching me on the way in, the amateur – and jabbed it straight into an eye. The tiny jet of blood that erupted almost went into mine. He screamed, but Eli jammed a dishcloth into his mouth.

When the knife was wrenched out I half expected most of Carey's left eyeball to come with it, but it stayed stubbornly in his socket, albeit cloven in half. I went to stab him in the head but the blade broke against his skull and half of it spun away across the bar. Incensed by the failure of my tools, I took hold of Carey's blood-spattered head – which was wailing, emitting primal hacking sounds – by his hair and smashed it into the counter. The skull relented, with a crack, and another crack, like eggshell. His body went limp and an ever-expanding circle of brain stain appeared on the bar-top where what remained of Carey's cranium impacted against it, in a harsh rhythm, until I got a bit of out of breath and stopped and let his body slide to the floor.

I noticed that Eli had refilled my glass, and I picked it up and took a sip.

'Cheers, mate.'

He was smiling a little. 'Cheers.'

I liked Eli. He was calm. Cool as fuck for a situation like this.

I blew cold air onto my forehead and pushed my hair out of my eyes.

The music had stopped.

I sat back down for a moment, appraising Carey's slumped form, and said, 'Hey, Eli, can you put that Kansas track back on? I was really digging that.'

CHAPTER TWO

Eamonn hadn't killed him, though that fact is very much a technicality when you stand there and let your mates stamp someone's skull all over the pavement just because they suspect the lad is gay. The ones with blood on their shoes had gotten life. We'd had over half the jurors on our side and Dad insisted a guilty verdict was unthinkable. But it hadn't been. Turns out, it had been very fucking thinkable. We'd all had fifteen years to think about it, or not think about it.

I waited with Eli in his car, both of us sipping iced beverages through straws. I hadn't wanted to go inside.

'*I'm drinking your milkshake, Eli,*' I said, laughing and slapping the dashboard.

He looked sideways at me, expressionless, lips clamped disapprovingly around the end of the straw, which was emitting a dry fricative hiss as the bubbly remains of his strawberry milkshake chased each other around the bottom of his plastic cup.

I stopped laughing. 'Sorry.'

Sitting here in the car park, I felt like I was doing a school run. But for the high walls and ominous grey, the curious halo of grass around its entrance, it could have been a college or a spa. It almost looked like a church inside, with its domes and towers and turrets, reverting to the role it was always meant for; place of judgement.

The morning's mission was simple; pick up Eamonn, take him home, have dinner with Mum and Dad and then... I wasn't sure.

'You ever think about London, Eli?'

He seemed disappointed with his sudden lack of drink, frowning. 'What, physically? Metaphorically? Philosophically?'

'To *live*, you tart. You ever think about going back?'

A smirk. 'Are you proposing to me?'

'Yes. Let's move in together.'

He shrugged. 'Business is good here. I don't miss it.'

'Ah, yeah, I forgot, you're a businessman.' I winked at him, glancing in the direction of the prison gates but seeing nothing. 'We have a lot of good stuff going on, you know. We could use someone like you. You wouldn't be bored.'

He wasn't giving anything away.

I shrugged. 'Just saying.'

'I thought you were here to look for a Japanese girl?' he asked, just when I'd resigned myself to dropping the subject. 'Are you saying you need my help back home too?'

'Truthfully' – *was I going to answer this truthfully?* – 'yeah, a bit. We've had some problems.'

'Like what?'

'If I tell you, do you wanna promise you'll think about coming over?'

He gave me a tight-lipped smile. I took that as a maybe. To my annoyance, Eli was someone who was very aware of how valuable an asset he was. He wouldn't be taken in with platitudes. I'd have to give him reasons. I'd have to give him a plan.

But I wasn't sure if I wanted him to know the full extent of how fucked-up a situation I'd left in London. Noel Braben, my business partner, was losing the plot big-time. We'd been screwed over, informed on, by one of our employees; a tiny little Japanese bitch. I could have fitted her into a shaving kit but she had somehow managed to steal tens of thousands of pounds in cash and drugs, and kill one of our most trusted employees.

We never said her name any more – Seven – especially not in front of Noel. Out loud, she existed only in pronouns.

What's more, the owner of our club, the Underground, had come back from Manchester to look into this sudden loss of profit. It was embarrassingly obvious to everyone that if Edie Franco had once again deigned to grace London with her presence, things must be bad.

Eli indicated his head at the prison gates. 'He looks like you.'

I followed his gaze and, for one horrible second, I thought there had been a mistake. They'd released the wrong person. The man with the small bag slung over his shoulder, walking tentatively towards the car, wasn't anyone I recognized.

'Jesus...'

I forgot the rest of my frappuccino and left it in the footwell as I got out of the 4x4.

The rugged thirty-five-year-old man stopped and gave us an awkward smile. 'Hey.'

Holy fuck, he did look like me. He had the same olive skin, black eyes, the same imposing build. The only difference was the hair. I'd kept mine long. His was shaved into a crew cut. He'd also started wearing an earring, I noticed.

He came towards me and we hugged for about the fifth time in our lives. No one in our family was into hugging apart from Mum, and even then we were more acquiescing victims than participants.

He felt wiry and adult.

'Uh, this is Eli,' I said, gesturing at the vehicle. 'This is his car.'

That was the first fucking thing I said, after fifteen years. What a tool.

Eamonn waved through the windscreen.

Eli waved back.

'How's it hanging?' he said.

I had no idea what to say. 'Um, good, I guess. How are…? Mum will be glad to see you.'

'Can I get a cheeseburger on the way home?'

I snorted. 'Well, yeah, if you like. Mum's cooking though.'

Every eldest child I knew had trouble getting their heads around the aging process when it came to their younger siblings. No matter how many birthdays sped by they always remained about twelve. I hadn't seen Eamonn since he was twenty-six. I'd spoken to him on the phone a lot but voices didn't age, not really, unless you were a smoker. In my mind he had halted at the age of fifteen, five years before he'd been sentenced.

'Yo,' Eamonn said to Eli as he bounded into the back seat, slinging his bag across the space.

Um, this is Eli. This is his car.

Eli glanced at me and smiled, but it was forced, awkward solidarity.

Eamonn would never have seen this house, I realized as we pulled up outside.

'You look *old*,' he'd said in the car, leaning forwards to slap me on both shoulders. 'Well, not old, but you look like…'

'Forty?'

'No, like Dad.'

I thought he looked like Dad too.

'Sick!' Eamonn exclaimed at the sight of the new place, where our parents had lived for the past eight years. 'Is Dad loaded now? Shit, we have a *veranda*. Mum must be psyched.'

I couldn't tell if his hyperactivity was masking nervousness. Eamonn had never been the type to be nervous over anything. He would walk into anywhere like he owned the place; a trait I'd always predicted would earn him a punch in the face.

Getting out of the car slowly, I slammed the door. The noise must have alerted my parents because in a matter of seconds the front door was open. I couldn't see Dad, but Mum peered out first, as if she wasn't sure the man we were bringing back was actually her son. But the recognition hit her, in much less time than it had taken to hit me, and she came flying out and down the steps to throw her arms around him.

Eamonn had dropped his bag by the car and I went back to pick it up for him. Eli was still behind the wheel, putting the entire vehicle between himself and the outpouring of emotion.

She was already sobbing, almost dragging Eamonn to the ground she was clinging to him so hard, like he was a crucifix. Our mum was a strong woman, built like a shire horse. When we were younger she'd been able to take us all in a fight.

Eamonn stood there and took it, lapping it all up like he was the fucking Pope on tour.

'It's all right, Ma, it's all right.'

'Yeah...' I went to say something, but no one was listening to me.

Dad was conspicuously absent and I raised my eyes to see him standing in the front doorway. Our eyes met and we nodded at each other, both unsure of where we stood in this tableau. Dad was an elder statesman of a man, with a full head of hair even in his sixties. He hadn't wrinkled like most guys his age; he only seemed to retain the most deep and proud lines.

'Ronnie, come here.' Mum waved her arm over Eamonn's shoulder, demanding participation.

I did as I was told and hugged her across my brother, my left arm jarring against his shoulder blade, still holding his goddamn bag.

'Paul! Paul!'

She directed the same gesture at Dad, forcing him to come down to us. I backed away at this point, giving them some space while he and Eamonn eyed each other. Dad held out a hand, 'Son,' and Eamonn took it with a thin smile, and then they hugged with the kind of back-slapping bravado that only men do.

Mum was still crying, and I sidestepped them both to put an arm around her shoulders and give her a squeeze. 'Oh Jesus, come here. It's all right, he's back, let's all have some fucking pasta, yeah?'

'*Language*,' she snapped at me through her tears. 'Eli, young man! Get yourself out of that car and come inside! You're staying for dinner, I insist, to thank you for picking my boy up.'

'*Oh dear God*,' I'm sure I saw Eli mutter under his breath as he left the safety of his car, smiling.

'So, what's for eats?' Eamonn beamed, striding on inside with Mum at his heels, leaving me standing with his bag. 'I'm starved!'

I want to go home, I thought, before I could even stop myself. *Fuck, I already want to go home.*

CHAPTER THREE

Eli went home after dinner, so I sat on the back porch smoking. It wasn't the habit for me, cigarettes, but they served their purpose at times like this, gave me time alone.

It wasn't an etiquette observed by everyone. After ten minutes or so, Eamonn came outside and joined me.

Our garden wasn't lit. Surrounded by trees, it was a black hole. The last time I'd been here they'd had a trampoline, for the rare times I managed to get the kids over. I suspected it might be still there, in shadow. I wondered if Dad ever had a go on it when no one was watching.

'Mum always thought you were the one who was actually gonna make something of himself,' he said.

'Oh, shut up, I'm not in the mood.'

'You have, though, haven't you? You've got that club, a proper business, house, kids.'

'I'm doing OK.'

'You sound so English, man.'

'I *am* English. I don't even remember much about living here any more, not school or anything.' I stubbed the cigarette out on the decking, dividing us with a tiny mound of ash. 'I remember leaving and coming back a lot, but it's not really the same, is it, just remembering the flights?

I remember more about what the airports looked like than our old house.'

I had a gut instinct that he had come out here to ask me for a favour.

He had sobered up a bit before coming to talk to me, but I wasn't impressed. He'd been back barely twelve hours and Mum had spent about sixty per cent of that time crying. He'd spent most of that time drunk on wine, his tolerance for alcohol gone.

'You know, I still wanna make something of myself,' he said.

'Good for you. The world is your oyster.'

'Why are you being such an asshole? I'm just trying to talk.'

'No, you're not,' I said. 'You're about to ask me if you can borrow some money or you're about to ask me for a job.'

He fell silent and looked at the ground.

I offered him a cigarette out of pity, but he shook his head. It must suck to be so fucking transparent. I thought fifteen years inside might have instilled some tact into him but no, he still had all the subtlety of a nail-gun.

'Look,' he continued, speaking to his hands, positioned as if he were holding some kind of invisible orb, 'I'm not gonna get work. You have any idea how fucked it is? Who's gonna hire me now?'

'I don't know, maybe you can try filling out an application form and getting an interview like the rest of the fucking world? Enrol in some rehabilitation programme to show some effort?' I shrugged. 'Just a thought.'

'This isn't fucking *England*. You can't just do that here when you've got a record. And like you've ever filled out an application for anything.'

'Er, yeah, I have. How exactly are you qualified to sound

disbelieving here? You haven't got a fucking clue what's been going on with *anything* other than the prison basketball league.'

'I could have done, if you'd visited or called or something! More than *four* times or whatever it was.'

Well, we both had each other there. I had him with failure and he had me with guilt. I lit a new cigarette because he wasn't going to go away and I needed something to do with my hands during the stalemate.

My life had always been an eight-hour flight away; that was how I was able to justify it. There had always been Rachel, my wife, that reason not to come back, then Ryan had been born, and Chantal so soon after. Whenever I thought about it, the distance, Mum, Dad and Eamonn, I felt taken over by this sickness in my gut.

'I'm not lending you money, Eamonn.'

'I don't want your money!'

'I'm not giving you a job either.'

'Oh, *come on...*'

'What am I gonna do, fly you back to England with me and put you in charge of something?'

He hesitated.

I laughed so hard I almost choked on smoke. 'Ha! Christ. No. Just no. In what fucking *universe* would I do that?'

'Your problem is that you still think I'm a kid, bro.'

'No, my problem is that I know you don't grow up in prison. It doesn't count. Believe me. You go in there young and you come out a fucking man-child.'

I glanced over my shoulder to see if Mum or Dad were in the vicinity, eavesdropping through the back door, but they weren't. I wondered if our voices could carry upstairs to an open window.

'Ron, you don't know me any more.'

'I never knew you before.'

'And whose fault is that?'

I wanted to stretch out and take a walk around the garden, maybe call my kids. 'I'm sorry if this sounds harsh, but you can't just have everything handed to you because you made the wrong choices.'

'Go on.' He leant back on his elbows, my words rolling off him. 'Ask me something.'

'What?'

'Ask me something. You say you don't know anything about me. How about asking?'

'No.' I stood up.

'Come on, just one question.'

'Shut up, *please*.'

'You can't think of *one* thing you wanna know about your kid brother?'

'Nope.'

'Nothing?'

'Just... *why?*' I spread my hands, cigarette between my teeth. 'That's what I wanna fucking know! How? *How* could you fuck-up so *fucking* hard? How did you end up just standing there, like a *prick*, while some guy gets his head kicked in by your fucking *degenerate* mates? You *fucking moron*. You *idiot*. I mean, who even gets themselves into that situation besides *you?*'

That was what I'd wanted to say.

I turned, looking down, and Eamonn stared right back at me with the defiance of youth, a thirty-five-year-old teenager.

'We both know I wouldn't have been sent down if I hadn't been your kid brother.' He raised his eyebrows, taunting me with those stupid fucking tramlines. 'They wanted to make an example of me. To scare you and Dad! And you guys didn't even fucking care. You didn't give a shit about family—'

'What do you think this is, the lost sequel to *The Godfather*?'

'You're too scared to admit you and Dad *owe* me. They got to you, putting me away. That's the only reason they didn't come after you guys harder.' He pointed at me. '*That's* why you don't wanna know anything! That's why Dad can't even look me in the eye!'

'I owe *you*? Jesus.' I shook my head.

'Yeah, you do! I took one for you guys! Hell, I took *fifteen!*'

'Because you were *stupid*. I'm not giving a job to someone who is *that* fucking stupid.'

He leapt at me.

I went to smack him down but he caught me off balance – stronger than he used to be – and I dropped the cigarette on my coat as we both went over the edge of the porch. I landed on top of him in a flowerbed.

'The *fuck* are you doing!'

He swiped at me but I had him pinned down. Reaching out, he flung a handful of soil into my face instead.

I rolled off him and scrambled to my feet. He did likewise and tried to kick me. I jumped back onto the lawn, swatting dirt out of my eyes, and he seemed to lose heart. Eamonn ground to a halt, standing with one foot on the grass and one in the flowers, and exhaled.

I brushed my coat off, scowling. 'Fuck's *sake*, this is expensive!'

'You're being such a bastard.'

He sounded like a boy then. It was hard to stay angry.

I rolled my eyes, hoping that nothing had stained. 'Thought you'd have learnt to fight a bit.'

'It was just the porch. It was luck you came out on top.'

'You tried to *kick* me. What are you, a little bitch?'

'Fuck off.'

'Well, I'm not the one who's going around kicking people.'
He snorted.

I put my hands in my pockets and looked at the black sky, and across the garden. Sure enough, tucked away where the lawn ended and trees began, was the trampoline. I sighed and started making my way towards it.

'Where are you going?' Eamonn called after me.

'There's a trampoline.'

I shrugged my coat off, dropped it on the grass – it was dirty now anyway – took off my shoes and climbed up onto the springs. With an awkward manoeuvre that made me feel about seventy years old, I rolled onto the mat and stood up.

'Why do they even have this?' Eamonn hopped around below me, trying to take off his trainers.

'For my kids.' I started bouncing. 'Makes no sense really, they're only here every so often.'

'Who's Eli?' he asked, climbing up onto the mat next to me and bouncing on the opposite side. 'That's his name, right? The quiet English guy?'

There was no safety net.

'He worked with Dad, ages ago.'

'He kinda creeps me out. Has that look of the guys inside you'd wanna avoid.'

'I think he likes the idea that he creeps people out.'

He gave me a shove in mid-air and jumped away. I could barely see the mat beneath our feet it was so dark. I could see Eamonn though, white teeth grinning. Springs creaking and exhales, coughs. I looked back at the house. The top lights were on, but no one had followed us out.

'Do you remember when we used to jump between the two walls outside the old place?' he said.

'Yup, I remember vividly the sensation of busting my lip open.'

''S what happens when you try and eat a brick, man.'

'Ha! Exactly what Dad said, the fucker. You were the one crying though, running inside screaming *"It's got blood! It's got blood!"* That was funny.'

Eamonn had to stop jumping before me. Smoker's lungs, I suspected. He sat down with his legs splayed, breathing hard.

I carried on for a while, enjoying the sensation of cool air whipping against my face, jogging him up and down a little. Maybe it was just because he looked so small below me, but I started to feel sorry for him. It was a dangerous emotion, pity. It could drag you into all sorts of crazy shit for the sake of making someone feel better about themselves. I was sorry that he'd had to spend fifteen years inside. I was sorry that he didn't know my kids. I was sorry for being an asshole, for not knowing what to say. Shouldn't we at least try to be better at being human? Damned as we all were, shouldn't we make the best of it?

Eamonn lay flat against the mat and with every pound of the springs he jolted.

The lights at the top of the house went out.

CHAPTER FOUR

Daisy

People said I shouldn't have gone back to work so quickly, after Seven left the way she did. Not least because every time I came in I found myself looking at the patch of floor I'd crawled across in a pool of my own blood after she'd shot me, all the way from the middle of the club to the bar. I'd caught her trying to leave with the stolen money. She'd convinced me it hadn't been her fault. She'd been my friend so I'd believed her, and I'd said that if her escape was to look convincing she'd have to shoot me first.

It didn't seem like such a big deal walking in that morning, the morning after the morning after the day Ronnie left. But then I'd thought it would be amusing to take a half hit of acid before I left the house so not many things were gonna seem like a big deal for the foreseeable future.

I was glad to be away from humans, inside on my own.

My boyfriend said he found the sight of nightclubs during the day depressing. But I found the opposite. Turn the lights down and fill them with people and I'd happily see any place nuked, but during the day they were unwanted space for me to relax in.

I kicked off my shoes and padded around in my socks, going upstairs to get the cash float out of the office and bringing it downstairs again.

Noel was never here in the mornings any more.

I should ask for a pay-rise.

It wasn't as if I was a fucking manager. But I didn't see anyone else here with the cash and list of stock to be ordered, or checking on the gun I'd insisted we keep under the bar.

Noel had commented that it was a bit 'dramatic and American' to keep it there, but then – as I'd pointed out at the time – he wasn't the one who'd been shot on the fucking premises.

Turning on the speakers, I put on some violin dubstep and zoned out.

It's funny how Hollywood makes it look like a gunshot wound to the shoulder is something you can run off. It blew my fucking mind how much that wasn't the case.

First off, you couldn't walk or run because the very impact of being shot, before the pain even starts, is like being hit by a train. For fuck-knows how long afterwards, you're on the floor looking up at the ceiling. No thought. No identity. No consciousness at all. When thought did return it was as if you'd forgotten even being shot. You start picking out faces in the copper pipes criss-crossing above you. Not entirely unlike the sensation of being on acid, right before the most nightmarish of trips.

You look to your left and your body has been replaced by some pulsing, gushing hunk of meat. There's just red. Your outsides have become blood and you think *I'm dying. I'm definitely fucking dying.*

But that doesn't bother you as much as you think it will because you can't move and there's no pain yet, just a swimming sensation like the floor is dissolving below you. But it's just your brain trying to deal, trying not to break down with trauma.

Then the screaming comes, the faint ringing that existed only in your head but you now realize is coming from outside you, that screaming, animal screaming... You realize that it's you, and you sound like you're dying.

You look at the state of your shoulder and think about touching it but you want to throw up at the sight.

The phone behind the bar rings and suddenly that sound becomes the difference between life and death.

You roll onto your right side and shout at it with your voice, voice you've only just remembered you have. But language – *fuck* – language is barely a concept. Words are broken – not going to save you – no fucking use to anybody.

You roll onto your back and push your entire body towards the bar with your legs, until you realize that's ridiculous and try to get to your feet, because the phone is going to ring off eventually and if it does you're going to die.

You cry, because even kneeling hurts. The entire upper half of your body is agony and you cry like it's going to help but it doesn't, so you put one foot down and ease all your weight onto that and you rise, blinded, until you can see the phone, but it's stopped ringing.

'*No! No, don't!*'

You lurch forwards, left arm hung uselessly across your chest, and scramble around the bar to the phone, and think, *I don't know anyone's fucking number.*

Then you look back at the trail of blood you've left behind and wonder how there's still any left in your body, and everything's gone numb and cold and you think that's a pretty solid symptom of *dying*, right there.

Your mobile is *right there.*

Your mobile. You pick it up and call Nic, because it didn't occur to you to call anyone else and you sound inconsolable and mental so he panics and then you explain:

'I've been shot, Seven was here and she shot me!'

'Where?'

'At work.'

'No, where did she shoot you, you fucking idiot!'

'Oh… My shoulder.'

'Get off the fucking phone and call an ambulance!'

'But… Can't you come?'

'What use am I gonna be, I'm not a fucking medical professional. Hang up and call an ambulance now!'

'But—'

He hangs up and it's such an unsupportive gesture that you start crying again. And then you call an ambulance, and on the way to the hospital later you consider that he might have been right. But you never tell him that.

You also never mention how you poured a third of a bottle of Grey Goose over yourself because that's what you'd seen in films, and collapsed to the floor writhing, smacking your head on the bar-top on the way down, because you'd never experienced debilitating pain like that in your fucking life. Luckily, before you had tried to be clever, a good deal of it had been poured down your throat, and the paramedics, when they arrived, didn't ask why you were covered in vodka.

I realized I'd been staring at the money in my hands and listening to the music and not much else.

Someone called, 'Hello? Anyone here?'

It wasn't Noel. It was a woman.

Fuck, try not to seem high, I thought.

Try not to seem high.

'Um… yeah!'

I put down the float but stayed behind the bar. I only felt safe in the vicinity of that gun now.

But I needn't have worried, at least not for that reason. It was Edie, the club's owner. She stepped down onto the club floor in alarmingly high heels and waved.

'Noel's not here,' I said, maybe too quickly.

'It's actually you I wanted to see,' she replied, taking off her leopard-print jacket and slinging it onto the back of a sofa booth. 'You have time for a chat?'

Edie, at close quarters, was fucking formidable. A right hook from her would probably take the nose off my face. She was slim but there was something hard about her; athletic, like a cheerleader or a swimmer. Her features were large and intensely defined. Nothing petite.

'Um… yeah. I guess so.'

I nervously emerged from behind the bar, concentrating too hard on walking normally. I hadn't banked on making conversation with a fellow human. Facial features on acid, even a tiny amount, appeared uncanny and alien.

Edie sat at one of the tables with her high heels up and crossed. 'Is the coffee machine on?'

'No, I… No, sorry, it takes about forty minutes to warm up.'

Words. Words. Focus on the words.

'Doesn't matter. Sit down.' Gesturing at the seat opposite.

I did as I was told, glad to be sitting again, trying to avoid her face, placing my hands firmly under my thighs so I couldn't fiddle with them. I could feel, at the edge of my consciousness, that I was dangerously close to freaking out.

'How long have you been working here?' Edie asked.

'Um, I don't know. A year and a half?'

'Ronnie mentioned that Nic Caruana put you forward.'

'Well, he... put me forward, yeah.'

'And Nic Caruana is your boyfriend?' A small and slightly vicious smile spread across her face.

'Kinda, yeah. Why?'

'No reason. Me and Nic go way back. Isn't he a love?'

I didn't like the implication in her tone, so I just nodded.

'So what exactly do you do here?' she continued eventually, patting her hair.

I hadn't interviewed for my job. Nic got it for me, because I'd been bored and wanted some pocket money to avoid freeloading off him. Every time I was asked for any sort of job description, it felt like a lie at worst and a blag at best.

'Well, I run the bar most days. I take bookings, process memberships, I order stock.' I tried to stop fidgeting but only succeeded in swaying left and right like a mental patient. 'I've hired people, like... I help interview girls who wanna work here. I close most nights. I organize the bill, like who's onstage. We have bands playing here now, which was my idea. If something's not working and Noel and Ronnie aren't around I get it fixed. Um... loads of stuff really. It probably sounds like more than it is coz Noel or Ronnie are here most nights. It's just recently with all the... stuff that's been going on they've been busier than usual. I think.'

Stop talking. For the love of fuck, stop talking.

There was a long silence.

She said, 'You seem like an enterprising young lady.'

I wasn't sure what to say to that, or what it was meant to mean.

'There was some trouble here.' Edie took her shoes off the desk, sounding grave. 'I'm not going to pussyfoot around you, my love. Noel said you were shot. I'm very sorry about that. If you were ever looking for any financial compensation then feel free to ask me anytime.'

It had never occurred to me that I might be owed anything. I shrugged.

'What happened?' she asked, eyeballing me, with eyes almost identical to Ronnie's. 'I know what the boys are saying, but you were here. This *Seven* they're talking about, she was a friend of yours?'

Christ, I thought. *She knows I'm fucking lying.*

'I don't really know that much. Seven worked here and we were... friends. Well, we talked a lot. Noel and Ronnie had been saying someone was informing on where they were keeping their... money, drugs and stuff. I didn't realize it was Seven until I came in one morning and found her looking for a bag of money I'd found in her locker. I tried to hold her up but she shot me and then she ran.'

'So you must have suspected, if you went into her locker?'

I hesitated. 'I don't think I suspected her of that. I just thought she was acting weird and hiding something. It might have been drugs or whatever. So I went into her locker that morning and that was when I found the bag.'

'And then?'

'On the way to the hospital I tried to call Noel but he wasn't answering. So I called Nic and then Ronnie and they both came.'

'Where was Noel?'

'Um, well, she drugged him. He was at his place.'

She raised her eyebrows. 'So she what? Broke in?'

'No, she didn't break in, she was... there...'

'With Noel,' she finished for me.

I couldn't tell if Edie had known that Noel and Seven were involved or not. She may just be confirming stories, or she could be pumping me for information and I could have just fucked over both my employers in the space of a minute. It was fucking terrifying. She was fucking terrifying.

She sat back in her chair and thought for a while.

I started chewing the hard skin around my thumbnail.

'As Noel put it so enthusiastically to me on the phone, you practically run this place when they're not here?'

'I guess.' There wasn't anything I could say that would make things worse at this point. 'He might be exaggerating a bit.'

'Have you fucked either of them?'

'Excuse me?' I almost choked out the words.

'I need to know that your relationship with your employers is strictly professional and not clouded by anything... else.' She waved her hand in mid-air.

'No! I mean, no. Never. I mean, Ronnie's married and Noel's... Just no. Even if I was single... No way.'

'Well, you seem repelled enough by the idea to convince me.' She grinned. 'Now, is there anything else you want to tell me?'

I hoped there wasn't. I wondered if she knew Noel was going to AA meetings again, but didn't risk mentioning it. I'd probably done enough damage for one day.

I shook my head and started to get up, sensing the interrogation was over. 'Look, Miss Franco—'

'Edie, darling.'

'Edie... I haven't got anyone into trouble, have I? Because Seven was really smart. No one would have suspected her, ever. Whether they were shagging her or not.'

I'd flushed red in the process of making my grand statement and I averted my eyes. Edie had the air of someone who, at any moment, might just crush your skull to see what it looked like inside. Ronnie had that same air too, but it was more unnerving coming from a woman.

'You haven't got anyone into trouble,' she said. 'But your concern is sweet.'

As she looked away from me for a second, over my shoulder towards the coffee machine, her features distorted into black gaping chasms, and I had to excuse myself and go upstairs, where I sat in the empty office and took deep breaths for ten minutes.

CHAPTER FIVE

Ronnie

I should have known that Eli would be a believer in favours. Not just the odd favour here and there, but the old-fashioned ideal of favours; the life-or-death ones you have to drag around with you for ever.

He had a look of purpose on his face when I saw him the next day.

'If you want my help,' he said, sitting upright and stern on the sofa across from mine in my mother's living room, 'then I have a proposition for you.'

I was Skyping Daisy, my employee back in London, and I waved at him as I tried to wrap up our conversation.

'When are you gonna be back?' she asked, not quite getting the hang of addressing the webcam and directing most of her questions to the thumbnail of herself in the bottom corner of her screen. 'Like, we could really use you being here. Edie is *not cool*. There's not much we can tell her without making it all sound like a...'

'Clusterfuck?'

'I was gonna go with *spunk explosion*, but yeah.'

Across the room, Eli's lips twitched.

Daisy did have a way with words. She adjusted her bleached blonde hair, eyes down on the thumbnail again. She looked hot on webcam. She was built for that kind of striptease, diminutive and wide-eyed, though how much of the wide-eyedness was due to the Olympian amounts of coke she snorted was anybody's guess.

It was such a waste having her work behind the bar, but her boyfriend wouldn't hear of her doing anything untoward, and her boyfriend wasn't someone to antagonize for shits and giggles.

'Ronnie, seriously, tell me what to say. She's interviewing all the staff like she's looking for someone to take the hit and I don't know what to say.'

'What's Noel said?'

'Noel isn't even *here*! Do we just tell her the truth or what?'

'Christ, no, are you *new*? We absolutely *don't* tell her the truth, the truth makes us sound shit.' I looked at Eli, rubbing the stubble across my chin. 'Love, I've got some stuff to do. Can we sort this out later?'

'Oh yeah, sure. I'll *manage*.'

Oh, just take your fucking T-shirt off, I thought. Daisy was smart, but it irked me sometimes how she'd come to address me and Noel as peers. Fair play, the girl had taken a bullet for us, but it didn't make her fucking Jesus.

'Cool. Later.'

I snapped the laptop shut and took a breath. I could have done without Eli hearing some of that, and he knew it. I wish I had the self-control to cultivate Eli's quietness; quietness was power.

With deliberation, I got up, made us both a cup of tea and brought the mugs back through to the living room. My parents were out, having taken Eamonn on a food shop like it was a bonding experience. Eli didn't appear to have moved, even blinked, but he thanked me for the tea.

'What's your proposition?' I asked.

He pulled the mug towards him and warmed his hands around it. 'You know when I left university and started up my first business, I was working with a partner.'

'What sort of business?'

'Small magazine, mostly political stuff.' He smiled. 'Back when I was a Marxist.'

'Er, no.' I almost laughed. 'No, I had absolutely no idea.'

'It was easier back then, what with there still being money in print publishing, but we did well. We were turning over a stupid amount of profit in five years. We had Sarah Mankowski writing for us at one point.'

He paused, as if I was meant to know this person and react accordingly.

I shrugged.

'She went on to write *Watching Them Burn*,' he said, in the tone of someone checking if I knew ketchup existed. 'Booker nominee 2002. It was a bestseller. Nothing to do with us, of course, she turned novelist much later. But it's been translated into twenty-eight languages. It's the *seminal* existential novel of the last fifty years. Do you even read?'

'For fun?'

A long hard stare, then a shake of the head. 'Anyway, I started this thing up. Then we had a board of members who'd invested money after a while, like with any outfit. After four years there was a lawsuit and they voted me out.' He ended on a shrug.

'And you...?'

'Well, you know I own magazines. That's what I've been doing the last decade.'

I'd had no clue what Eli did. I doubted if any of my family knew; he was so secretive. His money had always spoken for itself.

'What sort of magazines?' I asked.

'Teen magazines.' Deadpan.

'You what?'

'It's a huge market, Ronnie, and don't even get me started on the digital revolution. All the money is online now. Do you guys even have a website for your club? A blog or something?'

'Blog?' I spat the word out with the same incredulity as if he'd said 'anal rape'.

'We're digressing.'

'So what do you want me to do?'

He paused, testing the silence of the house. I noticed him notice a family photo up on the mantelpiece. A three-piece family photo of Mum, Dad and me. No Eamonn. I was surprised Mum hadn't taken it down.

'It's quite simple.' He sipped his tea. 'The guy I worked with was called Trent Byrne. He was someone I met at university, from a very rich family. We weren't friends but you know when you just... know someone can be useful to you? It was like that. But after the lawsuit, he disappeared.'

'In a *murdered* way or... just disappeared?'

'The latter.'

'How long ago?'

'Admittedly, I didn't keep track. But from what I can gather no one has heard from him for over ten years.' He frowned. 'Until last year, maybe just over a year ago, when a few of us, including me, started getting postcards. Some of them said nothing. Some were... weird.'

'Eli, I respect you.' I linked my fingers around my knees and looked at my tea. 'But I don't have that much time here—'

'I don't see how you can have any objection when I helped transform your ex-lawyer into chemical waste just the other night. I've also agreed to come to Chicago to help you find some Japanese girl who is of *no* importance to me.'

'No, it's not that.' I picked my words carefully, not wanting to sound ungrateful. 'It's just, I'm not sure what you think I can do.'

'That's not the point.' There was disappointment in his glare. 'I thought you, more than anyone, would understand that's not the point at all.'

'It's not that I don't understand, it's just…'

'You'd rather not.'

He couldn't have loaded the statement with more ice.

'Look, that's not what I mean. I've just got my brother out of prison and I have my kids back home, Eli, so I can't go all Thelma and Louise with you if this is gonna take months. I'm sorry.'

For a moment, Eli looked dangerous. But the expression was fleeting, misplaced, the knee-jerk reaction of someone who simply was not used to hearing 'no'.

He said, slowly, 'I don't trust anyone else.'

'That can't be my problem, come on.'

'No. I don't trust anyone else. You're the only person I know who can get things done, without trouble. I don't want any trouble.'

'What are you planning to do if you find this guy, Trent?'

Silence.

I snorted. 'You're planning to kill him, aren't you? This is a revenge thing?'

'I don't know where Trent is now… what he's doing, what his situation is but… I haven't ruled out that idea, no.'

'I'm not mad on the idea of committing more murder than

I planned. I'd quite like to leave this country via a plane rather than lethal injection.'

'I'd be doing you a favour coming back to London with you. It's important to you. Well, this is important to me.'

I hadn't called my kids yet. I put myself in their places, for a second, and imagined what it might be like for them to be without a father. I'd never done jail time, not like Noel, who had at least racked up a couple of months for varying levels of assault, a few overnight stays while drunk and disorderly. I just wasn't built for it.

'I can't shower with other men,' I said out loud, without sharing my train of thought.

Eli frowned. 'What?'

'Um, sorry, I meant I can't go to prison. Not for something like this, something that's so... fucking *unplanned*. Do you have any fucking idea how hard it is to pull off renegade stunts like this nowadays with satellites and forensics and all that?'

'If you want me to come back to London and for... Eamonn to maybe find some work.' He added the last part slyly, as if it were an afterthought.

'No.'

'If you knew how many times I've done favours for your father. When Marie was going through chemo and he was too busy to drive her to and from the hospital and you were in England, I did that too.'

'Don't do this, Eli.'

'Don't do what?' An impression of naivety.

'Don't you even fucking *try* and make this sound non-negotiable.' I didn't want to become angry with him, but it was hard to stop the warning tone from creeping in. 'I'm grateful to you, OK, but this is my life. Are you saying all those times you were driving Mum to and from chemo you were just racking up points in your column? Nice. Fucking classy.'

'No, I'm not saying that.' Still calm. 'I also helped you kill Carey.'

'That's completely fucking different, and you were *psyched* to help me kill Carey! Like you said, he was a lawyer so you were doing a public service either way. I've got nothing against... journalists.'

Eli looked about him for a spoon, took a pen out of his pocket and started stirring his tea with that instead. I forgot he always had to take his tea with a spoon in. It was an odd tick of his, always stirring.

'"Killing is killing, whether done for glory, profit, or fun",' he said.

I shrugged.

'You know who said that?'

'Nope.' I sighed and rolled my eyes to the ceiling. 'Anne Frank?'

'Richard Ramirez.' He raised his eyebrows at me over the rim of his mug. 'Say what you like about him, at least he wasn't a hypocrite.'

'Ha! You did *not* just compare me to a serial killer, you fuck!' I started laughing. 'Just because I said no. Why not just compare me to the Nazis too?'

Eli finished his tea and stood up, buttoning his coat, which he hadn't bothered to take off.

I gestured at him. 'Oh come on, let's not make things bad between us.'

'I'm not worried about that.' He smiled at me infuriatingly, and smoothed his hair back. 'I've done too much for you. I know you'll change your mind.'

CHAPTER SIX

It was as if Eamonn knew that the worst thing he could do right now, fresh out of prison, was fuck up. It was an evolutionary reflex for him, inevitable like breathing, fucking and eating. Eamonn had to fuck up. Sometimes when the phone rang when we were younger, I knew it was going to be about Eamonn, fucking up in some new and creative fashion. Every time he appeared to reach a peak, what I thought must be the utmost zenith of fucking up, he fucked up harder.

'Hey, Ronnie, it's Joe. I heard you were in town?'

Joe was the owner of JB's. It was Eamonn's favourite bar, one of the only places from our childhood that was still standing, and that had remained largely unchanged for over a decade. I should have known it would be among the first places he'd go as soon as Mum and Dad left him to his own devices for an evening.

'Oh, Christ.' I pinched the bridge of my nose. 'What's he done?'

'Sorry, I hate to talk to you for the first time in years when you're in town and call out your kid brother... but I'm *this* close to calling the cops on him, Ron. I don't wanna upset your dad. Come pick him up.'

For Joe, one of the most genial fellas I'd known here, 'this close' must mean very fucking close.

I'd been about to Skype with Ryan and Chantal. My laptop was open, about to sign in. I reached out and snapped the thing shut, again. Rachel was going to be pissed.

'When you're away you act like you don't even have a family,' she'd said, to my vehement rebuttal. 'You don't get holidays from being their dad, Ronnie. We're not something you get to have half-terms from.'

I was vaguely aware of Dad loitering just outside the living-room doorway. He knew what was going on just as well as I did. Eamonn's fuck-ups were like a sunrise to us, constant and rhythmic.

'I'll come get him,' I said to Joe. 'Fuck, I'll have to take Dad's car. Give me twenty minutes. Is he drunk?'

'Eamonn never needed to be drinking, Ron. He'd start a fight in solitary confinement.'

'He probably did,' I said. 'Righto.'

I ended the call and looked down at the laptop.

Dad came in and sat down.

'I'm gonna go pick Eamonn up,' I said.

Nothing had changed, not really. Not since we were teenagers. It was the same story, just with more stubble and expensive clothes and a larger reserve of resentment and bitterness to draw from.

'We need to talk,' Dad said.

'I know.' I sighed. 'Later. I need the car.'

'If he's drunk and throws up in that, he's paying for it.'

I spread my hands as I left the room. 'With what?'

JB's hadn't changed much. Still had the old sign hanging above the door.

HAVE A SIGNIFICANT DAY.

Joe Bishop liked to take old vinyl and stick them all over the walls and ceiling. Some were signed. Before he'd owned a bar he'd had two pretty successful albums in two pretty successful bands. He'd smoked heroin and launched terrifying amounts of alcohol into his body with the best of them – Keith Richards, Tom Waits – and it showed in the lines around his eyes and blotches of red dotting his otherwise handsome features.

'Ron! Good to see you, man!' Joe swung a hand into my back.

Behind him, I could see Eamonn sat in the corner with a sulk on, bottom lip thrust out and arms folded. There was a decent hum of activity. Jimi Hendrix playing. It always felt good to be in here, like a front room.

'I hope he didn't cause you too much hassle,' I said, shooting a harsh look in Eamonn's direction.

'Just a scuffle. Like a couple of old women. But it's not cool, you know, I don't want this place to get a reputation for being that kinda bar. You're looking well. Kids must keep you young?'

'Jokes. They take more years off your life than cigarettes, and don't even get me started on Chantal almost being a teenager, talking about *boys* and make-up and all that shit. The fucking stress of it.'

'Lock up your sons!'

'I'll just have to kill them all, Joe. There's no other way. Every spotty wanker who so much as *looks* at her is going straight under the patio.' I looked at Eamonn again. 'Speaking of kids...'

'I know what you think,' Eamonn said, not to us, but at the wall. 'But I didn't even start it.'

Joe and I exchanged glances.

'Punched a guy in the face, bit of rolling around on a table.'
Joe shrugged. 'Other guy scrammed when I split them up.
I didn't hear what happened.'

'Oh yeah.' I nodded. 'Totally blameless. I bet.'

Eamonn emitted a grunt of dissent, but said nothing else.

'All right, get up,' I said. 'Sorry about this, Joe. Let's have a
catch-up soon, yeah?'

The two doors of the bar's entrance slammed open into the
walls and four guys piled in. A boy who looked barely over
twenty-one, sporting a bloody nose and holding a fucking
baseball bat, pointed at Eamonn and shouted, 'That's him!'

'For the love of *fuck*!' I managed to exclaim before the
rabble tore towards us.

With almost tragic predictability, Eamonn threw his own
chair at them, narrowly missing me, and made a run for the
relative safety of the bar. Coward. It hadn't occurred to me to
bring a weapon – why the fuck should it? – so after missing
the first two of them I swung my arm successfully into the
third guy's neck.

It earned me a punch in the face.

'Ow!'

I threw one guy to the floor, took another by the collar and
headbutted him in the nose.

Bottles fell. Men shouting. Eamonn had been followed
behind the bar, and then Joe shut everyone up by screaming,
'*Everybody put your fucking hands up! Now!*' and I realized,
at about the same time as everyone else, that he was holding
a shotgun.

I raised my hands. One blow went to my eye, but it was
light. It wouldn't swell.

'You!' Joe yelled, turning the gun on Eamonn and the two
guys who had him pinned to the shelf of spirits. 'And you!

Out! Not you, Eamonn. *You!* You bunch of syphilitic fucking scrotums! Out of my bar!'

The remaining kids got to their feet and followed their ringleader sheepishly back towards the doors.

'Leave that,' Joe said, pumping the handgrip of his firearm when one of them went to retrieve the baseball bat.

I spotted Eamonn giving them a smug smile over Joe's shoulder. I lowered my hands, stormed behind the bar and cuffed him around the head. I caught his stupid earring and he recoiled, clutching at it. I was sorry I hadn't torn the thing clean out. An *earring*. At his age. How embarrassing. It made me angry every time I looked at it.

'Fucking hell, gimme a break!'

'Get in the car or I'll kick you through those fucking doors so hard it'll rupture the fucking space-time continuum!' I turned to Joe, rubbing my eye. 'I'm so sorry.'

Joe took off his leather jacket and started righting the chairs. The other customers, some of whom had left their seats in panic during the brief ruckus, were resuming their places, slowly raising the volume of chatter back to normal.

'He's never boring, I'll give the kid that.'

'Can I pay for anything?' I asked, scanning the place for any damage.

'Nah, you're all right. Just consider him temporarily barred.'

I couldn't tell if Joe was just unflappable, or whether he was being polite. Regardless, I took the opportunity to get out.

Eamonn was waiting in the passenger seat. I'd been psyching myself up for an outburst, the rant that he deserved, but when I was in the car, engine off, radio silent, I lost the will.

Instead I took out my phone and listened to a voicemail from Daisy. I didn't feel up to listening to the messages left by Rachel and my kids.

'Ronnie, I'm super fucking worried about Noel.'

That was the only sentence that stood out to me. Everything else she said was just noise.

'Ronnie, I'm super fucking worried about Noel.'

I thought of Eli and his smug exit earlier, took out my phone and started to compose a text. It said, *How long do you think this mental escapade of yours will take?*

There it was, in print, a fucking admission of defeat. I knew I'd only been saying no out of selfishness, because looking for another ghost while I was here was a massive inconvenience. But a bigger fucking inconvenience was sitting next to me in our dad's car, and I was gonna need all the help I could get.

Eamonn took a breath and began to say something.

'Shut up!' I snapped, jamming the key into the ignition. 'Do yourself a favour for once in your life and shut up.'

I met Dad out by the trampoline, where the O'Connell family apparently had all their serious conversations. It was safer than the house and not as exposed as the street, just two grown men sitting, side by side and conspicuous as hell. The neighbours would be bemused if they could see us.

Dad had given up smoking three years ago so I resisted the urge to light up in his presence, which was pretty unfair given that my stress levels around him tended to skyrocket. Rachel claimed that the main reason I'd left the country was because I couldn't do anything with my dad watching. In a way, she was right. He made me nervous. Things I'd always been able to do without any problems I somehow managed to screw up in front of him. His presence gave me a nervous limp, in all aspects of life, and it hadn't got better with age or distance.

'If your brother had to pick a place to sit,' Dad said, after a silence, 'and he had to choose between two armchairs and a rock, he'd choose the rock.'

I smiled a little. He'd said it before. It was the perfect analogy.

'He wouldn't hesitate either, or feel bad about it, he'd just sit himself down right there on that rock like "Yeah. Damn straight, this is my rock."'

'What are we gonna do with him?' he asked, letting the question hang there.

'You must have thought about this. We all knew when he was getting out.'

'I know, I just thought...' A sigh of abject disappointment. 'I thought...'

'You thought he might have changed?'

I felt awful saying it out loud. You shouldn't wish a fundamental change on family, like their personality was so substandard to you, but we'd all wished it of Eamonn. I think even Mum had, at times.

'Jail is serious. I thought it would have made him... think more. But it's like he hasn't even been gone.' Dad shook his head. 'And not in the good way. It's like this hasn't fazed him. If anything was gonna get through to him it was this, seeing what it's done to your mother and... he's acting like we sent him to summer camp. He's not even sorry.'

'I don't know, Dad, I think he's sorry, he just... doesn't say it like normal people.'

I was surprised to find myself sticking up for him.

'Are you going to take him back with you?' Dad asked.

'Do you want me to?'

He took a breath. 'It might be better.'

'For him or for you?'

'There's nothing for him here.'

'Why don't you give him a job then?'

He looked at me as if I were retarded.

'Dad, he's gonna need something to do.' I was starting to lose patience, but I was also losing my resilience to keep saying no. 'You know what happens to angry young guys with nothing to do? They start committing stupid crimes and get banged up because at least that gives them some direction. Maybe he just needs you to show a bit of faith in him?'

I knew what he wanted to say, but it was too harsh even for him to say out loud. Dad had never been one to fake emotion. He'd never forced a smile for anyone or anything and he wasn't going to start for his youngest son.

'We've tried, Ron,' he said. 'Maybe now it's your turn. If you have such *faith* in him.'

CHAPTER SEVEN

Daisy

It was half two in the morning and the last customers had left. I went upstairs to find Noel and he was in his office, doing something on his laptop that I couldn't be sure was work. There was a bottle of Newcastle Brown on his desk.

'You all right?' he asked, without looking up.

I shut the door. 'Can we talk about Edie?'

'If we must.'

'She knows about you and Seven, you know.'

His grimace became even more pronounced, but someone had to say her name out loud sooner or later. 'Fucking hell.'

Something changed in Noel's face when he'd been drinking for several days straight. His eyes were always too wide, pores open, skin sallow. The outlines of his features became.

I sat down. The silence felt like fresh air now that the club downstairs was empty. I could dimly hear the girls getting changed, chatting amongst themselves, but there was no music, no gross male braying.

'If Ronnie is away for a while, she's gonna pin this all on you.'

'I'm not fucking stupid.' He rubbed his forehead with both

hands, picked up the bottle to check it was empty and put it down again.

'I *know* that but I Skyped Ronnie today and he basically said "Yeah, whatever, YOLO", so sorry, but one of you has to be taking this seriously.'

Noel sighed. 'I fucked up. No point trying to lie to her about it, she'll find out sooner or later.'

'Then what are you doing about it? Have you found out who Seven was working for?'

'I am not sufficiently fucked to want to discuss this with you.'

'This isn't some fucking joke!'

'You see me laughing?' He met my eyes. 'We don't know who she was working for. Nic's looking into it for us but, honestly, your fella is expensive and Edie'll bring in her own people.'

'So you're just gonna take this? Not even try?'

'No, I'm accepting that... I fucked up.'

'Then *un*fuck up! Get Ronnie to come back off holiday and *un*fuck up!' I didn't have the balls to tell him to stop drinking. Not right then anyway.

'Isn't Nic coming to pick you up tonight?' Noel asked, blanking everything I'd just said and returning his gaze to his laptop.

Was I being paranoid? His lack of response, the lack of urgency from both of them, was making me feel as though I was just doing too many drugs and that I needed to get a grip.

'No, he's... busy.'

'I'll give you a lift.'

'Na.' I stood up, deflated. 'No offence, but I don't know how over the limit you are.'

'Fine, see you tomorrow.'

I stopped at the door on my way out, and saw him pick up the empty bottle, shake it and put it down again.

I stopped at the bar on my way out to pick up my handbag, checking to see if there was any acid left in my little blue phial. There wasn't, so I sucked the end of the dropper just in case, and walked home alone.

CHAPTER EIGHT

Ronnie

I had three weeks, according to Dad and according to Daisy, who I'd curtly informed over text. Three weeks to help Eli, three weeks until my flight back, three weeks before Daisy refused to continue holding everything together back home, three weeks for Mum and Dad to keep Eamonn out of trouble without my assistance. I told them to help him apply for a visa. It was a provisional gesture, dependent on him not fucking up in any terminal way before I got back.

It started at Eli's, where he met me with a rented 4x4 in his underground garage. It wasn't dissimilar to the one he usually drove, also black. Flights were too obvious, he said.

'So we're going on a road trip,' I said, finding it hard to be enthusiastic.

'See, you're already making it sound fun,' he replied, uncharacteristically peppy as he slung a couple of bags into the boot alongside a designer suitcase.

'Aren't we a little old for this?' I looked him up and down. 'I mean, we're both wearing two-thousand-dollar outfits. I've got kids.'

He smiled, enjoying my discomfort. 'Come on, I'll buy you an *I heart NYC* shirt on the way if it'll cheer you up.'

'This is gonna be like *Fear And Loathing*, isn't it? Except sober and no fucking fun.'

'Not if you count ProPlus as a drug.'

I sighed. 'So we're going to New York first?'

'Yeah, here's the itinerary.' He climbed into the driver's seat and handed me a thick dossier.

I took the folder and circled the car to get in beside him. I looked at the dossier and frowned. 'Eli, do you think it's maybe not the best idea to go around *printing* stuff out?'

'That's what shredders and fire are for. Calm down.'

'You haven't saved all this shit anywhere, have you? Like, online or on your desktop or something?'

A stern look. 'Of course not.'

I wished I'd worn something more appropriate; sunglasses or a fucking Hawaiian shirt or something that summed up just how disgruntled I was with this experience.

'Where are we going to sleep?' I asked, with genuine sorrow.

'Motels. Nowhere above one star in the cities, they take too much notice of people. Plus, if Seven is remotely smart for a female, she's going to know you'll be coming. The longer you can stay out of sight, the better.'

I grimaced. 'You know when you change that *h* to an *m* you lose a fuck-load of amenities. It's the difference between having a decent minibar or being stuck with a kettle and one of those dwarf hairdryers attached to the wall with curly wire. You know, the ones that have to come with warning labels like "Do not eat" because the place is full of mongoloids who need to be told that kind of thing?'

He started the engine and snorted. 'Yeah, exactly like that.'

'And there's no room service.'

'I know.'

'No, I mean it. Absolutely none.'

He drove us up the ramp and back out into the weak sunlight. 'So you won't be able to drink soy milk and order gluten-free burgers or whatever for a few weeks. It'll be good for you.'

I leafed through the pages and was amused to see he'd created a contents page, listing names and locations next to page numbers. It made me feel a little more at ease. It made me feel that, working with someone as meticulous as Eli, the next few weeks might not be as much of a disaster as I'd thought.

The first name on the list, just above the entry of *New York*, was Thomas Love. There was even a photo, when I turned to his page.

Thomas Love had moved to New York in 2006. Previously an accountant at a UK publisher, he had made the move to take over the same managerial position at the Larsson Group. Love had white-blond hair that reached his shoulders, severe cheekbones and an even more severe fringe.

'He joined our magazine briefly, for about six months, after graduation,' Eli said, with a glance down at the page. 'We were at uni together and he knew Trent quite well, both being super rich. They paired up for a bit after I was given the boot, throwing money at anything that interested them.'

'Does he sparkle when he goes out in daylight?'

A blank glare.

'Aw, come on, it was a book reference!' I raised my eyebrows. 'I thought you'd like that.'

'You don't read but you read *Twilight*.'

'Not by choice obviously, I've read parts of it to Chantal. It was awkward.' I shook my head, smirking. 'So why are we calling on this guy? They still in touch?'

'I know Trent would have contacted him at some point. We didn't all leave it on the best terms, but I don't think Love actually fell out with Trent.'

There was a silence.

I scanned the rest of the list.

Thomas Love. New York.

Cam Hopper. LA.

Trent Byrne. ?

Melissa de Ehrmann. London.

Between Thomas Love and Cam Hopper, I scribbled, *Seven. Chicago.*

I flipped Melissa de Ehrmann's page, the only other girl, and exhaled.

'O-M-*fucking*-G, Eli.'

'What?'

'What do you mean, *what*? She's hot.' I raised my eyebrows. 'Is this a recent photo?'

'From a few years ago.'

I didn't imagine a few years would make much difference to someone as attractive as Melissa de Ehrmann. She was skinny, so skinny as to be almost androgynous, with red curly hair and tiny childlike features, green eyes. In the photo she looked to be standing with a friend – cropped out – in front of a river somewhere, in summer.

'You ever tap that at uni?' I asked, only half joking.

Eli looked in the other direction. When faced with a question he didn't want to answer, he never became evasive. Instead he had an autistic habit of simply averting his eyes and not saying anything.

Interesting, I thought, and moved on.

'So tell me something about Trent Byrne then.'

'If I didn't know him better I'd say he'd changed his name

or something, but...' He pulled a dubious face. 'Why would he even feel the need? It wouldn't make any sense, it's not like he was some kind of gangster. He was just a businessman.'

'It's been a while. People change.'

'Yeah, but I could never picture Trent doing anything interesting enough to disappear over.'

'You know what they say.'

'No?'

'You know, it's always the quiet ones?'

I eyed Trent's photo. *Just a guy* would be how to describe him. *Just a guy.*

'The thing about psychos and people who do things like shoot up offices and fake their own deaths and stuff, they're always the quiet ones. People who knew them never say, "Oh yeah, he was the life and soul of the party. Always up for a laugh."'

He didn't seem convinced. 'Are you saying psychopaths can never be extroverts?'

I thought I might be onto something. 'Well, if they had more mates and went out more often, they probably wouldn't have developed all their social issues and have anger management problems.'

'But you're an extrovert.'

'And I'm an extremely well-adjusted human being.' I grinned, taking a cursory read of the accompanying biographical details on the hit list.

I knew Eli's expression would be condescending.

'I guess LA is gonna be nice this time of year,' I said, for the sake of noise.

'Fuck!' Eli slammed the brakes on and the folder fell off my lap into the footwell as we both snapped forwards.

I rubbed the back of my neck, looked up, and there was the

back end of a BMW in front of us, way too close. Windows were wound down. A defiant middle finger attached to a thick forearm was thrust in our direction.

'Fucking...' Eli snarled, unclipping his seatbelt.

He was out of his seat before I could say anything, coat billowing. I watched as he stormed up to the side of the BMW just as the offending window was promptly shut.

'Fuck you! Come out here and say that! Come out here!' He slammed both hands flat against the window as if he were about to smash through it with his head. 'What's your fucking problem, jerk-off? What's your *fucking* problem?'

Whoever the guy was, he revved his engine and drove off sharpish, leaving Eli standing in the middle of the road, frustrated and pacing, as if he was considering giving chase. The car behind us beeped and Eli made a violent gesture as he returned to his seat.

I didn't say anything. I stared straight ahead, mouth contorting as I tried so fucking badly not to laugh but I couldn't help it. It came out eventually in an undignified guffaw.

'Oh, like that ass-hat proves your point,' Eli scoffed.

'Dude, you're the one who blackmailed me into doing this *Kill Bill* fucking road-trip with you.' I picked up the folder from where it had landed by my feet and grimaced as the back of my neck twinged. 'Just saying.'

CHAPTER NINE

I hated New York City. It was an unfashionable opinion; well up there with 'I really enjoy touching kids', 'Cats are a waste of space' and other similar sentiments. It was as if a whole generation of people lost their grip on the idea of personal space and decided to push the human population upwards, in ever higher and ever narrower imitations of housing. There were adverts everywhere, neon spattered across the sides of every building like a rampaging capitalist Titan had ejaculated over the whole city. Even though I lived in London, so should have been used to this, it made me feel sick being here for too long.

Eli took us to a pizza place in Greenwich Village after the rental car had been hoisted into the air and left somewhere I didn't bother to remember. There were photos all over the walls, the manager or owner posing with celebrities and autographed faces in black and white. Eli had made a list of the top ten pizza places in the city and apparently this was the best.

'Tom won't be easy to talk to,' he said, folding a monstrous slice of pepperoni pizza in half and speaking around it as he shovelled it into his mouth. 'But he's most likely to know where Trent might be. I sent him a text in the car, asking if he fancies a meeting at his place tomorrow, hinted that it might be business-related.'

He grinned.

I wondered what kind of revenge he had in mind where Thomas Love was concerned. I was big on revenge, when it was righteous and fair. I'd never bought into the New Testament bullshit of turning the other cheek. An eye for an eye, that's what mattered. That's what had come first.

Eli and I had never talked about religion. In the next hour, I realized why.

He fixed me with a level gaze, and said, 'You should be an atheist, Ronnie. It surprises me that you're not.'

Eli said this kind of shit all the time to be provocative, so I managed not to become angry right away.

'Why?'

'Because you're not stupid. When you come across a relatively intelligent person you've got to assume they're an atheist. It's the only thing that makes sense.'

I looked down at the chequered tablecloth and sighed. 'Why would you even say that? It's like you *want* to have a fight right before you've got to rely on me for help.'

'I saw you say Grace, right then.' He nodded at my plate. 'Before you ate that, I saw you pause and, I don't know, *say* something in your head.'

'It's habit.' I shrugged. 'If I tell my kids to do it, I've got to remember. Got to set an example and all that.'

'But you believe it, don't you?'

I wasn't sure how to respond.

'Fascinating,' he said.

'You know Eli dies in the Bible from falling backwards out of a chair and breaking his neck.'

He smirked. 'Is that meant to trouble me? It's a story book.

I could write a story about a guy called Ronnie who rides a flying shark into an active volcano with a load of nukes strapped to him but it still doesn't mean anything.'

'Aren't you Jewish, with a name like yours?'

'My parents were Jewish.'

'And you didn't for a moment think they might be right?'

That smirk again. 'It's all stories. Why would I take them seriously? I read about four books a week when I was a teenager. Even if it's non-fiction you've got to take it all with a pinch of salt. You're reading one person's interpretation and that's it. With religious texts it's even more. You're reading dozens, maybe hundreds of interpretations of *fiction*.'

I felt a little sorry for him. 'It's there for a reason. Those stories are there to give you guidelines, teach you about right and wrong—'

'If you think the Bible teaches you right from wrong, then you must think you're going to hell.'

He didn't shy away from the direct accusation.

Everyone in the pizza place seemed quiet when he said that, like they were listening in to hear their fates. I tried not to think of other people in terms of the blip on their souls; it became too easy to slip into contempt, then hatred, than sadism, then chaos. Damned as we all were, shouldn't we make the best of it? Or, damned as we all were, an opposing voice so frequently said inside my head, why should any of us care?

'Yeah,' I said, finding it easier to vocalize than I'd predicted. 'We all are.'

'Then why worry about any of this?' Eli indicated at everything about us, with this funny little smile. 'If you're right, then no matter how fucked up things get, this is all better than where we're going.'

I wasn't hungry any more. The rest of my pizza went untouched.

I still haven't spoken to my kids, I thought.

That night, morbidly dossing around on my laptop in my single room, I looked up the Richard Ramirez interview that Eli had quoted at me and watched it on YouTube. The room was featureless, blank. The most exciting item it contained was a painting of a beach above the bed. There was a Bible on the bedside table.

Killing is killing, whether done for glory, profit, or fun. Men murdered themselves into this democracy.

Something about Ramirez, about his peculiarly compelling face and the way he spoke, reminded me of a man I knew back home, Mark Chester. Mark Chester was a contract killer. He was friends with Noel, and Daisy, but he was someone I'd cross the road to avoid. I didn't like the way he looked at people, like everyone was fair game. You could never tell if he was thinking about killing you or fucking you, I'd said to Noel tonnes of times, or in what order.

There are different sects of Satanism. The Satanist admits to being evil. We are all evil in one form or another, are we not?

It didn't sound like Satanism to me, admitting to being evil. Catholics admitted to being evil, to being sinners. Admitting to evil didn't mean worshipping Satan. That would be ridiculous. I snorted out loud to myself in the empty room and shut my laptop, thinking this Ramirez wasn't that fucking smart.

It was so loud here, so much louder than London. Nobody knew when to sleep here, when to just shut the hell up.

I still haven't spoken to my kids, I thought.

Thomas Love wanted to meet for brunch. *Brunch*.

'Is Thomas Love even his real name?' I asked, pouring a takeaway black coffee down my throat, unable to wait until we got to the café in question. 'He sounds like a porn star.'

'I don't think Love was his real surname.' Eli seemed thoughtful. 'But I don't know what he was originally called. Came from real upper-class stock though, whole family was from Ascot.'

We halted outside some upmarket place with flowers around its windows. 'Should have known it'd be somewhere like this.'

I peered through the glass and couldn't help but wonder if Love hadn't deliberately picked this place because he knew we wouldn't start anything. It was too crowded, too full of couples, businessmen, people you couldn't pay off or silence… I was glad we had bothered wearing suits.

Places like this reminded me why New York had never appealed to me in the same way that London did. London claimed to be a classless society, even if that claim was a barefaced lie, but New York was living this reality. The only people who could still afford to live here were the white, old and wealthy. It was openly hostile to the young, to aspirers. You couldn't afford to be an amateur any more. Not many places tolerated it. You had to emerge into the world a fully formed hardened professional or you'd be eaten alive, reduced to staring in a thousand windows like this until you either killed yourself, moved away, or stopped looking in at windows.

'Eli. Well, you haven't changed.'

We both turned in unison.

The only kind of arseholes who wore white suits were those who knew they could afford to buy another if it became tarnished. He had the same bowl haircut he'd been sporting in his photo, but the skin of his face was pulled back a little tighter now, was more artfully tanned. He looked like a rock star.

If Eli killed him, I realized I wouldn't lose much sleep over it.

'Tom!'

The two of them did that half hug half handshake thing that men did when they weren't sure how to greet someone and then parted, with Tom smoothing down his lapels and Eli smoothing back his hair, as if they'd both contracted something unpleasant.

'Your hair still hasn't moved,' Eli remarked, playfully swatting at his head. 'Is it made of plastic now too?'

'At least I still have hair.' Love swatted back, aiming for the edges of Eli's slightly receded hairline, and then spotted me. 'You must be Ronnie O'Connell. I'm Tom. Tom Love.'

We shook hands and he was stone-cold.

I looked around, half expecting him to have a bodyguard, but he was alone as far as I could tell.

He ordered a glass of wine with breakfast even though it was ten in the morning. The smell made me feel ill and I drank my coffee in double time.

'Trent,' Tom said, having just ordered eggs florentine. 'Now that's a name I haven't thought about in a while.'

'When was the last time you heard from him?' Eli folded and refolded his napkin.

'Must be three years ago now, maybe longer. He sent me a couple of postcards. Obviously I don't have them on me but I'm sure at least one is in my apartment somewhere.'

'You still have them?' I didn't think Tom seemed the sort to keep things for sentimental value; I imagined his apartment to be as sterile and white and minimal as the man sitting across from me. 'After all this time?'

'I liked the photo on the front. Burning palm trees.'

'Where did he send it from?'

'The stamp said St Louis, Missouri.'

'What was he doing there?'

'Teaching English... Probably. It's what he did after he left us. Melissa heard from him more recently, I think. From LA, she said.' Tom picked up his glass and smiled. 'No hard feelings about that, Eli. It was nothing personal.'

'Water under the bridge. Or something.' Eli downed his coffee like it was a shot of whisky.

I wondered whether they were alluding to business or Melissa.

'What do you do, Ronnie?' Tom turned his attentions to me, briefly.

'I run a gentleman's club in London. I also work in exports. I suppose I'm an entrepreneur, if you wanna get all French about it.'

Euphemism inside euphemism.

'So what brings you both out here? Is it really just to look for Trent? Seems a strange time to become so interested in his whereabouts. As I recall, you didn't take that much interest in him when he was alive—'

'You think he's no longer alive?' Eli sat up straighter in his chair.

'It's unlikely, I think.'

Tom was casting his eyes about for his food, as was I. Our eyes met while searching for a waiter.

The doilies were doing my head in. I kept pushing mine back and forth, hoping I could maybe slide it off the table.

'Maybe you should ask Melissa?' Tom's face split with an expression of utter elation at the sight of his breakfast being brought over. As it was set down he looked Eli in the eyes and said, 'She's the one who used to talk to him the most. Are you still in touch?'

I thought Eli was going to leap the table and throttle him, but a plate full of croissants and fruit was blocking him.

My gaze drifted downwards, out of habit, and I saw Tom was holding a gun down by the side of the table, imperceptibly, as if it were a mobile, or a cigarette. But it was there all the same, and it was aimed at me.

Tom picked up his fork with his right hand, speared a load of spinach and egg yolk, and ate with the nonchalance of a cat.

It was almost offensive he could function, I thought, with a haircut that infantile. It was the sort of haircut Noel would have taken a photo of and messaged to me.

I glanced at Eli, but there was no way to silently convey what was happening out of his view.

Tom wasn't going to shoot me. Not here. Not unless he had to. So I picked up my coffee, took a sip, and a bite of French toast. Then I said, 'Eli, I'm not one to make a drama but I thought you should know there's a gun being pointed at me this side of the table.'

Eli made to stand up.

Tom made a clicking sound with his teeth. 'Bad idea. Really bad idea.

Caught in an awkward crouch, Eli lowered himself back into his seat.

'You think I'd be so *stupid*?' Tom said, his voice low, a hiss.

Eli shrugged. 'Honestly … yes.'

'Yes, insult the man with the gun pointed at me. Very smart,'

I muttered, moving the doily around the table again at right angles. 'Fuck's sake.'

Eli shook his head. 'How did you know?'

'I've known you were coming *for years*. You're just the right brand of insane to hold a grudge this long. When I said you haven't changed, I meant it.'

Tom bared his teeth when he spoke.

'Who brings a gun to *brunch?*' I snapped, more to myself than anyone else.

Tom ate his breakfast with one hand.

I carried on eating because I was hungry and being shot on an empty stomach was an only slightly more tragic prospect than being shot whilst satisfied and eating bacon. It also took my mind off the silent stand-off.

Eli wasn't touching his food.

'I haven't spoken to Melissa for a while,' he said, straightening his cutlery.

I watched the couple at the table to our right, an animated Chanel ad, but they were oblivious, staring only at each other and occasionally at their iPhones. Great. No one notices when you're in a crisis yet if you were murdered in front of them they'd probably have the presence of mind to film it.

'She next?' Tom asked.

'What makes you think there is a next? I might just hate you.'

'You're looking for Trent, you came for me first... I'm getting the impression I should probably phone Cam when I leave. Of course you'd call on Melissa.' He decapitated his English muffin with the side of his fork without looking at the table. 'It was her that must have hurt the most, after all.'

I wondered if I could knock the gun out of his hands from

here, maybe disarm him. Not without causing a scene, and we couldn't be causing a scene right now. Not this early in the game.

I eyed the couple decked out in Chanel again, and then raised my hand to motion for a waiter.

The gun immediately disappeared, as I asked, 'May I have some Dijon mustard please?'

'Of course, sir.'

The waiter was standing in the exact spot where Tom's trigger finger had been, so much more helpful than he could have imagined.

Saved by condiments, I thought. *Fucking hell.*

As the waiter walked away, Tom stood up, glowering.

'Don't bother looking for me at home,' he said, moving away. 'You won't find me.'

Eli picked up his knife and fork, relief descending upon the table now that the firearm was concealed. 'You know I'll find you eventually.'

'I'm sure we'll continue this conversation then.'

Tom swept out of the café.

Not long after, the waiter brought over my mustard.

'Well, I suppose now it's interesting,' Eli mused. 'Paranoid old fucker.'

'Interesting is not the word I'd have gone for.'

'Now it's fun.' Straightening his cutlery again.

'How'd you figure that? If he thinks you're on some mad rampage, won't he try and warn everyone else?'

'He has no idea where Trent is, even if he did get a postcard. And he won't warn Melissa. He'll warn Cam maybe, but not her.' With some deliberation, Eli picked up a croissant and looked at it with unfathomable loathing. 'He hates her almost as much as I do.'

He wasn't going to explain if I asked him to elaborate, so I didn't for now.

For now, I gestured at Tom's empty plate and sighed. 'And he's left us to pick up the bill.'

CHAPTER TEN

'I'm going home.'

'Don't be melodramatic.'

'I'm not. It's a simple statement. I'm going home, then I'm going to Chicago.'

Eli caught up with me and grabbed my arm.

'*Fuck* off.'

'It's not as if your life was really in danger.'

'If it wasn't then, it fucking *is* now! How was I meant to know you were such a flaming nut-job that he saw a revenge plot coming for over a fucking decade? No wonder your old mate Trent has gone off the fucking radar!' I resumed walking, but couldn't remember where our hotel was.

'Wait!'

'No! What part of "fuck off" are you struggling with?'

Eli slowed, and for some reason I stopped with him.

He lowered his voice and turned slightly away from the bagel stand we'd halted next to. The man behind it surveyed us, arms folded.

'Are we really going to have a domestic in the street after *brunch*, Ron?' Eli said, deadpan. 'Is that what you're going to make happen right now?'

'Yep. Get domestic on me.'

'Fine.' Eli looked over his shoulder at the bagel man again, who was still staring at us. 'You *owe* me.'

'Like fuck I do. I can't take on the debt for all this shit you've done for Dad, it's not fair. Why can't he come with you, eh? If it's so fucking important.'

'Because is it *fucking* important!' he snapped, hands balled into fists. 'Of course I'd ask you before your father. You have twice the mind of that man, and you know it.'

The bagel man was freaking me out, so I started walking again.

'You're not going to make me stay with flattery.'

'Just come and search his apartment with me.'

'Why? So I can have a gun pointed at me again?'

'No, because... Oh come on, you can't turn down a good mystery. You really don't want to know where Trent is?'

'Why should I? I didn't know him.'

I sidestepped a child only to find myself facing a pack of dogs on a spiderweb of leashes. I turned and crossed the road, still with little idea of where I was going.

'Yeah, but you wanna know.'

'Why?'

He caught my arm again. 'A guy disappeared, no one knows why or where and you're telling me you have *zero* interest?'

I stopped again, because he was the only chance I had of finding our hotel. 'Yeah, I'm interested, but it's not about that. It's about a load of people who now know you want them dead, and are going to be waiting for you. I didn't sign up for that, this isn't fucking *Thunderdome*.'

'I told you, he won't have warned Melissa. Or Trent.'

'And you know that, how? You don't even know where Trent is.'

'Just… come to his apartment, help me find that postcard. If you still want to go home after that, then fine.' A fleeting moment of humility, but it was replaced with something like hate, a promise of hate. 'But I won't forget it.'

Great. I took him at his word and thought, *I'm going home.*

'Well, where the fuck are we staying again? Because I'm not going without a weapon.'

I wondered if I'd imagined that moment before, as he smiled at me. 'Neither am I.'

I walked into the building first. It occurred to Eli that the doorman might know what he looked like, if Tom Love really was as paranoid as all that. I'd changed into the most poncy outfit I'd packed, another one of my suits, and slicked back my hair. By the time it came to waving *'Afternoon'* to the guy behind the desk in the entrance hall, he didn't give me a second glance.

Making my way to the rear of the building by the fire escape, I let Eli in.

We took the lift to the fourth floor and Eli coolly shot the lock off the door with a silenced automatic.

It was as if Tom's suit had mutated, formed furniture and built itself property. Everything was impossibly and horribly white. It was like walking into an alien spacecraft, and not in a cool way.

'Jesus, how does any guy *live* like this? I'm afraid to touch anything.'

'He's severe OCD.' Eli was running his hands along the back of a pristine sofa. He could never deal with chaos. Maybe it's not so surprising that he expected this.'

'Hm.'

There were no pictures on the walls, nothing. Just the sofa, coffee table and a TV so large as to be horrifying. A black hole threatening to engulf everything else in the room.

Squinting, I made my way down the hall. The bedroom was no different, the wardrobes undisturbed. I could picture him having emergency luggage already packed and ready to leave. He must have had no attachment to this home, despite his best efforts to keep it spotless. There were a million things I'd return to my house for if I knew I was never coming back; maybe too many things. It was disgusting really, our infantile clutching at *stuff.*

'You sure he wouldn't keep all kinds of paper shit in an office somewhere?' I called back to Eli.

'He definitely said at home.' He appeared in the doorway, and went to part some of the hangers and suits in the wardrobe. 'He'd have a box for it. Just something to keep loose paper together in one place. Like that!'

He gestured at the suitcases and shoeboxes lining the upper shelf.

We both set about dragging them down in piles and opening them. Most of the cases contained other, smaller cases. But the shoeboxes had more. I watched Eli pick up a wad of bank statements and whistle.

'What?'

'If I gave a shit about money, I'd be jealous.' He put them to one side and pushed another of the boxes towards me. 'Have a look through there.'

I sifted through stationery, letters, a few scattered birthday cards, yellowed childhood photos and photos of his parents and then...

'Hey, check it.'

Burning palm trees.

DEAR TOM.

'Fuck!' Eli reached out and his hands stopped in mid-air, fell, jerkily came up again. 'Well, read it.'
I turned the postcard over.

DEAR TOM,

Sorry for not being in touch. I've been away for a while, teaching in St Louis. I appreciated your letter when Elsbeth died. Don't think it passed by unnoticed or unappreciated.

I'm going away for a while again.

We are hard pressed on every side, crushed; perplexed, in despair; persecuted, abandoned; struck down, destroyed.

Sincerely,
T.

Eli stared at me.
'He sounds cheery,' I said.
'Yeah, that got dark pretty quickly,' Eli remarked, reaching out and taking the postcard. 'What does the last bit mean?'
'It's a Bible quote, I think.'
Screwing up his face like a bad smell had entered the room. 'Trent wasn't a Christian.'
'Yeah, but it's not a proper Bible quote, the real one is... positive. My kids learn them at school, the good bits like that.'
'The bits that aren't about sodomy and genocide?'
'Yeah, *those*.'
Eli rubbed a hand over his face, collecting his thoughts.
'I don't know...' he said, slowly.
'Know what?'

'Whether to drive on to St Louis and worry about Tom later, or stay here and hope we get lucky.'

I cleared my throat. '*We* again, is it? Like how you slipped that in.'

'Like you're going to go home after reading that.' He thrust the card in my face. 'He was clearly losing his mind! Starts quoting the Bible and then disappears off the face of the earth. Are you saying that doesn't *intrigue* you?'

It had. The strange little message had given me a buzz, as if we'd uncovered a lost treasure map. But I wasn't going to make it sound as though enticing my interest was that fucking easy.

I snorted and said, 'There's still a psychotic albino on the loose so at the moment I'm more concerned about that.'

'Then we'll go,' he cut in. 'We'll go straight to St Louis. I'll deal with Tom later, but come on, Ron, help me find Trent.'

And then—

'You're not meant to be in here…'

We both turned, necks snapping back at this unfamiliar voice and the unfamiliar puffy white face with oversized comedy black eyebrows scowling at us.

I have no fucking idea how he got there; the doorman suddenly stood in the doorway, looking back and forth between us with his weapon still holstered but armed nonetheless. *What sort of doorman was fucking armed?* But it was his gaze coming to rest on Eli that made me move, the half whispered half muttered, 'It's *you*!' that propelled me off the bed and across the room to rugby-tackle the guy to the floor.

'Fuck!'

I must have almost pulled his arm clean out of his socket, as I dragged it across me and bashed it over and over again into the floor, before I realized it was carpet and wasn't making a fucking shred of difference, so I freed my right hand and punched him in the face instead.

Spatter marks across the white.

His gun was in my hand.

'How do you know him?' I jerked my head back at Eli, who hadn't moved.

The guy just glared.

'How do you know him?'

Looking away.

'I *will* shoot you,' I said. 'In the *face*.'

'Mr Love... made me keep his photo behind my desk.'

'Did he say who he was?'

'No. He just said if he was seen I had to alert him immediately, wherever he was.'

'Wait wait.' Eli clapped his hands together. '*Wherever* he was, you say? Do you know where he is right now?'

The doorman shook his head, but a little too late.

'No, I don't know where he is.'

'Yes, you do,' I said, driving the barrel into his throat.

'I don't, I promise.'

'Tell us where he is and we won't kill you before we leave. How about that?'

Eli crouched and rubbed his fingertips against the blood on the floor, creating streaks. 'I imagine he's offered to pay you a lot for this trouble.'

Silence.

'I'll take that as a yes.' Raising his fingers from the carpet, turning them over in front of his eyes. 'Let me tell you now, it isn't going to make any difference, because Tom is going to die either way. You can die with him if you want. But is he worth your life, *really*?'

The guy was thinking.

Eli said, 'He's not worth dying for, you must know that.'

Eyes moving from Eli to me, downwards to the gun under his chin.

He sniffed and said, 'Get the fuck off me and I'll tell you.'

CHAPTER ELEVEN

Daisy

I don't know what made me think it was a good idea to try and keep tabs on Edie and her phone calls. Maybe it was because of Seven and what she had done, giving me ideas. Maybe I just felt so disconnected from what was going on that I craved any insight. Or maybe everything seemed like a good idea when you were dabbing MDMA for breakfast. It was the only thing that kept me going to work without wanting to kill myself when I came home to an empty flat.

Nic was never there any more, so consumed was he by the search for Seven. Our other flatmate, Mark Chester, was also away. Both of them felt responsible for what had happened. Mark had told me himself: he should have seen it coming. Nic didn't need to say it; his absence spoke volumes.

'My phone's dead,' I said – hollered – to Edie in the middle of a shift over the house music playing over Xara's performance. 'Can I call Nic on yours?'

'Sure, honey.'

Edie was sat at a table of customers and barely looked at me as she handed her phone over.

I crouched outside the fire escape and scrolled through her address book. I glanced at my watch, calculated the time difference, and tried calling Ronnie. He might answer if he thought it was Edie.

He didn't answer.

Noel wasn't here again.

Prickles of anxiety, little claws grating against the inside of my breastplate.

I'm not paid enough for this shit.

I didn't sign up for this shit.

I'm not cut out for this shit.

I called Nic even though I knew he wouldn't pick up, just to make it look convincing, and then scrolled through the address book again. I didn't recognize any names. I went into her Calls tab and didn't recognize any names there either.

Paul O.

I copied a few of the numbers into my phone and stood up. The very act of becoming upright almost made me black out. All sound was amplified, the hum of traffic and activity on the main road becoming a mechanical whirr. My muscles went numb. I leant against the wall until my vision cleared and everything returned to normal.

Putting both phones in the pocket of my shorts, I took out my tobacco and started to roll a cigarette to steady my hands.

I started laughing. 'You're not losing it, you're not losing it, totally not, no way.'

The cigarette did nothing but increase my anxiety so I stubbed it out and called Noel again.

He wasn't picking up to either number.

Fucking figures.

'Hey, I don't know where you are, if you're at home or whatever but can you think about maybe, y'know, *coming in* anytime soon? It'd be super nice to not deal with all this shit on my own. Um… Oh, fuck it.'

That was the message I left. I wasn't confident he'd listen to it.

I went inside and gave Edie back her phone.

There probably was nothing going on, I thought; no relevance to the numbers I'd copied. I just needed to let my brain chemicals level out.

That night when I went home, Nic was there. He told me that Mark Chester was back from Russia and then he asked me to move out.

CHAPTER TWELVE

Ronnie

When I'd been younger, way younger, maybe before Eamonn had been born but it was hard to be sure, Dad took me on a ranching holiday in Oklahoma. On the second day he'd taught me how to skin a beaver and then later on he let me help him flay – but not actually hunt and kill – a cow.

I'd always thought of skin as an indisputable part of you, attached with the surety that your hands were to your arms or your lungs to the inside of your ribcage. Watching the skinnings gave me nightmares for years. I was horrified by how easily the skin came away. Far from being impressed with the efficiency of the method, I watched the knife nicking skin away from flesh, nicking away and nicking away, and it falling into my father's hands like it was *meant* to do that, like orange peel – no, *easier* than orange peel – and I told them I needed to go for a piss behind a tree and projectile-vomited instead.

In my dreams, I'd be doing something totally normal, like playing football, and I'd fall and nick a part of my skin, flaying it clean off. I woke up, always clutching at my arms, convinced my skin was no longer there until I had turned on the light.

Thinking about it, as we did the same thing to Thomas Love, strung upside down in another snow-white bedroom, that was probably why I'd got the tattoos on my forearms. They were nothing fancy, just my kids' names. But they were a small reminder that parts of my body weren't going anywhere.

Mine weren't, anyway.

I couldn't say the same for Thomas.

'What's wrong?' Eli asked, as I took a step back and supported myself against the nearest wall.

'Nothing. Really, go crazy. I'm just gonna sit for a second.'

I sat on the edge of the bed with my hands clasped in my lap. Even by my standards, this was too much blood. I lost the will to participate at around the time I realized Eli was using this extreme act of violence to lock me in, lock me into the alibi we'd have to share.

Thomas hadn't gone far, Eli had been right when he'd predicted that. He was too complacent and lazy to really go on the run; it would require too much effort when you could just throw money at the problem instead.

'Are you sure you're good?' Eli checked again.

'Fine, just go ahead.'

I didn't have to participate. Eli hadn't been the one to kill Carey. If I wanted to sit by and observe, there wasn't anything wrong with that.

It didn't seem to bother Eli too much. He pushed me aside some time after Thomas had stopped screaming through the tape across his mouth, and dug both hands into the sides of his face so hard I thought he was going to rip his skull clean in half.

I had been going to call my kids after we left the body, hanging, shredded and caked in blood, mouth lolling open, teeth and tongue gone. But I avoided it again. I had this mad idea they'd somehow be able to see the horror on me, through that telepathic link you get with your kids from time to time.

I had a missed call from Edie, I noticed. No fucking way I was dealing with *that*.

We made it past Indianapolis by the end of the day. It was a forty-hour drive from New York to LA, we ascertained from Google Maps. I'd wanted to more carefully plan our route to avoid tolls but Eli didn't care. He was all about the path of least resistance, though since killing Tom there was a noticeable spring in his step, exhilaration in the way he drove.

Our alibi was watertight, because New York was a city were Eli knew people. No one was going to follow us unless we got extremely unlucky.

It was in Bloomington, this quaint little place – well, quaint by US standards – lined with trees, that I finally found the time and place to Skype Rachel and the kids.

Eli parked outside a hotel, checked us both in and then left to do God-knows-what.

I loitered in my single room for a while, flipped through the room service menu and ordered a burger, some fries, 'slaw and three beers, taking advantage of the fact I'd talked Eli into choosing a slightly more upmarket place in the absence of anything scuzzier.

When food arrived, I took Eli's dossier out of my bag and spread it all out on the bed, in order of page numbers.

I knew enough people in LA to organize an alibi, surely. I scribbled a list of names, none of whom I'd spoken to face-to-face in a long time, and made a mental note to stop at a payphone and give them all a call.

Cameron Hopper had left Cain & Byrne way before Thomas Love, to work at the BBC, before moving to LA three years ago as a producer. He looked too rough for LA, too Scottish. I wondered if he'd got his teeth done yet. I heard it was mandatory once you got sucked into that scene.

He was a big guy. It wasn't as if we'd had the element of surprise in New York, but compared to Love, Hopper would be tough to take down. It was only very occasionally that size didn't matter in that regard. I'd read a news story a while ago about a guy high on meth, who fought off fifteen police officers while publicly masturbating. He was no man-mountain either. That was my definition of dedication.

A Skype call came through from my dad and I answered it with the webcam off.

'How's it going?' I said.

'Can you hear me?'

'Yeah, Dad, I can hear you.'

A pause.

'Can you hear me now?'

'Yep, I could hear you before.'

'Can you see me?'

'No, I haven't switched the webcam on.'

'Why?'

I took a deep breath and turned on my webcam.

My dad's face flooded the screen, pixellated. His eyes focused on me, then at the thumbnail of himself in the corner, frowning.

'Why can I see myself?'

'I don't know, Dad, in case someone breaks in, you can see them coming up behind you.'

He glanced behind him for a moment.

My dad was one of the smartest men I knew and things like

Skype floored him. It almost made me feel sorry for people of his generation, but at the same time it was something to envy. They only had to deal with one universe; the way they had escaped was by old-fashioned means, like books and music and maybe TV. But they didn't have to fight the lure of the multiverse, the layers and layers of code that now dictated a whole other personification of ourselves, our online doppelgangers.

'Where are you?' he asked, looking at the room behind me.

'Bloomington.'

'Where's that?'

'Are you just checking in, Dad?'

'Do you think Eamonn might have something to gain by joining you?'

I had to get up to answer the knock at the door that heralded the arrival of food, but I hoped that Dad had the time to appreciate my look of disdain. 'Er, why?'

He shrugged. 'It would make sense for him to get out of town, maybe see a bit of the country. It's not good for him here. I can see him slipping back into... old patterns.'

'Get him a job!'

'There's no point bribing someone into giving him a job for him to leave a month later.' He looked at me, brow first, how he always addressed me when he was pulling rank. 'Can you stay where you are for a couple of days?'

'Um, no.' I felt empowered by the computer screen dividing us.

'You could always make use of him? He could even help you.'

'No, I really don't think he could help.'

'Why not?'

'It's already too dangerous without adding Eamonn to the equation.'

'He could do with becoming used to how you and Eli work.'

'Like *adults*. That's how we work.'

I picked up my burger and tried to fold the entire thing into my mouth.

Dad watched me with blank features. 'Yes, I can see that.'

'If Eamonn wants to be useful, he can work on his. And I don't mean in a forge-it-to-fuck and make-shit-up kinda way. Anyway, how is Mum gonna cope with him coming back with me?' I asked, eyes on my food. 'You think this is unfair to her? She gets her son back after all this time and then he leaves the country.'

He looked pensive. 'We might not stay here for ever.'

'You're thinking of moving?'

'Maybe. It would be good for your mother to be around her grandchildren... and her own children.'

'You'd move the business too?'

Nothing. Just a non-committal downturn of the lips.

The prospect of being in competition with my own father or, worse, being subjected to his overseeing presence, was up there with the most stressful things that had happened in the last week.

'We'll think about it, Ronnie. Let me know when you're arriving in LA.'

'Is Mum there?'

'No.' He fiddled with something to the right of the screen. 'Be careful. Speak to you soon.'

The screen went black.

I thought about crossing the hallway to bend Eli's ear about this, but decided to save it for later.

There was a squeaking sound outside and I looked through my ground-floor window to see a black, white and chestnut cat sat on the grass, miaowing.

I left my room and opened the fire escape, glad of the distraction, and it followed me inside, bumping its head against my legs.

'Hey, what are you doing here, eh?'

I crouched to give it a stroke and it started rolling around on its back. It was wearing a collar; I checked. But there was no information on it. It looked healthy, felt skinny but not malnourished. It was probably just looking for company.

'You wanna come in and... drink something from the minibar?' I asked in an unnaturally shrill voice; the voice I reserved for babies, toddlers and small furry things. 'Come on, come here.'

I backed into my room, propped the door open with my shoes, and sat on my bed again.

The cat followed me in, after a few seconds' pause, and looked at me with wide green eyes.

'Come on.'

I patted the bed and it leapt up, starting to flex its claws in and out of the bed sheet, purring. I went to pick up one of the pages about Cameron Hopper's address but it ran over and started headbutting my hand.

I should buy the kids a cat, I thought. Rachel wasn't that keen on pets, reasoning that the majority of the work involved with looking after one would fall upon her, but the kids were old enough now to look after a kitten. Maybe it would be good for them, having a bit of responsibility.

Across the hall, I heard Eli's door open and close. He didn't come to my room, even though the door was slightly ajar.

For some reason, I was glad.

CHAPTER THIRTEEN

Daisy

The sofa booths in the Underground were way more com-
fortable than they appeared, I discovered after my first night
of sleeping on them. Even when everything was switched off,
the building itself never stopped humming. I'd been homeless
and slept in worse places than this. Wrapped in my sleeping
bag and relatively sober for the last ten hours, it was the best
sleep I'd had in weeks.

I didn't even feel angry with Nic. Most of what I was feeling
was anxiety; the dim wail of it in my veins at all times.

I didn't get up until quarter to eleven, around the time I
would have arrived on any other day. I rolled up the bag and
put it in my locker, applied some make-up and made myself a
coffee. I checked the gun was under the bar.

The staff doorbell went.

Seven. It's Seven.

I pushed the reactionary thought away.

Would taking the gun with me be too much? Too paranoid?

I decided it would be, and forced myself to go and answer
it unarmed.

A man was outside, walking away.

'Hey!' I called.

He turned. There was something instantly familiar about him.

'Are you looking for someone?' I asked.

'Daisy, right?'

Wide, smirking brown eyes observed me from under dark curly hair, and he was wearing a brown waistcoat, like he'd wandered out of a period drama. I felt as though I should be able to place him, if he knew my name.

'Yeah?'

'I'm Sean. Looking for Noel or Ronnie, are they in?'

'Er… no. Ronnie's not in the country, and Noel's off today. What did you want them about?'

He waved a hand. 'Ah, work stuff. Don't worry about it. Neither of them have been answering their phones so thought I'd drop by.'

'Ok. Anything I can pass on?'

He spoke with confidence, but didn't quite meet my eyes while talking. There was an air of customer service about him; confrontational insincerity.

'No, don't worry about it,' he said.

'Really? I can take a message.'

'No worries, love, really. I can call your other boss.'

'Edie?'

'Yeah.'

He gave me an awkward smile, waved, and walked away.

I went back inside to get the keys and then took a walk down the main road to smoke my morning cigarette. The longer I was conscious, the more rough I was beginning to feel. Or it was just sadness, the slow onset of realizing I wasn't in a relationship any more.

But what Nic and I had been doing for the last year was

so far removed from what most people would think of a relationship that it was hard to tell.

That I had nowhere to live was a very real concern.

That Edie was asking questions, trying to assign blame and punishment, was a very real concern.

That random guys were turning up at the club asking after my absentee managers was a very real concern.

That Nic had ended it – whatever *it* had been – seemed more abstract.

Thinking about him was putting me off smoking.

Across the road, outside a tube station, beneath the big red circle sign.

I dropped my cigarette and stepped into the road, whole body cold, shouting, 'Seven!'

She was walking away from me but I knew it was her, I knew her that well. The last I'd seen of her properly had been the back of her head. I jumped onto the kerb as I realized I was in the path of a taxi, and followed her, parallel.

'Seven!'

I waved my arms and thought better of it.

'Move!' I snapped, walking into someone's back and shoving her out of my way.

Seven wasn't looking at me, wasn't looking around at all.

I leapt into the road again, terrified of losing her.

What could you say to the person who shot you – even if you had, technically, asked for it – and fucked up your life and the lives of everyone around you? Sent Noel spiralling back into alcoholism, stole everyone's money and dissolved your familiar routine into chaos? No fucking idea. But I needed to look her in the eye and say… something.

I weaved in and out of the queue of cars on the opposite side of the road, searching for the back of her head.

I just wanted to look her in the eye.

I ran some way down the road, called again, 'Seven!'

But she'd gone.

I turned down side roads, searching for her. But she'd gone.

Tears sprang to my eyes, coming down brutally from the rush of adrenalin. I turned and started to walk back, tried to light another cigarette but couldn't, because I couldn't see and my hands were shaking.

If I had to pick a moment out of our timeline to remember for the worst reasons, it would have been when Nic called me at 23:17 and said I needed to get to 79 Bond Street. The time stood out so clearly.

Nic sounded far away and it wasn't the quality of the line. It was the weird, over-pronounced way he was picking his words.

'Daisy, I need you to get in the car and come to 79 Bond Street.'

I was on the sofa with my bare feet up on the coffee table, having just got out of the shower and painted my toenails bright green.

'Um, you sound super odd.'

'I just need you to come pick me up, right now.'

'Are you pulling a "no-questions-asked"?' I struggled to stay light-hearted but I went for it anyway.

'This isn't fucking funny.'

I went shrill. 'Well it has to be because you know I can't drive. Let alone drive your Audi, it's a fucking monster.'

'Just do it *now*. I know you can drive, you're just not very good at it, that's all.'

'Wow, nice. Look, I'm not going anywhere until I know what's going on.'

I could tell he wanted to shake me. It was a very familiar tone.

He said, 'I was working and it didn't go according to plan, OK? Mark isn't here, so I need you to come and pick me up.'

'From a job?' I swallowed. 'Seriously, you want me to pick you up from a job?'

'Daisy, I've been stabbed with a fucking potato peeler. Now shut the fuck up and get in the car!'

My first instinct was to laugh because it had to be a joke. But it wasn't because Nic just went quiet and I had to take my feet off the coffee table and take an unsteady step towards the bedroom. 'Um... what?'

'I thought he was dead. He wasn't. He got his hands on a fucking potato peeler on his way down.'

'Where are you? You sound... OK?'

'I don't think it hit anything too important but I don't want to see what happens if I sit in this pool of fucking blood all night. I haven't pulled it out yet in case I start haemorrhaging or... well, you're not stupid.'

'So you're just sat in this guy's kitchen?'

'Yes, I'm in his kitchen but I can't leave, I took the tube here.'

Now I wanted to cry. My fear of picking Nic up from a dead man's house equalled my fear of driving through central London. 'I can't. Nic, I can't. I *can't* drive!'

'Daisy just—'

'No, I can't do it!'

'There's *no one else*! Mark isn't fucking here!'

'Oh *fuck*!' Tears sprang to my eyes. 'You fucking *cunt*!'

'You can call me as many names as you like when you get here.'

He was so fucking unapologetic.

'Can you...? OK, fuck, can you at least stay on the line while I'm in the car?'

'No, my battery's low and you'll do better without the distraction. I'm gonna hang up now, but the front door isn't locked. I didn't shut it when...' He hesitated, to take a breath, and it was the first time any trace of pain crept into his voice. 'I didn't shut it. I didn't plan on being here this long.'

I couldn't believe this was happening. I was rooted to the spot with disbelief.

'Well... OK, I'll see you in a fucking *bit* then.'

I couldn't stop time and delay the next few hours for ever.

This was Mark's job. It was him who took Nic's emergency calls and I couldn't even fathom making it to the car without going to pieces. Those two were totally desensitized to violence and I'd never seen a dead body in real life. I'd never seen how much blood could leak out of a punctured artery. I didn't fucking want to. I'd never wanted to for a second.

I went into the bedroom and dropped the towel.

What did you wear to pick up your boyfriend from a crime scene that he'd created?

I settled on a pair of jeans that I didn't mind never wearing again, and a black hoodie.

My hair was still wet.

I could feel my heartbeat in my face, in my stomach.

Nic's car keys were in the bedside table.

I picked them up. They fell from my trembling hands and I burst into tears.

There was one deep lesion down the side of the silver Audi. But there was only the one by the time I parked some way down Bond Street. It was an achievement considering I'd spent the entire drive screaming.

Shivering as my hair drew the chill to my neck, I got out of the car and started wandering down the road. Inside one of these houses was a fucking horror show and I was entering stage right. I'd brought the first aid kit that we kept below the kitchen sink, which at least showed that I was thinking straight.

73, 75, 77...

People were around, arriving home, walking past in small groups of friends. But no one was watching me.

I walked up to the house and gave the door a nudge with my foot.

Slipping inside and shutting it quickly behind me, I found myself in a strange hallway. It was nondescript, painted blue. There was a coat stand upon which Nic had hung his coat before murdering the occupant.

'Nic?' I called, choked up.

'Thank fuck, I thought that was you.'

I half shut my eyes as I pushed open the door at the end of the hall, but even with blurred vision I could make out the blood on the floor.

'Daisy.'

I clapped a hand over my eyes to block out the scene and Nic repeated, 'Daisy, come on. Just look at me. Don't look at all that shit. Just focus on me.'

His voice was weaker than usual.

The tap was dripping frantically. It said a lot about the state of him that Nic hadn't got up to turn it off.

I opened my eyes and stared at him, but it wasn't enough. No one was blinkered enough to block out a dead body when it was in their field of vision. It was slumped against the cupboards like Nic was. To me it looked like a cartoon; white and puffy like the Marshmallow Man.

Stay Puft, I thought.

I began laughing hysterically, and Nic didn't seem surprised.
He was sat up, hugging himself with his right arm.

But he was alive.

'That's quite a normal reaction,' he said.

'It... he looks like *Stay Puft*.'

He frowned.

A couple of tears fell. 'The marshmallow man. And I scratched your car!'

'That's fine, don't worry about it. Come here.' He beckoned at me.

I took a few steps and reached out across the pool of red to grab his hand. The blood on his skin had dried. He smiled at me. In a moment, the shock gave way to numb and I thought I could probably do this. It wasn't so bad. Then the numb became nausea.

The man's throat had been gashed, along with some stab wounds to his chest. He'd been wearing a red Snoopy T-shirt.

'Come on, I knew you could do it. Help me up.'

'Do you need me to...' I shook the first aid kit.

'No, I just need to get to the car.'

'OK.' I took another step and watched blood soak into my red Nikes. 'How do you want to—'

'Just stay there. I won't put all my weight on you, I promise.' He shifted a little, dragging on my hand, and pushed back against the cupboards to find his feet.

I was surprised by how much his pain affected me. Maybe this was love; being willing to do fucked-up shit like this. That was the first time the possibility of love had sprung to mind around Nic. A dead man in a red Snoopy T-shirt brought us closer than we'd ever been.

He put one of his arms around my shoulders and I said, 'What was the deal with this guy? You've never been this... shit.'

'I thought he was dead but as I was leaving he grabbed the nearest thing and just went for me. Fucking lucky he wasn't more ambitious with his choice of weapon.' He laughed darkly. 'I got complacent.'

'No, I mean why did you have to kill him?'

Nic tried to shrug and put us both off balance on our way out. 'I don't know. I don't always ask.'

CHAPTER FOURTEEN

Ronnie

'Look.'

Eli nodded at some indeterminate spot in the distance.

My sunglasses cast everything in a glow that was both golden and completely blinding. I'd paid about two hundred quid for them as well, a price that seemed justified only by their aesthetic; because they sure as fuck didn't help me see anything.

'What?'

'Hitcher.'

I took the glasses off and let my eyes adjust to the expanse of beige dust and the odd skeletal tree. He was right. A stick-like speck on our windscreen grew into a fully formed man, with his arm outstretched into the road, thumb up. A large brown bag was on the ground beside him.

Eli slowed the car.

'You're not seriously thinking about picking him up,' I said, unable to hide my incredulity.

'Why not? We could just find out where he's going.'

'He could be a fucking murderer or something.'

He snorted and gave me a pointed look, as the car slowed and slowed.

I sighed. 'OK, fine, I get you.'

We pulled over and Eli leant out of his window. 'Where you headed?'

'St Louis, but you don't have to take me the whole way.'

The guy was Australian. He was also pretty weird-looking, even for someone being picked up in the arse-end of no-named outback, with no discernible signs of humanity in sight. He had the overly trusting brown eyes of a four-year-old, staring out from a lumbering panda-like body. He was wearing a leather hide jacket, smart trousers and small, round, John Lennon-style glasses. His hair was dark and pulled back into a ponytail.

Eli exchanged a glance with me.

'What's your name?' I asked.

'Jimmy.'

He looked like an Indiana Jones villain.

'Yeah, come on, we're stopping in St Louis for a bit.' Eli unlocked the back doors and smiled.

Jimmy picked up his bag, which looked to be made of the same dead animal as his jacket, and slung it into the back before clambering in. He grinned at us over his glasses.

'Really nice of you guys, thanks.'

'No worries.' Eli started driving again. 'What were you doing all the way out here?'

'Oh, just wandering.'

'Were you in Bloomington or something? There a ranch out here?'

'Yeah, yeah. Was staying with a friend. Nice to meet you guys, by the way. You're English, that's wild!' He thrust a huge palm through the middle of our seats. 'What are your names?'

'Mark,' I replied, reaching back to give the hand a shake.

Eli did the same.

'Thomas,' he said.

'Where you headed after St Louis?'

'LA.'

'Wow. A road trip. With all due respect, you don't look like the kinda fellas for it.'

'Well, you don't look like the sort of person you'd find at the side of the road in the middle of nowhere.' I eyed him in the overhead mirror. 'You out here burying a corpse or something?'

'Haha! No... Hahaha! Nothing like that.' He paused, unable to maintain the momentum of his theatrical laughter. 'Besides, if I was out here doing that, wouldn't I have at least thought about how to get back?'

I couldn't take my eyes off his bag. It looked like animal hide, but I couldn't tell what kind. It was tan, and thick, a dark brown. For a moment, I entertained the delusion that it might be human. But then I ignored the theory and asked, 'Why are you in America?'

'I was doing an engineering degree,' he said, staring out of the window like a dog, 'in Zurich, but I hated it, I got really bored. So I dropped out and went travelling instead. I was in England for a bit, then France, then a bit of Asia, then I came here... I think when I hit Santa Cruz I'm gonna head back over to Asia again.'

'Your parents must be loaded,' Eli remarked.

He shrugged.

I frowned. 'What's your bag made of?'

'Oh this?' He looked down at it and gave the bag an affectionate stroke. 'Goat.'

'Right.'

I was unconvinced, to say the least.

'Want some rum?' Jimmy reached into the bag, that looked to be the size of an entire adult goat, or the torso of an adult human being.

Eli motioned at the steering wheel. 'I'd love some but...'

'You? Mark?' Jimmy held out a bottle of Havana Club.

His glasses were several sizes too small for his ginormous head, I noticed. They were slipping down his nose resolutely, no matter how many times he pushed them up.

He can't have bought them, I thought. He must have acquired them from someone.

'Oh, why not,' I said, and took the bottle.

There was a funny smell in the car now, I was sure of it. I was also sure it was coming from the goat bag. It smelt like smoked meat. I sipped the rum slowly, paranoid that it might be drugged or something. But it tasted normal. I suppose it always did, regardless. You weren't meant to know if someone had spiked your drink. That was the point.

'Where do you come from in Australia?' Eli asked.

'Melbourne. Well, just outside Melbourne, this small town called Bairnsdale. You wouldn't have heard of it, it's tiny. We had a bowling alley, but it shut.'

There was something infinitely sad about that statement.

'We'll take you to St Louis, no problem,' Eli said, taking the bottle of rum from my hands and gulping some down. 'What's in St Louis for you?'

'I'm meeting a girl there,' Jimmy said, hand slung across his bag with this mental little smile on his face. 'She's the love of my life.'

We ran into a pothole and the car jolted. It disguised the second bemused smile that Eli and I exchanged, wondering who the hell we had invited into the back seat.

'What are you guys doing in LA?' Jimmy asked.

'Assassinating an old foe.' Eli flashed teeth in the overhead mirror.

Jimmy slapped his knees and laughed.

Eli laughed too.

We reached St Louis by sundown, with *Goat Bag* – as I'd rechristened him – yakking away in the back. It was like having a toddler narrating the journey. Eli was howling, but in a good-natured way; I think he had taken to the Australian.

'Doesn't this place have the highest murder rate of any city in the US?' Goat Bag asked, as if he was asking about the weather.

'I don't know.'

'Yes.' Eli nodded. 'They don't put that in the guidebooks, though it is one of the first facts that comes up on Google.'

'You know anyone here?' Goat Bag leant forwards and rested his chin on the edge of my seat.

'No, we were just gonna check in somewhere for the night,' I said, involuntarily shifting away.

'Want to come party with me and Amy?'

Amy was the name of the girl he was meeting; the 'love of his life'. She was Canadian. Most likely another upper-class drop-out with too much parental money to spare, like him.

'Where?' Eli asked.

'She's at a house party. That's why I have rum.' Goat Bag shook his bag at us. 'Come on, guys.'

'Yeah, come on.' Eli goaded me with his expression. 'Let's go party.'

'How old are you, Goat Bag?' I asked, looking back with concern. 'Like, *honestly*.'

'Twenty-two.'

'Jesus.' I shook my head. 'Am I gonna have to come just to make sure you don't do anything stupid?'

'Marvellous.' Eli sat back, starting to admire the outlines of St Louis out of the windscreen. 'That murder rate statistic seems unfair. I mean, look at it. It's gorgeous.'

He was right. Maybe it was only because we were seeing it in half-light, the sort that photographers would use to make everything seem softer than it actually was. It didn't look so much like a city in this light, an ugly manmade blight on the dust-scape; it looked like hills, mountains, something more benign than a super-structure crawling with viruses.

'Do you have a satnav?' Goat Bag asked, encroaching into the front.

'Yeah, knock yourself out.'

Eli handed the dormant device back, and Goat Bag fiddled with it in his strange cumbersome hands. They could snap a neck, I thought. Just crush a skull between his fingers like an egg.

According to the voice emitting from the satnav our destination was twenty minutes away. It didn't even seem to take that long. I took several more gulps of rum and realized I definitely wouldn't be getting around to calling my kids tonight.

Eli parked below a tower block, encircled by a serpentine fire escape.

'I don't know if it's OK to park here,' he said, with the air of someone who could afford any ticket that was slapped on him.

We got out of the car and I noticed the building we were heading towards was behind a locked iron gate. From somewhere in the sky I could hear a drumbeat, or a bass line, thrumming down.

Goat Bag was not fazed by the gate.

'Hey!' he hollered over it, both hands cupped around his mouth. 'Hey!'

A second, where we stood unacknowledged in the dark, and then, 'What?'

'We're looking for a party!' Goat Bag yelled. 'Is a girl called Amy in there?'

The voice was located above us.

'*Fack* knows, man. You wanna come in?'

'I have rum!'

Another pause. '... OK.'

'I like you, Goat Bag,' Eli said with a grin, as the gate unlocked itself and began to slide open. 'Unlocker of gates.'

'Bringer of liquor!'

I rolled my eyes. 'Come on, let's do this.'

'It's a party, *Mark*. Not war.' Eli winked at me.

'It's evidently been a long, *long* time since you've partied with twenty-two-year-olds,' I replied, feeling conspicuously decrepit. 'God, I hope there's Class As in there.'

We walked up to the building's entrance, but there was no one there.

Goat Bag tried the doors, and just as we began peering at the buzzers we were accosted by the same voice that had shouted from the sky at us.

'No, up here.'

I turned, and found myself addressing a bearded Hispanic man, smoking pot, crouched on the brick wall encircling the porch.

'Up where?' I said, as he looked us all up and down.

'Here.'

The man took a drag on his spliff, stepped backwards off the wall and vanished.

Eli darted past me to leap the wall. Goat Bag did the same and I followed them, landing on grass. I looked left and the three of them were scampering towards the bottom of the fire escape.

I couldn't remember if Eli had locked the car. Was this a dodgy part of town?

This is ridiculous, I thought. *We're not sixteen any more.*

Up the fire escape we went.

Most of the windows were curtained but every so often I'd catch a glimpse of someone inside, looking back at me with an expression of resigned vacancy. The music got louder.

A woman in her forties wearing a see-through nightgown…

A guy practising guitar cross-legged on his floor…

Nothing. Maybe a leg leaving a bedroom doorway…

A man was watching Jimmy Kimmel…

No kids in this building.

The music was physical now, a sensation in my nerves.

We reached the ninth floor and I realized Goat Bag and Eli had followed the Hispanic man through an open window. I ducked, clung to the window frame and felt for my footing on a bedroom floor. Through an open door in front of me there were lights, and people moving back and forth across them like a peep show.

I thought I'd lost Eli but he reappeared by my side, grabbing my arm. 'That guy's got MD.'

'Well, thank fuck.'

I reached into my jacket to try and roll myself a cigarette, but Eli was pulling me through into the apartment and I couldn't get hold of my filters.

'Where's Goat Bag?' I asked, but no one was listening.

'Here.' Eli pulled me into a kitchen.

The light was mortuary bright.

The Hispanic guy was saying, 'Bomb?'

'Ah, I hate doing it like that,' I said, as someone handed me a coke-coloured drink that tasted like petrol. 'I'll just dab.'

The Hispanic thrust out a clear sachet of white powder and I licked my finger and stuck it in. It didn't taste like MDMA, but maybe they cut it differently over here nowadays. I washed it down with that vile drink.

'You Mark?' the guy said.

'Who're you?'

'Luiz,' Eli answered for him, as if he was already high. 'He's in a band.'

He's in a band! Like it was the most exciting statement in the fucking world...

''S my after-party,' Luiz elaborated, gesturing at his kingdom.

'Right.'

I started to roll a cigarette again.

Goat Bag appeared, leering over those absurd glasses. 'Come and meet Amy!'

'In a sec.' Concentrating on not overfilling the paper, taking more concentration than usual... 'What's the name of your band?'

Not caring about the answer...

Could have been anything...

Eli said, 'You're a proper hippy, yeah?' sounding so London again all of a sudden.

'I travel a lot so... you develop an appreciation for things man did not make.'

'Do you believe in God? This guy does.'

Looking up, blearily, thinking that Eli probably meant me. Tobacco.

'We are all Gods, we all have the power of creation—'

'We have the power to give and take life,' I said. *I wasn't sure that had been MDMA.* 'We didn't create the universe though, did we?'

'We do, with our consciousness, with our perception.'

'Mate, we'd still exist whether I close my eyes on you or not.'

Definitely not MDMA.

Fuck...

'Was that MDMA?' I asked.

'No, 's ket.'

'Ah, no, *fuuuuuck.*'

That was from Eli, not from me.

I took my jacket off because I was sweating, and walked back into the hallway. If it was ket I needed to be alone, right away. On the floor in the living room there were three mattresses. A guy was on his knees, gesturing in the direction of what I guessed was the bathroom. It was hard to tell, because he kept shouting, *'Snow! Fucking snow!'*

There was definitely no snow. No snow.

Goat Bag had his arm around a girl, both of them sprawled on the floor, and she looked like she'd stepped out of the fucking sixties. She had a wreath of flowers around her head, for fuck's sake.

Eli said, 'Amy?'

I didn't realize he had come with me.

I looked down, thinking that I should roll a cigarette, but my tobacco and papers were gone.

The girl laughed and said... something.

Sound was coming in and out of focus.

Fucking goddamn shitting ketamine...

I desperately wanted to lie down on one of the mattresses but they were mostly occupied. I could lie down next to Goat

Bag and his Canadian girl but I knew I wouldn't be able to get back up again. Those mattresses would suck me in.

The girl laughed and said something else.

I turned and walked back towards the kitchen, but the kitchen wasn't there. I opened the door to the bathroom and some girl was being fucked over a sink by a guy with too many facial piercings and I said, 'Sorry, sorry,' and backed out, and I knew some little shit was going to have taken my tobacco.

I could smell weed – should try and track some down. It might help.

'It's so sweet how they met, and within, like, fifteen minutes he was telling her he loved her.'

I had no idea who was talking until I about-turned and saw Eli, and we were in the kitchen again, with Luiz.

'Who?' I asked.

My tobacco and half-rollie were on the side, where I'd left them, and my coke-coloured drink.

'Jimmy.'

'Who's Jimmy?' Luiz asked.

'Goat Bag.' I started laughing, unable to roll the cigarette to save my fucking life. 'I swear, his bag's not a fucking goat...'

Luiz looked confused. I couldn't work out if he was standing or sitting, but he was holding a guitar. Best to just not look at him... He had too much facial hair. I didn't trust men with too much facial hair.

'Where's my jacket?' I asked, climbing out of the window.

Down the fire escape, I couldn't tell if I was following Eli or Goat Bag, or neither of them.

I sat on a step for a moment, but my tobacco was gone.

Face down on the road outside, outside the gate, concrete eating my face, saying, 'Goat Bag! Find jacket!'

He left a bottle of rum by my head, next to the goat bag. This wasn't Havana Club. This was Kraken.

'Goat Bag! Tobacco!'

Black and white tentacles lapping at me.

Eli waving his hands and shouting something.

Lying on the pavement beside me, shouting, 'I am *impaired*!'

'My life! … In that bag! Goat Bag, go!'

I stared at the kraken in this sea of concrete eating my face, until I blacked out.

CHAPTER FIFTEEN

There was a diner on the corner of a street near a monument of a man's head flipped onto its side. Apt, I thought, as we passed it in the car, with my face pressed against the window because I didn't have the strength in my neck to lift it off the glass.

The café/diner place was called Terry's. That was it, just 'Terry's'. I *love* Terry. I'd have turned for Terry that morning, or that afternoon, or whatever fucking time it was when I came to.

'Tuna melt,' Eli said, staring down at the yellow tablecloth and the back of his hand. 'Black coffee, please. But a fucktonne of cheese in that melt, please.'

Goat Bag – *Goat Bag, sat to my right!* – said, 'I'll have blueberry pancakes please, with a side of fries, and a latte.'

I blinked myself alive, reborn from the K-hole, and said, 'Bacon, fried eggs, French toast, fries, sausages. English tea, if you have it. Please.'

The waitress looked at the three of us as if we were on drugs – ironically – and left. I wondered what we looked like: pale, eyes like pinpricks, veiny cling-film skin. I tried to raise my hand from the table and it shook, so I put it down.

I realized I was wearing my jacket.

Joy!

I had no energy for joy, but I almost raised a smile. Clutching the lapels, groping inside the pockets, I found my wallet and tobacco.

'Holy shit-bags, guys, you found it!'

'All Goat Bag,' Eli said, with a salute. 'I was busy being... impaired.'

Goat Bag laughed. 'He means that literally. He was lying on the ground next to you waving at me shouting, "I am impaired!" It was pretty funny.'

'Seriously?'

Eli raised a hand as if in supplication. 'I am impaired.'

'Aw, it was nothing.' Goat Bag was all humility, smiling, still wearing those glasses.

'He climbed over that gate, you know, right back up the fire escape into that hell-hole, found your jacket, and made it back out. The man's a hero.'

'Just say you owe me a drink. Or it can be my thank you for driving me here.'

'Goat Bag, I'll buy you a drink you can fucking *swim* in.' I checked my wallet again, just for kicks, and slumped face down against the tabletop. 'I'm a father, guys. I am actually a father of children. I can't be K-holing at my age. I fucking *hate* K.'

'Accidental K is the *worst*,' Goat Bag agreed.

'The worst,' I echoed.

I looked up, most of my head still enfolded in my arms.

'Yeah, and some of us didn't sleep in the car all morning.' Eli rubbed his eyes. '*Some* of us had to drive away, pull over, eat a packaged salad and get the fuck on with it.'

'I need food so much, I think I'm going to fucking die,' I mumbled. 'What happened to... thingy? Amy?'

'I'm meeting up with her again later, we're gonna catch a flight to San Fran. She was fine, she could see I needed to take care of you guys.'

He gave me an affectionate pat on the shoulder that felt like being assaulted.

'You wanna catch our flight with us?' Goat Bag asked, with the kind of deranged sincerity that only existed in the young.

'We need to shoot off, really.'

I was glad Eli had replied for me.

'Well, it was fun having an adventure with you guys.' He chuckled to himself. 'What exactly are you up to in LA?'

'Assassinating an old foe,' Eli said again, smirking.

'If you don't wanna tell me, you don't wanna tell me.' Goat Bag held up his hands. 'But I'm glad you picked me up.'

'Is your bag made of human skin?' I asked, my head bursting.

Goat Bag laughed, and laughed and laughed.

Our food arrived and the three of us lapsed into silence as we inhaled it and ordered seconds, with a shed-load of fries and more coffee.

There was something he wasn't telling us, but that was OK because we weren't telling him anything either. He had still climbed into a godforsaken building to get my jacket for me.

I was sorry to leave him. Goat Bag didn't come back to the car.

I opened the door and as I got into the passenger side I woke up Luiz, who'd been passed out in the back seat.

He awoke with his fists raised, screaming, 'Yeeeargh *what*!'

'Jesus, what the *fuck* is he doing here?' I gestured at Eli.

Luiz patted himself down and his eyes widened, cartoon-like.

He snarled, 'Which one a'you sons of bitches has my *facking* wallet, eh?'

*

'How well do you know this city, Luiz?' Eli asked.

The three of us were parked in a lay-by necking three different types of energy drink.

It was the most dishevelled I'd ever seen Eli. His hair, that had been perfectly slicked back the night before, was now hanging at several different angles like the top of a pineapple.

'Pretty well, I live here for over a year now. I move on soon, I think, but I know it well.'

'You think you can find a way of tracking this man down?'

Luiz took the photo of Trent and examined it. 'Maybe. How long was he here for?'

'We don't know. We just know he ended up here on his way west. He was a teacher for a while. Don't know which school though.'

'I'll need a day or two days, maybe.' Luiz tucked the photo inside his collar and started to roll a cigarette. 'In return, you can find my money that was in my jacket last night. I just got paid, cash as well, man, there was two hundred 'n' seventy-five dollars in there.'

'Wait a second, that wasn't your apartment?' I rested my hands on the steering wheel, trying to get used to the idea of driving again.

'No. I think that's why the fuckers kick me out, after they found my money.'

'How did you end up in our car?'

He spread his hands, cigarette between his lips. His eyes said, *Beats me, man.*

'We're really gonna stay here for a couple of days?'

Eli shrugged. 'We have the time. We know Trent was here.'

'What is his name?' Luiz asked, patting his chest.

'Trent Byrne. He might have been going by something else.'

'What else do you know about him? Why you looking?'

'Personal reasons,' Eli said, searching for cheap hotels on his iPad.

'What did he teach?'

'English. Before that he was a publisher, journalist, businessman.'

'What did he do?'

'Why do you want to know?' I turned in my seat.

Luiz held up his hands. 'It makes it easier for me to find him, or find someone who knows him, if I know what he's done. He's not memorable, easy to describe. I show this photo to people, they ain't gonna remember. I tell them something about him that stands out, it makes them more likely to remember.'

'Honestly, we don't know why he disappeared,' I said, picking at the label around my drink.

Monster.

At least Red Bull had some pretensions. *It gives you wings.* Monster was everything it said on the label: *We will pump you full of drugs.*

'So you are... gangsters, huh?' Luiz lit his cigarette and opened his window. 'Don't worry, you are doing a terrible job of hiding it. But that's good for me, you can get my money back.'

'I think we should split up,' Eli said, addressing the both of us. 'We'll all cover more ground.'

'How do we know we can trust you?' I asked Luiz.

'Why not? What would I do with a photo of a man I do not know? Sell it on eBay?'

'You have a weapon?' Eli asked.

'At home. You ask like I will need it...'

'You ever kill someone with it?'

'Yes.' Luiz smiled, seemingly unable to find his lighter.

'If you're such a hippy, how do you justify killing people?' I raised my eyebrows.

Luiz looked at me pityingly. 'People. You say it like we are special. *People.* I have no place in my heart for people.'

'We should take him with us,' Eli remarked. 'I like this guy's philosophy.'

'If I help you,' Luiz continued, finally finding his lighter, 'you can pay me the amount of money I've lost. Or you can find it for me. Your choice.'

He was like some deranged Jesus. All hair and mad brown eyes and a thousand bracelets and necklaces.

Luiz eyed Eli, taking a long-awaited drag. 'You were named after Eli from the Bible? He was a judge? A judge, am I right?'

'How do you know he's called Eli?' I tensed.

'He tell me last night, when he was wasted.'

'Oh… Right.' Glancing at Eli, I nodded. 'Seeing as we're all on proper first name terms now, my name's Ronnie.'

A roar of laughter. 'Well, I am glad you are on my side, Judge Eli. This guy, he's not feeling me so much.'

'You can go with him,' Eli said, smirking at us. 'I'm sure you'll find loads to talk about.'

CHAPTER SIXTEEN

I was surprised that anyone in a school would agree to talk to someone like Luiz, but the advantage of speaking English as a second language, he told me with some mirth, is that most people assumed you were retarded, and therefore harmless.

'Where are you actually from?' I asked, while we waited in another reception area.

Cliques of teenagers made their way to classes behind a pair of glass doors.

We'd been to four schools. It was entertaining at first, like a field trip, but the novelty had quickly worn off. I hated teenagers. Even when I'd been a teenager, I'd hated teenagers.

'Puerto Rico,' he replied.

'You got family here?'

'No, I came here to work and I send money back every month, to my mother.'

'You came over here illegally?'

A sideways glance. 'Yes, I came here *illegally*. I have a passport now though, my real name and everything.'

'My family were Italian immigrants, so I can't really have a problem with it.'

'People do have a problem though. But it is better to be somewhere you're unwelcome but you can live, than somewhere

where everyone loves you, but you have no work and no money. I could have worked for the drug bosses when I was twelve, but my mother wouldn't let me.'

'So you came to work for the drug bosses in the US instead?'

He spread his hands. 'What she doesn't know, won't hurt her. At least here you know where you stand. You're not so much "under a thumb", as you say. If you're good, you can make something of yourself and people respect that. What is it you do anyway?'

'I run a nightclub, and I... I guess I'm one of the UK "bosses".' I shrugged. 'Though I don't feel much like a boss right now.'

'I come over to the UK and I'll work for you, eh.'

'It seems to be all the rage,' I said, sighing. 'It's like I put out a fucking Craigslist ad.'

The glass doors were pushed open and we both fell into silence.

A woman approached us, in a long green skirt. Owl-like glasses.

'I'm Vice-Principal Lukehurst. Can I help you?'

'Hello, it is pleasure. My name is Luiz and this is my colleague, Ron.' Luiz reached out a hand to shake hers, and I noticed his English became noticeably worse. 'We are here to ask questions about former teacher here, Mr Trent Byrne.'

He handed her the photo before she could reply or take it all in. For the first time that day, recognition appeared in someone's face.

'I'm sorry,' she said, still looking at the photo. 'Who did you say you were again?'

'Luiz, and Ron.' Luiz beamed at her, as if that were all the explanation she needed.

I managed a half-smile.

'I mean, who do you work for?' she said.

Luiz mocked confusion, so much so that I almost laughed. 'I'm sorry, I do not understand.'

'We're private investigators,' I cut in. 'We're looking for Trent Byrne, following some criminal allegations, and we were hoping to speak to someone who knew him.'

'You're English,' she said, blurting it out.

'Yes.'

She couldn't work out what to make of either of us, this odd couple of Hispanic and English that had appeared in her reception, and she didn't want to deal with us either, which played to our advantage.

She took a step back, taking the photo with her, and mumbled, eyes still on Trent's face, 'Wait a moment, I need to... You should speak to Principal Bosman. He might be in a meeting but... wait here.'

Luiz shook his head as she walked away, and waited until the glass doors swung shut again to speak. 'Retarded, see. She would never have spoken to two Americans.'

'She wouldn't have spoken to a crazy bearded semi-literate fucker on his own either.'

'You may be right there. Eh, look, here she comes.'

Vice-Principal Lukehurst indicated her head at us, and we let ourselves into the now-empty corridor.

We were led past a gym and outside into another building. Across the way I could see kids running around a track.

It took a while, but Vice-Principal Lukehurst hung back and said, in a conspiratorial tone, 'I didn't know Trent that well, but I knew he was strange, from the start. If you want to ask any more questions or you don't think he's being straight with you, come and find me after. Some people here don't like to talk about these things. They worry more about the press than the kids' welfare.'

'We'll keep that in mind, thanks,' I said.

The sign above the entrance to the school had said *Owen Whitfield High School, 'Believe & Achieve'*.

Vice-Principal Lukehurst knocked on a door to an out-building.

A voice replied, 'In a minute.'

'Who's Owen Whitfield?' I asked, to pass the awkward time standing just off the racetrack, in view of the science labs.

To my surprise, Vice-Principal Lukehurst smoothed down her skirt and checked the ground before sitting on the concrete steps. Evidently 'In a minute' translated to quite a while in her mind. I was tempted to sit with her, but thought it might be inappropriate.

'He was a leader in a roadside demonstration protesting the eviction of local farmers from their homes, right here in Missouri in 1939.' A small smile. 'It was partly because the school was named after him that I applied to work here.'

'Were you saying earlier that you don't think Principal... Bosman was likely to speak to us?'

'He won't be eager to talk about the Trent business. He hired and fired him. Didn't even speak to local press about it when they asked.'

'What happened?'

'Later,' she said.

Not long after, the door opened and a gym teacher in absurdly short shorts left the building. We were left standing in front of a short and ill-looking man who had one too many buttons open under his blazer.

'Principal Bosman,' he introduced himself, reaching down from the upper step to shake both of our hands as Vice-Principal Lukehurst hurriedly stood up from her seat on the ground.

Even standing above me, he only drew level with the top of my head.

He said, 'You fellas want some coffee?'

'Um, no, I'm good.' The building we were led into was a temporary classroom, and it smelt damp.

'Should I stay?' asked Vice-Principal Lukehurst.

'That won't be necessary.'

If I wasn't mistaken, Principal Bosman actually waved her away, like a toddler.

'I'll have coffee,' Luiz said, curling the tips of his moustache.

There were rows and rows of wooden desks, a few old computers, and a coffee machine at the front of the room where a projector should be. It looked like the only thing still used on a regular basis.

I sat on the edge of a desk and Luiz sat at one of them with his fingers linked, like a student.

Principal Bosman turned on the machine, and it sputtered to life with dry rasps.

'Takes a while to warm up,' he said, patting it. 'How do you know of Trent Byrne?'

I wasn't sure how to answer this. It seemed like an odd question to open with.

'I don't know him, but our client does. There have been some criminal allegations that we can't go into, and we've been trying to track him down. The last anyone heard of him he was teaching here.'

'That was a while ago.'

'Yes.' Luiz frowned. 'Why did you fire him?'

'I thought you'd already know.'

I offered, 'There's not much record of it in the press, anywhere really. We thought it best to come to you, in the absence of much public information.'

Principal Bosman looked pleased with himself. 'Well, I worked hard to keep all that... unpleasantness out of the papers. Terrible for the school, and not fair... not fair on the good teachers who work here and not fair on the kids, to tarnish them with that. Personally, I think it would be for the best if Trent were locked up.'

Luiz looked about him for the photo but it was still with Vice-Principal Lukehurst. 'So, what happened? He wasn't no sex predator, was he? He didn't touch the kids?'

'God, no.' The principal recoiled from the suggestion. 'No, nothing like that, thank Jesus. No, he was... inappropriate but, I like to think, never in that way.'

The coffee machine whirred like a spaceship.

'No, it was brought to my attention by one of the teachers who no longer works with us, and then later on by several of the children, that Trent was using his class time to give ungodly lectures.'

'What's that meant to mean?' I asked, not liking where this was headed.

'When I say "ungodly", I mean just that. He was giving lectures about... about Satanism.'

He said the word 'Satanism' in a whisper. It was almost lost in the roar of the coffee machine.

'Satanism?' Luiz almost had to shout.

'Yes, the worship of Satan, the devil, whatever you want to call him.' The principal pulled at his tie. 'I never heard any of them myself, but I did see some of the literature he began distributing. It was then I was forced to fire him. Some parents called in, asking why their child had been given these blasphemous pamphlets, asked me if it was my idea of a joke...'

The memory was clearly still a sore one.

The coffee machine reached its anticlimax, with a sigh, and spat out some coffee. The principal took the resulting mug and handed it to Luiz, who looked unimpressed with its contents.

'Do you have any of the pamphlets left?' I asked. 'Are any of the students who heard those sermons still here?'

'No and no. For obvious reasons, we didn't keep anything.' He sat on the edge of the desk at the front, lost in thought, and then rubbed his hands together. 'Is there anything else you wanted to know?'

Luiz took a sip of coffee and winced. 'Do you know where he go after you fired him?'

'No.'

'Was he friends with any of the teachers here who might know?' I added.

'No. Sorry.'

Luiz and I looked at each other, and I stood up first. 'Well, thanks for all your help, Principal Bosman. We'll see ourselves out.'

'No, I wouldn't hear of it,' the principal said, as though anxious to make sure we were off the premises in person. 'I'll walk you to reception.'

On the way out, Luiz lagged behind and tipped the remainder of his coffee onto the edge of the playing field.

We never did manage to find Vice-Principal Lukehurst again, but we left a message for her with reception just in case.

We suspected she was being watched.

There were a group of young 'uns in their twenties sat not far from us in the bar, barely seven feet away. I was finding it hard to keep up with what Eli or Luiz were saying, too distracted by their smartphones.

I hated them now. I hated how the species had evolved to depend on a permanent black rectangle stained into the palm of your hand.

'I have family in LA,' Luiz was saying. 'Well, friends who are like family, as good as family.'

Eli was picking the label off his bottle of beer. 'It doesn't matter how you know them, it only matters that they won't say anything, no matter who comes asking after us.'

'These people are trustworthy.'

Eli looked at me.

I shook the trance out of my expression and said, 'Huh?'

'These people are trustworthy,' Luiz repeated.

I shrugged. 'That's great, right.'

Eli didn't look convinced. 'Maybe we should just stick to the plan—'

'Eli, nothing we've done so far has remotely resembled your fucking plan,' I snapped.

'How do we really know we can trust you?' Eli directed at Luiz, ignoring me.

I spread my hands and returned to eyeballing the smartphones.

A waitress had been standing by their table waiting to take their food order for what felt like several years, her smile becoming less and less sincere, reduced to a human lampshade in the face of social media.

'How do you know you can trust anyone?' Luiz was saying emphatically.

'Well—'

'Have we not already helped each other?'

The group were now getting the waitress to take photos of them posing with their drinks.

I realized that both Eli and Luiz were waiting for me to

answer a question. I turned, picked up my beer and went, 'What?'

'Are we fucking *boring* you?' Eli asked with insufferable slowness. 'Do you want to move to another fucking table?'

'I don't get your point, that's all. You're happy to go to this guy's party, take his ketamine, have him go around schools waving Trent's photo and carry a gun for us, but you don't want him in the car and now you don't wanna stay with people who are vouched for.' I shrugged.

I was glared at like a husband who had just undermined his wife in a public argument. Eli returned his gaze to Luiz and I tried to repress the uprising of anger in my chest.

It must have taken them almost twenty minutes just to order drinks. Did they not think that the people working here had anything better to do?

'"Trustworthy" seems to be a word that has different definitions according to different people—'

'You trust me when you need help, but don't trust me when I need a ride.'

I saw one of the girls in the group talking to a guy, maybe her boyfriend, whose eyes kept sliding downwards towards his screen. She'd be better off taping the thing to her forehead, I thought.

'Trust...'

'The idea of trust...'

'Who do you trust?'

'Why do you trust...?'

'Trustworthy isn't some fucking label...'

'It has to be earned.'

I stood up.

The others didn't watch me go. It was as if I was moving in the space between universes. The kids didn't look up when

I approached them, but then why would they? They barely looked up to interact with each other.

I picked up one of their phones and dropped it in a full pint glass.

Now they were looking.

Taking the pint glass and slapping my palm flat over the top, I shook the pint of beer and smartphone like a mixologist, before slamming the glass back down in the middle of the group.

There were no exclamations, not even a mild protest.

The bar went silent.

'Cheers,' I said, and left.

When we finally, thank fuck, got out of St Louis, Luiz was sat in the back of the car drinking energy drinks. I don't recall them having another discussion about trust again, and no one talked about the smartphone pint.

CHAPTER SEVENTEEN

Daisy

It wasn't that I thought Noel would do anything stupid, like kill himself. But I knew how low-level depression could transform one day into a sudden tiredness with everything. In my experience the decision to end it all wasn't a slow burner. It was a snap. Like walking out of a club and past a kebab shop and you're vaguely aware of being hungry but then – *bang* – you've never needed food more in your life.

I'd walked Noel to an AA meeting that morning but he refused to go in, so we sat on a wall outside and smoked. I didn't vocalize my disapproval; I didn't feel able.

It was chilly.

Noel told me about a time he tried to kill himself in a sea cave and it didn't work. He walked out of his family's holiday home, into a cave a few miles along the seafront, and took as many pills as he could. By some stroke of fortune, either good or bad depending on how you looked at it, someone saw him and called the coastguard. By the time help arrived, Noel had thrown up most of the pills anyway. It was much harder to kill yourself than he had envisioned, he said.

'I tried to kill myself once,' I chimed in, as if we were

acknowledging a mutual love of pasta or something equally banal. 'When I was younger. It was a weird phase I went through. I totally meant it though, at the time.'

'Did it work?'

We both laughed. For some reason that was always the first question people asked.

I relit the end of my cigarette. 'It wasn't even dramatic. I'd just...'

'Had enough.'

'Yeah.'

'See, look, we're talking about personal stuff.' Noel spread his hands. 'Who needs AA when we can just be each other's therapists?'

'You'd have to start paying me a butt-load more than you're paying me now.'

'You know, at my first meeting at AA our group leader, Si, he told us that some of us were gonna die. Straight out. No sugar-coating. I'm not sure parts of AA actually work, some of it is bullshit, but Si was always really in-your-face about things. I liked him for that.'

'What did he say?'

'First time I went, he told us all to take a look at the guy on our left, and then at the guy on our right. Then he said, really matter-of-fact, "Alcoholism kills one in three people who suffer from it, so only two of you are going to get out of this alive."'

I grimaced. 'Fuck. Harsh.'

'Better harsh though. It's all a bit...' he waggled his fingers under his chin mockingly, 'touchy-feely sometimes.'

We both looked over our shoulders at the church hall. I thought about calling Ronnie and maybe putting him on speakerphone.

But Noel asked, 'So how did you try and kill yourself then?'

'Oh, pills, same as you.' It didn't bother me talking about it now. 'You know I'm allergic to everything, antibiotics, penicillin and all that? Well, because of that I basically had a pharmacy in my room of these different medications I'd never finished. So I just took everything I had, put them in a bowl and started taking them in my room.'

'Why did you put them in a bowl first?'

Of all the questions he could have asked, I found that one quite weird.

'I don't know. It just seemed neater.'

'So what happened?'

I slid off the wall and stretched, pacing. 'I'm not massively superstitious... but my mum lost her credit card the year before when we were on holiday in Spain and we never found it. She had to cancel her card days before we flew back and we just thought it had been pickpocketed.'

Noel was frowning.

'No, trust me, this is going somewhere,' I said. 'I was opening this pack of painkillers with Spanish writing on them and this card just fell out right into my hand. It had my mum's name on it, and then it hit me – it was *her* credit card that she'd lost on holiday, from a year ago. How weird is that?'

He nodded, slowly. 'Pretty weird, I guess.'

'What were the chances that, just as I decided I was gonna kill myself, this lost card reappears in my hand? I didn't even register it was my mum's at first, I had to read her name like four times, I thought it was just something that came in the packet.'

Did I sound manic? Probably.

I lapsed into silence and flicked my cigarette butt into the gutter.

'So what happened after you found the card?'

'Oh yeah. Um… I started laughing, like… mental laughing. Then I started crying. Then I just… snapped out of it. I couldn't top myself after that, it would be absurd. So I went upstairs and threw up everything, then I went and told my mum I'd found her card – just coincidentally – and we had a laugh about it. It was like two in the morning and I just walked into her room and gave it to her. I don't think she knew what actually went on.'

'I always found it weird that someone got me out of that sea cave.' He shrugged. 'It was so remote. The chances of someone being there and seeing me go in, and then calling for help. It was nil.'

'You ever thought about doing it again?'

'Yeah… But then again, no. It didn't work the first time. I don't think I could cope with how sad another failure would be.' He slipped down from the wall to lean against it. 'What about you?'

'Na.'

I started walking alongside him in the direction of the club, zipping up my jacket and wishing I'd worn tights.

'It gave me this feeling like I wasn't supposed to die yet,' I said.

'Thought you weren't superstitious?'

'I'm not. But I think that's why I've never thought about it since. It felt like I was being told that I wasn't meant to die yet. So I figured that when it's my time to go, I'll go.'

There was a silence.

I found myself frantically scanning the pavements now, looking into every face for Seven. I hoped that Noel didn't notice. It didn't occur to me right away that he was probably doing the same thing.

'That's why I've never tried again too, if it makes you feel any better,' Noel said, sniffing. 'Just seemed like too much of a coincidence. I'm not superstitious either but… well, maybe I am. Who cares really? Not like we're religious or anything.'

'Yeah, we just believe some higher power thinks we're special enough to tell us it's not time to die.' I smirked. 'I think that might be narcissism, eh.'

'Yeah, it's fucking weird. Let's never talk about this to anyone else.'

'Fine by me.'

CHAPTER EIGHTEEN

Ronnie

I called everyone I knew in LA, everyone who could have owed me a favour, which came to a total of three people, and they all turned me down.

The closer we got to LA, to Cameron Hopper, to where Trent had apparently been most recently according to Melissa, the faster those forty hours flew by, and the more I started to panic. Luiz found less to talk about and it was no longer entertaining to sing along to the Proclaimers or something else clichéd.

I Googled Trent's name on my phone in the car, and found nothing. Mostly links to articles about Nine Inch Nails and Trent Reznor. I Googled his name alongside Eli's, and found one reference – just the one – to their magazine. There was a tiny photo of him, Eli, Love and Melissa, smiling for the same camera, and they all looked very young. Trent was wearing glasses, but that was the only distinguishable change.

'Trent doesn't sound very LA from how you've described him,' I said, the endless desert outside my window making me feel as though I had sight problems. 'He looks like a pale little geek. I mean, as leads go, the idea that he's in LA is less than second-hand. It's a rumour of a rumour.'

'We're going there anyway.' Eli shrugged, flexing his fingers around the wheel. 'Someone like Cam, he'd go there to make something of himself, become *someone*. Trent would have gone there to disappear.'

'If you could sum up Trent in one sentence,' I said, just for the hell of it, 'what would it be?'

Eli frowned. 'He was the sort of guy who would order the soup starter from a set menu.'

Luiz said, 'What does that mean?'

'Boring,' I said.

I watched Luiz nodding in the overhead mirror.

'Who are your friends in LA again?' I asked.

'Irish friend I know for years. His name's Cathal. I've warned him we're coming. He... how do you say? He *knows* the score.'

From somewhere upon his person Luiz had produced a pair of scissors and a hand-mirror. He was now hunched over and squinting at himself, trimming his beard and moustache.

'Do you think Trent may have still been teaching in LA?' he continued, blowing hair onto the floor.

'It wasn't as if he was charged with anything.' Eli sounded hopeful.

'Yeah, but he'd have a record after being fired.'

'This may be a crazy idea,' Luiz said, as if our journey up until now hadn't been. 'But we should check into Satanist groups, no? There must be Satanists in LA.'

'Of course there must be, it's LA.'

I took out my iPhone and typed, with as little conviction as possible, *LA Satanist groups* into a search engine. There were mostly descriptions of films being made, crackpot sites about Satanism in Hollywood, that kinda thing. It was only when

I put some effort into it, now the radio was off and I needed to make progress just to alleviate the boredom, that I started to stumble across things.

'Ever heard of the Cecil Hotel?' I asked Eli.

'No,' Luiz said.

Eli, eyes narrowed, 'Yes.'

'Really?' I looked at him. 'Where?'

'I don't know. Why?'

'There was a murder there recently and there are a load of articles saying it was a Satanic sacrifice.' I scrolled down. 'Girl was found dead in a water tank and it was passed off as a suicide even though she was naked and there was no water in her lungs. Everyone at the hotel was drinking and showering in cadaver water for two weeks before anyone found her.'

Luiz grimaced. 'What does it have to do with your man?'

'Well, it's not just that murder. The Cecil apparently has a reputation for attracting drifters... Been loads of murders and suicides. A lot of nutcase sites claim it's a Satanist hotspot. If Trent was into that, he'd probably have checked in at some point. It's called Stay On Main now and it's been refurbished a bit, but maybe some of the old staff are still there.'

'Worth a look, definitely.'

I glanced back and exchanged a look with Luiz. Neither of us looked thrilled.

'Where is it?' Eli asked.

I saw Luiz cross himself and it reassured me somehow.

When we finally hit LA, it was an oppressive blot of identical houses that had the same colour scheme as the desert; yellow and beige, yellow and beige. Cathal's house, when we reached it, was one of those impossibly large ones that only seemed to exist for fictional families on cable TV. Why did they all need so much goddamn space?

I sat up from where I'd been lying across the back seats, feeling a hundred and fifty years old and like my body had been drained of fluid. 'Are we there yet?'

Eli had slumped into an uncomfortable angle in the passenger side, and only managed to shake his head to indicate any response.

Luiz – who had been driving the last hour – beeped the horn.

'Fuck, hell...' Eli mumbled as he almost slid into the footwell.

'Man, *hello*!' Luiz didn't acknowledge either of us as he got out of the car.

I opened the back door, the one that I was leaning against, and didn't so much exit the vehicle as fall out of it.

I righted myself and peered through the windows at the man Luiz was hugging.

'Come! This man has food and beer!'

I could smell the food.

Eli and I both managed to raise weak hands and mumble, 'Hi.'

My shirt was stuck to my back.

It became clear very early on, before we had even polished off our first helpings of pasta, that Cathal wasn't someone we were expected to use euphemisms with. Luiz told him our entire story within twenty minutes, and Cathal nodded with an expression of mild interest, but nothing more.

He looked almost Italian in ancestry – though he assured us there was nothing in it – with a heavy brow, thick but meticulous beard, and overly defined mouth. He could have been handsome, if not for his small teeth and hippy style of dress. He also had a lazy eye, I noticed. His left eye didn't move in sync with his right; it stayed eerily stationary.

'Well, you're both welcome to stay here,' he said, with no trace of an American accent. 'Anything you need.'

His living room was vast. Even though he claimed to have a wife and three children, who were staying with her parents for a fortnight, there was no trace of them. It was as if he had expunged all evidence of their existence as soon as the front door clicked shut. I looked everywhere for a photo, maybe something childlike, but it was a four-bedroomed bachelor pad and, yeah, he was wearing a wedding ring but it looked awkward on his finger.

I didn't trust him.

'You collect art?' Eli asked, casting his eyes across the walls.

Any free space was crammed full of images and paint, oil, canvas, prints, record sleeves, and old photos.

'I collect loads of things: art, coins, antiques, furniture, books, shoes... I have more pairs of shoes than my missus!' He laughed. 'When I was young and we lived in Ireland I used to collect dead things.'

'Er, dead things?' I glanced at Eli, but he wasn't looking at me – he was chugging his beer.

'Yeah, roadkill,' he elaborated, like that was totally normal. 'I used to cycle around picking them up from the sides of the roads and put them in a basket on the front. Then I'd bury them at home and leave a little number marking where I found them, so I could match their grave in the garden with where they died.'

'Parents must have been worried, eh?' Luiz laughed, getting up and slapping Cathal's knee.

In the kitchen, we could hear him helping himself to more food.

'Er, have you heard of a place in LA called the Cecil Hotel, by any chance?' I asked, getting out my phone and realizing I didn't know his Wi-Fi password. 'By Skid Row.'

'I have actually. I remember reading about that girl they found in the water tank, horrible, fucking horrible, man. I mean, to not find her for that long, it...' He put a hand to his chest like he was having trouble digesting. 'You don't wanna think about it, it'll put you right off your lunch. What do you guys want with the place? You following a lead?'

Eli shrugged, putting his bowl on the floor. 'It's unlikely he'll be there any more. But he might have been, that's the important thing. It's not a lead as such, more of a—'

'Hunch,' I finished.

Luiz leant against the living room doorway, face full of pasta.

Cathal leant forwards. 'I was a bit obsessed by that hotel when the story came out. If you like I can show you all the stories I found on it. I made a timeline, it goes back to the nineteen twenties. Richard Ramirez stayed there and Jack Unterweger in the nineties. Hell of a place. Really, a hell of a place.'

Eli only hesitated for a moment. 'Er, yeah, OK.'

I noticed he had taken out his notepad and pen at some point and started scribbling things down. One of his *to-do* lists.

'You guys can head upstairs and take a nap in any of the kids' rooms if you like, don't worry. I'm not gonna keep you awake.' Cathal got up and stacked our bowls. 'Just let me get you my scrapbook. You'll love it, eh.'

CHAPTER NINETEEN

Daisy

From what I could tell, it had taken literally no time at all for Ronnie to go from indifferent and sarcastic to full-on fucking crazy town. Noel and I had only been on Skype with him in his office for half an hour and I felt like we'd fallen down a rabbit hole of weird.

'So let me get this straight,' Noel said, sneaking a look at me that said *Wtf?* 'You're following one of your friend's business associates to a haunted hotel in LA?'

'Former business associate, he's been missing for years.'

'And this has anything to do with you, *why?*'

I was leaning on the back of Noel's chair and I could smell something alcoholic in the room. Ale, beer, could have been whisky. He didn't seem drunk. It must have been coming out in his sweat. I took a step back and surveyed Ronnie.

He said, 'I have to do this for Eli, guys.'

'Why?'

'Because, honestly, he's the best person I can think of to come back and help out right now. You know we can't keep bleeding money into Mark Chester and her fucking *boyfriend*.'

'Ex-boyfriend,' Noel corrected, without any prompting from me.

'What?'

'Ex.'

'Oh, right, whatever.' Ronnie shook his head. 'But the point is, I owe him. Seriously, I'll get him to Skype you guys soon, you'll see. He's trustworthy.'

No 'sorry'. Nothing.

I leant down again. 'Do you know a guy called Sean? He was here looking for you.'

'He doesn't need to worry about that,' Noel cut in, way too quickly. 'I'm handling it.'

'Sean?'

'Ron!' I couldn't see Noel's expression, and I looked down to check the thumbnail of his face on the screen too late to gauge whatever telepathic exchange had just happened. 'It's fine.'

I threw up my hands and went to sit on the other side of the desk, not bothering to hide my disgust from Noel, who was ignoring me. Turning in the swivel chair, I lowered the back until I was almost lying down to listen to the rest of their conversation, hanging my head over the edge towards the floor.

'What's the deal with this hotel then?' Noel asked.

'It's not haunted… well, that's bullshit. But it's fucked up. There's been lots of suicides there, women jumping out of windows and killing the people they landed on. There was a girl dead in the water tank for two weeks before anyone thought the water tasted funny.'

'Jesus.'

'It's a magnet for freaks from all over.'

I stopped spinning. It had hurt when Ronnie skimmed over my relationship status. But what seemed like an atomic bomb going off in the centre of your life didn't often register on anyone else's radar.

'Fuck this shit,' I muttered, pulling myself up.

Noel barely glanced over his laptop as I left the office.

On a more sinister note, I wondered, did the fact that I was no longer with Nic mean I had no leverage? It was Nic who had got me this job in the first place. Without a renowned contract killer at my back, what power did I have? It could have been the paranoia, the drugs or whatever, but I was looking into the future and seeing a massive fucking elbow edging me out. And then what? Back to the squats and minimum wage and skipping for food? Fuck that. It was me holding everything together. Me.

I'd stopped in the hall.

This place was as much mine as it was theirs. I wasn't leaving.

My fingernails dug into my palms.

I wasn't leaving.

Just let them try and make me.

I went downstairs and a couple of the girls were rehearsing dance routines onstage in hoodies. Retrieving my mobile and some cigarettes from the bar, I went outside and thought it over for a few minutes before calling Edie.

It was hardly a betrayal. I wasn't Seven. But it paid to keep my options open.

CHAPTER TWENTY

Ronnie

I fell asleep fully clothed in one of the bedrooms upstairs without even kicking my shoes off, and when I woke up nine hours later it was four in the morning and the house was empty.

I excavated grime from the corners of my eyes and wandered from room to room. The one I'd been sleeping in was clearly occupied by a girl, but it was sparse.

The other kid's room – a boy, by the looks of it – had the appearance of being slept in, but when I looked out of the window our car was gone.

I went downstairs and found a note on the kitchen counter.

Going to talk to some people.
Luiz with me.
E.

I felt inside my crumpled jacket for my phone. All the fuss about bringing him with us and then suddenly they were inseparable.

The note didn't explain where Cathal was though.

I ran a glass of water from the tap and downed it.

The house was silent. He definitely wasn't sleeping.

I looked out of the living room window, but could only see the lit-up driveway and not much of the neighbouring houses.

'Cathal!' I called, just in case.

Nothing.

I tried the back door and it was unlocked.

Did I really want to see what Cathal was doing in his back garden at four in the morning?

I did, I decided. If we were living with a serial killer it would be best to know.

Taking off my jacket, I rifled through one of the drawers for a slim little filleting knife, and went outside. The garden was unlit. I couldn't see any borders but I could feel a stone path beneath my feet so I followed it into the darkness.

I could be Skyping with my kids or with Rachel, I thought. The longer I went without doing it, the more monumental a task it became.

Most of the sky was blacked out by trees as I continued to feel my way along the flagstones.

There was a light. As I squinted, it became three lights, emanating from the windows of a workshed, a wooden box, a man-cave. He could be doing anything; making a table, or welding. I just couldn't help but imagine it was more likely he had some poor soul chained up and ready for a ritual sacrifice, a kidnapped woman being held as a sex-slave maybe—

I stopped because it was none of my business.

But we were staying in this guy's house. I had to know.

I held the knife down by my side, out of sight, and edged towards the shed.

I put my ear to the door, but couldn't hear much. In a slight crouch, I skirted around and peered in one of the windows. Dew soaked into my socks from the long grass.

There was a worktop, a microwave, glass implements and smoke coming from somewhere. I craned my neck to get a better look and Cathal's face appeared through the glass.

'Fuck!' I started, falling away from the pane.

The door opened behind me and I hurriedly put the knife in my back pocket.

'Wanna come in?' Cathal asked, hanging out of the doorway.

'I, uh... couldn't find anyone in the house.'

'And you thought I might be hiding something?'

He presented the inside of the shed with a sweep of his arm, and it became apparent that no human being was chained up in this space. It was mostly desks and weird instruments, like a lab.

'Searching for a cure for cancer?' I said, looking for a place to lean and settling for one of the worktops.

The fish knife dug into my arse and I straightened up again, as Cathal did something with a beaker of water over a bunsen burner.

'You're not far wrong,' he replied, looking over his shoulder.

'Really?'

'You ever heard of Ormus?' He picked up a tiny plastic pot full of white powder and held it out.

I studied it for a moment, but it was just white powder.

'No.' I handed it back. 'What is it, a drug?'

'It's a combination of precious metals in an unusual atomic form, where the atoms don't form any bonds with each other. Gold, silver, cobalt, nickel, copper, couple of others. You won't find it on the periodic table though.'

'Why?' I tried to sit down again but couldn't.

'It's not scientifically recognized.'

'Why?'

Cathal locked onto me with this intense stare. 'Because it can cure pretty much everything.'

I frowned, not sure how he wanted me to react.

With awe, I guessed, going by the expectant way he was looking at me.

'Um... really?'

'Yes.' He opened a drawer beneath one of his worktops and took out a bag of capsules. 'I started taking them nine years ago, when I was diagnosed with eye cancer.'

He reached up to his left eye, hid it for a moment, and when his hand came away again it was gone.

I jumped at the sight of the pink empty socket. 'Shit!'

'It's a glass one.' He opened his palm and there was his eye, dark grey, staring up at me. 'It was spreading though. Eye cancer is a bugger, it can reach your brain like *that*' – clicking his fingers, 'turn into tumours and stuff.'

'Um... so...'

He put his glass eye back in, blinking it into place as if it was a contact lens. 'I got on the Internet and ordered these as a last resort. I stopped chemo, it was making me sicker. Within a year, the cancer was gone. My oncologist didn't know what the fuck was going on like.'

'And you weren't doing any other treatment?'

'Nope.' His eye lit up. 'And what's more, my hearing got better, the sight in my right eye became perfect, my blood oxygen levels are like I'm a teenager. It literally *reversed* the aging process. I water my plants with the stuff. Here, take some.'

'So why aren't you a multimillionaire then?' I took the bag of capsules and eyed them with suspicion.

'It's actually illegal to claim you can cure cancer if you're not one of the big-boy pharmaceuticals in America.' He sat down on one of his wooden chairs and shook his head. 'Most of the research is going on in Canada. But I make a tidy amount selling Ormus on the Internet to people like me.'

'But that makes no sense.'

'It makes perfect sense, Ronnie, eh. No one makes money out of healthy people. All these drugs we're being peddled, they cover symptoms but don't tackle the illness, keeping you hooked on medication for ever. If Ormus was out there for everyone... Fuck, the pharmaceutical industry would be dead fish.'

I suppose that did make sense. I took a handful of the capsules and glanced up at Cathal, who nodded.

'Take a load, seriously. I'd rather you believe me than pay anything. If you're up for it, Ormus oil is a trippy drug too, kinda like acid.'

'OK, thanks. I might hold off on the tripping balls but... OK, I'll take these.' I put the bag in my pocket. 'So what are you doing in here at stupid o'clock? Making it?'

'You extract Ormus rather than make it. But no, I'm doing something a bit more experimental.'

I couldn't work out whether he was a nutter or not. He seemed to make good points, but then a lot of conspiracy theorists did. The one thing that gave Cathal some credibility was his money. He clearly had a lot of money and you couldn't afford to buy a house like this without peddling a decent product.

'Like what?' I asked.

When Cathal turned away again I took the knife out of my pocket and hid it behind a pile of books. Then I sat down. When he turned back he was holding tiny fragments of something in his outstretched hand.

'Making gold,' he said.

I almost lapsed into a smirk. 'What, extracting gold? From Ormus?'

'Kinda. It's more like using Ormus to transmute other metals into gold.'

I laughed a little, hoping he'd take it in good spirits. 'Fuck, man, here I was expecting you to have sex slaves tied up in here or be part of a cult or something, but you're actually doing something *more* mental than that. Alchemy, really? Can you show me?'

'My method isn't perfected yet. I almost went and gave myself mercury poisoning last year. But give me a piece of silver before you go and next time I see you it'll be part gold.'

'How would you do that?'

'Can't tell you. I'd have to kill you, eh?' He winked at me with his real eye.

I glanced back towards the house. 'You mind if I make myself a coffee? Then I'll see about giving you bits of silver.'

'Help yourself, man. Make one for me while you're at it. The boys should be back soon.'

I couldn't find a window in which to pick the knife up discreetly so I left it there.

It was lighter outside as I walked back towards the house.

In the kitchen I took out the bag of capsules. They didn't look like they had magical properties, but then what did I expect them to do? Glow? Dance about?

I opened a few cupboards and then laid eyes upon a glass jar of coffee by the kettle and a cafetière.

'Fucking a,' I muttered.

There was a key in the front door, Luiz and Eli's excited tones, shoes being scraped against the mat...

'Hey!' I called.

'Trent lived at the Cecil!' Eli blurted out, bounding into the kitchen. 'He *lived* there!'

'Fuck *yeeeeah, boy*!' Luiz screeched.

'How'd you know?'

'We asked around people, spoke to some homeless guys and the security guards.' Eli looked wired, as if he had taken some coke.

'And they said?'

'They said… well, they said to come back in the morning. But they recognized Trent from the photo, said he'd lived there for *five or six months* last year. *Lived* there.'

'Where's Cathal, he asleep?' Luiz pointed at the ceiling.

'Na, he's in the garden making gold.'

'Huh?'

'In the garden,' I said again. 'In his shed out there.'

'Wicked, man.'

Luiz let himself out of the back door and I put the Ormus capsules in my pocket.

Eli was staring into space, flicking his fingers against each other. After a while he said, 'In one of Trent's postcards to me, he said he was in the clutches of something… *evil*. He said he wasn't himself, that he had only come to long enough to write that postcard and send it.'

'What?'

'I didn't tell you because I thought you'd find it too bizarre. I should have told you though.'

'Have you still got the postcard?'

'No, not that one. My w— It got thrown away. Luckily it wasn't forgettable but it didn't give me the chance to check where it had come from or glean anything useful.'

'So you don't want to… kill Trent?'

'No. Yes… I don't know. As I said, I don't blame him as much as I do the others. If they all ganged up on him he would have gone along with anything they wanted. Especially if Mel convinced him, he always loved her most.' Flicking his fingers, not looking at me, picking at his lips. 'He wasn't a malicious guy. I once caught him standing in a storm outside the tube on my way to our offices, and he'd brought a stack of umbrellas to hand out to people who had forgotten theirs. Like, this was a guy who went vegan before it was cool because he actually gave a shit about animals. He was so fucking... bland.'

'But he asked you for help. You personally. That's why we're here?'

He nodded.

'Why the fuck didn't you say anything before?'

'I didn't think you'd be as interested by a mission to go help a guy out.'

'As opposed to killing him?'

He shrugged, as if it was fucking obvious and I just lacked the self-awareness to see it. 'Thought it would seem insipid.'

'Really?'

'Weak, innit.'

'Maybe you don't know me that well.' I folded my arms.

He chewed at his nail and said, insincerely, 'Maybe.'

CHAPTER TWENTY-ONE

The Cecil Hotel was a tall cement block by LA's Skid Row. It wasn't the sort of decay that existed so visibly in London. The sheer number of homeless was breathtaking. On the short walk from our taxi to the front of the hotel I was sure I could see about two drug deals happening in plain view of the security guards.

They didn't seem to care. They only cared that none of these people got inside.

The Cecil was gold-topped and bordered by a fire escape, with a grand sign and three American flags above its double doors. Frustrated grandeur, like the rest of LA. Inside, everything was still gold, but tired and bordering on beige.

This was where Trent Byrne had lived for five months.

I wondered what he could have been doing, wandering these halls for so long.

Above me there was what looked like a stained glass window in the ceiling. Even though it had seen better days, I wouldn't have had the Cecil pinned as a murder hotel.

Eli had taken Trent's photo up to the reception desk. I could hear him talking to a receptionist, asking how long the lady had worked there and who was in charge.

I walked down the lobby and out of earshot. There were

faux marble statues next to towering pot-plants and stone plinths, as if they had tried to recreate a scene from Ancient Greece. Everything about this place repelled me. Whether it was genuine foreboding, or whether I'd become biased due to Cathal's scrapbook of atrocities, I didn't know.

'Ron!' Eli waved me back over. 'We can check out Trent's old room.'

The receptionist gave me a nod.

He had probably slipped her a fifty-dollar note or more.

I eyed up the two security guards either side of the lifts. Eli waved his key at them but they didn't take much notice. I guessed they were there to enforce a strict 'No guests' policy.

We went inside, and the doors of the lift slid shut.

Eli pulled a face and said, 'This place is creepy.'

'Wouldn't even stay here a night, let alone five months.'

'Enough to drive anyone insane after that long. It's like The fucking Overlook.'

I wasn't sure what that meant.

When we stepped into the eighth-floor hallway, I realized that the reason for my sense of unease was the lighting. I found myself having to squint.

It was quiet.

The floor was like polished bathroom tiles.

'We can talk to the manager once we've had a look,' Eli said, turning the key over in his hand.

They'd given us a proper key for the room, I realized; not a key card. This place really must be old.

The hallway was dotted with circular mirrors.

'How long was that girl's body in the water tank before people noticed?' I asked.

'Two or three weeks.'

We stopped outside Trent's old room and exchanged a look.

You go first.

No, you.

Then Eli let us in.

The room was tiny and smelt stale; the kind of smell you'd get in an old peoples' home. A bed, a chair and a small TV. That was it. He must have been using a communal bathroom.

It was one of the most depressing places I had ever seen. Looking back and seeing the four deadbolts on the door just compounded the misery. I ran my hand over them and wondered if Trent had watched them from his bed, feeling as unsafe as I did now.

'Because when someone knocks on your door at the Cecil, it isn't room service,' Eli had said, while reading an article on the Internet.

He pulled the grubby covers from the bed, turned the pillows, checked the empty drawers in the small table, but there wasn't enough stuff in the room. If Trent had left something here, it would be in plain view.

I looked behind the TV. Nothing. I checked the drawers Eli had already opened, but found nothing but a Bible.

He opened the window, which didn't have a lock, and peered at the fire escape.

The tile from the hallway had been replaced by carpet; greenish brown, scuffed. There were burn marks on the walls.

'Drug dealers used to rent these rooms for clients to shoot up in,' Eli told me, sitting down on the bed. 'I read that paramedics used to be here all the time picking up people who had accidentally overdosed.'

'I'd OD if I had to stay here.' I leant against the small table, trying to see the room through Trent's eyes again, but it was as blank and featureless as the man himself. 'I don't think

Trent would have left anything. Not that would still be here after this long. I mean, what would be the point? Unless he knew someone would be searching for him. We'll be better off talking to the guys downstairs.'

It took a long time for Eli to say anything.

'It has to mean something,' he said eventually, still sitting.

'What? That he stayed here?'

'Yeah, of all places, he stayed here in the fucking *murder hotel*. Then he disappeared.'

To feel as though I was contributing, I got on my hands and knees and checked under the bed, but there was nothing there either. It was madness to think there would still be a trace of him here when he had left virtually no trace anywhere else.

I ran my hand along the sombre radiator, scratches there and scratches on the wall behind, parallel and frenzied, almost like a tally.

Eli saw them too.

I wanted to say, 'Fingernails' but it seemed too speculative, so unnecessarily morbid, that I didn't.

Fingernails.

'Come on, let's go downstairs,' I said, getting up.

Eli nodded, turning the key over and over in his hand again, then he got up and followed me out. At the last moment I went back and took the Bible with me. It didn't seem like the sort of place to provide the word of God.

Eli tried to order some bourbon while we were waiting for the manager but the Cecil's bar only served tea and coffee. It was nearing six in the evening and I knew we both wouldn't sleep, but we sat with double espressos anyway, in brown armless chairs.

'Salvation.'

'What?' I started when Eli broke the silence.

He nodded at the floor of the lobby and at the stained glass ceiling. 'You should know that, right? It's a Christian sign of salvation and deliverance, the eight-pointed star.'

I stared at the gold star encircled in black and white on the floor and at the red star depicted on the ceiling.

'No idea,' I said, bracing myself for one of his caustic remarks, but he didn't elaborate.

The manager of the Cecil, a man who tried to walk with a commanding sort of presence but who only succeeded in making himself look neurotic, joined us after twenty minutes or so. He'd probably had to deal with a lot of shit, I thought as I looked him up and down, being the manager of a place like this.

'Edward Saxon,' he introduced himself to us, with a weak handshake.

'Elias.'

'Mark,' I said.

We all sat and Saxon crossed his legs, one thigh over the other like a woman.

He said, 'You're here to enquire about—'

'May I have a spoon?' Eli interjected.

'Excuse me?'

'A spoon, for my coffee.'

Saxon jerkily stood up again. 'I, er... of course. I'll find one for you.'

He walked in the direction of the kitchens, next to the bar. After a minute or so he returned and handed Eli a teaspoon.

The second time Saxon sat down he looked in serious discomfort, watching Eli stirring his coffee as if it were disturbing behaviour.

He said, 'You're here to enquire about one of our former residents?'

'Yeah.' Eli took the photo out of his coat again and handed it across the coffee table. 'This is him, from about ten years ago. He probably looked very different...'

'No, I know him.' Saxon held the photo up to his face. 'You're right, he changed a lot but this is undoubtedly him. Who exactly are you, if you don't mind me asking?'

Eli made to take the photo back but Saxon kept hold of it. 'I'm an old friend of his. He disappeared a while ago, and I've been trying to find him. He hasn't left any forwarding addresses. It's as if he's vanished off the face of the earth.'

'How did you find out your friend stayed here? If he didn't leave any forwarding address?'

'He mentioned to someone that he was staying here.'

'You know, we have to respect a customer's right to privacy, to a point.'

'But what if a customer's life was in danger? Or he had disappeared in suspicious circumstances?' I said, raising my eyebrows. 'You'd want to cooperate, wouldn't you?'

'Are you with the LAPD?'

We both shook our heads.

'Private investigators then?'

'No, we're just friends of Trent's,' Eli said, in an over-pronounced tone that no one but me would recognize as a sign that he was about to lose his temper. 'Something bad may have happened to him and we just really need to know what he was doing here and whether he gave any indication of where he was going.' He added, for good measure, 'His family are going out of their minds with worry.'

Saxon frowned and adjusted his suit. 'He didn't strike me as a man who had any family. Or friends, for that matter.'

'How did he look?'

'He looked... in the most polite way I can put it, like any other transient. We weren't sure if he was a drug addict or not quite there in the head, but he wasn't right. We had the impression he was someone who might have fallen upon hard times, lost his job or something and needed a place to go.'

'Did he look different to that photo when he was staying here?'

'Yes.' Saxon glanced at it again. 'He had a small beard, greying. He was very lined and was pale, almost like a meth addict. He was very polite, though, kept himself to himself and didn't leave the hotel very much. After a while he had befriended the doormen and most of housekeeping. They all liked him. He was strange, but I liked him too.'

'Can we speak to any of these people?' I asked.

'Penny, in housekeeping. She got to know him well. Better than any of us. She won't be in again until tomorrow morning though. If I tell her to come in half an hour early, you can come back and speak to her then? About eight-thirty?'

'That would be great, thanks.' Eli had relaxed now that Saxon had opened up.

'You said he never left the hotel much?' I added, wired from the espresso.

'No, he'd emerge every few days. Sometimes he wouldn't come out at all. But security said he used to walk around the halls a lot.' Saxon gestured upwards at the tower block above our heads, the eight-pointed star. 'Maybe he did it for exercise or to gather his thoughts, I don't know. But to my knowledge he never bothered anybody.'

'No, he wasn't the sort who ever bothered anybody.' A sharp line had appeared between Eli's eyebrows. 'You haven't got any footage of him, have you? From the corridors?'

'I can... see if we have anything.'

I started flipping through the Bible on my lap. 'Do you provide these in the rooms?'

Saxon pursed his lips. 'No. Why?'

'No reason.'

Someone had written in this Bible, scribbled in the margins.

Eli glanced at me, saw some of the writing, but didn't mention it in front of Saxon.

There was a sugar bowl on the table between us. I took the spoon out of it and, when Saxon wasn't looking, put it in my pocket.

We left not long after that.

Walking back to the car, a homeless guy grabbed Eli's arm.

He wrenched it out of the man's grasp, thinking he was about to lose his watch, but the guy wasn't armed. He was gibbering through swollen and cracked lips, eyes rolling in his head; a mental.

I took Eli by the shoulder and steered us both around him.

'Cecil means sixth,' the guy lisped after us. 'Cecil means the devil, the devil...'

CHAPTER TWENTY-TWO

Daisy

I always knew on some level that Nic was going to kill me. I even considered putting it in writing somewhere a couple of times, as evidence were I to go missing and my body never found. But that seemed insane, so I never convinced myself to do it.

Choking on blood, I spat out a tooth, rolled onto my side and scrambled to my feet to keep running.

Where, fuck knows.

Sucks to be me.

I thought it would be somewhere like this; a grey concrete warehouse, the pretext of somewhere secluded to talk.

Mental, right, the trust we put in people. Mental, that I'd fooled myself into trusting Nic when he was built to destroy, paid to destroy. Why should I be any different from the other humans he'd wiped out of existence?

I ran at one of the first-floor windows and expected to crash through it like they always managed to do in films. I rebounded off the glass, smashed my fists on it, screaming. But no give.

'Help me! Hey, *fucking help me!*'

He dragged me back by a fistful of my hair and threw me to the floor.

'Nic, please, I don't know what you think I've done—'

'Shut up!'

I rolled out of reach as he went to kick me again, struggling to do much more than scrabble away.

'I know I should have told you about Seven, I know. Fuck... please...' I dug my fingernails into his wrists as he pulled me upright again, just to smack me back down. 'Nic, please—'

'I don't give a *fuck* what you have to *say*!'

I tried to breathe, couldn't, coughed up more blood.

Gonna die.

He picked me up again, shaking me by my bad arm.

Gonna die.

Should've told the truth.

I was always gonna die because of this.

His blue eyes were slits, barely open, as mine stared into them, waiting for it... waiting for it...

Held up by the front of my shirt, bunched up in his fist, my feet scraping the floor, waiting for it...

I started crying. It was the worst thing I could have done in front of him.

'Nic, please... Nic, I'm sorry.'

He didn't give a shit.

I was blacking out, waiting for it...

Of course he didn't give a shit.

'Sleep is shite at the moment, to be honest,' I said, spooning three sugars into my flat white. 'Keep having nightmares.'

Mark Chester, mine and Nic's former flatmate, looked me up and down with concern.

It would be easy to resent Mark, if I didn't know him so well. He was prettier than me, had better skin, better cheekbones, bigger eyes, and being well over six foot he wore a pair of skinny jeans better than I ever could.

He was also the only person I knew who killed with less remorse than Nic.

'But the place is OK for you, no?'

'Oh yeah, yeah it's great, Mark, thanks. Beats sleeping at work.' I snorted. 'As long as you don't need it for anything?'

'It's just somewhere I store things, paperwork and stuff.' He shifted in his seat, stabbing at his green tea to enforce brewing. 'You don't mind that Seven stayed there?'

'I don't think it's haunted, if that's what you mean.'

'No one feels shittier about this than me, love.'

He'd said it so many times. I met his eyes, startlingly green – so green I thought he had taken to wearing coloured contacts – and spread my hands.

'I'm fine. Really, I'm fine. Like, it wasn't pleasant getting shot but... working there, it's probably one of those things that was gonna happen sooner or later anyway.'

'You know I told her she was like me, when we were working together. I actually told her she'd be good at doing my job.' He shook his head. 'Should have had some clue that she already *was* good at it.'

'It might not have made a difference. She was really fucking clever. Give her credit for that.'

Seven had been clever, manoeuvring around us like a big cat as Noel and Ronnie suspected everyone else, even each other.

And I'd let her go. I'd let her shoot me.

I'd let her go and I didn't know if it had been the right call.

We both looked around, at faces, out of habit. Every

conversation felt like it was recorded now. It was exhausting being on the lookout all the time, even in bland Hampstead coffee shops like this one.

'I keep seeing her everywhere, it's driving me insane,' I said, with a forced smile. 'But I'm so sure it's her, I'm sure she's still in London.'

'What, seeing her in a "I'm tripping balls most of the time" way?'

'No, in an "actually seeing her" way. I swear, I'm not making it up. She hasn't left, I'd bet my life on it.' On second thoughts, I gestured at a businessman sitting alone by the window on his iPad. 'His life. I'd bet *his* life on it.'

'I'm not sure she would stay in London, considering. And I've had some leads elsewhere.'

'Really? I mean, where have you been looking – Japan? London would be the last place you'd look for her, right. She'd know that.'

He hesitated. 'I'd know if she was still here.'

'Like you *knew* what she was going to do last time?'

Silence.

I rubbed my eyes. 'Gah, sorry, that was harsh.'

'Not entirely unfair.'

I wondered what it felt like for someone like Mark, with his infamous one hundred per cent success rate, to feel at the mercy of a situation.

He put his sunglasses on, and took them off again two seconds later. He was dressed entirely in black, with long sleeves covering his mosaic of Russian prison tattoos. The ones on his hands could rarely be hidden though; the tiny marks on the backs of his fingers. They were more restless than usual, moving to cup themselves around his eyes, creating a sun visor.

'Wish the weather would make its mind up,' he muttered.

'Noel's kinda shitting himself about this money,' I said. 'They can't afford you much longer.'

He shrugged. 'I'll still be looking, whether they're paying me or not. Maybe don't mention that to them though. Can't have too many people knowing I can be bought with a challenge.'

'*Gurl*, please.' I spread my hands.

'A gurl gotta make rent, honey. Know what I'm sayin'.' He rubbed his thumb and middle finger together. 'Gurl needs her dollar.'

'*Can I get a Amen!*' I drank some of my syrupy coffee. 'Well, it makes me feel better that you'll keep looking. Has, um... has Nic talked about it?'

'No, he's really absent. I'm not living there at the moment.' He pinched the bridge of his nose. 'Fuck me, love, how did things get so fucked?'

Would things be so fucked if I hadn't let Seven go?

I could feel the weight of it in my throat.

But that wasn't coming out, ever.

'What's going on with Edie?' Mark asked, dissatisfied with his tea, frowning at it.

'Why?'

'Gossip.' He grinned. 'Ammunition. Curiosity.'

'I'm speaking to her later but I think Noel and Ronnie are in for a firing, whatever being fired by Edie entails. She's calling someone in America a lot, though that may be family stuff, I don't know. Just think it's a bit of a coincidence with Ronnie being out there.'

'You got a number?'

I repressed a grin as large as his. 'Well, as you ask, I do.'

'Knew you'd have something. Want me to check it out?'

'Please. I Googled it but you're probably gonna do something more James Bond with it.'

I pushed my phone across the table and Mark copied the number into his.

'Whose side are you on then?' he asked, picking up his tea and giving it a tentative sip.

'I don't know if there are sides yet.'

'But if there were?'

'I don't know. Whose side would you be on?'

'Yours, love.' He nodded. 'Seriously. You have me on your side anytime you want.'

It was hard not to feel overwhelmed by the gravity of that statement.

I wanted to run some ideas by him, use him as a soundboard, tell him my suspicions that Edie might be setting me up to take over the club. But it seemed premature before speaking to her. It wouldn't be that simple. Best to stay quiet and collect as much information as I could, then hopefully pick the option that resulted in the minimum number of people getting shot.

'What have you been having nightmares about?' he asked, putting his sunglasses on again.

'You don't wanna know.'

'Maybe lay off the psychedelics for a while.'

I looked up from my coffee. 'What makes you think...? How do you know about that?'

He checked his nails, palm flat, like a woman. 'It's still my business to know everything.'

'Are you still seeing that Russian guy?' I asked. 'Roman?'

'Roman Katz? When I can. He seems distant lately.'

'Aren't Russians generally distant?'

'No. No, the opposite. Coming from a country where you have to hide what you are, that makes you guarded. But they're not distant people. They're abrasive, grounded. They're the people I like speaking to most, actually.'

'But Katz seems distant?'

He fell silent for a while. I noticed that under his eye, along one cheekbone, he had some glitter smudged into his skin.

'I know it's hard to believe,' he said, raising his eyebrows, 'but I've been broken up with a couple of times. Just a couple. You get to recognize the signs, months in advance sometimes. You realize you're choosing your words around them more, worrying more, and you're not even sure why until it ends and you realize you'd felt it coming.'

I'd felt it coming with Nic. He was right. Even if it felt like you'd been pushed out of a moving car, break-ups were never a surprise.

'Have you ever killed an ex? Or like, castrated them or something?'

He grinned, checking the people around us. 'No, shh.'

'You must have been tempted?'

'It's less of an urge when you know you actually *could* kill them.'

'I always thought Nic was gonna kill me. I had nightmares about it all the time. It's actually the reason I'm not sleeping that well...'

'Why? Did he ever give you the idea?'

'No, it's just... who he is. Sometimes the only way I could ever see us breaking up was with him killing me. I get the impression that's how most of his relationships end, especially after *whatshername*.'

'Clare. His boss's wife. He didn't kill her though.'

'Yeah, I know. To be honest, the only person I could see him staying with for ever is you.'

The atmosphere shifted, almost imperceptibly. I went up to the counter to get a croissant.

When I came back, Mark pushed the rest of his tea away.

'Have you guys always been platonic?' I asked, unsure why I kept pursuing the subject.

He went to say something but I cut him off, groaning, 'I can *literally* see you about to say something about *actual* Plato. I have read his book about "man-love", OK, because *you* were the one who lent it to me. Just answer the damn question without being an arse.'

'You know me quite well.' He laughed, flicking crumbs off his jeans. 'Nothing sexual has ever happened between us, no.'

'But?'

'But nothing.'

'Bollocks.'

'What do you *want* me to say?'

'That you're in love with him.'

'So are you,' he replied, without hesitation.

I nodded. That was a satisfactory response.

What was the statistic? Two women a week killed by a current or former male partner? One every three days? So today it was me, instead of someone else.

Stupid fucking shit that goes through your head when you're about to die.

I die the same way every time, thumbs crushing my throat, spitting blood down my front, trying to say, 'Please, please, please...' but not able to say anything. And crying. The crying was fucking unforgivable.

That's how I wake up eventually; crying.

The fucking worst.

And these nightmares started way before me and Nic broke up.

I started smoking a massive joint before I went to bed, and that sometimes kept them away.

It made getting up in the morning traumatic. But I figured that's what MDMA was for.

CHAPTER TWENTY-THREE

Ronnie

I took one of Cathal's Ormus capsules before we got in the car the following morning, but didn't feel anything. Ingest white powder and you usually got some sort of buzz, maybe a loved-up or anxious sort of emotion at worst. But no, nothing.

It didn't bode well for the spoon, which I'd given to Cathal with the brief challenge, 'This is my spoon, make it gold for me.' It hadn't been the spoon from the hotel either, which I'd realised most likely wasn't made of solid silver. The spoon I'd given him had been bought from a rundown antique shop next to a cafe where I'd stopped for coffee.

I didn't mention either the Ormus or the spoon to Eli, but I was disappointed. I made a mental note to take a few more later.

Saxon didn't meet us, but the receptionist – a boy this time – told us Penny was waiting in the same place we'd spoken with him the day before.

A male receptionist made more sense, I thought. I wouldn't want to work here if I was a woman, given the place's history.

Penny was in her forties, of Mexican heritage, maybe Puerto

Rican. There was something in her features reminiscent of Luiz. She gave us a nervous curtsy instead of shaking our hands, and we refrained from sitting until she did.

'Mr Saxon said you wanted to speak about Trent?' she said, hands clasped in her lap. 'You are friends?'

'Yeah, old friends.' I nodded.

She seemed disbelieving. 'Trent never spoke about friends.'

'We haven't spoken for years,' Eli said, almost whispering, as if he was afraid of scaring her away. 'He's disappeared and no one seems to know where he is. We're very worried about him. Did he mention anything to you about what he was doing here or where he was going?'

'He liked to help me clean his room. He didn't need to, but he said it made him feel guilty watching me work while he did nothing.' She shook her head. 'He never said anything about why he was living here. People usually choose here because they have nowhere else to go.'

'Did you find him strange?' I asked. 'Did he ever act strange or say anything out of the ordinary?'

Her eyes slid sideways. 'Um…'

'Did he ever say anything that scared you?' I asked, rephrasing.

'He didn't scare me.' But she looked as though she wanted to say something else.

We both stayed silent, watching her decide what to say.

'He didn't scare me, but sometimes he would say things I didn't like. But as soon as I told him to stop saying these things, he'd apologize.'

'What did he say that you didn't like?'

Her hand went to her neck and I realized she was wearing a silver crucifix.

'He would say things about Satan.'

That was it. That was all she offered.

'Like what?' Eli pressed.

'I don't want to say them.'

'Did he have a Bible in his room?' I asked. 'There was a Bible in his room, even though you apparently don't provide them here.'

She seemed to shrink. She touched the crucifix, smoothed her hair, looked away, looked back at us and said, 'Please don't tell Mr Saxon. I left Trent a Bible in his room, to help him. I thought he needed it. I think it is still there, he didn't take it with him and I left it there, just in case.'

Eli's eyes widened for a moment.

'He said the Cecil is a gateway to hell,' she said, catching her breath as if the very words might snatch her from salvation.

'What?'

'A gateway to hell,' she repeated, with fearful eyes. 'He said, when he was talking one day, that this was a place of baptism, where sinners would be cleansed or punished.'

I thought of the girl in the water tank and my stomach turned.

Eli glanced at the eight-pointed star on the ceiling and thought I didn't notice.

'Do you believe him?' I asked, not liking where this interview was going. 'A lot of bad stuff has happened here. Doesn't it scare you?'

I wondered if she'd drunk any water from the taps while the girl had been in there, or whether Saxon had. I was surprised anyone would ever take a job here after that. They should burn the place down, consecrate the ground and be done with it.

'At work I'm not scared,' she said, indicating her head at the entrance. 'I have worked here for seven years and nothing bad has happened to me. The men outside. They are the ones who scare me.'

'And Trent didn't say anything about where he was going?'

'Not to me, no. Talk to Robeson. He works on the door sometimes. Sometimes Trent would talk to the men outside, but I don't know which ones. The... *bums*, Mr Saxon calls them. I don't like that word.'

'The ones from Skid Row?'

She pursed her lips at the very mention of the name.

I didn't ask anything else.

Eli must have also sensed that we wouldn't get much more out of her, because he leant forwards, his hands linked on his knees. 'Thanks, Penny. You've been really helpful. Is Mr Saxon in today? We were hoping to talk to him about seeing some of the video footage you may have of Trent?'

'No, he's not.' She shifted. 'I need to go to work now.'

'No, right, of course you can.'

Eli gave her leave to go.

When she was far enough away, small heels clicking on the luminous floor, I turned to him.

'I don't wanna hang around in LA for days.'

'I have a feeling Saxon was counting on that. He could tell we weren't staying.' Eli pursed his lips, thinking.

'I don't suppose it would look good if it got out, the hotel staff divulging private information about guests.'

'What? Compared to the *glowing* publicity of a girl's body ending up in the water tank and five or six decades of murders and suicides?'

'You make a good point.'

He swivelled and watched the reception desk. 'We could see if this Robeson is in today?'

'If he's not, we have to go.'

The boy from behind reception was approaching us, thick eyebrows lowered, making everything he did seem mysterious. He made a beckoning motion with his fingers, which raised the two of us from our chairs. He was clutching a small package down by his side, which he held out to me when I reached him first.

'Mr Saxon put this aside for you. He said to make sure you got it.'

It was a wad of letters, postcards and scribbles, about two inches thick and tied with rubber bands. The piece of lined notepaper on the top read *Trent left these behind. Maybe you can find a use for them. E.S.*

Eli almost snatched it out of my hands. 'Did he say anything else?'

'No, that's it.'

'No CCTV? Video?'

The boy shook his head.

'Wicked. We'll take it.' I started to drag Eli towards the exit, muttering, 'Let's not push our luck now. We can always come back later.'

Both Cathal and Luiz were out when we got back. I spent most of the afternoon with my laptop in the garden shed thinking about maybe Skyping my kids, but mostly researching the relevance of water and corpses in Satanism.

I cast my eyes over some of the equipment, trying to gauge how Cathal was coming along with turning the stolen spoon into gold, but there was no sign of it. His alchemy appliances looked like customized microwaves. Maybe I should have marked the spoon in some way, so that he wouldn't just swap it for another, but it was too late now.

I had a text from Mark Chester, back in the UK, asking when he should fly to Chicago to meet me. The idea of looking for Seven seemed distant now, almost irrelevant, compared to looking for Trent. Irritating, considering that the former directly concerned me and the latter didn't.

It was my lack of concern that was the problem. I hated talking to Noel when he was drinking. I hated Seven with such a visceral repulsion that I didn't want to see her again, even if it was to kill her. Daisy... Daisy was just another problem. I wasn't yet sure why.

I took another Ormus capsule and dry-swallowed it.

Give me a few days, I texted back.

We don't have a few days. I'll have to meet you there, came the insolent reply.

I knew he was right, but I couldn't bring myself to care. I'd rather stay here in the shed, avoiding everyone for ever. The idea of never seeing any of them again. Well, it didn't fill me with dread...

Putting my mobile down, I clicked on one of the articles I'd found. Four men in Bangladesh had been arrested in 2010 for murdering a bricklayer, cutting off his head and burning it in a kiln. Apparently the owners of their business had wanted to produce redder bricks, and a fortune-teller had told them a human sacrifice would ensure the desired colour. Apparently neither the owners nor the fortune-teller had ever been found. I wondered how easy it would be to convince someone to do something like that if they were desperate and uneducated.

It couldn't be hard. After all, I'd been taking capsules full of God-knows-what on the word of a man who said they could cure cancer and turn metals into gold.

There was a tap on the door and I started.

Eli stood there, looking uneasy.

'Anything interesting in Trent's pile of crap?' I asked.

'I haven't looked yet, I've been trying to get hold of Cam but he's not available.' He shifted. 'There's two guys here to see Cathal.'

'Where are they?'

'In the living room. They just came in.'

'Did you tell them he isn't here?'

'I haven't told them anything.'

We both paused. I felt my pockets, remembered I'd left my gun in the car, and slowly followed Eli out into the garden and back up towards the house.

'Are you carrying?' I asked.

'No, it's upstairs.'

'Do they look dangerous?'

'They don't look chill.'

We stepped into the empty kitchen. There was a magnetic knife rack against the wall, a metal strip with about eight knives stuck to it. Before I could venture near it the two men came in. They were wearing suits, like they were in the fucking Matrix. They were both also conspicuously blond.

'Cathal Sheedy?'

Without even glancing at each other, I replied, 'Yes?'

Their hands went simultaneously to their waistbands and I dived for the knife rack. My fingers curled around the handle of a wimpy chopping blade and then I was in a crouch. I looked up, forearm raised, and everyone was on the floor. Eli must have rushed both of them. I leapt to my feet and rammed the blade through the chin of the one nearest to me.

A jet of blood hit my eyes.

'Fuck! Fuck!'

I dropped the knife, or left it sticking out of the guy's face. I didn't know. I swatted blood off my fingers, feeling around for the sink, everything stinging like hell. Then I remembered my shirt and rubbed the sleeves across my face.

Eli came into focus, his knee across a man's neck. The other one was dead and the knife was on the floor not far from his hand; he must have pulled it out of his chin before he died.

'Eli... you...' I pointed at him, trying to wipe more blood out of my eyes.

He reached up and realized his ear was bleeding.

We both looked at the ceiling and saw two bullet holes.

I hadn't heard the shots being fired.

I checked myself, but appeared to be fine.

Eli returned his attention to the man beneath him. 'Why do you want Cathal Sheedy dead?'

The man glanced at me.

'I'm not Cathal, genius,' I said.

'Then why...' The man choked. 'Why did you say you were?'

'To see what you'd do.' I went to the sink and ran the cold tap, dashing some water into my eyes.

'Then it's none of your business.'

Eli searched the man's pockets and the inside of his jacket, tucked the gun into the back of his trousers and stood up. 'Kinda is our business now, I'm afraid, and we can *make* you talk to us, you know.'

I started and yelled, 'Fuck, get him!'

But it was too late. I saw the man's hand go to his mouth, and by the time Eli reached him he had started convulsing.

Eli recoiled, and we watched as he went into a violent seizure, eyes bulging, rolling back in his head, before he went still. It looked like a terrible way to die, veins and eyes straining.

'That escalated quickly,' Eli remarked.

'Fuck's sake. What the fuck is Cathal gonna say when he gets back and finds this in his kitchen!' I snapped. 'We just fucking killed them, that's not *escalating*! Jesus Christ, what's *wrong* with you? As if we haven't got enough on our plates without...' I gestured at the bodies.

I wasn't sure why but I was angry with Eli for this. Regardless of what Cathal was mixed up in, I was irrationally certain this wouldn't have happened if he hadn't brought us here.

He hadn't reacted to any of it. Instead, he started examining the bodies.

He said, 'I don't think Cathal'll be as surprised as you think, if he's the type of guy who has two professionals sent to kill him. They're not run-of-the-mill thugs.'

'Of course they're not, they were carrying suicide pills. You know who carries those?'

'Spies.'

'Or soldiers.' I ran the tap and rinsed my face again. 'You know what, have you seen his kids' rooms? They seem weird. What do we even know about Cathal apart from what Luiz has told us?'

'You think Luiz knew about this?'

I gave him a shrug that said *I don't even fucking know*.

'I'm not cleaning this up,' I said, somewhat stroppily.

Eli appeared to remember that his ear had been obliterated and tried to stem the flow, grimacing. It was only when he did that that I realized how much blood was collecting on his clothes.

'I'm sure he'll have a first aid kit somewhere,' I said, thinking of the garden shed first, then hesitating. 'You think...? No.'

'What?' He went to the sink, ran the tap and tried to awkwardly position his ear under it.

'Doesn't matter. Just thinking.'

Leaving him with his head in the sink, I went back to the shed to get my laptop. Once inside, all of Cathal's equipment had taken on a more purposeful appearance. I opened and closed a couple of the drawers, but doubted he'd have left his stash of Ormus capsules in here.

He couldn't be onto something, could he?

Ridiculous, I thought, as I searched for a first aid kit. People deserved to die for loads of plausible reasons; alchemy and curing cancer weren't among them.

Sheedy, I thought. What a ridiculous made-up surname.

When I went back up to the house I gave Eli two Ormus capsules and told him they were painkillers, just to see if anything impressive happened.

CHAPTER TWENTY-FOUR

There were Power Rangers on the chest of drawers, but teddy bears on the bed. I picked up one of the figurines. Ryan had been too old for this shit for years. He'd done away with teddy bears when he was three. How old were these kids?

I opened some of the drawers. The clothes were neatly folded and ageless.

Returning to the landing, I shouted, 'This guy doesn't have kids.'

From downstairs, 'Does he have a wife, you think?'

Into the master bedroom I went. Again, it was too tidy. But something was off. Rachel's closet was nowhere near as ordered, and there simply weren't enough clothes. It looked like the sort of stuff I'd buy if my mission was to disguise myself as a woman.

Into the bathroom and there was just men's stuff.

It was a man's house.

'Is no one fucking *normal* any more?' I went downstairs and neatly stepped over the bodies to light a cigarette in the back doorway.

Eli was sitting on the floor against one of the cupboards, dosed up on Ormus and real painkillers and holding a tea towel to his ear.

I looked at the holes in the ceiling. 'I didn't hear those, you know.'

'*What?*'

It was enough to crack me for a second, and we both grinned.

'Seriously though,' I continued, inhaling, exhaling, inhaling again, holding the smoke, 'my ears aren't ringing or anything. They weren't using silencers either.'

He nodded. 'I once read about a guy whose eyesight improved so much during a hostage situation that his prescription had to be lowered after.'

'The human body is off its tits sometimes.'

Eli took the tea towel away from his ear, grimacing, and managed to laugh.

'Well?' he said, gesturing at the mess.

'I'll go search the car.'

I threw my cigarette away and bent to rifle through the men's pockets. One of them had keys, but no other ID was forthcoming.

Outside it was, if possible, even quieter. I guess that was the idea of suburbia, cutting yourself off so no one could hear you talking, having sex, cooking, dying.

They hadn't parked in the driveway so I ventured into the road, pressing the unlock button on the keys.

There were a couple of drives not completely shrouded by hedges and trees, but no curtains open.

About twenty yards away, a small dark blue Honda made itself known by beeping. I could tell immediately there was going to be nothing there; it was second-hand. I jogged over and opened the driver's door.

Nothing. Not even empty crisp packets.

I shut the door behind me and levered myself into the back,

checking the seat storage, under the cushions, and clambering into the front again to check the glove compartments. There was one smartphone.

Locked.

The car smelt of smoke.

I got out and jogged back towards Cathal's house. As I did, a dim rumble and a pair of headlights found me.

I slowed to a walk as the car did, and it was Luiz who leant out of the window.

'What you doing in the road, man?'

I stared at them both, put the phone in my pocket and walked away.

I expected Cathal to – well, I'm not sure what I expected. I didn't expect him to shake his head and reach out to grasp my shoulder.

'Boys, I'm sorry, eh. Fuck. I guess it was always... I'm sorry.'

Eli, who may have been on the verge of an overdose, waved from the sofa. 'You're not a dull landlord.'

'He should go to hospital,' Luiz said in an undertone.

The three of us were standing in an awkward row in the kitchen, huddled shoulder to shoulder awaiting instruction from Cathal. It was his mess, after all.

'Well,' he said, eventually, scratching his beard.

Then he went upstairs.

I exchanged a glance with Luiz, and followed.

'Hey! Um, so what? You going to help us clear this shit up?'

He looked back at me. 'No, I can't.'

'What do you mean, fucking *no*?'

He ignored me, disappearing from sight. In the bedroom I could hear doors banging, a dragging sound, the noises of someone packing.

I looked over at Eli, who still had the tea towel pressed against his ear and his eyes shut. Luiz seemed as lost as me. So I took the initiative and stormed after Cathal.

'Oi! We're not fucking done here.'

He had gone into this spaced-out, eyes-down state. I couldn't be certain he was hearing me as he threw clothes into the vast suitcase he'd dragged onto the bed.

'Hey!' I grabbed his shoulder. 'What the fuck is going on?'

He flinched out of my grasp but his eyes were still downcast.

'What are you doing?' I stepped into his path on his way back to the wardrobe. 'Hey! What, you're going to run away? Who were those guys?'

He still wouldn't look at me.

Like arguing with a fucking woman.

I slapped him.

It seemed a prissy thing to do, probably hurt my hand more than it hurt his face, but I had to snap him out of it.

He glared at me and I thought he was going to throw a punch.

Go on.

But it wasn't a glare. It was wide-eyed fucking fear.

He sniffed, looked away again, and walked around me to get to his clothes.

This time I didn't stop him.

'Cathal, look, I don't know you.' I sat on the bed, next to the suitcase. 'But those guys were pros. If you run away, they might come after us. You should tell me why they were here at least.'

'They won't come after you,' he said.

I sighed.

'Then help us bury them.'

'I haven't got time.'

'What about Luiz? Does he know what's going on?'

'No.'

Those weren't appropriate clothes to flee in, I thought, surveying his baggy jeans and Aztec shirt. The last thing you wanted to look like when you were on the run was a vagrant.

'Take my scrapbook on the Cecil,' he said, going into the bathroom and coming back with hands full of products. 'In fact, take anything. Take anything you want.'

He zipped up the case and took it downstairs.

I stayed in the bedroom for a while, listening to him and Luiz conversing in rapid tones. My phone was in my right pocket and the phone from the car was in my left. I didn't know what to do about Eli; he wouldn't go to a hospital so we'd have to make do.

Going to the top of the stairs, I watched Cathal carrying appliances out of the front door from his shed, loading them into his car. I sat on the top step and scrolled through my phone, looking for anyone we could stay with.

After a while even Luiz stopped trying to intervene.

Cathal shut the back door and I stood up. 'Cathal, come on! Let us help you!'

He pinched the bridge of his nose.

'What about your wife and kids?' I ventured.

He looked up at me and actually smiled.

It was almost funny, I thought. I guess it had to be.

Cathal reached into his pocket and then held out a wrangled piece of metal.

I realized, as I looked at it in my palm, that it used to be a spoon. It had changed colour; wasn't entirely silver.

Eli said, 'Maybe I should go to the hospital,' and it jolted me out of my reverie in time to see Cathal leaving, with Luiz in tow.

He looked back at us apologetically and said, 'I'm going with him, guys. I'll call you, I promise.'

It seemed so fucking inconsequential that I didn't answer.

Then they were gone, and I was left standing in the doorway holding a repurposed spoon.

Eli started laughing.

CHAPTER TWENTY-FIVE

Daisy

It was colder than it should have been on Hampstead's West Heath. Beautiful though. It would be an amazing place to take an acid trip, with all the flowers and shit. But I was sober as a fucking Tuesday morning and wasn't in the mood to look at *nice* things.

This was the second day I'd sat here, headphones on and listening to Caribou beneath the pergola.

It boiled down to me knowing more than them, I realized. That's why they all thought Seven was in Chicago or Japan or Timbuktu. Noel might have been able to contradict them if he was capable of doing anything right now. He'd known her, I reckoned. But not as well as me.

Seven said the only place you could go in London to feel like you weren't in London was the Hill garden and pergola on Hampstead Heath. She used to eat her lunch here when the sun was out, no matter how cold it was. In fact she said she preferred it when it was chilly. Less people.

Every so often I moved to another bench or walked to the pergola and sat on one of the walls, watching faces.

Maybe I'd just been wasted for too long, creating a black hole of time where recovery might have been, but I had definitely reached that stage of a break-up where every morning felt like the end of the fucking world. I woke up, remembered what had happened, and wanted to be unconscious again.

And I kept crying for no reason. It was making me tired, all the spontaneous crying.

I kept composing a text to Edie and deleting it.

'Come on, Seven, where the fuck are you, you crazy bitch?'

She was still in London, I fucking knew it. I could feel her lurking, as if the bullet she'd embedded in my shoulder had given us some psychic link. Like it was Harry Potter's scar or something.

I laughed out loud to myself.

Mark had told me once that the interesting thing about the word 'nemesis' was that it used to refer to the deep hatred of a part of yourself. Your biggest enemy, your sabotage, your end, was a part of you. Was Seven my nemesis now? Nemesis didn't mean any old enemy; it was the need to destroy a malignant part of you. My aching, stiff and scarred shoulder was her.

I'd been high at the time. It sounded cooler then.

None of this made a difference to Mark. He was still going to Chicago whether I thought she was there or not.

Nothing I thought made much difference to anyone, it fucking seemed.

I watched another girl walk by with her boyfriend.

I hated how couples fell into that walk; the girl always slightly on the back foot, being led along like a pet. I hoped me and Nic had never looked like that. But then neither of us had ever been into walking along hand in hand.

Gay, as Nic would have put it.

I'd walked into every pub, club and bar in the West End

looking for Nic once. If I had to sit here for a week, or a month, I'd do it. There were worse places to be.

'Do you think you're managed well?'

I wasn't sure how to answer that question. It was the first one she asked. Not even a *How are you?* Just straight to business.

Actually, to be fair, she had asked if I'd wanted a coffee.

I'd been invited to a late lunch with Edie at her house before work. I'd never been there before. It was kinda like her; disproportionately large and intimidating for something quite feminine. I'd heard rumours that she had a kid, but I couldn't see any sign of him. Unmarried, but then women like her – fucking powerhouses – often were.

She was wearing jeans, which was weird to see.

'Um...' I'd only just started to take off my jacket, not sure where to sit. Her kitchen looked like the inside of a fucking spaceship. 'Managed?'

'At the club.' Edie had her back to me for a time, making coffee in one of those fancy coffee-making Italian things. 'Do you think you're managed there well?'

'Honestly' – and I meant it this time – 'I don't really feel managed.'

'You feel like the manager?'

'Well, yeah. I don't mean I'm unmanageable.'

'Would you like to be?'

'Unmanageable?'

She smiled. 'Manager.'

I hadn't expected her to come right out and say it. Ronnie and Noel didn't say anything to me straight any more. It was as if, after what Seven had done, every woman was tarnished.

Wives had left them – though I guess Ronnie's was still hanging in there by a fucking thread for the sake of the kids – and lovers. Next their employees, their friends...

I'd thought I was Noel's friend, but I'd probably never be seen as his equal.

'What, like, co-run the place with Noel and Ron?'

'No. Run the place. Daisy, can we not be so fucking "British" about this?' 'British' was placed in air-quotes. 'I've never got the impression you were into all that coy bull-crap. That's why I think you'd be perfect.'

I decided, finally, to sit down at the breakfast bar, on a stool that was far too high for me. It tipped backwards. It was lime green and impossible to balance on. I never understood why rich people insisted on using these displays of abstract art as furniture.

'You know I'm not some big-shot drug-dealer, right?' I watched the silver Italian thing sat on the hob and speculated as to whether it was actually doing anything. 'Like, if I was a manager I'd just be... y'know, a manager.'

She shrugged, sitting opposite me with ease upon another lime-green monstrosity. 'It seemed like a good idea at the time. Everyone was making money and I liked them. No, really, I can see that look on your face... But I do, I love those boys.'

'You know what happened wasn't their fault.'

She stared at me and raised an eyebrow.

'OK, it wasn't entirely their fault,' I conceded. 'But I was Seven's friend and I didn't see what was going on either.'

'But you did see what was going on. That's why she had to do that.'

I touched my shoulder. I might have imagined the twinge when she nodded at it. With all the drugs and the imposition of the outside world I hadn't thought about it in a while.

'I heard about you and Nic.'

I wondered how she could possibly have known, unless she'd spoken to Nic herself.

I made some non-committal – maybe vaguely disgusted – face.

'I've never known Nic to have a girlfriend,' she said, not getting the hint or just steamrollering over it.

Sometimes I'd been painfully aware of how easily I adopted that label for convenience. I'd been more a lodger at first, in the absence of a place to stay. But if you hung around in the same place and had sex with the same person and shared breakfasts for long enough, I guessed that made you their girlfriend by default.

It was none of her fucking business, so of course I didn't say any of this out loud.

I went, 'Oh.'

'I just want you to know I'm not offering you this because of who your boyfriend is, or was. Because that's what I would suspect, if I was in your position.'

The thing on the hob reached a crescendo.

She stood up and removed it, poured me a coffee and pushed it at me.

I was too self-conscious to ask for milk or sugar. To ask for anything else at this point seemed like pushing my luck.

'So what would happen to Ronnie and Noel?'

'They'll be fine, or they won't. They're adult men, why should you look after them?' She eyed me. 'Daisy, aren't you sick of looking after them?'

I sniffed the coffee and it smelled like bitter European shit but I drank some anyway, to appear sophisticated.

'I guess... you're right.'

She shook her head and said, 'There's something so weak about men.'

'Well, yeah,' I had to agree.

'I really want you to think about this offer.'

'Oh yeah, I am thinking about it. Really.'

'You think if I offered Ronnie and Noel more power on the condition they sell you up the river they'd deliberate for even a second?'

I looked away, out through vast glass windows, into a garden made entirely of stones. 'No.'

'Never do anything for a man when he wouldn't consider doing the same in return.'

'You mean anal?' I blurted it out with a peal of nervous laughter that had been hovering at the back of my throat.

Thank fuck, Edie laughed too. 'Business *and* anal.'

I drank more coffee, smirking. 'I once asked an ex why he wouldn't have a three-way with another guy. A devil's three-way.'

'What did he say?'

I put on a ridiculous macho voice. 'Uh, I just couldn't have my dick that close to another guy's.'

She rolled her eyes. 'Sad.'

For a second I forgot who she was. But then I remembered and stopped laughing.

'Is your real name Daisy?' she asked.

'No.'

'What is it?'

'Eh. Ick.'

'On our books you're... Well, you never gave us your bank account details, I know the boys pay you in cash. You're nameless.'

It seemed pointless to put up a fight.

'It's Catherine.'

'Catherine...?'

'Murray-Spinks. No one's called me that for years. Only my parents really, and I ran away when I was like sixteen so… it's Daisy.' I looked at the stone garden again. 'Look, I want to take your offer.'

There was a glimmer of a smile. Good-natured or not, I couldn't tell.

'Are you sure you don't want to think about it?'

'I've thought about it.'

'Well then.' She stood up and filled the silver thing with more water.

I forced down some more coffee even though it was making me feel sick.

'You'd tell me if you knew where that girl Seven was, wouldn't you?' she said, without turning around.

I wondered who her friends were, and whether they were bigger and badder than my friends.

'Oh, I dunno, me and my fucked-up arm will have to confer and get back to you.'

She still didn't turn around, so I couldn't tell if she was convinced.

CHAPTER TWENTY-SIX

Ronnie

I had never slept in a car before. It was the first of too many times.

I tried to get some strategy out of Eli but he was drowsy and delirious.

'Eli, do you have info on Cameron Hopper?'

'It doesn't matter, we have to find Trent.'

'Do you think we should go back to the hotel?'

'We just have to… find Trent.'

Find Trent. Find Trent.

It was like someone had broken him.

Mark had been calling but I hadn't been picking up. Was he in Chicago now, waiting for me? Did I give a shit?

I shut my eyes again, slumped in the driver's seat.

Eli was unconscious now, in the back.

I didn't have it in me to spend the night like this.

Taking a couple more of the Ormus capsules, I got out of the car and walked along the road for a stretch. We'd parked down a side road, obscured from view in a lay-by. I don't know what I was expecting to find; a motel maybe, a bar. We couldn't check in anywhere with most of Eli's ear missing and bound with a bloodstained tea towel.

The air was so warm, like clammy hands.

My phone started ringing, but it was a Skype call.

Eamonn.

He said, 'Where *are* you?'

'Honestly, no fucking idea. Outskirts of LA, I think.'

'Dad said you're going to Chicago.'

I couldn't remember saying anything to him about Chicago, but I took his word for it.

'I think so. I mean, I am. I just... maybe. I *might* be going to Chicago.'

'You don't look good, bro.'

I paused. 'No... No, I guess I don't.'

Any other time I would've smashed him for a comment like that.

'Dad's given me a few jobs to do,' he said, as if I might be proud of this.

'Oh yeah?'

'Yeah, he said he did the same for you once upon a time, so I should give it a try.'

A mutinous thought – that Dad might be pitting us against each other – sprang into my head, but I ignored it. I'd surpassed all that years ago.

'That's great,' I said, thinking that I might get off the hook if Eamonn could flourish in employment here.

'And he said it might make you feel better about me going back with you if I kinda proved I could do something here... kinda thing.'

As if he had read my fucking mind.

'Well why don't you just stay here and work for Dad?' I said, starting to walk again.

'Why would I do that?'

'Because it makes sense.'

'Because you really don't fucking want me to come home with you.'

'*My* home, Eamonn. Not yours.'

'And where the fuck you think mine is?'

I looked around me, at a load of stern blank houses and hedgerows and a few lights on but not the lights of anyone we knew. I wasn't even going to be able to steal someone's Wi-Fi.

'Let me come to Chicago with you or something,' he said.

'What? No.'

'It might help.'

'With what?'

'Making you think I'm worth shit.'

I don't know whether it actually hurt me, knowing that he thought I held him in no regard.

If it had been Rachel Skyping me, or one of my kids, I wondered whether I'd have answered.

'Look, I can text you when I'm getting on a flight,' I said. 'I'll fly from St Louis and let you know. Come if you want.'

His face broke into a smile.

'Huh, thanks.' That was all he said; he didn't push it.

There was a pause. I'd left my cigarettes in the car.

'Dude,' Eamonn said, snorting, 'where *are* you? Like really.'

I said, 'I really don't fucking know.'

We couldn't stay in LA, with Eli in this condition. But I liked order and I like conclusion, so I checked Eli into a motel on the outskirts to sleep it off, and took the car back into the city.

It was too hot for a jacket or smart trousers. I was dressed in jeans and a T-shirt with hipster sun-drenched scenery across it. It felt good to be driving alone.

I took the car across the bridge and along the waterfront.

Traffic wasn't bad. The brown water appeared blue. I did a couple of laps and then brought the car in past the gorgeous lake next to a small campus.

Students were rowing across it.

I glanced at the passenger seat and checked I had everything I needed; papers, photos, postcards. And most importantly for this trip, the phone belonging to the men who had been sent after Cathal.

There had been a school shooting in Arkansas, the radio blared. Eleven children dead and the shooter had turned the gun on himself. Someone was saying, *'Teachers should be armed, able to defend themselves in situations like this. How many lives could be saved if more of us were carrying guns?'*

I parked and started walking down the main road. To my right were lines of trees and greenery, on my left a Fine Wine & Liquor, a carwash, people looking at me strangely for walking so far, for looking so much like a foreigner in my own country.

Checking my phone to see if I was heading in the right direction, I almost caught the eyes of a bearded man coming out of Black Fire Tattoo, with his forearm wrapped in cling film and a look on his face like he really wanted to punch a fucker.

I was on the right course. Five more minutes down the road and I was at the door of a place called PhoneDoc, an orange and green building that looked like it had been made out of Lego.

Inside I was told to wait, and I took a seat on a red leather sofa in the corner, watching the staff out of the corner of my eye and wondering if they would believe my bullshit story about my lost brother and his locked mobile phone.

Just imagine Eamonn really is lost, I thought. That'll make you more convincing.

No, think about Ryan. You care about Ryan.

I clenched the iPhone between my palms until a woman with long black hair almost down to her waist came over to talk to me.

'What can we help you with, Mr...?'

'O'Connell. It's a bit of a weird one, I'll be honest. My little brother, he's just got out of prison and... well, you don't care about that, but he's been missing for a couple of days and he's left his phone.' I indicated the mobile. 'We don't really know who his friends are any more and we were hoping you could unlock his phone so we'd have some people to call.'

She sat down and took the phone off me. 'This is your brother's phone?'

'Yeah.'

'And his name is?'

'Ryan. O'Connell.'

She had artificially full lips, but they suited her. 'You have any documentation to prove this phone is your brother's?'

'He... barely has any documentation. Our dad bought it for him.'

I didn't look like the sort of man who would steal a phone. No matter how long she spent eyeing me up, there was nothing about my demeanour that would place me in the lower classes.

'Can I see some ID?' she eventually asked. 'It'll cost you thirty-five dollars.'

It was a rip-off.

I smiled. 'Sure, anything. We just want to find him.'

I gave her my passport. She scanned me a couple of times, and then took the phone away.

The iPhone was back in my hands within three minutes and I was back on the street, looking over my shoulder once at the girl behind the desk.

There was nowhere to eat on the main road so I went back to the car and started rinsing the phone for information. But there was only the one number saved, and there was no name attached. No photos. The only number populating the call history was the number saved into the Contacts folder.

'Fuck me,' I muttered, taking some deep breaths.

Checking my watch and finding I was doing OK for time, I called the only number.

The line clicked open on the second ring and I said, 'We need to talk.'

Someone – a man – said, 'Who is this?'

'This is a guy who knows you're after Cathal Sheedy and your men did a piss-poor job of taking him out due to a case of mistaken identity.'

A pause.

'So you're the reason they didn't come back?'

'Feedback for next time: make sure they actually *know* who to pull weapons on. But that's beside the point, I want to give you Cathal. And to avoid you sending anyone after me on some ill-advised vendetta – and I promise, it *will* be ill-advised – I'm going to tell you where he is and who's hiding him. But only if you leave me alone.'

Rustling.

I strained for a hint of background noise, but it was like he was sat in an empty room.

'Do you know who we are?' he asked.

'I'm guessing government or similar, but I don't want to be a part of this. We were stopping over at Cathal's for a few nights on a friend's recommendation. 'We didn't know him. We've got other stuff to do. If I give you this information, go find Cathal and leave us be.'

'You killed the men we sent before.'

'You obviously weren't that invested in them if they were carrying cyanide pills.'

'True.'

My heart was beating as if I was on a run. I could hear it.

'So you are government?' I asked, to fill air.

'Something like that. So where is Cathal hiding?'

'According to a friend of his who went with him, he's hiding with some of his more… prominent friends. Cameron Hopper, you heard of him? Works in TV. Anyway, he's keeping Cathal on the down-low. He can do that apparently. He has money.'

'And how do you know this?'

'We were offered the same protection if we wanted it.'

'… Cameron Hopper.'

'Yes, that's the name. Find him and you find Cathal. Now do I have your word that I'll never hear from you again?'

A pause.

The line died.

Some kids started screaming from across the lot, as their car went through the wash.

It was too hot. I got out of the car and went for a walk around a small lake next to a prep school, unable to relax despite the cooler breeze.

I hadn't been given any reassurance that we weren't going to be followed.

The phone in my pocket buzzed and I jumped, causing some passers-by to look at me with alarm, but I realized it was my own phone and the incoming Skype call was from my mum.

Seizing the moment, I answered it.

She said, 'Son, we're so worried about you. I just wanted to check you were OK.'

Having cancer hadn't done anything to increase her fear

of death, but her fears around her children had skyrocketed, I'd noticed.

'Mum, I'm fine,' I said, flashing a smile before turning the camera out towards the lake. 'Seriously, take a look at where I am.'

And the lying utopian scene had the desired effect.

CHAPTER TWENTY-SEVEN

It was a thirty-nine-hour drive back, for Eli. I didn't tell him I was only going half the distance. I also didn't tell him about the unlocked phone. Whatever came of that, we'd know the outcome in due course.

If his ear was still hurting, he wasn't mentioning it any more. He just insisted on driving – I suspected to keep his mind off it. If we hit a pothole or a sharp bend in the road I caught sight of him grimacing, tilting his head this way and that.

He pulled us over onto the side of the road in a place called Victorville, which seemed to be comprised of nothing but beige rock and rubble, scrubland. We both got out of the car, squinting behind our sunglasses and grumbling about the heat, and spread Trent's letters and papers across the bonnet.

There was no wind save for what was created by the occasional vehicles speeding past. It felt good to be in open space. Just being able to look down a road and see a view – unblocked – was comforting.

'How much of this is biblical shite?' Eli asked, frowning. 'Sorry, biblical *stuff*?'

I didn't want to return to it all right away. Instead I took a short stroll alongside Interstate 15 and then turned left into the scrubland between the leafless trees, not caring that the dust was clinging to my shoes.

I still hadn't spoken to my kids and I hadn't been able to find the will to give Rachel an excuse, or even a reply. The weeks had been lost.

About twenty yards from the road I found a jagged chalky rock and sat down. If I shut my eyes I could almost pretend the sounds of cars were the sea, the wind whistling through the trees, or something else natural that came in waves.

There were faint footsteps, scuffs, a voice saying, 'Fuck.'

I opened my eyes, looked right and Eli was hopping about on one leg, trying to tip some stones out of his shoe. His left foot hung and swung in mid-air, flailing in a faded blue sock, trying to find balance. After a while he gave up, put the shoe back on and came and stood above me, taking care not to block the sun. I noticed he hadn't brought any of the papers with him.

Neither of us said anything.

He looked about him for a suitable place to sit, sighed and sat down on the ground.

I managed a small laugh, a barely audible exhale through my nose.

His lips twitched.

We both looked in separate directions and sat there for I'm not sure how long, until Eli started to catch the sun on the bridge of his nose. Just two guys in suits, three and a half ears, sat in the wasteland between civilizations, just off the interstate.

I thought about how people did it in this day and age – left society and all its invisible structures. You couldn't. Not in the age of satellites and smartphones, when everyone wanted to know where you were, where you had been, what you had bought, what your net worth was, what you were contributing with your failures and your dubious successes.

Not so long ago it would have been possible to walk off into the wilderness and never come back, elevate your existence to the singular everyday concern and comfort of survival, with nothing to worry about except what to eat and where to sleep. Food, warmth, shelter, hunting. No job, no money, no expectations, no hierarchies, no banks, no wealth, no ideals, no politics, no concept of the globe, of a market or economy, because there would be nothing to sell, nothing to buy, nothing to decipher, or boast about. Just back in the food chain, where we belonged.

Wouldn't that be lovely? I thought.

The sun beat down.

I took my sunglasses off, rubbed my eyes and swallowed.

Eli stared at the summit of a hill, like he was about to take off his jacket, run towards it and never be seen again.

This was the best we had, without the ability to disappear, so we made do with moments like this.

Finally, I thought, one moment of fucking peace.

I drove for the next nine hours – until my vision blurred and I started to lose my depth perception – before I felt able to pull over again, this time into a motel car park on the outskirts of Albuquerque. It was forty-five dollars a night, for two rooms that weren't next to each other. No bloody Wi-Fi in sight.

The landscape here was impossibly flat, with bursts of brown shrubbery that looked strangely ordered, as if someone had planted them in rows.

After a quick change of clothes we convened, sitting cross-legged on the floor of Eli's room, to look at what

Edward Saxon had given us. The light had almost died. The curtains, specks of mould creeping upwards from the hems, were shut.

We split the small pile and I flicked through half-heartedly.

'Do you think anyone would deliver pizza out here?' I asked, leaning against the foot of the bed with my legs out in front of me. 'Otherwise I think we're eating out of the vending machine. If there is one.'

Eli got up before even starting to look at his papers. 'I'll go ask at the front desk.'

Forty minutes later, during which we had talked only about the premiership and why all bands from the nineties were reforming, a spotty guy arrived at our door in uniform holding two double pepperoni pizzas. He looked deeply unimpressed with us. We were well out of the catchment area for delivery, but Eli had offered him a seventy-five dollar tip in cash.

I considered suggesting beer, but Eli was reading now and I felt pressured into finally doing the same.

Trent's handwriting had worsened between the postcard he had written to Thomas Love and this haphazard collection of notes. Before it had been in elegant loops, like that of a teenage girl. Now it was slanted and erratic, dipping and swerving, barely able to maintain a straight line. Not every word was legible.

'Can we sort them into biblical and non-biblical?' he said.

His hair was devoid of product, his shirt was mostly undone and slanted across his torso, the skin underneath beginning to tan and his shoes greying with dust. The punctured ear was still being held in place, with a bandage now. If I asked him about the pain he never replied.

I wondered what the hell I looked like.

They do not crowd each other, They march everyone in his path;
When they burst through the defenses, They do not break ranks.

They rush on the city. They run on the wall; They climb into
the houses, They enter through the windows like a thief.

Before them the earth quakes, The heavens tremble, The sun
and the moon grow dark And the stars lose their brightness.

'Locusts,' I said, handing out the piece of paper. 'Or demons,
it could be a metaphor. It's from… I can't remember what part.'

'Weeping and gnashing of teeth?' He had a Post-it stuck to
the end of his finger.

'Yep, standard. Bible pile.'

'He wasn't even a Christian when I knew him.'

'Well, he doesn't seem like a Christian now.' I ate some
pizza and grimaced at the thought of the Cecil. 'Why would
he go and stay somewhere he thought was the gateway to hell
if he was a Christian? I think he's a nutcase who got obsessed
with the occult.'

'But Trent wasn't *into* all that! He's not *evil*. You can see a
budding nutcase a mile off and that just wasn't him, it *wasn't*.
Maybe there is something wrong here…'

'What, he's possessed or something?'

'No, I mean, that's ridiculous… That's ridiculous.'

But he didn't say anything else.

I said, 'Well, maybe Trent *was* the sort who would pick up
a machine gun and shoot up an office, take heroin, download
kiddy-porn; how would you fucking know? You didn't *know*
the guy. No one did, by the sounds of it.'

I thought I'd actually hurt Eli's feelings. He looked so
troubled by the idea.

'Or he really was in trouble,' I added, trying not to turn the
analysis into a confrontation.

He turned another postcard over.

This is Disneyland.

'*This* is fucked,' he said, attempting to slick back his hair with nothing. 'That's what this is.'
I found a postcard in my pile.

Man – Dig those crazy Los Angeles freeways.

Eli stared at the faded pink Disneyland card as if he was about to cry. 'He just had money, that *was* it. He opened up to Melissa, or at least he talked to her more. I suppose I always found that interesting too. Melissa didn't talk to just anyone.'
'So what was Melissa to you?'
'Colleague. Associate.'
'Just a colleague?'
'It doesn't matter now,' he said, unable to subdue a lie. 'I just need to know. I can't go back with you to London until I know what the fuck happened with him.'
It's about Melissa.
'Because you've come too far now?' I said, as if I was following him.
Maybe they had an affair.
Melissa and Eli, or Melissa and Trent...
He indicated the paper and cards, shaking his head. Look at it, it's... bizarre.'

Blessed are the destroyers of false hope, for they are the true Messiahs – Cursed are the god-adorers, for they shall be born sheep!

'Eli...' I said softly.

It was addressed to Edward Saxon, at Stay On Main.

There was a stamp from Staten Island.

I flipped the postcard it was written on, and involuntarily grabbed Eli's forearm.

'Eli! Staten Island. This picture is the Staten Island Ferry.'

'You think he went to Staten Island?'

'It was sent after he has been in LA, otherwise why would he have addressed it to Saxon? I mean, Staten Island is a weird choice, there's nothing there.'

Eli dropped his head forwards, as if he had run a great distance. 'Well, at least now we have somewhere to go.'

I understood perfectly now, I thought. *It's definitely about Melissa.*

CHAPTER TWENTY-EIGHT

I went to a late-night bar just off the road about three hundred yards back, where they had free Wi-Fi, and sat in a corner to do some online stalking of Melissa de Ehrmann. Everyone – apart from Eli himself it seemed – had an online presence, especially if you were an entrepreneur. They had LinkedIn and Twitter and all that shit. Noel was too scared of computers to handle anything like that but I loved it. It could only be good for people like us, with so many new ways to dig up dirt.

I wasn't sure if this place did table service, but I waved the young bartender over anyway. He approached me with apprehension, saying, 'Er, you order at the bar.'

'Yeah, whatever. Can I get a Guinness, please?'

'Er… Yeah. Yes, sir.'

He almost bowed as he moved away.

It was one in the morning. There was no one else here.

Melissa did have a LinkedIn account.

Connect.

She had been an editor of fiction for about six years before becoming a writer herself, and relocating to Paris. She'd written two novels, a book of poetry, did copy editing on the side, and had apparently moved back to London in the meantime. She also translated novels from French to English and from English to French. There was nothing about her personal life on here.

I stared at her photo. This was a more professional one, with a white background and sepia lighting. Old girlfriend? Eli didn't seem the type to maintain a girlfriend. Maybe she was a relative, though they looked nothing alike…

Facebook. That fucking goldmine.

My Guinness was brought over.

'*Public*, fuck yeah!' I raised both my fists in victory as I opened her profile page.

The bartender gave me a polite nod.

Her profile wasn't that old. It only went back to 2009. Not nearly long enough ago to contain anything about Eli. But I scrolled through her photos anyway.

However…

'What?' I mumbled, spotting something familiar.

It was a photo of Melissa and Eli, an old one. In fact, it was the photo he had given me in her dossier. Only now I realized that it wasn't a friend who had been cropped out. It was Eli. Eli and Melissa were standing in front of a river, arms around each other like some sort of… couple.

'No,' I said, out loud.

I clicked on the photo, enlarged it, and stared for a while. It didn't look real. Eli was smiling.

Fucking weird.

Melissa's hand was on Eli's shoulder. There was a ring on her finger. *That* finger.

'No fucking way!'

I looked around the bar, as if I could find someone to share my incredulity. There was no way in hell Melissa de Ehrmann could have been Eli's wife. Eli couldn't have had a wife. Especially not a wife who looked like *that*, and…

And he wanted to kill her.

It *was* about Melissa.

Were they still married? I guessed not, given the amount of time that had passed. There was a chance they still could be, but the evidence pointed towards a divorce.

I sat back, the photo still large and ostentatious across my screen.

I'd been dragged on a deranged revenge mission, but it hadn't been the deranged revenge mission I'd thought it was. Had all this talk about his business, about his associates, about betrayal, killing Thomas Love and chasing this ghost, Trent Byrne, around a continent, just been a smokescreen?

I saved the photo, kept it open in a separate window, and scrolled down her timeline as far as I could go.

All stories.

I remembered my Guinness and took a gulp.

Most of her posts were music videos, quotes from books I didn't recognize, quotes from poems I didn't recognize.

I heard a Fly buzz when I died, The stillness round my form was like the Stillness in the Air, Between the Heaves of Storm.

Some photos she was tagged in, from Paris. All the comments were in French.

I wondered what her voice was like. It almost didn't matter; French sounded hot on anybody.

I hated people who posted shit like this all the time.

There were no public photos of her with any other men. No new husband or douchebag boyfriend for Eli to become jealous over.

Relationship status was blank.

I opened Twitter in another tab and checked if she had an account but I couldn't find one. No Instagram either. I typed her name into Google Images and she came up a few times, mostly at publishing events, some generic tags in Getty Images, a few from book signings, readings, Amazon links, a personal website...

Another glance at the door. Another gulp of Guinness.

Melissa's website mostly consisted of links to her social media. She did have a Twitter account, I discovered; I'd just been misspelling her name. There was also a gallery of images and a *Contact Me* page.

I hovered over the blank box, awaiting text.

I wrote, *Have you spoken to Elias Cain recently?* but deleted it.

I wrote, *I'm a friend of Eli's* but deleted that too.

I paused, and drank some more Guinness.

The music in here was weird, some repetitive beat with a woman's voice singing over it.

I wrote, *Do you know what happened to Trent Byrne?*, filled in the return email address with my business one, and clicked Send before I could think too much about it.

I Googled Cameron Hopper, but there was no recent news on him.

Opening another tab, I typed Trent Byrne into Google, Facebook, Twitter and LinkedIn.

Jack. Shit.

For a joke, I added the word *Satan* to my Google search.

I closed Facebook, Twitter and LinkedIn straight away, and trawled through several pages of Google results. It didn't help that most of the results were about Trent Reznor. But after all the NIN articles, something caught my eye and I stopped. It was a tiny news story from a few years ago.

Satanic Substitute Teacher Suspended.

That was the headline. Below it were two or three paragraphs; Trent Byrne, substitute English teacher, had been suspended for preaching Satanism to his classes. At first I thought it was about St Louis, but this had happened in LA, at one of the poorer schools. Apparently he'd 'distributed Satanic literature and given anti-Christian lectures' to the children, and he'd also had no comment to make about it.

That was it. There wasn't even a photo. I had no way of knowing if this was even the right Trent Byrne, but it had to be.

I bookmarked the page and emailed the link to Eli. I thought about the postcard and the burning palm trees. If I'd had the postcard with me I'd have tried typing some of the stuff he'd written into Google, but I made a mental note to try it later or get Eli to do it.

An image came to mind, from my previous forays into Google while looking for the source of one of Eli's quotations: a photo of Richard Ramirez with his palm open, the lopsided pentagram held out to the court.

'There are different sects of Satanism. The Satanist admits to being evil.'

Ramirez had stayed in the Cecil too, when he had been breaking into people's houses and raping them and killing them. According to Cathal's scrapbook he used to discard his bloodied clothes in a dumpster before climbing up the fire escape.

They enter through the windows…

I thought back to the guy who had taken Eli's arm, eyes rolling around in his head like a chameleon's.

'Cecil means six. Cecil means the devil.'

The eight-pointed star.

The girl in the water tank.

I started to feel a bit odd – not scared or anything, just a bit odd – and shut the Trent Byrne tab. I didn't want all this shit in my head, all these strange coincidences and connections.

'Can you play something more upbeat, buddy?' I called out to the bartender, grimacing and making a mental note to never use that word again.

'Like what, sir?' he asked, making his nervous jerky app-roach.

'I don't know, Bon Jovi or something. Just something… happy, you know?'

The music stopped abruptly, but he must have become distracted because he didn't replace it with anything.

I didn't stay long after that.

The walk to the motel seemed longer and darker on the way back.

CHAPTER TWENTY-NINE

The following morning, I noticed I had an email from Melissa's website when I was in the car the next morning. Flinching, I killed the screen and started playing Angry Birds instead. Eli paid too much attention to his surroundings for me to risk reading it in front of him.

We stopped briefly for gas outside Oklahoma and I ducked into a wooden shack masquerading as a toilet to read it.

The email said, *Who is this?*

That was it.

A little disappointed, I leant against the side of the shack and typed, *A friend of Eli's.*

I watched the four words vanish and stared at the phone for a while, as if she might reply instantly despite the time difference. I asked myself what I wanted to achieve with this secret dialogue. Was it for the sake of undermining Eli? Or did I really suspect that he had another agenda?

'Are you going into labour or something?' Eli banged a fist on the side of the shack. 'Come on, let's go!'

As I made to unlock the door, my mobile vibrated.

I looked down.

The email said, *Don't contact me again.*

'Um, a second,' I said, pausing.

I had to say something. This would be my only chance for miles.

Call me later. Trust me, it's in your interest.

I gave her my mobile number, hoping I could rely on her curiosity. People like that had no self-control; they had to know. It was a much more common trait in females, I noticed. Men could walk by any open doors and speed past a car crash without thought, without a lost second of sleep. But women had to know things.

'Ron!'

Another bang on the side of the shack.

'Jesus, OK!' I slammed the door open, hoping it wasn't a conspicuous overreaction. 'Keen, much?'

Eli stared at me as we swapped places.

I went to stand by the car, glanced at my phone, but there was nothing.

Walking to the doorway of the store, I peered in. I wondered how many armed robberies they had out here. It wasn't as if there were any police stations in the vicinity to respond to a panic button.

The man sat behind the counter met my eyes.

I nodded and smiled.

He must have a shotgun by his knees, I thought.

I heard Eli enter the store behind me.

'You're not from round here?' the man behind the counter said, with the tiniest of inflections.

'No, passing through,' I replied.

'Where to?'

'Home,' Eli said.

'We don't get many expensive-looking suits around here,' the man said, taking a twenty dollar bill.

I saw his eyes drop to our waistbands, but my gun was in the car.

Eli selected a postcard from a cylindrical rack by the till, nodded at it and then held it up to me.

USA ROAD TRIP.

There was a gaudy drawing of the White House beneath the bubble writing, scrawled across blue sky.

'For posterity,' Eli said.

As he slapped it on the counter I saw the man's eyes flicker downwards, his crossed arms twitching for a fraction of a second.

I went to lean against the car in the sunshine. My mobile started vibrating but it was an Unknown Number. Eli was coming, so I cut the call off and put my phone in my pocket.

Eli stuck the postcard to the dashboard.

I just had to hope that, if it had been Melissa, she'd call again.

'I don't think this kind of extended holiday is appropriate, Ronnie. Given the circumstances.'

Now it was Edie on the phone.

'It's hardly a holiday. I was meeting Eamonn out of prison.'

'And that was how long ago now?'

'Do you want me to fill in a timesheet for you, boss?'

It was terrible for Eli to be witnessing this. I hoped the signal would cut out.

She said, 'If you want to remain one of my managers, you're going to have to start acting like one.'

'It can't be helped. I'm sure Noel will be fine until I get back.' *Lie.* 'This is personal stuff, and I'm also helping Mark chase a lead on Seven, if that means anything to you.'

'I'm not interested in what you *say* you're doing.'

'I'll bring back Seven's head on a platter, how will that go down?'

'It's your head you should be concerned about.'

And the bitch *actually* hung up on me.

It wasn't the signal.

She hung up like I was nobody.

I flushed, heart pounding with rage, and Eli pretended not to notice.

About eighty miles down the road he pulled us over again, adamant that he wanted to buy alcohol. We were still nowhere near a motel and night was falling. Both of us were too wiped, too jittery, to drive any more.

When are you getting here?

Mark Chester, in Chicago.

I don't know. Soon.

Bro, when you going to Chicago?

Eamonn, in Philadelphia.

I don't know. Soon.

Bitch hung up on me...

There wasn't much in this town. We weren't quite in the suburbs but I could see a liquor store to our right and a kids' park to our left across the road. It was humid.

'I haven't been on swings for years,' I said.

'I never used to play in parks.'

We crossed the road.

I couldn't imagine him as a kid. I couldn't imagine him ever wanting to *play* with anything, in innocent fashion. Eli would play with things like a cat, batting them back and forth until they died.

'What did you do?'

'I used to have lots of models, animals and dinosaurs and stuff.' Eli took out a pack of cigarettes and lit one.

'Yeah, me too, and cars.'

'My mum said that I never used to move them or speak or make-believe voices or anything like that. I used to just sit there and watch them.' He made an expansive gesture with his hands, cigarette clamped between his teeth. 'I used to do everything in my head. I'd arrange them and then look at them. To the outside it looked as though I was doing nothing, but in my mind it made perfect sense. I could see them moving and hear them speaking. Then, when the time came, I'd move them all into a different position and do it again.'

'That's well creepy.'

He shrugged. 'Yeah, it probably was. Just this kid sat on his own staring at toys, not making a sound. Must have seemed like the kid from *The Omen*.'

'You basically are now.'

He shot me a grin as we stopped outside the liquor store, waiting for him to finish his cigarette.

'I wasn't as creepy as one of my friend's brothers,' he said, snorting. 'He was a really intense kid and everyone was scared of him. This was when we lived in Boston, by the way, so he also played with his dad's gun way too much.'

'Did he ever do anything?'

'He used to bring his dad's gun with him everywhere. When he was fifteen he cornered us in my back garden and made me and my friend play Action Man with him.'

'Doesn't sound so bad.'

'Yeah?' He raised his eyebrows. 'He made us play at gun-point. We were eight.'

I put my hands on my hips and nodded. 'OK. Yeah, OK.'

'Put me off Action Man for life.'

He dropped his cigarette to the ground and stamped on it,

and as we were about to go inside we heard someone call to us from the shadows.

'Hey! Hey, mister! Excuse me…'

I looked over Eli's shoulder into the dark. There were four kids in their late teens loitering beside a vending machine; three boys and one girl. They were all dressed in black, two of the guys had long dreads and piercings, and the girl had light blue hair.

'If we give you some money, can you buy us some beers?'

Eli waved a hand. 'Get lost.'

'Aw, come on, it doesn't cost you anything,' the girl said, pouting.

'Yeah, *no*.' I laughed, glancing at Eli.

He had one hand on the door, but he was smiling a little.

'Maybe it doesn't cost us anything.' He indicated his head at the storefront. 'Say we buy you some beer. You should come and share it with us in the park.'

I saw the group exchange glances, sizing us up. What was our threat? Probably nothing. We looked rich after all. We had no reason to want anything from them really.

'You want us to come to the park with you?' one of the guys checked, hoisting his rucksack further up onto his shoulders.

'Yeah.'

I wasn't sure what Eli was doing, but I decided to let it play out.

Another pause. A silent conferral.

'Well, um… yeah OK, I guess.' Another of the guys shrugged. 'Let's go.'

I shot Eli a questioning look – *What's going on here? What is this game?* – but he ignored me. He continued ignoring me walking around the store.

The man behind the counter didn't seem to suspect

anything. I suppose he couldn't imagine that someone would spend upwards of forty dollars on a bottle of brandy for a ramshackle band of youths.

When we went back outside the group had moved further afield, towards the other side of the road.

Eli took the brandy out of his paper bag and handed it over.

They had probably never held a bottle of anything so expensive.

'Come on then,' Eli said, walking up to the edge of the park and neatly stepping over the low wire fence.

'What are your names?' the girl asked.

'Eli.'

I glared at him as I stepped over the fence after them.

'Mark,' I said, hesitating. 'What are yours?'

'Jade.'

The boys' names I didn't really absorb, but I was sure one of them was called Martin, maybe Simon. It didn't matter. The girl was sort of attractive. But then it was dark and her voice was husky, which probably accounted for about forty per cent of what I found attractive about her.

Eli had jumped onto one of the swings and was propelling himself back and forth.

'What are you guys doing in town?' one of the boys asked, stepping up onto the one beside him.

The other two guys had found the tyre swing.

'Yeah, you on holiday?'

'You picked a shit place for it.'

'What are you visiting here? Family?'

Eli leapt into the air and launched the swing over the bar back onto itself. He landed with a dull thwack, like a gymnast, and turned to look at us. 'No, we're on business.'

'What sort of business?'

One of the boys, pushing his friend with one hand, took a gulp of brandy with the other and coughed. 'Must be important if you can spend this much on brandy for a bunch of strangers? You just have money to throw away?'

The boy standing on the swing had one of those annoying miniature beards sitting on the bottom of his chin.

'You should never keep hold of money,' Eli replied. 'It's not that important.'

'You'd only say that as a privileged capitalist,' Jade said, taking up residence on the swing that Eli had vacated, swinging it back over the bar with a clang.

'Yeah, check your privilege, Eli,' I said, amused.

I watched them climbing onto the various structures and didn't feel moved to join in. Eli handed me the brandy on his way past, on the way to the red rope climbing frame in the shape of a pyramid.

'You're capitalists, just as much as us,' he said, hoisting himself up onto the ropes and swinging under and over.

A derisive snort came from the swings to my right.

'What makes you say that? We don't exploit people, we don't drive cars, we're vegan, our carbon footprint is less than zero—'

'But you still came here on a transaction. You did what I said on the promise of something, that's a transaction.'

'Yeah, but we could leave if we wanted.'

'Could you?'

Eli stood at the top of the pyramid, surveying the area.

It was impossibly warm. I was starting to miss a change in temperature.

'Yeah, we could,' Jade said.

I walked up to a roundabout and gave it a shove. It rotated, empty.

Eli held out his arms for a moment, Jesus watching over Rio de Janeiro, then he started climbing down.

He said, 'You are capitalists. You are privileged. Look at you, you're white. You're straight, I assume. Three of you are men. You think you've dropped out of society because you don't have a Facebook account and don't drive or have jobs? You think anyone who lives on Skid Row would congratulate you? Do you think any of them give a shit what your carbon footprint is when your parents probably make five- or six-figure salaries? In fact, do you think they can afford to give a shit what *their* carbon footprint is? Or what they eat when they don't know when they're going to eat next?'

The boys had stopped swinging.

Jade didn't, but her feet were scuffing the ground.

They didn't contradict him.

Eli's feet touched the floor.

'But we could leave,' one of the boys said, eventually, standing up like he had authority.

'And I ask again, could you?' Eli spread his hands and as he did so his jacket pulled back from his hips to flash the gun tucked into his waistband.

At first I didn't think any of them had seen it, but Jade gasped.

The boys looked to her first, then to where she was pointing.

'Fuck, man, chill out, what the fuck!'

'What?' Eli stood dead still.

'You didn't say you had a *gun* on you!'

'Why have you got a gun?'

'Look, calm down—' Jade started.

'I thought you guys were leaving?' Eli looked at me, smiling.

The boy with the stupid beard took a step forward and put the bottle of brandy on the floor. 'Hey, man... just don't hurt us, OK?'

'What makes you think I would hurt you?'

Eli didn't improve the tableau by taking out the gun and holding it out, making all four of them retreat several steps.

'Look, we didn't mean to piss you off!'

Eli frowned.

I didn't move, transfixed by the sight. They probably assumed I had a gun too.

'Leave, if you want.' Eli had his finger around the trigger. 'Or stay and play.'

'What?'

'Try to leave... or play?'

The kids looked at each other, hands shaking, eyes wide.

'What?' Jade asked again.

'If you're going to stay, then *swing*!' Eli snapped.

'Eli, come on,' I said, laughing but not quite feeling it.

'What?'

He looked at me and I swore there was something wrong with his face.

'Nothing,' I said, meaning it. 'Carry on.'

Jade shrank back against the chains, a few tears leaked from her eyes, her feet scuffed the ground for a moment as she pushed herself forwards and backwards on the swing. There was a creak, a scrape of iron. The boys were frozen.

Eli turned to them. 'Well? I thought you wanted to play on the *roundabout*?'

They cowered.

'Then play!' Eli said. '*Play*.'

I'll never forget that sight, I thought; the sight of four young 'uns all dressed in black and trembling, crying with fear as they swung back and forth on the swings, pushed each other around the roundabout, climbed the climbing frames with weak limbs.

I started laughing. I couldn't help it.

Eli stood in the middle of the park with his gun outstretched, like a conductor.

Every so often I would catch his eye and he would grin, his face splitting open with utter glee at the nightmare playground he'd created.

We must have been there for almost an hour.

I was crying with laughter – *yes, definitely laughter* – sitting on the ground with tears streaming down my cheeks.

Jade was sobbing just over from me, swinging back and forth the whole time. There was a tiny pool of urine on the ground below the swing.

I couldn't stop laughing, no matter how much I tried.

CHAPTER THIRTY

We didn't find a place to stop after that. Eli just drove, with manic sleepless eyes. We could have been going in circles for all I knew. On and off I kept laughing, then after a while it was just tears of exhaustion, dry and acidic.

He had drunk too much brandy to be allowed on the roads, but it was as though he'd burned the alcohol up with his insides. I noticed his hands twitching up and down the wheel. The world must have looked like a video game.

'If I fall asleep, you won't crash, will you?' I mumbled.

He shook his head.

I sank down in my seat and looked at my emails but there was nothing.

It felt unlikely that I'd sleep, so I pulled Trent's Bible, notes and postcards through from the back seat.

I glanced at Eli, giving in to a restless need to provoke something.

'Why didn't you mention that Melissa was your ex-wife?'

Nothing.

His expression didn't even change.

I shuffled the papers. 'Eli.'

'How did you find out?'

'It was on her Facebook page.' I wished he would look at

me. 'I checked it out because... Well, something about this wasn't adding up. This whole thing isn't about her, is it?'

He ignored the question.

'Fuck's sake, you can't just pull your usual shit of pretending not to hear me.'

Nothing.

'Eli.' I sat up. 'Eli!'

'If it was about her, why would you care? She was on the list anyway.'

'Oh, shut the fuck up about the list. If this has all been about settling a score with your ex I'll run this car off the fucking road!'

'Why would it bother you?'

'I left my *family* for this!'

'You would have left them anyway.'

'What's that supposed to mean?'

Yellow light flashed across his face. 'You know what I mean.'

'No, *explain*.'

He smirked. 'You get married because your parents and a book written by the Latin-speaking elite tell you that's what you should do; you reproduce; you cater to this forced unit and repress everything that makes you human—'

'I doubt you have much insight into what makes people human.' I rolled my eyes.

The car wobbled for a moment and I checked he was still looking at the road. He was still looking at it, only he was grinning now.

'I think my idea of what makes people human is more advanced than what your book says.'

'Why are you calling it *my* book?'

'*Your* book preaches pure violence, you know. Joy in

atrocity! That's the beauty of the Bible, really. That's its genius. It creates the very concept of the sin that it claims to have the solution to.'

The car wobbled again and I involuntarily held onto the door handle.

'It describes humans revelling in excess and sin and degradation in a way that can *only* make it sound appealing. It shows you a way of life we relate to more than any moralistic self-denial.'

'I don't agree.' Knuckles tightening. 'You don't believe in anything, that's your problem.'

'I'm just not delusional. Humans are animals. We're just grey squirrels who have been lucky enough to invent guns so we aren't reduced to ripping each other's throats out with our teeth.'

'We're more than that, Eli. Squirrels are just vermin, they don't know right from wrong.'

'And yet we choose the latter anyway, almost every time! What does that say about us?'

'Not all of us do, if we can help it.'

He laughed. 'Ron, you enjoy violence more than anyone else I know.'

'I don't enjoy it.'

'Bullshit.' Now he looked at me, as we shot underneath a bridge and into a tunnel. 'You know that when you're causing pain, killing someone, you are more yourself than you've ever been.'

'That's not true.'

'Then why haven't you spoken to your children since you've been out here? Why have I never heard you speaking to your *precious* Rachel or even your parents telling them you miss them and that you can't wait to be back? Because it's a lie. They're there for theatre, to show the outside world and pretend that's who you are. You haven't spoken to them because *this* is what you enjoy. *This* is who you are.'

'You're talking rubbish.'

'Am I?'

'You haven't slept in two days!'

We were drifting closer to the wall and Eli's gaze was turned on me.

'Eli.'

He stared at me.

Drifting. A jolt.

'Eli, for fuck's sake!' I made a grab for the wheel and the vehicle juddered left and right.

He pushed me in the chest, to my side of the car, and swung us back across the divide. G-force punched me in the chest and I stared into oncoming headlights.

Eli wrenched the wheel to the right and I felt the force of the van we had been driving into whip past us. I saw an image of my own shattered bones, human flesh welded into dashboard.

A horn wailed and faded.

'*Are you fucking crazy?*' I shouted.

The Bible and postcards had fallen into the footwell. My right leg was twitching as the bright-eyed face of Audrey Hepburn stared up at me from the front of a postcard.

For a moment all I could hear was my heart, then the steady hum of the engine again.

We left the tunnel into natural darkness, out of the psychedelic nightmare of lights.

Eli rubbed his eyes, as if he had shocked even himself, and said, 'Maybe we should pull over.'

'Maybe we should.'

'Could you sleep here?'

'I don't know, not the best fucking time to ask.'

He smiled. 'You know there's no reward, Ronnie. There's nothing in the afterlife waiting for us, to absolve us or punish us. There's just... nothing. You must know that.'

'Stop it, I'm too...' I couldn't even finish the sentence. 'I can't listen to this shit right now.'

'How shit would it be to realize that you'd lived a life devoid of fun and experience to appease someone who *doesn't* exist, to prepare for a reward that *doesn't* exist?'

I don't whether we'd just been driving for too long, or whether I was too tired to expect any rational reaction, but the idea almost made me want to cry. Those dry tears of tiredness were still coming, but only from one eye now.

Eli started looking for a rest-stop, and I realized he had managed to dodge my questions about his ex-wife.

I said, 'I think you're lying to me.'

No confirmation from him either way. He started undoing the bandage around his ear with one hand.

I checked my pocket and I didn't have many Ormus capsules left.

We had pulled into a lay-by with a pay phone and some portaloos, the sort used by long-distance lorry drivers, couriers and armed sex offenders.

It didn't surprise me that Eli could sleep sitting up. It was a nice gesture, by his standards, to let me lie down on the back seats. If I twisted my face away from the window I could avoid the yellow glare, but sleep was impossible.

Eli's ear was healing much better than I thought it would. I entertained the idea that it might have been the Ormus, even if it was unlikely.

I sat up and my limbs had atrophied in the stiff attempts at sleep. Eli didn't move. He was like a shark; I doubted he ever entered any kind of oblivion, just floated forwards, barely changing position until prey entered his line of vision.

Rubbing my eyes, I opened the back door and swivelled until I could manoeuvre myself out and shut it again quietly. Outside, it was cool. I took my jacket off and let goosebumps rise along my arms. If a nuclear bomb were to drop on one of the big cities, it might not even affect us here. We were that far out. It was a comforting thought.

When I'd been younger I thought World War Three was starting every time I heard helicopters over my house. I thought within a matter of minutes my windows would explode inwards, the street and the bodies of my neighbours coming through into my room. War had seemed a lot more real back then, weirdly, when I had less concept of it as something that happened to other people in other countries. Getting older had made me complacent, allowed me to indulge in fantasies about the collapse of society and civilization without worrying about having to experience it first-hand.

I took out some pot that Eli had confiscated from the kids, before he had finally let them flee the park in tears, and rolled a joint.

My mobile started to ring.

My first guess was that it might be Melissa, but it wasn't. It was my UK landline, and I didn't want to answer it.

'Come on,' I whispered, looking down at it in my hand.

Home.

'Come on.'

Home, calling.

My stomach felt tight, invaded and toxic with guilt. The sensation crept up my neck and across my shoulders into my forehead.

What was I doing, staring at the call like it was unwelcome? *Home*, calling.

It rang off.

Relief, for a moment.

A pair of headlights appeared in the distance and hummed their way towards me. The car passed with a penetrative growl, speeding up at the sight of me, and then there was calm again. I imagined the driver wondering what I was doing standing by the side of the road staring at my phone.

A lot of violent opportunists might stand at the sides of the road hiding firearms, luring people into stopping before stealing their cars or worse.

Missed call: Home.

After a sickeningly long time, I called *Home* back. It rang four times – I wondered if whoever had called might have gone back to bed – but then the line clicked open.

'Dad?'

The voice was distant, pixellated, but so unmistakably Ryan's, in this dark and nameless place. I glanced back at the car and Eli was still propped up in the driver's seat, eyes closed, shoulders a little slumped.

'Hey, champ, how's it going?'

My voice sounded alien, talking with any trace of love or familiarity.

'Oh, just school stuff. Mum said you were on a road trip?'

'She did, yeah? I am, with an old friend.'

'That's so cool. What are you doing?'

'Mostly pretending to be cowboys.'

'Literally? That's so gay.'

'Yeah, literally.' I shut my eyes and started pacing. 'We were staying at this ranch with a friend of ours, and we've been riding horses, shooting guns, rounding up livestock and wearing Stetsons. Pretending to be Clint Eastwood, that kinda thing.'

'How come me and Chantal couldn't come? That sucks balls!'

'Hey, hey, language. You can come next time. Gimme a break, when you have kids you'll know that sometimes you need a holiday with your mates. Plus, your uncle was getting out of prison and I needed to be here for him. That part wasn't fun. It wouldn't have been fun for you guys.'

'Have you shot anything?'

Choked up, for a moment. 'We shot a few birds, and a squirrel.'

'Are there Indians where you are any more? Apparently there are still tribes around, but are they, like, proper?'

He sounded so London I almost couldn't stand it. I wondered if I sounded ridiculous to him, whether I'd gotten my accent back. I'd lived in England for so long that listening to American accents sounded like a piss-take of human speech.

'Native Americans, Ryan. They're not Indians. But no, they're not here.'

'Why?'

'Just not that kinda area, I think.'

'Didn't the cowboys kill them off? Dad, we did it at school. The settlers hid diseases in the gifts they exchanged, we looked at a poem about it.'

I paused, crushed by unfathomable upset, and said, 'Really?'

'Yeah, they pretended to give them Western things, like blankets and stuff, but really they were giving them smallpox. We learnt about it in history. It was one of the first examples of chemical warfare.'

'Jesus, they teach you about chemical warfare in secondary school now?'

'Dad, you know I spend, like, *all* year doing the Holocaust.'

'Yeah, but in that much detail? When I was your age we used to get exam questions like "*Hitler: Why?*" and just deal with it.'

'Yeah but you're, like, a hundred years old.'

'Education's gone downhill from then on, Ryan.'

'Since the Stone Age.'

I laughed. 'Yeah, and we had the cane. We had proper discipline, boy. Plus, I was way cooler than you at school, and smarter.'

'There's no way you were cooler.'

'You're, like, *two* foot tall.'

'I've got Holocaust and Native American genocide banter.'

'Bitches *love* Holocaust banter.'

'Lolocaust.'

I had to stop, almost keeled over with mirth.

An angry wail split the air either side of my head and I leapt, whirled around and saw Eli jolting himself out of sleep. My heart pounded, we both stared at each other in confusion, and then I realized he must have fallen forwards against the horn.

I wanted to walk over to the car, drag him out onto the ground and kick him in the face. But the moment was already lost.

Ryan said, 'What was that?' and the moment was gone.

I couldn't answer him.

Eli mouthed '*Sorry*' at me through the windshield and put the window down.

'Where are you, Dad?' Ryan asked.

'We're at a pit-stop,' I said, no trace of familiarity left. 'On the road. Gonna have to go.'

'Don't you wanna speak to Mum or Chantal?'

'I'll call back.'

At the time, I didn't know that was a lie. I watched Eli through the windscreen, wiping his face in the sun visor mirror, unrepentant.

'OK, love you.'

'I love you too.'

I looked at my phone and then ended the call. Alone again, with Eli, by the side of the freeway. Home wasn't here any more.

CHAPTER THIRTY-ONE

Daisy

I hadn't planned what I was going to do when I saw her.

It had been fuck-knows-how-many-days of nothing, and then suddenly she was there. She was sat on one of the benches drinking a bottle of something and I didn't know what to fucking do so I just dropped. One moment I was walking, holding a deli sandwich, and the next I knew I was falling sideways like a tree onto the rain-soaked ground behind some bushes.

A woman who'd been walking behind me had stopped dead. I looked at her with raised eyebrows like *Move, bitch!* and she hurried past.

Seven hadn't seen us. Or if she had she was hiding it well.

My elbows were bruised, maybe bleeding. My sandwich was on the ground.

It was her. She was a little way away, but it was her.

Was it?

The girl was definitely sitting like Seven, but then how many different methods of sitting were there? Fuck's sake. Her clothes were similar, but black jeans and an Aztec-print coat were hardly solid identifying features. Her hair was longer than I remembered, but then it would be.

Shuffling along, rodent-like, I tried to close some of the distance between us.

It occurred to me that I could call Noel or Nic and let one of them deal with this. But this wasn't about them. It would absolve me, but I didn't want to be absolved. I wanted... To what? Kill her? Talk to her? Punch her in the face and move on?

There was nowhere I could go; only left or right, not forwards. So I stayed where I was, obscured by foliage, blinded by the million tiny reflections of the sun in fallen rainwater.

Every so often someone walked past but didn't make any fuss. In London you got used to seeing weirdos. You just avoided eye contact and walked on.

Seven looked up a few times, and I realized she had probably picked that bench precisely *because* it gave her a view of the rest of the garden. No sneaking up on her from here.

So I waited, until my knees seized up and my shoulders hurt, until the cold permeated the rest of my body and I was shivering, struggling to keep my balance. After fifteen minutes or so I sat cross-legged on the ground.

Seven took out her phone and started texting someone. She shook the empty bottle of something, stood up and left.

I wasn't ready, had fallen into a kind of trance. Both my knees clicked and my shoulder blades cracked as I limped after her.

'Fuck, ow, fuck... *Fuck.*'

Everything hurt. The gunshot had aged my body. I forgot sometimes I must still be recovering. The cells that had bound themselves back together must carry some trace of that impact for ever, like a mute traumatized child. They could go through the motions of living but they were still rigid on the inside.

Skirting the bushes, I sprinted across the clearing.

She'd disappeared.

I took a left, then a right, and she was there again, heading across the Heath. Not directly back towards the tube, where it was crowded, but taking the exit across an open expanse of grass. She was acting like someone who expected to be followed.

The nearest tube from that exit was Golders Green.

I stayed well back, almost out of sight.

As she reached the edge of the Heath and vanished, I started running again.

Only the dogs noticed. A couple of terriers ran with me until the grass ended.

But...

I'd left my handbag behind the bushes.

It didn't matter. Only Seven mattered.

But it did matter. My fucking Oyster was in there. My wallet and phone.

I stopped – the shittest fucking James Bond ever – then pressed on. I could catch up with her before she reached the tube. Wasn't sure what the fuck I'd do with her then. But catching up with her was a start.

Breaking into a run, muttering, '*Fucking leave your fucking bag, stupid fucking bitch, fuck.*' I reached the road, left the Heath, ran for the nearest station... Everyone was in my way, fucking *everyone*. It was like the very city wanted to hide her.

But then she reappeared, for a moment, and without thinking I shouted, 'Hey!'

I know she heard me because she didn't turn around and she walked faster.

'Hey!'

People started getting out of my way.

'Hey! Stop!'

She didn't.

I had this idea that I might just stop her and scream in her face, slap her or something. Now that she was so close I didn't feel so ambiguous. She'd fucked up everything. She'd lied about everything. I wanted to hurt her.

'Hey! Fucking *look* at me...'

I took her by the shoulder, swung her towards me and shook her by the shirt she was wearing. But she was the wrong height – I didn't notice until she was in front of me – and when I looked into her face, it wasn't Seven.

It wasn't Seven.

I should have felt embarrassment, holding this poor girl by the lapels like I was about to knock her teeth out...

She was saying, 'What? What – get off me!'

... but there was just disappointment.

I didn't let her go so much as push her backwards, spitting, '*Urgh. For fuck sake*,' as if this was her fault.

She hurried away.

Tears pricked at the corners of my eyes but I blinked them back, not wanting to make more of a spectacle of myself. I put my hands in my pockets and forced my feet to walk at a stroll-like pace back towards the Heath, as if this had all been totally fucking normal.

I couldn't believe it hadn't been her.

From where I'd been watching in the park, it had been her. It couldn't have *not* been her.

When I thought I was far enough away from the scene of the incident, I broke into a run again, back across the grass towards where I'd left my bag.

It was still there.

Un-fucking-precedented.

I knelt down behind the hedge to rifle through it, finding

my belongings untouched. London hadn't wanted to fuck me over today after all.

When I picked up my phone I had two missed calls from Noel and a text that read, *Seven's in London, call me, N.*

CHAPTER THIRTY-TWO

Ronnie

'Hello? Hello? ... I don't know who this is, or if this is your idea of a joke. But stop contacting me. Eli, if this is you... I expected better of you. Stop it. Bye.'

I looked down and the dust rolled across the road thirty feet below.

Eli had kicked up a fuss about checking in anywhere and insisted on sleeping in the car again. I could see him down in the lot, black mass in the driver's seat, sitting up and facing straight out. I felt as though we were drifting more and more to the opposite ends of a spectrum; paranoia and confrontation, disassociation and run-of-the-mill sadism. If we drifted any more we'd probably come full circle and meet in the middle again, both equally sick in the soul.

Maybe we were both turning into Trent?

The thought upset me, so I listened to my voicemail again.

I'd been unable to sleep in my motel room so I'd come out and climbed the scaffolding propping up one side of the building. The air was fresh up here. Occupied buildings looked like a switchboard, dots of light in the distance flickering on and off.

Melissa's voice was higher than I'd expected it to be.

Eli would hate it if he knew about the message, that I had access to something he didn't.

I looked down at the lot again and called Melissa's number back. I didn't expect her to answer, and she didn't, so I called her again just for the hell of it. Three times and it would freak her out, but twice was acceptable.

The line clicked open and then there was silence.

No greeting, from either of us.

It was I who broke the stand-off, when my fear that she might hang up overpowered my urge to win the virtual staring contest.

'I'm a friend of Eli's,' I said.

She didn't reply.

'This is really important. He doesn't know I'm calling.'

'If you're a friend of Eli's, wouldn't I know you?'

'You were a bit before my time. Also, he was more a friend of my dad's.'

'And he is?'

'Surname's O'Connell.'

'Was his wife called... Marie?'

'Yeah, that's my mum.'

'I went for dinner at their house with Eli, a few times. Your mum is lovely.' She paused. She spoke very fluently for someone who must have been uneasy. 'I remember them saying their son was in prison.'

'That's my younger brother. I've always lived in London.'

'What's your name?'

'Ronnie.'

'Ronnie O'Connell.' Another pause. 'Maybe Eli has mentioned you.'

Not in the past tense, I noticed. She didn't speak of him as if he was in the past.

My heart was beating with uncomfortable vigour. 'Has Eli spoken to you recently?'

'No. We didn't remain *friends*.'

'How much do you know about Eli? His work and—'

'What's this about?'

'Would he hold a grudge against you for any reason?'

'He holds grudges for longer than anyone I've ever met.'

'He asked me to help him look for a guy called Trent Byrne.'

'The last I heard of Trent he... wasn't himself.'

I was amazed I had a signal up here. The line was so clear.

'From what we can gather, he did go insane at some point,' I said, figuring that I had nothing to lose by being open with her.

'Why are you looking for him?'

I hesitated. 'Eli wants to settle an old business dispute.'

'He wants to kill him,' she said, as though she was rolling her eyes.

'Um...'

Silence.

'It's OK,' she said. 'I was married to the man.'

'Yeah but—'

'People don't change. Empathy isn't something you grow into.'

'Then why were you married to him if he was such a sociopath?'

'Well, he had other good qualities.'

She laughed, fleetingly.

This was weird, I thought. Yes, this was definitely weird.

'This can't be just about Trent,' she continued, in the absence of any groundbreaking contribution from me, 'if you're contacting me. Am I right?'

'Yeah. Thomas Love is dead. Cameron Hopper likely is too.'

'Ah.'

No trace of surprise. Or concern.

'Did my name appear on some sort of list then?' she asked.

'How... How did you know?'

'Eli loves lists. He loves them more than ticking off any of the things on them. It's only the creation of the list that matters to him. Whether it's carried out or not is usually always irrelevant.' She sighed. 'He never was good at finishing things. But there were lists all over the house.'

'Why would you be on the list?' I asked.

'Because it would make no sense to leave me off it, I suppose.'

'You don't sound worried.'

'I'm not. I don't think you have to worry about me. Though if this was a gesture of concern, thanks. Ronnie, was it?'

'Yeah, Ronnie O'Connell.'

'Your mum was really nice. I'll probably be seeing you.'

'Melissa,' I said, disliking the vague sexual thrill that pulsed through me at the enunciation of her name, 'do you have any idea what happened to Trent?'

'It was something to do with his niece, I think.'

'I didn't know he had family.'

'Well, he used to. I only know because he talked to me about personal stuff a bit more than everyone else. Maybe because I actually listened... But when his niece died he changed. She was only twelve.'

'How...?'

'Look, I've got to go into this meeting quickly. Can I call you back in half an hour?'

I looked around. 'Um, yeah. Yeah, I haven't got anything else to do.'

'OK.'

She hung up, and I rested my chin and arms on the metal

bar in front of my face. Physiologically, I felt as though I'd just been in a fight, or fucked someone really hard, or jumped from a moving train onto a grass verge.

Down from me, Eli slept.

His ex-wife was calling me back in half an hour, and I was sitting thirty feet up some scaffolding above the world, arse-end of America, thinking that maybe I'd been lied to across the country and back.

I stood up, enjoying the pleasant clacking of my feet on panelling.

Half an hour. I made a note of the time on my phone and put it on the floor to climb to a higher tier. The more I was a slave to telecommunications, the more I wanted to throw it clean off the scaffolding. I couldn't promise to myself that it wouldn't happen if I took it even higher.

My shoes didn't gain much purchase on the slick rungs, meaning that I had to haul myself up with my arms for most of the climb. When I reached the roof, though, it was worth it. The air was even heavier with silence and darkness.

I sat and let my legs hang over the edge. I couldn't even see the car any more.

> They rush on the city. They run on the wall; They climb into the houses, They enter through the windows like a thief.

I had a dream once that a demon was climbing down the walls of my house with black elongated limbs that stretched and rounded corners, clung to windowsills and dragged a humanoid body down the length of two floors. In my mind, demons looked exactly like humans. They didn't have horns and pitchforks or tails. They weren't red or scaled. They were blackened featureless humans with long fingers.

My phone started vibrating, rattling below.

I climbed down the ladder.

It wasn't Melissa though. It was my home phone from Philadelphia.

I stared at it until it disconnected and a breeze cooled me.

Eamonn couldn't come back to London, I decided. I couldn't inflict that upon Rachel or my kids, and Noel and Daisy would hate him. But it was just as obvious that Eamonn couldn't stay here. He had left his place in the queue of society and now he couldn't return to where he'd been before; everyone had moved on and he had to go to the back of the line alone.

I tried composing a text to Rachel asking if he could use the spare room, but I knew it wouldn't be sent. Rachel didn't appreciate warnings. We got married the day after I proposed and we decided to have kids at the moment she discovered she was pregnant. Before that there had been no discussion. It was one of the things I loved most about her; her complete and utter aversion to reductive future planning. She'd deal with it better if Eamonn just appeared on our doorstep.

I lay with my back flat against the wood. With no lights surrounding me, the sky lit up, you could kid yourself you were seeing right into another galaxy.

Melissa sounded more relaxed when she called back. She startled me with vibrations against my chest, and I knocked the back of my head against wood as I jerked awake to answer the phone.

'Where are you?' she asked. 'You sound as though you're outside.'

'I am, I'm... somewhere in the central states, no idea. Eli's driving.'

A dark laugh. 'He's a terrible driver.'

'I'd say *enthusiastic*.'

'Trent's niece died of cancer,' she said, moving from one subject to another with disorientating fluidity. 'There was some family trouble over the church, their family church, funding this experimental treatment, but they refused. Then Trent tried to sue them for... something. There's an article about it somewhere, about the man and his niece trying to sue God. But it didn't come to anything, and then she died and Trent just left.'

'He tried to sue God?'

'Well, the Church as God's representative, but it was a news story.' She sighed. 'It sounds funny, but he was heartbroken. His niece was like his own daughter.'

'You know he became a Satanist?'

'... No. But then I'm not surprised, if that's what's happened. Where has he been? The last time I got a postcard from him I think it was marked Los Angeles.'

'He was staying in a hotel for months. The Cecil, by Skid Row.'

'That makes me so sad, to think he never recovered.'

'We think he might be in Staten Island now. That's where we're headed anyway, and then we're coming back to London.' I frowned. 'Are you sure you're not worried?'

'I'm not worried.'

'But why?'

'I know Eli better.'

I wondered where she was. There was no background noise forming an outline around her voice.

'Trent's not a bad person,' she said. 'He'd never hurt anybody.'

'A few people seem to think he might have done. Eli thinks so.'

'What do you think? Do you have any opinion on this at all?'

'I didn't really have a choice. Eli's done a lot for my family.'

'But do you think Trent is a bad person?'

I shrugged. 'No. Losing your mind doesn't necessarily make you bad.'

'Where's Eli right now?'

'In the car, asleep.'

And she hung up.

Down below in the parking lot, Eli must have woken up because he turned the headlights on. As he did so I looked up, and the stars had disappeared.

CHAPTER THIRTY-THREE

'There's a city around here with a population of just over eight thousand,' Eli said.

'Isn't that more of a town?'

'A city technically. I don't know.'

'A town wearing a city's suit,' I said, smiling.

'They have a tank in their police force.'

'Why?'

'I don't know, probably just to play with.'

I looked in the vague direction of my gun and shrugged. 'I'm not sure we're the best poster boys for gun control given—'

'Yeah, but we actually need them. It makes more sense for us to carry guns than a shack full of cops to have a tank.' He took his eyes off the road to smirk. 'I'd also like to think we're very responsible carriers.'

'It's not a toy,' I said.

'Blatantly is.'

The landscapes were all beginning to look the same, or maybe we were retracing our steps so accurately that we really were seeing the same things twice.

A speck appeared at the side of the road, looking as if it were waving at us.

For one mad, glorious second, I thought it was Goat Bag.

I had no idea what he could have been doing on this stretch of road, waiting for us like he'd crawled through a wormhole.

But the black insect-like body on our windscreen grew into nothing, not even a person. It was a tree, or a misshapen naked weed, wrapped around a vandalized signpost. I wondered who had been out here to vandalize it.

'I thought we might see that mad Australian again,' Eli remarked, as if I'd said something out loud.

'Yeah, me too. How close are we to St Louis now?' I asked.

'Dunno, ten miles or so.'

'Drop me off there.'

'What?'

'Drop me at the airport.'

'The fuck?'

'I *need* to go to Chicago. You knew this. It's what I'm here for.'

'You can't be serious? Not now?'

I didn't reply.

Another figure by the side of the road, another hitcher. We both watched him grow in size and stature, until he definitely wasn't Goat Bag, and he zoomed by.

Eli didn't say anything. Maybe he would continue to not say anything until he hoped it was too late, and he could just drive by the airport like I hadn't suggested leaving.

'I can meet up with you again in Staten Island. But... I mean, wouldn't it be good for you to chill out for a few days? We could both do our own thing and then we'll finish this. I promise we will finish this.'

He touched his ear.

'Two days,' he said.

'It'll take as long as it takes.'

I didn't quite understand why he seemed so pissed off.

It was as if my leaving, even temporarily, was messing with his sense of order, going against his *plan*.

'I can't just sack off this Seven thing. I'm here for Noel as well. Everyone back home, they're expecting this.'

I should have told him what I knew about Trent, but I didn't. It was the knowledge I had any sort of upper hand that gave me the strength to leave.

Not for the first time, I began to get the creeping sense that Eli had some other agenda that existed just out of my reach. But I didn't have long to dwell on it because before long I was on a flight and the idea slipped my mind again.

That one hour and fifteen minute flight was the shortest I could remember. No texts for a time, no calls, no social media. No conversation either. I even booked my ticket on my phone outside Lambert–St Louis International Airport in order to cut down on human interaction.

It was one of the ugliest places I'd ever fucking seen, like a nuclear bunker. Lumps of grey and tinted glass and a stunted little tower.

I spent all the spare time before my flight in the bathrooms.

It wasn't just the fluorescent lights. I looked as if I'd climbed out of a grave.

I texted Eamonn and Mark saying I was coming to Chicago, mostly so that Mark could meet me at the airport, and spent the flight staring out of the window feeling sick.

I wondered what Eli was doing, as G-force hit my stomach during the jagged landing.

He had driven away in silence, without a goodbye or a glance back.

It could be the last I saw of him.

Eyes down as I walked out into O'Hare International, following the trippy tiling, until I looked up and saw part of London standing in front of me, wearing black skinny jeans and a leather jacket and eyeing me with a, 'You look terrible.'

'Thanks.'

'No really. I don't fancy you at all.'

I thought he was going to hug me – Mark was a hugger – but he frowned and settled for taking a couple of steps towards me with his hands in his pockets.

'Did you find him?' he asked, as we began walking.

'What?'

'The guy, Trent. Did you find him?'

'Oh, no. After this I'm flying back to meet Eli and tie this shit up.'

'Who's Eli again?'

'Family friend.'

'Ronnie.' He stopped at the entrance.

I was dying for a cigarette, itching on the inside. 'What?'

'Are you OK? You seem…'

'I'm tired.'

'OK.' He indicated his head. 'My car's over there. Do you want something to eat or…?'

'No, I'm fine.'

I didn't like the way he was looking at me.

'OK,' he said, again, and didn't pursue it.

He didn't pursue it in the car either, which I was grateful for. The last thing I wanted, ever again, was to sit in another fucking car. I sat to the very far side of my seat, desperate to sleep. I kept looking to the side expecting to see Eli, and Mark conscientiously avoided speaking.

I chuckled to myself, watching Chicago go by.

It had an optimism about it that you rarely found in cities

further east. It was cleaner and saner. It was cold, had a real chill in the air, which I liked. But it wasn't as caustic and ugly as New York, wasn't as self-satisfied as Boston, wasn't as quaint as Philadelphia, wasn't as bat-shit fucking crazy as New Orleans, wasn't as kale-juice-no-dressing-Bikram-fuckery as LA, wasn't as *stoked, bra* as Santa Cruz, wasn't as… well, Houston was all right.

'Have you spoken to Noel recently?' he asked at one point.

'No.'

Our hotel was gorgeous. Mark had booked a twin room and I didn't even care. After sharing a car with Eli, after spending way too much time forced into each other's personal bubbles, I found I didn't care much for personal bubbles any more.

I dropped my bags near the door, went into the bathroom and showered for an hour. I looked at myself for a long time. I'd lost weight. There were heavy black circles under my eyes.

I put on clean clothes and it didn't make much difference.

Mark was by the window reading. I had to hand it to him, he was fine to be left in his own company.

Eventually, I sat on one of the beds and picked up the room service menu. I hadn't noticed what the name of the hotel was; an independent place called the Palmeira.

Our room had rooms of its own. I approved.

'Is she here?' I asked.

Mark put his book away. 'She'd better be. I had a tip-off from a friend.'

'Which friend?'

'A Russian.'

'How good a friend is he?'

An assured smile. 'Good.'

'If she's not here then you don't know where the hell she is, do you?'

'I've never failed a job like this, Ron.'

'Every record has to come to an end sometime.'

The statement hung there between us, and Mark was the one who chose to move on from it.

'Do you want to tell me what you've been up to?' he asked.

'Chasing a born-again Satanist from St Louis to LA and back. You know, standard.'

'Sounds like my kinda territory.'

'Well, I might tell you more about it after I've eaten.'

I'd sent a text to Eamonn before getting on the plane, but I couldn't see a reply.

CHAPTER THIRTY-FOUR

'*I don't know what's going on out there, Ronnie. But I don't feel like you're being my husband any more. All we want to do is talk to you. Your kids... We don't know whether you're alive or dead every day and... You know what, forget it. Just don't expect me to be waiting at the airport for you with a stupid smile on my face, OK?*'

I played Rachel's message a couple of times and was shocked by how little it affected me. Her role as my *wife* – whatever that word had meant to me – seemed diminished.

Synecdoche.

Was there ever a word so custom-made for dehumanization? It is the very definition of how serial killers – any killers, any abusers – think. To reduce a person to one defining feature is their art form.

Men are better at it than women. When I was younger I could fuck a woman for no other reason than I was fascinated by a squint in one of her eyes. She was the squint. That was the only thing about her worth identifying. I don't even like you, I have no interest in your hopes or your dreams or your future or what dubious effect you're going to have on anything in the world or even whether you're enjoying this – because you're just a squint and you're indifferent to experience – but I'm going to fuck you, just focus on that squint, because I kinda like the way your right eye squints like that, like that, like that...

You can shoot a police officer if they're just a uniform, nothing more than an empty outfit hanging in the wardrobe. You're not shooting the man, you're shooting the clothes – the uniform, the icon that represents everything that makes you hate and feel downtrodden – because that's all they are. Uniforms were never alive before anyway. The person is incidental. The uniform is all you hate.

You're not stealing a car. You're looking for wheels. Stealing a car isn't nearly as bad as stealing wheels. Anyone could steal wheels.

How easy it is for an employer to fuck over the people who work for him when they're not people, not really; they're hands. Hired hands. The help. You can fire the help – the hands – condemn their entire family to starve and live on the streets because hands don't have families and help is just a concept.

You see guys shouting out of cars, addressing girls as legs. Legs don't get harassed. Legs are just legs. Good luck trying to hurt a pair of legs' feelings.

You could rape a skirt, a gash, no problem. You couldn't hurt or kill a skirt any more than a uniform.

There's a reason why, at war, you're never ordered to fire at a human, a person. There's always a name – gook, towel-head, whatever. You blew-up thirty towel-heads today and there's no way you gave a shit. How could you?

Because hands don't have families and help is just a concept and wearing a towel on your head is stupid.

My point is...

Well, what is the point?

Synecdoche.

What a wonderful quirk of language. How comforting to know that the very way we speak is designed to justify our basest desires.

People will always find ways to do damage to people.

As long as you never have to think of them as people.

Then it's fine.

It's fine.

Because hands don't have families anyway and help is just a concept and voices mean nothing.

'It's been hard without a good photo of her,' Mark said in the car.

'Do we not have one?' I asked, surprised.

'Only one from Facebook but even that isn't great. Impressive really. I would've thought it was impossible to be this absent from the Internet nowadays, especially at her age.'

'No.' I hadn't known her well enough to know whether she was into social media or not. 'You'd have to talk to Noel about stuff she was into. I could do a bit more online stalking for you if you like. I'm good at that.'

'I think Noel knew her even less than we did.'

'He was fucking her though.'

'Yeah, so he can't be objective.'

I was still so fucking tired. Ten hours' sleep and still so fucking tired. I pulled down the sun visor as we sat in unmoving traffic and shut my eyes. My dreams had been haunted by weird figures, things my subconscious must have made up because I'd never seen anything like it in waking life. Last night it was a man, wearing some ill-fitting blue shirt, walking on tiptoes, knees slightly bent, arms and hands twisted up behind him like wings, stretched to full extension. He stalked me between buildings, far enough away for me not to run, but close enough to fill me with dread.

Mark had shaken me awake. Apparently I'd been muttering. I wondered if I'd ever talked in my sleep in front of Eli.

'What went on in LA?' Mark asked, taking his hands off the wheel and killing the engine for a spell.

I sighed. 'We were looking for someone and it just got a bit weird, that's all.'

'Weird how?'

'Weird as in… I don't know how to tell you. It's not even about Trent. It's everyone who was around him who's become weird. It's like this guy was so mental that wherever he went he left this trail of fucking bat-shit insanity. We killed one of Eli's old business partners, which made sense, but Eli skinned him alive. Then there were these hitmen sent to kill a guy we were staying with, and I sent their boss after someone else, so I think he's dead too now. And we still don't know where Trent is.'

'Want to tell me about him?'

'Trent? He seemed like a nice guy, but he lost the plot when his niece died and…'

Mark waited for me to finish, but I didn't.

'What is it about him that scares you?' he asked.

'I didn't say he scared me.'

Some douche on her way to work stepped in front of the car as Mark was restarting the engine and I reached across Mark to slam the horn. She started and spilt her coffee over the bonnet.

'Move it, you fucking ass-piece!'

Mark snorted. 'Hasn't taken you long to slip back into old habits.'

'People aren't so fucking sensitive here,' I said, as the woman hurried away and we crawled forwards another couple of metres. 'Did you not speak to Noel about Seven before coming out here? You didn't think he'd have had anything useful to tell you?'

'No.'

'You don't think Daisy knows anything?'

'Daisy doesn't think Seven has even left London. But my source is trustworthy, he wouldn't send me out here on rumours.'

'I know you and Seven were quite close. Noel said you were helping her out with all that shit that happened to her family. The murders.'

'I thought we were close. But all the best liars are shape-shifters.'

'Like you?' I smiled. 'No offence.'

'None taken. We all are to some extent. I think the idea of a fixed self is debatable.' He shrugged. 'And I think that being *yourself* with someone – if *yourself* even exists – doesn't apply to the people you think it does. I've felt less myself around people I've been fucking than some of my friends. Do you feel like you're being *yourself* with Rachel?'

'Yes. That's, like, the whole point of being married, isn't it. So you can just... be yourself.'

But I wasn't thinking about Rachel. I was thinking about Eli's ranting in the car. '*You are more yourself than you've ever been.*' His glee at reminding me of how much I wasn't longing for home, clinging to home, in the way I'd thought I would.

'I'd like to have met Eli,' Mark said, as if he'd been following my train of thought. 'He sounds rare.'

★

I'd come to Chicago for a stake-out, I realized. A stake-out Mark had already been conducting by himself for three days, either in his car or sitting in the window of the same coffee shop. The exact tip-off this Russian had given him was that a young Japanese girl had been working with a gang of armed robbers in the South Side, near Englewood.

He hadn't seen her yet.

'A few girls who fit the description arrived through O'Hare International in the weeks after Seven disappeared,' Mark assured me. 'Nothing totally conclusive because she'll be using a fake name and will have changed her appearance at least slightly. But there were enough to make it worth checking out thoroughly.'

'So what makes you think this particular girl is Seven and not just some rando?'

'Mostly the description. Half Japanese, hard-arse. He said she was new in town, spoke with an English accent.' He glanced at me, smiling reassurance. 'It's not much, I know. But everyone seems very protective of her too, no one has been talking. Well, not without some persuasion anyway.'

I didn't feel much like smiling back.

We got out of the car, parked on the bottom floor of a multistorey, some way from Englewood, but not far enough. I didn't know Chicago that well, but when I'd briefly thought about moving here in my mid-teens for college, Englewood had been one of the places I'd been told to avoid.

'I know you might think New York has the best pizza,' Mark said, as we walked down a street of mostly restaurants. 'But it's like pizza for ants compared to this place.'

I kinda zoned out, stopped and sent Eli a text asking whether he was back in New York or Philadelphia, and when he was heading to Staten Island.

'Ron?'

I didn't notice that I'd halted.

'Ronnie, are you all right?'

It hit me. I no longer gave a shit. I didn't care if we found Seven or not. Fuck this. Fuck mystery Russians. Fuck Noel back in London. Fuck Daisy and her self-satisfied questioning. Fuck Eamonn and fuck Dad and his palming-off of the worst of his creations onto me. Fuck everyone fucking up in such a repellent fucking *human* fashion. I wanted to go to Staten Island, find Trent and go home.

We were on the outskirts of a park. Mark standing some way away, looking over his shoulder.

'I'm not staking out this building with you,' I said.

His gaze fell to my phone. 'Why? What's happened?'

'Nothing.' I put the mobile in my pocket. 'Nothing's happened, I just... Let my brother help you or something. I think he's coming here and I'll tell him to meet you. I'm... I'm going to the airport.'

I took a step back, about-turned and started walking.

It used to appeal to me that Chicago's streets were cleaner than most, but now it made me want to retreat. Not even vengeance was enough to keep me here, station me outside a building searching for someone who meant nothing to me. I didn't even feel hate. I'd fucking transcended hate; I'd transcended all these emotions now.

'Trent isn't your problem, Ron.'

'I don't care, I've got to go.'

'Go where?'

'*Go!*'

I stopped, rocking backwards and forwards on the balls of my feet as if I was going to run. But I was paralysed by indecision.

'Where, to Staten Island?'

'Yes, probably. I don't know.'

I flinched as Mark tried to take my shoulder, and realized I'd put both hands to my head.

Why was I here? Why was I here? Why was I here?

'*We skinned Thomas Love alive in New York, hung him upside down and pulled it off in fucking reams, it came off in pieces, and then Cathal Sheedy gave me this... spoon after a guy chewed up a cyanide pill in his kitchen. And before we left I told their faceless boss to go after the wrong person.*'

The memories came back, and I didn't think I was repeating them out loud but I looked at Mark and knew it had been speech rather than thought.

I said, 'We went to a hotel where a girl died in a water tank. I don't care if she's here. I mean... I don't care if Seven's here. Not the girl. Seven's not *important* to me any more, what's important is just... I need to find Trent for Eli, and then get back to the UK to protect my fucking club from fucking Edie Franco.'

'Ron, you looked as though you hadn't slept in days.'

'I need to go.'

He tried to stop me and I lost it, grabbing the front of his jacket.

'If you try and stop me *I'll kill you.* I'll fucking kill you.'

He didn't resist, probably because he didn't believe I'd actually hurt him. But I wanted to, for the hell of it. Because there was pressure in my head that needed releasing.

I walked, putting distance between us, struggling to breathe and thinking, *Am I having a heart attack?*

There was a bar, so I headed for that, through the swinging doors and into the restrooms where I threw up in the sink. My arms quivered, struggling to support my weight as I vomited grey bile. Then I backed into an empty cubicle and shut the door, slammed down the toilet seat and pulled my knees up to my chin.

The door and walls were dark green.

I cupped my hands over my mouth and nose. I couldn't breathe, or I was breathing too much. I was having a heart attack. This was what a heart attack felt like, a fist punching you repeatedly in the chest while screaming, *Breathe! Breathe! Breathe!*

I reached for my gun – in my pocket or in my waistband, inside my coat – because I was going to shoot myself in the head. But I'd left it in one of the cars.

For some reason, that took the edge off.

I wasn't going to shoot myself, because I couldn't, and I wasn't having a heart attack, because I could breathe now, now that everything had stopped shaking...

I put my hands out and braced myself against the cold walls.

Outside the restrooms, I could hear some dim activity.

I stood and pushed open the door of the cubicle. I saw myself in the mirror, breathless and sweating, glowing with adrenalin.

It was so quiet.

I smoothed back my hair, rubbed my hands over my face, and left the restroom.

To my surprise, Mark was waiting for me outside the bar.

I accepted the cigarette he offered.

'Do you want me to drive you back?' he asked.

I hesitated. 'I'm just gonna go to the airport.'

'Well, then I can drive you.'

'You don't have to, I'll get a cab.'

'Are you sure you don't wanna stay another night and... make up some sleep?'

'No, I'll sleep on the plane,' I lied.

I didn't particularly want to be accompanied on my abdication, for the clearing of my desk, but Mark ended up driving anyway, which I suppose was nice of him.

But he didn't belong here. He was one of those foreign things now, another call to avoid.

Before we got in the car there was a vision of my future, where I looked at him and felt I was on the verge of committing an act of extreme violence. I could just kill him to remove him from my peripheral vision. In my mind I took my gun and shot him twice in the stomach and chest, and we both jerked with the sound of the impact and then I walked away. The idea was almost hypnotic. I even felt the spatter of blood, and it didn't move me at all.

'One thing though,' Mark said, and I braced myself. 'Why are you carrying an old spoon around with you? You said someone gave it to you.'

I snorted. 'It's a souvenir, I guess. Apparently it's made of gold or something.'

'OK. Well, everybody needs a hobby.'

Checking my phone in the car, I had an email from Melissa.

Daisy had stopped trying to contact me, I noticed.

Mark would mention this to Noel, I knew he would. But Noel wasn't here, and it wasn't as if I had to go back.

CHAPTER THIRTY-FIVE

Daisy

I ran into him somewhere on the South Bank because that was the only place he was happy to talk. It had become an over-cast and dramatic evening, which was fitting as Noel wanted to conduct himself like he was in a fucking spy drama.

'Noel!'

'Walk.' He took me by the arm and dragged me along the riverside.

'Dude, calm down, no one's listening.'

'I don't know if we're all being followed.'

'God, Noel, get *off*.' I slowed my pace and managed to reclaim my arm. 'Where did you see her? Are you absolutely sure? Because I thought I saw her today and—'

'It *was* her.'

We took the ramp down from the Centre and walked past the green.

He continued, 'I know you think I've been doing fuck all with my time off, just getting off my face or whatever, but I have been doing stuff. I knew she was still in London, I don't know how but... you know how you just *know*?'

'Yeah, I know.'

'I knew if she was still around she wouldn't be able to stop going to certain places, National Portrait Gallery and shit like that. I took her there once and... Anyway, I've been going there to wander around.'

'How often?'

'Every day, pretty much. Security there think I'm mental but I'm not a hobo so they couldn't exactly chuck me out.'

'And you just saw her there?'

'Well yeah. I didn't expect it so I hid round a corner, just in case there was one person in the fucking place who *didn't* think I was insane.' He brought us to a halt, looked around, then indicated his head behind us and started walking in the opposite direction. 'So I followed her all day, until she went into a restaurant around Covent Garden. I got a few photos, look.'

He handed me his phone.

I squinted and cupped my hand around the screen. I could make out a few blurry shots of Seven from behind, a couple taken from inside the Gallery that had her in profile, and then I recognized someone.

'I know him,' I said, pointing at a stocky waistcoated man standing with Seven outside a restaurant covered in ivy.

'Sean. I remember you mentioned he stopped by.'

'Yeah, and you got really weird when I tried to ask Ron about it.'

We stopped by a bench, facing the water. Noel began to sit down but the wood looked damp and he thought better of it. His desire not to be overheard was being overcome by his desire to be warm.

He pointed at one of the huge cafés under the South Bank and we pulled out chairs beneath an overhang, in the vicinity of some heaters.

I was starting to get agitated by Noel's furtive glances.

He took his phone back. 'Sean is someone I've known of for a while. Irish guy who pretty much just worked for anyone. He even applied... Well, "applied" may not be the right word. He offered his services to us once like four years ago but we had enough people and there was something off about him. He was way too easy to get on with. You know the type.'

'Yeah, those friendly people. Suspicious as fuck.'

'Yeah, right. Anyway, he probably doesn't think we remember him. But we've kept tabs on him, on and off. He tends to work for' – he lowered his voice in a way that made me snigger – 'foreigners.'

'Careful, *they* might hear you. Who's he working for now then?'

'Russian arseholes. Sure of it.'

'For serious?'

'Yep.' Noel waved a waitress over. 'Can I have a double gin and tonic, love?'

I raised my eyebrows.

'Sorry,' he said, 'did you want anything?'

'No.'

He tapped his fingers against the silver tabletop. 'This is actually doing my head in.'

'Have you told Ronnie?'

'Why would I? You know Mark called and said he turned up in Chicago and had some kind of mental breakdown.'

'What?'

'Yeah.' He seemed incredulous. 'Apparently he showed up for two minutes, had a meltdown and left. Mark thinks he's gone to Staten Island looking for someone else.'

'Damn.'

'Yeah. This doesn't bode well. He's meant to be the stable one.'

'What about Edie?' I ventured.

'Up to something but I'm not sure what. Everyone's fucking *tainted*, Daisy.' He pulled a face, as if he could smell it. 'Everyone's fucking untrustworthy. I fucking *bet* Mark's Russian mates tipped him off about Chicago to get him out of the way, but I can't tell him that because he fucking works for them most of the time. Who knows who he'd side with?'

He made a good point. As much as I did trust Mark, considered him a friend, I didn't know how far I could believe his claim he was on my side if I found myself opposed to one of his long-time employers. It wasn't my tattoos he had scrawled all over his body.

'What about Nic?' I asked.

'I just don't know.'

'Maybe choose your moment. But I think you can trust him.'

'You think?'

Wow, I thought. He was actually considering my opinion.

'Yeah, I think you can. But don't discount Mark completely.'

'Why?'

'He has something to prove.'

A long gin and tonic was placed in front of him and he took out the straw to down half of it.

He stared into space for a long time, watching people walk by. 'It was an absolute mind-fuck seeing her again. Didn't know whether I wanted to hug her or kill her.'

A pause.

'Kill her,' he added. 'No, I wanted to kill her.'

I nodded. 'I thought I saw her a couple of times. It was like that "I want to die" feeling of seeing an ex but way worse.'

'Do you think she ever thinks about us?'

'I don't know. She was always good at ignoring stuff.

With her parents, she never thought about it. She told me she never even cried. If you can repress something like that, you can probably repress anything.'

He looked crushed.

'But it's not like she didn't have a conscience,' I added.

Had we even talked about this properly before? I wasn't sure any of us had.

'Sometimes I think she did it all because I hurt her. You know, went back to Caroline for a while. But that just makes it all about me and it was probably all about fucking money.'

'She did care about you, from what I could gather...' I paused. 'It might have been something that got out of control. Like, maybe it started off as one thing and became something that she couldn't get out of.'

I realised that I was just parroting what Seven had said to me to justify it all, in the club right before I gave her permission to shoot.

He frowned. 'What do you mean?'

I shrugged. 'I'm thinking out loud.'

I zipped up my grey Harrington and Noel finished his gin and tonic.

'Maybe I should have just fucking ended it, right there.' He grimaced. 'I'd be in prison right now but at least it would have been over.'

'But it wouldn't be over, would it?'

He rolled his eyes. 'It'd be some fucking relief though. And being banged up would be the easiest way to quit drinking. No G & T's in there.'

We both scrolled through the photos again, and sat in silence.

CHAPTER THIRTY-SIX

Ronnie

Judas got a bad rep. People threw his name around as an insult but they had it wrong. He had a role, like all of us. When you thought about it, we could all hope to be that relevant in the grand scheme of things, part of *the plan*.

The Satanist admits to being evil.

It made sense. Without sin, without these betrayals and disobediences, transgressions, without these deaths, goodness would mean nothing. The very things we prayed for would mean nothing.

Judas must have felt a similar vindication, even as he hung by the neck with his intestines spilling out of him like a rope ladder. He must have felt a similar conviction to mine, sitting on the plane back to Philadelphia.

I didn't go straight home, but took a taxi part of the way so I could stop off in JB's for a drink.

Blessed are the destroyers of false hope, for they are the true Messiahs – Cursed are the god-adorers, for they shall be born sheep!

I sat at the bar and ordered a bourbon from another girl

with blue hair who looked so much like the girl from the park it was uncanny. I did a double-take and watched her out of the corner of my eye.

Joe appeared from the cellar.

'The wanderer returns! Alice, don't let this man pay for a drink.'

They rush on the city. They run on the wall; They climb into the houses, They enter through the windows like a thief.

I took Cathal's spoon from my pocket and placed it on the bar. 'I met a guy in LA who can extract gold from base metals.'

'No shit? You mean alchemy?'

'No, it's different somehow. I don't know really.'

'I think you met a good conman, Ron.' Joe gave me a gentle smile as he filled the dishwasher.

It was five in the afternoon and I was one of only a few people in.

'Maybe,' I admitted.

Joe picked up the spoon, gave it a careful examination, and handed it back with a sceptical expression.

Where could Cathal and Luiz from St Louis be now?

Where was Goat Bag and the love of his life?

They felt so fucking distant, like they hadn't existed at all.

'You look different.'

'Well, it's been a few years,' I said, taking out my smoking paraphernalia and spreading it across the bar-top.

'No, since I last saw you.'

'It was a weird road trip. Eamonn been flouting his ban?'

'He's like a puppy, you can't stay mad at him, can you?' He shook his head. 'He's been behaving himself though, even asked me about some shifts last week.'

'You'll hire him?'

'Fuck no.' He laughed. 'But bless him for asking.'

A group of kids stood up across the bar, putting on coats. I glanced up, sipping my bourbon, and recognized a couple of them. Out of the corner of my eye, I tried to place their features. Two of them I'd seen here before; the ones who'd been scrapping with Eamonn. Not the one who'd had the baseball bat, but the others. One of them had taken a swing at me.

I downed the rest of my bourbon, and reckoned I could leave my bags here for a spell.

As the kids left I stood up, took my tobacco with me as if I was leaving for a cigarette, and followed them outside.

I thought, from the King James Bible,

And deceiveth them that dwell on the earth by the means of those miracles which he had power to do in the sight of the beast; saying to them that dwell on the earth, that they should make an image to the beast, which had the wound by a sword, and did live.

One of them was wearing a khaki coat with a fur hood. Another was wearing some sleeveless beige cardigan like a full-time douche.

There were more people around than I might have liked and it was starting to rain, but sometimes you had to roll with the opportunities presented to you.

Khaki split away from the group and I halted a little way away while they said goodbye to each other in an awkward back-patting way. I chose between him and Cardigan, and followed Khaki. He was heading for a car.

It amazed me how many people continued to enter their

homes and their vehicles without looking around them first, without assuming they might be being followed.

He'd parked down a narrow street, only one pavement, a maze of bins and no people.

Khaki took out his keys, pulled his hood back to show straw-coloured hair, and I cast my gaze about us before grabbing the back of his neck and smashing his face forwards into the roof of the shoddy little car.

He dropped his keys.

His nose broke and he crumpled.

It was so easy to hate the young.

Hidden by his car, I braced myself against the roof and kicked him where he cowered on the ground. Then I pulled him up, punched him down and kicked him again, pulled him up, punched him down and kicked him again. He didn't make a sound.

I looked for his car keys and picked them up, while Khaki lay bleeding.

Opening his car door, I dragged the kid to his feet and shoved him inside.

I don't think he got a good look at my face before both his eyes were swollen shut and clouded with blood.

Reaching past him, where he was quivering and groaning on the seat, I put his keys on the dashboard and shut the door. I could have locked him in, thrown the keys away, but I wasn't a monster about it.

Vengeance, swiftly dealt.

I retracted my hands into my sleeves to wipe the blood off.

Upon turning, we were alone. I wasn't sure if anyone had been watching us before, but they weren't now. The rain had worsened but it was refreshing. I hadn't felt rain for a while.

I walked slowly towards the main road and realized I couldn't remember which way I'd come.

People ducked into shops around me. Everyone looked too far away and yet too close.

Eli hadn't got in touch yet, which was worrying.

I turned left and spotted the establishments I recognized and those I didn't.

Not even breathless, not even sweating. I'd expended no energy on Khaki. The violence had taken nothing out of me; it was more like letting something move through me, like the inhaling and exhaling of oxygen.

My hands emerged from my sleeves and most of the blood had gone.

I re-entered JB's and couldn't read the expression on Joe's face.

If he knew I hadn't gone out for a cigarette, he didn't mention it.

'I'll be back in again before I go,' I said, slinging my bags over my shoulder.

'Be safe, Ron.'

'I'm safe as houses.'

I stood in the doorway – *Have a significant day!* – and let the rain hit me for a moment before hailing another cab. I was so glad of it. Too much heat brought out the crazy in people.

'Bro, you look sick!'

I frowned at Eamonn across the dinner table, a vat of pasta and fresh tomato. He hadn't got on the plane, it transpired. It was probably for the best. I couldn't imagine Mark babysitting him for an unspecified length of time.

'Do you mean that in a good way or do you mean *ill*?'

Eamonn snorted and said, 'You're so old.'

I directed my condescension into a plate of mozzarella and tried to remain zen. There was some brilliant repressed savagery at my fingertips. It was making me feel unstable and out of place at the family table.

'Have you guys heard from Eli?' I asked.

Mum said, 'No. Did everything go well? You look thin.'

'It went OK, we're not quite done. I need a few days in Staten Island.'

'What do you want with that cesspit?' Dad chipped in.

'There's someone there Eli wants to speak to, in a face-to-face way.'

'Can we talk about what's happening with you two?'

Eamonn and I glanced at each other and for a moment found a glimmer of solidarity.

'As you know, we think it would be a good idea for Eamonn to be taken under your wing.'

Simultaneously:

'I don't want nothing to do with his *fucking* wings.'

'My wings are *fine*, thank you.'

'God*damn* it.'

That was Mum.

'I'm sorry, I don't mean to...' She put a hand to her heart, then her hair. When it had grown back after chemo she developed a nervous tick of checking it was still there. 'But this isn't a joke, you know. Your *lives* aren't a joke to us. Sometimes I feel like neither of you realize just how precious your lives are.'

'Trust me, no one's been laughing.' I looked down at my lap.

'Eamonn, you need to think about what you're doing.'

'I am thinking—'

'No, I mean *think*. Not just asking your friends for jobs. Think about what you want to do with your life. You wanted to do things once, didn't you? Well you have your chance now. If you waste it we might as well not even have you back.'

I made an awkward creep across the table with my right hand, going for more pasta.

Dad glared at me and I retracted it.

Eamonn seemed deep in thought for once. I didn't buy it.

He realized Mum was still watching him for a reply. 'Yeah... Yeah, Mom, don't worry. I'm thinking about stuff, I'm just... getting used to being out, that's all.'

'He needs a routine,' Dad said.

'I'm not a new *fucking* puppy,' Eamonn snapped.

I muttered, 'You are a bit though.'

He pushed his plate away – 'I'm being excused' – and left the room.

Mum stood up as well but I beat her to it. 'I'll go.'

'Ronnie, he needs to understand—'

'Yeah, I get that, but he's been dealing with prison guards for the last fifteen years. You really think he needs talking down to right now?' I glanced down at the table, and pointed at the pasta. 'Save that, I'm not done.'

It struck me, as I was going upstairs, that I was expecting to see Eamonn's teenage room. But we didn't live in that house any more. I didn't know what they'd done with his stuff. Surely they wouldn't have been insensitive enough to get rid of it.

I knocked on his door.

'What?'

Opening it, I realized his new room looked more like a

guest room. It was green and beige. I half-expected to see a towel folded at the end of his bed. The only thing that seemed like his was the Xbox in the corner on top of a chest of drawers, wired up to a small TV.

Maybe his stuff – his real stuff – was still in the attic.

'You coming in or just wanna take in the view?'

Eamonn was sitting on the floor, leaning against his bed. He made an expansive gesture with his arms.

I sat beside him, staring ahead at a white wardrobe.

'Some heavy shit went down with you and Eli, didn't it.'

I nodded. 'We never found that guy.'

'You know Eli's fucking mental, right?'

I smiled a little. 'I think that trip would have sent anyone a bit mental.'

'No really, he's fucked up.'

'He's all right.'

'OK, man. I'm just saying.'

'Why do you have to keep making things so hard?'

He shrugged. 'It seems more interesting.'

'Did you ever want to do anything other than get into trouble?'

'Na, not really.' He made a face. 'Even at school I didn't enjoy any lessons, I just wanted to piss everyone off more than anybody else.'

'Everyone has a talent apparently.'

'It was in third grade.'

'What?'

'When it started properly. Like, I've always been into getting into trouble, but in third grade I had a fight with this kid. I can't even remember his name now, it's not important. But we had a fight and he put me through a glass door outside the cafeteria and it smashed.' An odd little expression of glee came over him. 'It was the most trouble I'd ever been in. I was sent to the principal's office and she just didn't know what to say to me. I was in so much trouble I didn't even get punished in the end, they never called Mom and Dad. We were just kinda... left alone. That's when I thought, "OK, this is how you get through life".'

'What, by being in trouble?'

'No, not just that. That's not enough. You always have to go bigger than everyone else.'

'I had you worked out young. I always knew that if we were in a fight and you threw a plate at me I had to throw a fucking toaster back. Eventually you'd run out of ways to throw an even bigger tantrum and just shut the fuck up.'

He laughed. 'We were such dicks to each other.'

'We *are* such dicks to each other.' I sighed. 'Look, I know you're coming back to London with me and I'm sorry if I'm making you feel fucking unwelcome about it.'

'I'm basically being kicked out.'

'Yeah, I know. But you can come stay with me for a bit if you want. Like, we've got a spare room, that's what it's there for.'

'Won't your missus mind?'

I hesitated. 'Well, I've put up her bloody relatives before, so... And I know people, I can probably get you a bar job or an office job as long as you don't fuck up everything.'

'Aw, man, that's like the nicest thing you've ever said to me.'

'Enjoy it. That's my nice quota fulfilled for the year.'

My phone vibrated with a text in my pocket and somehow I knew this time it would be Eli. We were connected now, by some psychic call to arms.

'Well, you know, nice talk,' Eamonn muttered.

While calling Eli, listening to the line ringing, I passed Dad on his mobile talking to someone in the hallway. He ducked into his study and it wasn't until later it would even strike me as weird.

CHAPTER THIRTY-SEVEN

Melissa called me again, at night. It might be that she didn't remember the time difference, but more likely she wanted to catch me slightly off guard. I jerked awake, confused at the sound of my alarm before realizing it wasn't my alarm and it was four in the morning.

I'd been having the dream about the birdman again.

I got my hand on the phone before it rang off.

'I wasn't entirely honest with you,' she said, as if we'd never stopped talking.

'I... What?' I sat up, rubbing my eyes.

'LA wasn't the last time I heard from Trent.'

'You what?'

'Did I wake you?'

'... Yes.'

I tried to stand up, almost fell, found the light and then wished I hadn't because then I couldn't fucking see. My eyes scrunched up against glare. She was silent for a moment, giving me time to adjust by way of apology.

'He called me, quite recently. But he wasn't making much sense. It was quite upsetting actually. Maybe that's why I didn't mention it. It was one of those things you just try and forget because it seemed too horrible to be real.'

'Why the change of heart?'

'I don't know, because you told me you were going to kill him?'

'Yeah but... that hasn't changed.'

'I know, but the more I thought about it, the more it seemed like maybe it was a good idea for someone, you two, to find Trent. Maybe it would be better for him that way.'

'Better than letting him live?'

'Yes.'

'So what did he say?'

'It didn't make much sense, he was rambling. He was talking about Titian. He used to say that my hair was like a woman in a Titian painting. When you said he became a Satanist some of the things he was talking about made more sense. He was talking about plagues and something about how he wanted to rid the world of all unwanted things, including himself. He said he didn't have control of himself, that he was being made to do things. God, it was creepy, you know.'

I sat on the edge of the bed, then lay down again.

It struck me that the light under the door might seem odd to anyone who was awake and I went back to flip the switch again, casting me and Melissa's voice into darkness. It was a turn-on, talking to her like this. I hoped she wouldn't notice. Or maybe that was her ploy.

'He said the world was full of unwanted children and that God hadn't helped them. I thought he might have been talking about his niece. He said God was a lie because he left unwanted children to fend for themselves.'

'Did he say where he was?'

'The phone he called from was a payphone in Staten Island. I looked it up because... well, it was worrying. I thought he sounded ill.'

'Where was the payphone?'

'It was in Willowbrook. He said he was there to find where the children were buried.'

'The what?'

'Where the children were buried.'

I grimaced. 'Where the...'

'Children are buried.'

'Fuck.'

'I know.'

We were in silence for a while. There wasn't much that could have been said. The buried children were enough of an illustration.

'Do you know what he might have meant by that?' I asked.

'Maybe. You know about the missing children in Staten Island that were never found?'

I couldn't think of anything I wanted to know less about, but I sighed. 'No.'

'It started off as an urban legend, a serial killer or a bogeyman that abducted children. But then the urban legend became real. Children did go missing. I think only one was found.'

'You think Trent...'

'No, this was decades ago, in the eighties. I think he might have taken an interest in it. It might have been what he was referring to, I don't know. But if he was talking about buried children and he was in the area...'

'Where are you now?'

'I'm sorry?'

'Where are you now, London?'

And she hung up on me.

I wasn't tired any more. I felt out of breath. I sat up and opened my laptop, eyes adjusting to the glare.

Eli had sent me some sort of documentary about the place

called Willowbrook. For a second, a mad conspiracy took root in my mind, that he and Melissa had been talking to each other somehow, thinking up a story to send me.

But obviously not.

It was easy to become paranoid, in the dark, with strangers calling you.

Obviously not.

I searched for Cameron Hopper again and a shiver went up my spine and along my arms, raising the hairs. Cameron Hopper, a well-liked Scottish TV producer based in LA, had been found dead in his home, having committed suicide by slitting his wrists in the bath. Those who knew him were said to be 'in shock'.

In shock.

I thought I'd feel accomplished somehow, but I didn't. With him gone, with the trail for Cathal cold, they – whoever *they* were – could come after us now.

It wasn't as if the man at the other end of the line had known my name, but that seemed inconsequential. They seemed like the sort of people who would be hooked into satellites, who could lean down to read a newspaper over someone's shoulder from orbit.

I copied the article, from some gossip site, and emailed it to Eli.

Then I got back under the duvet to watch the documentary he had sent to me.

Between that and the image of Cameron Hopper, suicided in his home, I didn't get any more sleep that night.

The Staten Island ferry remained one of the ugliest fuck-ing things I'd ever seen. Fittingly, it resembled a large and unwieldy piece of litter. I suppose they'd picked the colour orange because they'd wanted it to look inviting and jolly. But it looked like toxic waste. A floating crisp packet.

Eli pulled over so we could look at one of them half-submerged in the Hudson, decommissioned.

But we were wedded to the car; I wasn't going anywhere without one, so we took the half-hour drive instead.

I found that's what I'd come to expect from following Eli now, having all my least favourite aspects of humanity thrown into my face. But he spared me the ferry, thank fuck.

'Was that you?' was the first thing Eli asked me when we were standing side by side staring at the monstrosity. 'The day you left me in the motel. Did you kill Cam?'

'What? No. Look, it happened only yesterday.'

'No, that's when they found him. Was it you?'

'No.'

He stared.

'Eli, no. What do you think this is, some conspiracy?' I laughed, and stopped abruptly when it seemed too much.

'It just seems... out of character.'

'It's been a long time since you knew him. Maybe he changed.'

'Maybe,' he murmured.

'Anyway, that thing you sent me about this place,' I said, with caution, 'about the missing kids and this place we're going. Are you suggesting that Trent might have something to do with them?'

'No,' he said, giving the same answer as Melissa. 'It was too long ago. It's just something that may have attracted him, that's all.'

'And how did you get a hunch that he was in the area?'

'I asked around.'

'You... asked around.'

'Yeah, while you were taking your long weekend I started asking about Satanic hotspots in Staten Island. When I got here I asked a few of the locals, reporters, and every answer came back to this place. Willowbrook. So I sent you that documentary so you could get up to speed.'

I tried to eyeball him but he was watching the decommissioned ferry. He must have spoken to Melissa; it was the only explanation. How else would he know?

'Well, to be more accurate,' he suddenly added, 'there are rumours of cults meeting in the ruins of this place. Apparently people say they hold Black Mass there and offer sacrifices, that sort of thing.'

'And the reporters you spoke to, they told you about the experiments and the fucked-up stuff that used to go on?'

'Yeah, the entire institution was the subject of an exposé in the seventies when a journalist managed to get inside. Kids were being injected with TB, fed each other's faeces, left crawling around in the dark with no supervision because of understaffing or whatever. So no wonder the site attracts fucking mental cases now.'

'Did any of the reporters recognize Trent?'

'No, but a local police officer thought he did. He said he stopped and searched someone for acting suspiciously a couple of months ago, but didn't take him in as he thought it would be a waste of a cell. The guy didn't have any drugs on him but he was muttering a lot of shit about the devil and being possessed.'

'OK. OK, so Trent might still be around.'

'Trent would have no other reason to be in Staten Island if it weren't for the Willowbrook thing. It just seems to fit.'

'You don't think he'd have come here to... carry on teaching or...'

'I don't think he'll be getting another teaching job after being fired twice, even if it is in this shithole.' He paused. 'The officer told me there's loads of homeless people living in the tunnels under the woods. There's a whole community of them, just living down there in the dark like rats, and the council leave them to it. Can you imagine?'

He sounded way too happy at the prospect.

'No, not really.'

America was fucked, I realized. As a Western country we had failed. We were a social experiment that had gone horribly wrong, that had driven half of its subjects insane and forced them underground, and had turned the other half into hedonistic psychopaths.

Even to look at, everyone here was an extreme compared to the stubborn mediocrity of people in England. People were either emaciated to the point of shadows or had turned themselves into trudging, listless tanks.

'Did you speak to anyone else about this?' I asked.

No reply.

'Did you speak to Melissa?'

If it was possible, he gave me even less of a reply. An icy gust of wind rushed in from the water and the shell of the boat seemed to groan.

'Look. I just wanna know.'

'He'll be there,' Eli said.

'And you're so certain of that, how?'

'I just know. He'll be there.'

He got back in the car.

I followed suit, and we travelled in relative silence for the rest of the drive.

In fact, all he said before we reached the hotel was, 'I'm looking forward to coming back to London with you now.

I didn't think I would but, with more consideration, it'll be like seeing an old friend.'

I was too busy judging the squalor of these houses to pay him much attention.

'Christ, if I had to live here I think I'd kill myself,' I said at one point.

And Eli nodded.

CHAPTER THIRTY-EIGHT

In some areas around Willowbrook Institution the trees had collapsed, sagging under the atmosphere. Branches and withered vines, blackened and mottled with disease, snaked along the ground and climbed buildings.

Eli slipped through the closely knit trees with the ease of a jungle cat. He didn't seem fazed by the place. On the contrary, he seemed, like he was arriving home.

I followed, wishing I'd stayed in the protective cocoon of the vehicle, feeling spiked foliage scrape my ankles and snag on my clothes. I wondered if anything here was poisonous. Everything looked ill. Plant something in the ground here and it'd grow up deformed.

Eli bounded up to the laundry and industrial building.

'Do you know where the tunnel entrances are?' I asked, uneasy about disturbing the silence.

'No.' He glanced back at me. 'But then, I've never lived here.'

'You suggesting we *ask* someone?'

We both looked around. The place was deserted.

'You'd think one of the homeless who live here would know.'

Even compared to Skid Row, the idea of sleeping here

horrified me. Though maybe it was harder to be scared of places like this when you knew that monsters didn't really exist; when most people looked at you and thought you were the monster. The people who claimed they'd been chased out of the woods by screaming wraiths had probably just come across a person trying to sleep, a person more terrified on a daily basis than they could understand.

Eli pushed aside branches, averting his face as the tendrils swiped across his cheeks, and climbed through a cavernous window.

'Really?'

'We're not going to find anything out there, are we?'

I looked at my smart, dust-covered shoes. I had a gun. This wasn't the UK, I thought. I have a fucking gun and I won't be chastised for using it. It was, perhaps, the only thing as a country we were doing right.

'OK, wait.'

I pushed aside the same branch and followed Eli. As I jumped to the floor I was sprung back up and lost my footing. The ground was carpeted with coils of wire; old mattress springs and fuck knows what.

'This is the laundry building?' I checked.

Eli was observing some graffiti; nothing Satanic, mostly just racist.

'I don't know,' he murmured. 'I don't know much about this place. Maybe we should split up?'

I raised my eyebrows. 'Fuck, no! You know all horror movies start with splitting up. It's the fucking *worst* idea ever.'

'This isn't a horror movie.' He looked back at me and smiled, the web of branches across the window casting a veil across his features. 'You're scared?'

I took the bait. 'Fine. We'll split up. You have a signal?'

We both checked our phones and I at least had four bars.

'Well, if I end up getting chased through the catacombs by the fucking Slender Man I know you'll have my back, eh. How long do you think it'll take to get any emergency services out here?'

He didn't seem bothered. Maybe he just had no imagination.

'I'll meet you back here in half an hour,' he said, and walked through a hole in the wall to our left.

I'd never explored abandoned buildings as a child. There hadn't been many near us. Even the boarded-up places in the suburbs never interested me. I waited outside while my friends ran from room to room, graffitiing, setting things on fire, committing acts of random destruction as boys are wont to do.

It was a lack of interest, I told myself, but it ran deeper than that. Maybe it was because I believed in hell, was able to believe in things you couldn't see, that I felt an almost paralysing fear when faced with an alien enclosed space.

It was OK for other people. For them, the only monsters they could imagine were human.

There was a torch on my phone, I reminded myself as I stuck my head out into the corridor.

'Fuck fuck fuck fuck fuck,' I sang to myself under my breath, to lighten the atmosphere.

Not far from me I could hear Eli walking, scuffing, kicking things out of his way.

It was dark, but I could see that the walls were practically rainbow-spattered. It should have been cheery but it wasn't.

Had Trent Byrne walked down this corridor? Had he put out his arms and maybe trailed his fingers along the plaster?

I held out my hands and tentatively touched the walls.

Light poured in from the holes in the ceiling, down

through the third and second floors and the exposed piping, reminiscent of the design I had in my own club.

'Ron!'

I went for my gun before I registered that the voice was Eli's, and the word was my name.

'Fuck,' I spat, beads of sweat dotting my forehead. 'Jesus fucking Christ.'

'Come and look at this!'

I returned to where we'd climbed in and followed Eli's call. I tripped and kicked out as wire coiled around my ankles like sentient plants.

Eli was in the next room, crouched by a broken wheelchair and shining his phone at the wall.

'That's fucking creepy,' I said, eyeing the wheelchair.

'No, that's not what I meant.' He beckoned. 'Look at this.'

On the wall, on the verge of being lost but not completely illegible, was an eight-pointed star.

'There's a few of them,' he said, shining the phone-torch up the wall and across the doorframe.

'Could be coincidence.' I shrugged. 'Not as if eight-pointed stars aren't a thing most kids get into doodling.'

'Pentagrams maybe, but not eight-pointed stars. They wouldn't be what most people would scribble if you asked them to draw a star.'

I wanted to explain it away. 'But it's just... So many people come through here. It's unlikely.'

Eli stood up, shaking his head. 'No, we're close.'

'He's probably gone now.'

'But we're close. We're closing in, Ron.' He clapped me on the shoulder as he left the room. 'We're closing in!'

I stood there watching him go, then went back to my corridor. There wasn't much here but drawings and rubble, but I stopped as I reached a shallow staircase leading down. I could go and get Eli, but that would have looked pathetic.

My children would do it with no fear. I knew them. They'd always been braver than me. They refused to believe in God for a start, which I minded less from a theological perspective and more because it must be terrifying for them. The idea of believing in nothing; a full stop, darkness, chaos, coincidence, the idea that we were just deluded barely progressive organisms that had lucked out by developing on the right piece of rock flying through space, surrounded by billions upon billions of other rocks, balls of gas, surrounded by nothing, no consciousness, just speeding towards an end with no point...

I looked down the stairs.

Was there no point?

I switched on my torch and descended.

The basement rooms. Now these motherfuckers were dark. The claustrophobia made it hard to catch my breath. I walked from room to room, shining my thin beam across old chairs and rusted bedframes.

'Fuck fuck fuck fuck fuck...'

After watching the documentary that Eli had sent me I kept expecting the light to hit some hind legs, the stunted feral limbs of malnourished children.

'Trent,' I called, as if he were a wayward cat. 'Trent! Here, Trent! Here, Trent, my boy...'

My beam fell across an old gurney, with the restraints still hanging off...

A face...

'*Fuck!*'

I dropped my phone and the beam flew across the room, plunging me into black.

Scuttling.

I scrabbled towards the light. My gun was forgotten, I just wanted vision. In the dark all I could see was the face. There had been a face.

I thought I was going to throw up.

Finding my phone, I shone it upwards, to the doorways and staircase.

Nothing.

I took out my gun.

'Who's there?' I shouted, sounding more dangerous than I felt.

Of course there was no reply.

The better part of my brain, the part not flatlining with fear, was already telling me there had been nothing there.

But I knew there had been.

There were footsteps on the stairs and I held out my gun, saw my shaking arm and felt disgusted. It was as if my dad was here. I was fine, but now my arm was shaking. I was an unsteady, hyperventilating fucking limb.

'Ron? You all right?'

It was Eli.

I lowered my gun and all evidence of the shaking arm disappeared.

'Yeah, I'm fine.'

'I heard you shouting. Thought you had found someone.' He appeared in the doorway with his own beam of light, more powerful than mine. 'Or someone had found you?'

'I thought I saw something. It was nothing.'

It wasn't nothing. I could still hear that movement across the floor.

We're closing in, I thought, turning the gurney behind me and giving it a kick. *We're closing in.*

CHAPTER THIRTY-NINE

Daisy

As I said earlier, this isn't a film. I didn't look up and see Noel waving from across a river. But sometimes a hunch is a hunch.

His absence weighed upon the Underground with more gravity than usual. At other times when he hadn't been there, by definition I just imagined him elsewhere, probably drunk. This time I came into the dressing rooms and asked Gail, 'Is Noel upstairs?'

She shook her head.

I sent him a text straight away, saying, *Where u at boi?*

'Did he say where he was going to be?' I asked.

Gail paused, hands to her hair. 'No.'

'Has he been in at all?'

'Um...'

'Gail, just like *focus* on me, yeah? On my face, yeah?'

She stopped fiddling with her hair slides and frowned at me.

'Has. Noel. Been. In?'

'No, what's your problem?'

'Fuck's sake.' I looked at my phone again and turned. 'I'm gonna be late.'

'Hey, what? We can't open without you!'

'How long have you worked here, Gail?' I gestured around us at some of the other girls. 'You can organize this shower for a bit, right? *No offence*, guys.'

I left through the staff door, already calling a taxi. As the call connected I spotted one across the street, cut it off and tried to get through to Noel instead. He wasn't answering and hadn't acknowledged my text.

I was panicking, and maybe that was enough of a warning.

I gave the driver Noel's address in Marylebone and tried to call him again.

'Fuck, Noel, just *answer*.'

I texted Ronnie, asking him to text Noel. He'd be more likely to respond to Ronnie. But it was still going to be too late.

This isn't a film. No one arrives in the nick of time because there would be traffic or a delay on the Victoria line. Or you'd miss the premonition altogether because you'd be buying lunch, and you might feel a creeping panic or anxiety in your gut but then you felt like this all the time because this was London and you'd been taking so many drugs that your body chemistry was essentially fucked...

I called Noel again.

The taxi driver eyed me in the overhead mirror but didn't say anything.

'Noel, if you get this can you just send a text or something? You don't have to come in but can you let me know you're all right?'

What if he wasn't at home? The thought hit me as his building came into view. I wouldn't know where else to start.

I got out of the taxi without paying.

'Oi!'

'In *a minute*,' I yelled. 'I'll pay you in a *minute*!'

He might have been with Caroline, I thought, as I ran up to the doors and hammered on all the buzzers.

The entrance hummed and opened itself.

I powered upstairs.

He wasn't with Caroline, I knew.

I reached his front door, banged on it and shouted, 'Noel! Open the door!'

No movement from inside.

'Noel, I fucking swear I'll—'

The door opened and Noel was staring at me. 'What are you doing here?'

'I...' I hadn't realized I was shaking, red-faced, out of breath. 'You're here.'

'Yep.'

'You're not at work.'

'No.'

'Why?'

'I'm off.'

'No, you're not.'

'And you came here to tell me that?'

There was something odd about him. I looked him up and down and pushed past into his flat. It stank in here, a real *man* smell. Women never managed to pollute a space with their degeneration like this. When women degenerated they still managed to be fragrant.

'What are you doing?'

He glared, still standing by the door. 'Nothing.'

'You seem weird.'

'*I* seem weird? Daisy, go back to work.'

I hesitated, feeling stupid, but only for a moment. There were a couple of empty bottles on his coffee table but not that many, not enough for a drinking session. I craned my neck so I could see the contents of the bin and then stomped into the kitchen.

'So you're just taking the day off?' I asked.

I opened and closed a few cupboards. Fridge was empty.

Noel shut the front door and came into view to roll his eyes. 'Yes. What do you want me to say?'

I walked up to him and peered into his eyes. They were watery, tired, maybe bloodshot.

'I don't know,' I said.

Moving down his small hallway to the bathroom and bedroom, he snapped, 'What are you *looking* for?'

I halted and looked over my shoulder.

He scowled back.

I put my hand on the handle of the bathroom door, watching for a reaction.

He stood there, stiffly, with his arms folded.

In the bathroom I crouched to rifle through the under-sink cabinet, stretched for the one behind the mirror. In the bin there was an empty pack of something. *Epilim*.

'What the fuck is this?'

'It's medication.'

'For what?'

'It's a… mood stabilizer.'

I found another empty pack. 'And this?'

'An antidepressant.'

'Why are they here?'

'I finished the course, I'm due another prescription.'

'You expect me to believe that?' I stood up, crushing both of the packets in my fist. 'You just *happened* to finish them at the same time?'

'Well… yes.'

'How many did you take?'

'It's none of your business.'

'I'm not leaving then.'

'Yes you *fucking* are.' He half-heartedly tried to take me by the arm.

'No!' I snatched it away. 'I'm gonna wait here until I'm convinced you haven't done something really fucking stupid and I don't have to call an ambulance.'

'Fine! Just... What are you gonna do, just stay here in my bathroom?'

'No.' I barged past him again. 'I'm going to sit on your sofa and *watch* you.'

'I'll go out.'

'Fine, go on then.' I leant against his sofa and waited.

He hovered, inclining his head towards the door but failing to move his feet.

'No,' he stammered. 'No, it's my fucking house.'

'Of course you weren't going out.'

'Why?'

'Because you've ...' Neither us wanted me to say it but I forced the words out. 'You've just fucking topped yourself and if you go outside someone's going to call an ambulance once you pass out.'

'I haven't *topped* myself.'

I got my phone out and dialled 999.

'What are you doing?'

'If you haven't, then you won't mind me calling paramedics to come look at you.' I held up the mobile, thumb poised over *Call*. 'They're not going to have to pump your stomach if you haven't taken anything, right?'

He said nothing.

My voice shook a little. 'Right? Because you haven't taken anything? Right?'

It had all been posturing until then, just stomping around to make myself feel better. I hadn't been certain, until then.

Noel picked up the beer bottles from the coffee table and went to drop them in a bag of recycling under his kitchen sink.

I followed him.

'Noel—'

'It's none of your fucking business.' He leant against the side, taking deep breaths.

'It fucking *is*. How fucking dare you! What, you're just gonna sign out, just… what, *leave* the rest of us here to deal with your shit? *Fuck* you! You don't just get to run away because you're not having fun! You think *any* of us are having fun?'

'Can you just get out of my face?'

I punched him, in the face. It hurt more than I was anticipating.

He clapped a hand to his cheek and for a second I thought he might punch me right back, so I started shouting, *'If you don't go and throw all that up I'll fucking kill you myself, you selfish piece of shit!'*

I blocked his path when he tried to sidestep me, and we stood head to head.

'This isn't fair,' he said.

'Life's. Not. Fair.'

'Who… the fuck… are you,' he said, 'to tell me there's something to live for?'

'I'm not telling you there's something to live for.'

'Then what are you *doing* here?'

'I'm just not letting you go *now*! You can't leave me to tidy up all this shit by myself, you've got to just…'

'What, just put up with it?'

'Oh grow up,' I scoffed.

I pushed him again, for good measure, and he grabbed me by the wrists. 'Fucking stop that!'

'What, are you gonna hit me? Go on! Go on, I dare you!'

'For fuck's sake…'

'Good luck keeping this up when you've got an ambulance here and little cartoon birds are flying around your head!'

'Christ, do you ever stop fucking *talking*?'

He pushed me away with disgust and I caught myself in the doorway, hurting my shoulder.

Noel held the bridge of his nose for a moment.

'Get out,' he said.

'No.'

'Daisy, fucking *get out* or I swear to God I'll…'

It had never crossed my mind that he would hurt me. It still hadn't, really. But I couldn't stand there for ever, in protest.

'If I don't hear from you in fifteen minutes I'm calling an ambulance,' I said, storming out.

'Yeah, you fucking do that!'

And he slammed the door.

On the verge of tears, my shoulder aching again for the first time in a while, I sat down in the hallway. I swallowed back the urge to cry, watched the clock, and waited.

CHAPTER FORTY

Ronnie

I had the dream again, before Eli woke me from my nap and said we were going back that same evening. The man dressed in cheap blue tat was getting closer, shuffling behind buildings. I got a better look at how he was walking, with his arms contorted back, straightened and upwards like wings, fingers splayed. He was standing on his toes and with his knees bent, like an injured stork.

Even if he caught up with me he didn't look capable of harm. He looked as though his limbs could be bent and broken like straws. But it was the way he moved that gave me the creeps...

'Ron, time to go.'

'Argh, fuck.'

I swung my legs out of bed and felt, for some reason, that this might be the last time I ever woke up. If we went into those tunnels tonight, I thought, that's where we would be staying.

Everything was so dark. Light was struggling.

I waited for Eli to get out of the car first, which he did.

We left the headlights on but they only followed us so far.

'Should we try a different building?' I asked.

'Yeah, I'm not sure laundry is where it's at.' He gestured at a spire, which could almost be mistaken for a tree. 'There's an entrance to one of the tunnels in there. Apparently they were concealed in case any patients worked out where they were and tried to escape.'

'OK.'

I wasn't OK, at all.

It was surprising just how much you could see when your eyes adjusted to moonlight. Eli said it would be better to let our eyes learn to cope with the darkness rather than blind each other with torch beams before we got inside. After the first minute I could see more than outlines. I could even see the thread-veins across leaves. I could see markings against brickwork.

Then Eli switched on his torch to get a better look inside a window.

'How will we even recognize him?'

'We might not.' He tentatively checked the window frame for glass. 'He'll recognize me though.'

I turned on my own torch and climbed into the building.

Somewhere inside, there came the scrape of feet against ground, voices...

'Shit!'

Even Eli sounded startled as we both fell into instinctive crouches and turned the lights off. I had my hand on the butt of my gun, though in this darkness I wouldn't be able to see who I was firing at. No moonlight here. Not a sliver.

'What the *fuck* was that?' I snapped, as quietly as I could.

The whisper still seemed to reverberate.

'Better to know we're not alone sooner rather than later.' Eli adjusted his crouch until he was in a position to spring. 'If it's him—'

'If it is him... he'll know this place better than us, even in the dark. He'll—'

There was a scuff of shoes in the doorway and we both leapt to our feet.

'Fucking show yourself!' I shouted.

'Don't shoot, *fuck*, don't shoot!'

Eli took one hand off his gun to shine his torch directly in front of us, and I lowered my weapon at the sight of a young couple almost shitting themselves with fright. Their hands were in the air and faces wide.

'Are you security?' the dude yelled, shifting in front of his girlfriend. 'We're sorry, look, we're really sorry, we were just looking around...'

'Fuck.' Eli breathed a sigh of relief and rested the butt of his gun against his forehead. 'No, we're police. We're looking for someone and had a tip-off he was here. I suggest you go home.'

'Yeah, we will. We'll go.'

'Have you seen anyone?' I asked, glad that I could sound assertive when called upon. 'Why are you kids even out?'

The girl piped up, 'Well, you know there's rumours that the kids who vanished were kidnapped by this bogeyman called Cropsey. He's meant to haunt the woods.'

'Cropsey?'

'Yeah, he's a ghost story.'

I shone my beam at the girl's face and she squinted. She was wearing a necklace of shells.

'In some of the stories he's a ghost, but most around here think he's just some homeless guy. Maybe a mental patient who never left.'

Eli motioned his torch at them. 'You know anything about the Satanic groups that come here?'

The guy said, 'Yeah, but no one's ever seen them. It was

a stupid idea for a date but we just thought it would be creepy. Fun-creepy.'

'Has there ever been any evidence of these rituals?' Eli asked.

She said, 'There's some graffiti back there, but not much. It's mostly talk. And the missing kids, but no one ever found them so...'

The boy looked pretty spooked now, just letting his date talk.

'The guy we're looking for, he's pretty dangerous. So we recommend you go home, OK?' Eli was hilariously serious for a moment. 'Don't approach anyone else you run into.'

'OK, we're sorry. We're sorry.'

She took hold of her partner's arm and hurried him over to the window frame, climbing out one after another. I could hear them exchanging profanities as they ran across the field towards the road. They'd be bricking it all the way back to civilization and beyond that, I thought. But at least they were able to leave.

'We should have checked...' I trailed off.

'What?'

'If Trent's been living here, we should have checked if there were any more disappearances. Since the eighties, I mean.'

Eli looked away and moved on as if I hadn't spoken.

I wondered if he was deliberately trying to split us up, and then followed him. Fuck that. I wasn't doing this one alone. Not tonight. We either both got out of here, or neither of us did.

I kicked away rubble and wire, and felt my way along the corridor.

'Where did you hear the entrance to the tunnel was?' I asked.

Eli shone his torch at the ground, searching for the promise of stairs nearby. 'The basement. There's gonna be beds turned on their sides and leant against the wall to hide it. Anyone who goes down there must put them back every time.'

'Anyone who's crazy enough to go down there.' My eyes were starting to itch from the dust in the air.

'Scared, Ron?'

He smiled at me. I saw him, even in the gloom. I couldn't fucking believe that he was smiling.

'Fuck. Off.' I stopped. 'You're dragging me into a tunnel full of crazy homeless and psycho ex-mental patients. They're all gonna be like Gollum down there!'

'They're not gonna have these though, are they?' He waved his firearm at me.

'No,' I conceded. 'But they have the element of surprise.'

'The more you keep talking, the more surprise they'll have.'

I wanted to retort, but he had a point. I caught up so we were walking side by side. I was thinking, *Both of us leave, or neither of us do.*

At the end of the corridor that would never end, we found some stairs. I peered into unused dormitories. There were rows of unmade beds, frame after frame standing there like fleshless carcasses.

As we went down into the hole, further and further, I wondered if Eli was still smiling.

There were curtains pinned to the walls and draped across furniture.

Who was still putting up curtains down here?

Eli was dragging an old bed to one side. I stood back and stared for a second before remembering to help. We lifted it off the floor and Eli let it fall to his left. The metal clanged and rattled to the ground and it took a long time for the angry echoes to die down.

Without any conferral, Eli walked into the tunnel.

It didn't look like a tunnel so much as the end of the world. The beams from our torches seemed swallowed by it.

Eli didn't seem to mind; he vanished into the dark as if he could see perfectly. It hadn't even broken his stride.

'Come on, it's fine,' I heard him call, like I was a nervous swimmer being coaxed into a pool.

'I'm not sure it is.'

'You get used to it.'

'See anything?'

'No.'

I took a step forwards, unsure where to put my feet.

'See anyone?' I called again.

'No.'

Something brushed against my foot and I leapt sideways, stumbling against something jagged and metal.

'Fuck's sake! Eli!'

'What?' The dim beam of light ahead of me halted and turned, sweeping across the floor.

'We're not going to find anything down here, we can't even fucking *see*!'

The beam shone into my face. 'It won't be any different coming back in daylight, we're underground.'

'This is fucking stupid. I'm waiting back here. You can give me some fucking signal if you find anything.'

'A signal, like what?'

I turned, my head starting to ache with the concentration required to not fall over something. 'I don't know. Shouting like hell and shooting something will probably be enough.'

There was an ominous quiet.

'I can't believe you're not coming with me.'

I couldn't find Eli with my torch any more. 'Where does this lead to? Maybe I can find the exit and come from the other side?'

'It's out in the grounds somewhere.'

'Out in the grounds' meant *above* ground, which was good enough for me.

'I'll be out there,' I said, unsure whether he could hear me. 'I've got a good sense of direction. If this tunnel goes in a straight line, I'll find where it comes out.'

Nothing back.

Taking a last look at the gaping hole, I turned and tried to find my way back to the staircase. I stood in the middle of one of the dormitories, a doorway in front of me and a doorway behind, and didn't recognize anything.

On second thought, had the dormitories been upstairs or downstairs?

Beds stared back at me. At least in the tunnel I'd had Eli's footfalls to give me some purchase on the space. The lone sound of my shoes on this floor was unbearable and inconsistent. I felt surrounded by the furniture suddenly and I paced towards the nearest doorway.

I didn't know if I was going in the right direction.

At the far end of the dormitory was a crucifix nailed to the wall. I was surprised it hadn't been looted.

I wondered if it had been there when the kids were being infected with hepatitis and tuberculosis, experimented on like rodents. Maybe that's why no one took it with them? It was as infected as everything else. The mattresses left leaning against the wall were stained deep with blood and crying and faeces and disease and semen and ugliness.

I kept moving, out of the dormitories and up some stairs. They weren't the same stairs as before; I didn't recall the cave-in down the centre, leaving them cloven like that. But I didn't care. Up was an improvement.

Everything was so fucking yellow. The walls had a sickly, jaundiced glow.

I took the corridor to my right. If I had my bearings, the tunnel was directly below. A door at the end promised to lead out of the building but it didn't. It was a windowless office. In the middle of the room, expectant, was an operating table. The leather was worn. Grey belts hung from the sides like lifeless arms.

There was no other exit.

I scanned the room, pacing around it with my eyes on the floor. It was covered in smashed glass. The phials and jars had probably been raided decades ago for cheap highs.

I crouched, putting my gun on the floor, and pulled a couple of drawers out of the overturned desk in the corner.

There were still papers, I was surprised to see.

I coughed into the cloud of dust that billowed into the needle of light emanating from my phone.

A lot of the writing was too small for me to read, but about four pages down, bent out of shape and almost illegible, was a parental consent form. *Tests.* That was how they had phrased it. Not anything so alarming or intrusive as *experiments*, but *tests*. Without that signature, without consenting to that paragraph, this child would have no place at Willowbrook.

The signature was smudged but the name printed beneath it was Darick West. He couldn't have had any idea, I thought. How could he? He couldn't have known that *tests* meant forced infection with hepatitis, diseased injections, the ingesting of other children's excrement...

Worse, maybe he *had* known. Maybe he'd just wanted the kid off his hands.

I tried to imagine signing one of my children away. I even tried to give Darick West the benefit of the doubt and imagine what it'd be like if one of them suffered from a disability that made their life unbearable to witness. But it didn't work.

No matter which way I looked at it there was no empathy, no understanding.

I looked up at the operating table and my eyes caught something in the gloom, something moving from the doorway. I tried to stand, fell sideways over the desk and grabbed the head of the table.

An explosion of noise, too much for my mind to cope with.

I heaved myself up. I'd forgotten my gun on the floor and I sprang back for it, aiming it at the space where the disturbance had drawn my eye. But there was nothing there. I lowered myself to retrieve my phone.

'Eli?' I called.

It hadn't been Eli.

I stepped over the desk, carefully placing the operating table between me and the exit. The door itself was gone. All the doors were gone for some reason.

One more time – 'Eli?'

No scuffling of feet. No face. I wasn't even sure I had seen anything.

I lowered my gun, slowly.

I crossed the threshold of the empty doorway and looked at the floor but there was no obvious disturbance in the dust. I don't know what I'd expected; cartoon-like footprints.

'Fuck's sake, *really*,' I said out loud.

I only needed to get outside. It was hardly *Crystal Maze*. Leave the building. All I needed to do was leave the fucking building. Why was I looking for a door when I could use a window?

Crossing into the dormitories, I climbed out into a wall of thistle and trees that hadn't been cut back for fifty years. I had to put my gun away to navigate it. I followed the building, clinging to the wall and skirting my way past holes, peering into rooms and seeing rows of latrines.

Foliage ripped at my back.

Paper-thin scratches on my cheeks.

When the building stopped and I staggered out of the undergrowth, I inhaled as if I'd been underwater. Now I could see the path back to the car.

I started walking towards it, brushing nature off my coat and out of my hair.

Both of us leave, or neither of us do.

I stopped.

What if Eli ran into trouble? What if he ran into Trent?

I looked back at Willowbrook and thought I saw Eli standing at one of the holes-for-windows. I raised my hand to wave. It didn't wave back. It was human, but it wasn't Eli. It wasn't Eli.

It wasn't Eli.

'Shit!'

Looking back at me, at the hole-for-window, wasn't Eli.

My gun and torch meant nothing. I tore back towards the car.

Flooded with fear. Fucking ringing with it. Sentience gone.

Get to the car.

Get to the car.

Get to the car.

It came into sight and my velocity caused me to slam straight into the bonnet.

If I got inside and started the car I'd have a mobile weapon. I could drive to the entrance, blast my way through the forest and find Eli, run right over that faceless breather in the window.

Shutting the door and locking everything, even checking the sunroof, I stared back at the buildings. I started the engine and the purr of the vehicle surrounded me, drowning out the humiliating thump of my heart.

I put the gun down on the seat next to me, shaking.

'Fuck...' It made me feel better, the senseless repetition of this word. 'Fuck fuck fuck fuck...'

I checked if I had any calls from Eli. I tried ringing him but it went straight to voicemail. He must still be underground.

Everything was locked. I checked again, and one more time to be sure.

I placed both hands on the wheel, almost rattling it loose.

Unblinking, I watched and watched the path, the trees, but no one came walking.

I wouldn't be able to drive back through the forest towards the tunnel, I realized. It was too dense. I was going to have to leave the car to get Eli.

Both of us leave, or neither of us do.

My gun felt light and ineffectual in my grip.

I took deep breaths for a few seconds before unlocking the doors.

'Fuck, Eli,' I muttered, getting out of the car again. '*Fuck, Eli!*'

CHAPTER FORTY-ONE

Even the moon had disappeared on the second time around. No natural light. Nothing. Even nature was conspiring against me. But then, nature wanted all of us dead in the end.

My eyes were fixed on the hole-for-window, but there was no face or human outline, no movement. If there was, I'd shoot it, I decided. Fuck questioning, fuck thinking, fuck logic, fuck humans and the value of life, fuck Trent Byrne and whatever had happened to him. If something appeared in that window, even for a moment, it was getting shot.

'Eli!' I shouted into the void.

It didn't matter if the thing knew I was coming. It was probably watching me right now. The more I announced my presence the more likely we were to avoid each other, like stamping through long grass to avoid snakes.

'Eli!'

Into the trees again, reopening old scratches, clearing centimetre after centimetre of space. Unbidden, the image of being cornered by some skeletal creature in this claustrophobic mess leapt into my mind. I felt sick, pushed it away.

I stopped, looked at my phone and tried calling Eli with my back against a tree, but there was no answer and no ringing.

I pushed forwards. My foot hit something metallic.

I couldn't tell if I had passed the window I'd climbed out of, but I felt as though I'd been walking for longer. Just as I thought I should have been reaching a turn in the building, the trees cleared and I stumbled into a clearing.

The ground had become dust and dirt. I shone my light around and the trees were thinner here, anaemic and leafless, creating a rough path to my right.

I followed it.

The forest hummed and whirred, making it impossible to hear if someone was following me or not.

I had no idea what the other entrance to the tunnel would look like, or whether it would even be visible.

'Eli!'

The path seemed to end. The building turned another corner and there was nowhere for me to go but back into the forest.

That didn't make any sense.

I followed the edge of the clearing in a circle, moving away from the walls and windows. About twenty-five yards away, when the trees started to become intrusive again, I spotted something.

It was as if someone had tried to create a bonfire, a haphazard pile of leafy branches and dead bushes all piled atop a half-buried wheelchair. I was reluctant to approach it, as it meant putting my gun inside my coat, but I took hold of the wheelchair's handles and shook it out of place. The wheels spun easily when tested, but more easily backwards...

I wheeled the artificial compost heap out of place, and saw it had been shielding a concrete hole.

It was a steep drop with a steel ladder embedded into the wall. At the bottom – by the looks of it – was a tunnel leading under the building.

'Oh, Jesus fucking Christ.' I fell into a crouch, shone my light down, and covered my eyes. 'This is *fucked.*'

I stood up, turned and found the third rung of the steel ladder with my left foot, torch wedged between two fingers as the rest of them clung, claw-like, around the ladder. I descended into the abyss, thousands of miles from home, and wondered how I had got here, how far and how deep into the earth I would follow Eli.

Sometimes I caught myself looking at him and thinking he was the devil himself. Why was I climbing into the tunnel to rescue him? Eli wouldn't need rescuing. Not from this. He belonged here.

Still... he hadn't come out the other side.

I felt for rung after rung until I hit solid ground. I was faced with the same dilemma as earlier; either keep on into the tunnel or wait here.

Taking out my gun. 'Eli!'

A pause, then I tried again with, 'Trent?'

Saying his name out loud dispelled some of my fear.

'Trent! You in here?'

'*Eughm.*'

I stopped dead.

It might have been a word, distorted by how confined we were, but it hadn't sounded like Eli's voice. It didn't sound entirely like a person.

'Eli? Is that you?'

It must have been. I just hadn't heard him properly. It must have been Eli. It *had* to have been.

I moved on. At least moving forward would provoke something sooner or later.

There were no footsteps apart from mine.

It could have been an animal.

I couldn't think about it. Just keep moving forward...

Don't think.

You didn't think before.

Not thinking brought you here.

'Eli, are you still fucking here?' I reached out and leant against the wall. 'Can you hear me?'

'*Gotta be quick, gotta be... quick.*'

This time I heard words and they were closer than before.

I jabbed the light before me like a weapon.

'Who's that?' I called. 'Eli? Show yourself!'

Tapping, like fingers drumming against metal.

I backed away, squinting into the tunnel.

The tapping stopped.

It was replaced with a scraping sound, feet being dragged against ground, then the same frantic rodent-like scrabble as before.

'Fuck—'

I turned and ran.

Barely ten strides and I ran clean into the ladder, busting my lip open.

Not even pausing to put my torch or gun away I hoisted myself upwards, deaf to everything. Two fingers weren't enough to grip and I slipped, my gun falling.

I was about to leave it and keep climbing but...

What if the thing got hold of it?

The idea was too grim to handle and I let go, dropping four or so feet and scrabbling about the floor. My knees jarred, and just as I found the butt of my gun—

Footsteps—

Something grabbed my wrist and I fired twice, both shots above my head and I was screaming into someone's face, screaming into mine.

Eli...

'Ron! *Ron*, fucking get a fucking grip!'

Eli. It was Eli.

'*Ron!*'

It was Eli.

I stopped. Even this close, almost nose to nose, it was hard to make out his features. But it was definitely him.

'Eli?' I lowered my arms and pushed him away. 'What the fuck was that?'

'What?'

'*That!*'

He stared at me without comprehension and it made me lose my shit.

'Don't fucking look at me like you don't know what I'm talking about, *that!*' I jabbed my gun over his shoulder. 'You didn't hear that?'

'Ron... there's nothing there. I just walked all the way through.'

'*Bullshit!*'

He frowned. 'Are you OK?'

I shook him by the collar. 'You're fucking *lying*! You *know* you're fucking lying! How can you just stand there and—'

'Get off!' He swatted my hands away and took a step back. 'The trees, the dark, it can make you hear and see things.'

'When I came out of the forest I saw someone standing in the window. It was a person, Eli, and you were down here. It wasn't you.'

Even as I kept talking, I knew I sounded crazy. But even as I kept talking, I knew I wasn't.

'What were you doing in the forest?' he said.

'That's not...' I sighed. 'That's not the point. I was round the front and I saw... You know what, never mind.'

I didn't know who was lying, who was mistaken, why we were on opposite sides. I couldn't believe that, even after all of this, I didn't know him well enough to tell for sure when he was being truthful. He had no reason to claim to have not heard that voice. Why would he lie about something like that?

'You really didn't see anything?' I said eventually.

'No. It's deserted.'

'Then why does it emerge here?'

'What?'

'This ladder leads up to a clearing in the woods. It doesn't go to another building.'

'It should.'

'You think it splinters off anywhere?'

He hesitated. 'I don't know, maybe I missed something.'

My heart rate was still insane, arteries overflowing with adrenalin. What disturbed me more was the possibility that I might have imagined it. How did you carry on once you'd admitted to yourself that sometimes you saw and heard things that weren't there?

I still had bullets. 'OK, we can check.'

'You OK?'

'OK as I'll ever be.'

This time I felt more prepared. I took the right and he took the left, shining our lights along the walls.

'People have been down here,' Eli observed.

'How can you tell?'

'Because I didn't trip over anything. It's being kept clear.'

'The entrance back there was hidden by a load of bushes on a wheelchair.'

'So this must go somewhere...'

'Sideways, not just forwards and back.'

I started dragging a hand along the wall. The tunnel was wide enough for about three people; two people and a gurney in width.

After a while, when we had built up pace, my hand fell into air and my light fell into another tunnel.

I backhanded Eli's shoulder and he stopped.

'I didn't even see it,' he said.

The brief sense of empowerment evaporated. I put my palm against the wall and followed the corner.

'It's meant to lead to the operating rooms,' Eli said, following me. 'The health centres.'

'Labs?'

Now I was stepping into the light on the floor. The walkway was still clear.

'Why would you come back here?' I asked, my voice now significantly quieter. 'If you'd been shut off here for your whole childhood, why would you come back?'

'*Because* you've been shut off here for your whole childhood? If you were suddenly faced with the world, having never seen it before, wouldn't you want to return to somewhere familiar, whether it was good or bad?'

I caught sight of some colour, out of the corner of my eye.

WANT TO COME AND PLAY?

In red.

I knocked my fist against the graffiti and called, 'Hello?'

'What are you doing?'

'I want them to know where we are.'

'Why?'

Tapping, like the sound of a dozen rats from far away.

I stepped back until my shoulder knocked against Eli's, torch resting on top of my gun.

'Sounds like dogs,' he said.

'Yeah, you keep telling yourself that. I'm sure dogs wrote that shit all over the walls too.'

He moved past me and there was a horrifying crash.

The noise zigzagged off the walls and ceiling with a violence that seemed to be visible in the air.

I almost fired into Eli's back with shock, but then realized he had walked into a gurney. It had been left across the tunnel like a roadblock. We'd just tripped someone's alarm.

'Suppose that gurney just arranged itself into that position, eh,' I said, shoving it to one side.

Tapping again.

Not rats.

Not dogs either.

'I think we should go back,' I muttered.

'Why?'

'We don't know how many there are.'

Rustling from way behind us.

'And they know these tunnels better than us.' I took Eli by the shoulder.

'But—'

'I really think we should go back now.'

'But can't you hear—'

'Let them follow us out.'

He shrugged me off.

'Eli, for fuck's sake.'

'*Gotta be quick, gotta be quick.*'

From behind us, too close, *way* close, close enough to make me run, without even thinking, past the gurney, light strobing, illuminating nothing and distorting everything. I didn't know if Eli was running with me. There was too much noise. My footsteps echoing, maybe not my footsteps at all...

'Eli!'

I called over my shoulder and ran into something solid that swung open, heavy metal. I careered through it and went to slam it shut behind me before remembering, again…

'Eli!'

But he wasn't here.

I swung and aimed my torch at the new space, pushing the door shut with my shoulder. Something flew at me, casting light against gnashing front teeth and holed gums and eyes that looked like Eli's – it looked so much like Eli – before my phone dropped and skidded away, and I was left blind and at the mercy of touch and noise, so much noise, my hands around a throat.

I emptied my bullets into the mass throwing itself against me, not thinking about direction. Forward, only forward. There was hacking, putrid breath against my face.

The thing went limp and fell, obscuring the thin sliver of light picking out an arrow of dust particles on the floor.

Clicking clicking clicking clicking…

I looked at my trigger finger, still convulsing. I couldn't make it stop.

The door behind me opened.

'Ron?'

I didn't trust that the voice was Eli's. Eli wasn't here.

'Ron, are you OK?'

I stared at the door's outline in the dark.

It swung open slowly, metal creaking against hideous metal.

Eli shone light at his own face.

I looked at the form on the ground.

Lodging my foot under flesh, I turned it over. It had been lying across my phone. As I bent to pick it up, Eli crouched with me, and we both shone light into the thing's face. All my shots had entered its torso, leaving artful crimson spatters across an already soiled shirt.

My mouth was dry, useless to language. 'Trent?'

He shook his head. 'I don't know.'

'I thought it was you.'

He looked at me, with no expression.

'I thought it was you,' I repeated.

I had visions of the creature's limbs coming off in my hands as we carried it out of the tunnel and through the dormitories, out via the same hole-for-window that I hadn't been able to find on my way back alone.

It almost made me have to drop him, the idea of his arms coming away from his shoulders and being left holding them like a pair of ski poles.

Even worse, I began to fantasize that it wasn't dead. It wasn't enough to feel the lack of pulse, the staggering dead-weight, but I had to stare – really fucking stare – at those bullet holes, to the point that Eli stopped, dropped the feet and asked, 'Do you need a moment?'

Blinking. 'I'm fine.'

'Are you sure?'

'Yeah, why?'

'You're quiet.'

Ironically, I didn't have anything to say to that.

He said, 'I really did lose you, you know.'

'I know.'

'I got there as fast as I could.'

'Yeah.'

'And you're still alive.'

'Eli, I'm fine.'

I thought it was you, I thought. *I thought it was you and I hadn't hesitated to kill it.*

In the glare of our torches and the light from the moon, it didn't look like Eli. I don't know what had made me see the resemblance. The dark did that to you apparently. Without any reference, a familiar point, your mind starts to conjure recognizable things.

I thought it was you.

I wondered if it was obvious to Eli that 'I thought it was you' translated so easily to 'I thought it was you, so I killed it.'

Such a hideous yet inevitable accident it would have been, to kill Eli in that darkness.

Hideous, yet inevitable.

'Lucky you got him before he bit you,' Eli remarked. 'He might have had rabies or something.'

'Probably did.'

'Like I said.' He shone his torch into the thing's mouth. 'Dogs around.'

We could both see that it wasn't Trent.

There was blood all over me.

I mimicked Eli's pose and pulled back the creature's lips to reveal blackened and veined gums, not many teeth left to bite with but the front ones were still intact. He must have thought that was lucky, maybe. Still had a smile to show the world if he needed it, while the insides of his body decayed and rotted out of view, like a family pet that had crawled under a veranda to die.

Letting the lips fall back into place, I backed away.

Blood, I remembered. All over me.

I climbed into the driver's seat to get away from people both alive and dead. But Eli followed.

We sat for a while, side by side.

He said, 'We can always—'

'I'm going home.'

It must have been true this time, because he didn't fight me.

CHAPTER FORTY-TWO

Daisy

We both drank water with trembling hands; mine from crying and his from vomiting. It didn't take long for me to become amused by how terrible we looked, sat in front of the sofa rather than on it.

'What could possibly be funny?' Noel muttered, as I started giggling.

'What *isn't*?'

I gestured at the two of us and he nodded. 'Ah, yes. Fucking hell, the state.'

His under-eyes were black, and the rest of his face drained of colour.

My cheeks felt red and swollen.

We sat shoulder to shoulder, so close because it was reassuring to feel that he was still there, even if it was begrudgingly. The inside of the flat had darkened as the sun disappeared outside, but neither of us could be bothered to turn a light on.

'Do you think anyone's ever killed themselves just because they've needed to know?' I mused.

'Know what?'

'What actually happens when we die.'

'Dunno, the options seem shit either way.'

'Big dude in the sky or…'

'Nothing.'

I shrugged. 'I'm not an atheist, so…'

'I think I'm half-atheist. I don't think there's a big man up there or… down there. But I think it's an all right thought, the idea of rotting down in the ground and being food for plants and trees and all that nature shit.'

'That's not atheist, that's just being a fucking hippy.' I watched him for a reaction and he managed to laugh.

'No one's ever called me that before.' He drank some more water. 'I don't know how Ronnie does it, believing in all that wank full-time. It must do his head in. No wonder he's so fucked.'

'Do you think he's coming back?'

He glanced at the living room window. 'I don't know.'

'Maybe you should start thinking about that.'

'Edie's been thinking about it, hasn't she?'

'Can you blame her?'

'She wants you to manage the place.' He gave me a side-eye. 'I'm not an idiot, despite appearances. You know she's not gonna let you do it alone, she'll have someone in mind to keep an eye on you. She might… even be selling up. Huh.'

He paused, as if he'd surprised himself.

'She could be selling up,' he repeated

'What does that mean for you guys?'

'Well, I won't cause a scene. I fucking love it, it's my home. But I fucked up, I can take the hit and move on. Ron won't go quietly. He'd burn the club to the fucking ground before he gets elbowed out. But she'll know that.'

'Do you think Ronnie knows?'

The most animated of shrugs. 'I know fuck all about Ron

right now. The last time we spoke he was going on about a mental place in Staten Island and he thinks he's met a guy who can turn metal into golf.'

'Golf?'

'*Gold*. Gold, not golf. Fuck, you'd be the shittest alchemist ever.'

It seemed frivolous to laugh for too long.

'So you haven't told him about Seven then?'

'Na, not the sort of thing you do over Skype. We can deal with that when he gets back, if Edie gives us time to deal with it.'

'I might...'

He looked at me before I had the balls to finish the sentence.

'I might be able to give you some time.'

A smirk. 'Look at you, Mr Big-shot.'

'Well, she's listened to me before. Maybe she'd listen if I just... asked.'

'Maybe it'd turn out better for you if you just kept your loyalties a bit closer to your chest.' He nodded at my chest, with meaning. 'But thanks for the offer, you cheeky fucking upstart. You wanna take on the Russians for us as well? Seeing as you're the fucking *Don* now.'

'I just saved your arse, didn't I?'

'Yeah, great, I'm not gonna be able to sleep for twenty-four hours in case you have me sectioned.' He leant his head back against the sofa and sighed. 'While I have to stay awake, wanna have sex?'

'Don't take this the wrong way, you're usually an all right-looking guy, but at this precise moment I'd rather lick a tramp.' I patted his leg.

A shrug. 'Worth a try though.'

'Always worth a try.'

He raised a fist and I bumped it.

A phone started ringing. We both stared at each other until I recognized it as mine, and I scrambled for my pocket.

It was Ronnie. But it wasn't just Ronnie who came back.

CHAPTER FORTY-THREE

Ronnie

London was a village, I realized; an incestuous, bitchy, horrible little village. People had no concept of living anywhere it was impossible to function without a car. You could walk everywhere you needed to. Roads were the width of two cars only. Buildings were crammed in, compact, not stretched desperately across every inch of free space.

You couldn't do what Eli and I had done here. The very law of statistics dictated that someone would be close enough to witness a murder. There was an audience for everything.

I hated it.

I thought I hated America, with all its space and anonymity. But no, it was this I hated; the people.

Eamonn had been staying in mine and Rachel's guest bedroom for a fortnight and was already grating on everyone apart from the kids. He was great with the kids.

I sat up on our kitchen counter and watched Eamonn playing a trampoline-based game of basketball with Ryan and Chantal in the garden, springing back and forth from the safety nets and laughing.

'How long is he going to stay here?'

I looked across the room at Rachel straining some coffee. 'Until he can afford somewhere by himself, I guess.'

'By himself? In London?'

'Well, he'll probably have to get a flat-share...'

'OK, and when's that likely to be?'

'When he gets a job.'

I could tell she wanted to ask when that was likely to be as well, but she didn't.

Things had been weirdly formal between us since I'd returned, as if I was a butler. Too many *please*s and *thank you*s for my liking.

I thought it might sometimes be like this for women; having to reacquaint themselves with someone before feeling at ease with the former levels of intimacy. But it felt deeper than that.

'It's complicated,' I said, answering the question she hadn't asked. 'I'm not going to just hand him a job, because how will he learn if I do that? He needs to seriously think about what he's going to do with his life. If he does, he could really have a go at making a new start here.'

'You won't give him a job even if it helps us?'

'He's the one who needs help right now.' Once again, I was surprised to be sticking up for him. 'He been out of society for fifteen years, the kid doesn't know where he belongs any more. The most important thing we can do is make him realize he's at least a part of the family. Ryan and Chantal love him, you can't argue with that.'

She hadn't taken her eyes from the cafetière.

'Is he dangerous?' she asked.

I realized that was the question she had been working towards all along.

'No.'

She watched Eamonn slam-dunking on the trampoline, tackling Ryan to the mat while Chantal keeled over, breathless with laughter. Rachel looked as though she wanted to go out there and drag them both inside.

'You've never quite explained to me why he ended up in prison,' she said.

'Yeah, I have.'

'You've said he was charged with accomplice to murder but you didn't say why.'

I really wanted some coffee – my eyes slid down towards the waiting mugs and cafetière – but I thought it would be an insensitive moment to bring it up.

'His friends, these guys who he was hanging around with at the time, kicked a man to death and Eamonn was there. He didn't land a blow but he didn't exactly stop them either.'

'Yes, you've said that. You know you've said that. But why did they do it?'

'Um.' There wasn't any good way to phrase it. 'They thought he was gay. I don't know if he was... But I guess that doesn't matter, does it? They thought he was.'

It took a lot to make Rachel look this horrified.

'Is he some kind of neo-Nazi?'

'What? Fuck, no. How could you jump to that conclusion?'

'That's what neo-Nazis *do*.' Her gaze snapped back in the direction of Eamonn and the kids. 'I'm not sure I want him here around the kids.'

'He didn't do it!' I snapped. 'Eamonn's a lot of things but he's not a murderer.'

'But he was clearly with hanging around with people like that.'

'He was scared, Rach. I know you might find this hard to believe but sometimes you can't always run to the police.'

I was getting flustered. 'How come you're only bringing this up now? He's been here for two weeks.'

'And I think two weeks is long enough, I don't want him to start thinking this is his house and assume he can stay rent-free for ever.'

'He's not on fucking holiday, Rach!'

There was a silence. We never swore at other. Not in sixteen years of marriage.

A peal of laughter came drifting in through the window.

I slid down from the side and went to hug her. 'I'm sorry.'

She acquiesced but it wasn't returned. Her body felt unyielding, like a mannequin. I retreated after what felt like the expected amount of time, and hoisted myself onto the side again.

Eamonn was in the role of goalkeeper now, trying to keep the kids' shots out.

'And I'm sorry, I really don't like Eli.' She sounded as though she had been keeping these complaints pent up for a while. 'I know he's your friend and your parents have known him for years but he gives me the creeps; I don't want him in the house any more.'

'Why don't you like him?'

'I just...' She shook her head. 'I don't know, I just don't.'

'Has he said anything weird?'

'No, it's not even anything he's said, it's more how he looks at people.'

'He's just a private person, Rach.' I shrugged, determined not to acknowledge her completely valid point. 'I know he can make people uncomfortable because he doesn't talk that much and he seems a bit... autistic maybe. But not letting him in the house, that's a bit much. Especially if you can't even pinpoint why you don't like him. I mean, if you could give me an example...'

She sighed. 'No. Just forget about it.'

'No, seriously, if you wanna tell me something about him you don't like then go for it.'

It was a dickhead move but I couldn't help it. I wanted Eli here. No, I *needed* him here.

She glared at me and walked out, leaving the coffee strained but not poured; an irritating, but effective gesture of defiance.

That evening I dropped into the Underground to check on Eli.

I saw him talking to Daisy at the bar and she was laughing. Daisy flirted with everyone – it was in her make-up, how she interacted with the world – but it still bothered me. I wasn't sure why.

'Can I get a word?' I said to Daisy, indicating upwards.

Daisy, to my chagrin, glanced at Eli.

He circled the bar. 'Don't worry, I'll cover you. I can't make cocktails though.'

She shrugged. 'Neither can I, mate. They get what they're fucking given.'

I walked off and up the stairs, looking over the club floor and deciding that everything seemed to be running smoothly.

Coralie was dancing onstage, lights turning from purple to gold to red, and no one was inappropriately drunk or loud. In fact, it was nicely quiet. But everything that wasn't outdoors and bathed in natural light felt like a tunnel now.

Daisy followed me upstairs and I could feel dry amusement radiating from her.

'What's up with you?' she asked.

'How's Eli getting on?' I asked back, ignoring her. 'You seem to be getting on *well*.'

I pulled out the swivel chair and sat down.

Daisy remained standing, hands on her hips. 'Honestly?'

'Honestly.'

She went and shut the door. 'I don't like him.'

I faltered. 'What?'

'You know he's completely insane, right?'

'He's...' I thought of Eli, standing in that tunnel of blood, *the beast*, and lied, 'not insane. What are you talking about?'

'Ronnie, I know he's your friend but you said to be honest. He's crazy town.'

I began to smile, taking it for a joke. 'Oh shut up, Daisy. You're kidding?'

'Er, no.'

'But you guys seemed to be getting on. I mean, you were all...' I made a vague wiggle of my hips in the chair to demonstrate flirtation. 'You were giving him the total "fuck me" routine.'

'Ha! I was all...' She mimicked my gesture in her leather hot-pants, 'was I?'

'Well, yeah, you were hair-flicking and all that.'

She snorted and sat down opposite me, turning a few times in the chair. 'Look, I hate tonnes of people who come in here, but you give them a customer service smile, don't you? You can't be honest with everybody about what you think of them, you'd never get any business.'

'I'm surprised. I thought you guys were hitting it off.'

Daisy raised her eyebrows. 'I'm surprised *you* couldn't tell when a girl is faking it.'

I frowned. 'What exactly don't you like about him?'

'I told you, I wouldn't trust him. I don't even know what he wants, money or whatever, but he's just got this look on his face like... he just wants to be entertained. I was asking him loads of questions about what you guys got up to in the States, and when he didn't want to answer he just didn't. It's weird. He just stares at you until you ask something else.'

I resented that the *women* were rallying against us.

'Don't you think you're exaggerating?'

'No.' She was totally serious. 'Trust me, I have a radar for fucked-up men.'

'You're going out with Nic Caruana and you claim to get psychic *vibes* about people?'

A long, drawn-out pause, then she shrugged. 'Touché.'

'Eli's going to keep Edie off our backs. That's important.'

'I know. Doesn't mean I have to trust him.'

'Well, in situations like this, don't trust anyone. That's the only smart thing you can do.'

'*You* trust him though, don't you.'

I paused. 'He's done a lot for my family. I don't have any reason not to.'

'Maybe you're right,' she said in a monotone. 'Maybe it's just me.'

It was a platitude and we both knew it.

'Daisy, am I missing something?' I asked.

She folded her arms.

'I mean it, be straight with me. Am I missing something?'

'I don't know. I mean, I don't know him like you do and it could be nothing.' She turned circles in the chair again. 'I guess just keep an eye on him, make sure he isn't trying to get *you* to do something.'

'Do what?'

'I don't know, *something*. He's gonna want something. Just can't work out what, that's all.'

CHAPTER FORTY-FOUR

I went to see Noel at his flat. I had been putting it off for too long. It was the galling predictability of it that I hated; the endless conversations about AA, drinking, the pessimistic generalizations about life, his bloodshot eyes and paranoia.

He buzzed me in without a word and I took the lift up to his floor, wondering if it might have been better to send Daisy instead. Her methods of coping with Noel in this state were better than mine.

It also helped that Noel was tragically in love with her and would do almost anything she asked. He didn't know it yet. But I knew how Noel got when he liked somebody.

He had left the front door open.

It smelt like a smoker's flat again. It was the only way he could say 'fuck you' to Caroline now she had gone.

Noel was sitting in his living room, cigarette in hand, laptop open on the coffee table.

I didn't offer a greeting and he didn't look up. Instead I sat on the arm of the sofa and listened to the tinny music coming from the laptop speakers. I dropped my bag on the floor and took my coat off.

'Well, here we are again,' I said.

Before I had kept that sentiment to myself, but this time

I wanted him to hear it. Every time I found it harder and harder to sympathize. I realized that probably made me a shit friend, but I couldn't help it. I didn't know why he couldn't just... *not* do this.

'The place hasn't burned down without me,' he replied, nonplussed, checking his fucking emails or something. I almost shut the laptop over his fingers.

He didn't look as terrible as he had on other occasions. I thought – with some sadness – that it was probably because his body had acclimatized to being poisoned.

'When are you going to go to a meeting?' I asked.

'I don't want to go to a meeting.'

'Well, you are.'

'They don't work.'

'How would you even know if they work? You've never been to more than five in a row.'

'I'm not like those people who go to things like that.' He sat back and at least looked at me. 'Why is everyone so desperate to have a problem?'

'You *do* have a problem,' I said.

'Who is it a problem for?'

'Everyone *but* you, you selfish fuck!' I stood up. 'You think Edie is just gonna let you wander back in once you're done with this tantrum?'

'No, I've never thought that.'

Nothing on his face even flickered.

'Sometimes I think you only do this because we put up with it,' I said, spreading my hands. 'Do you want to tell us what to do this time? Or do we wait for you to snap out of it?'

He grimaced. 'Honestly, I just want to be left alone.'

I decided to go for a different angle, sitting down again. 'Look, I know you had feelings for her—'

'Of course I had *feelings* for her, she's my fucking wife.'

'I'm not talking about Caroline and you know it.' I gave him a stern look. 'I know you think you could have done things differently, we all do, but it's happened. It's done.'

He didn't say anything. He was glaring though, which was an improvement.

'This. Isn't. About. Her.'

I laughed at him. 'You fucking liar.'

I'd wanted him to spring right out of the sofa and punch me in the face, really go for me, but he just stared with these big sad eyes and said, 'It was personal. She left me a letter.'

This was news to me.

'Well, a note,' he elaborated, realizing that his rollie had gone out and relighting it.

'Saying what?'

'Sorry, mostly.' He rubbed his forehead. 'I think I'd actually care less if she'd done us over without the apology. I'd have some respect for her just being an ambitious fucking bitch. But it was the note that got me.'

I slipped off the arm of the sofa and sat next to him.

'So, what, you're just going to let her win?'

He shut his laptop, ceasing the electric whine of what-ever band had been playing, and plunged us both into silence.

'She's already won,' he said. 'And I think I'm all right with that.'

'Yeah, you seem all right.'

'I'm so fucking tired of fighting it. It's so hard. I keep thinking I'll reach this point in life when things stop being hard, but it doesn't fucking stop.'

'No, it doesn't.'

I wished I could tell him something different. This wasn't

Disneyland. Santa Claus didn't exist and the world wasn't going to reward you for being a good person.

'You can't just hide from everything,' I added.

'Can't you?'

'Not unless you wanna go live underground somewhere.'

I laughed nervously.

Noel seemed to be giving the idea some consideration.

'We can get Nic to find Seven,' I suggested. 'Or we can stick with Mark, if you'd prefer, even though he costs a fucking leg.'

'Ron...' He sighed.

'OK, Mark then. He's international, isn't he?'

He raised a hand. 'Ron, there's something we need to talk about. Should've opened with this really, but me and Daisy weren't sure... Well, we weren't sure how to go forwards with it.'

'What are you talking about?'

'Seven's still in London, we've both seen her. We both saw her talking to a guy I recognized. Daisy recognized him too because he came to the club claiming to be looking for us. He's called Sean and—'

'OK, OK, get to the fucking point.'

'He's mates with Roman Katz.'

'Katz, the Russian?'

'Yeah, the Russian.'

'The Russians who Mark Chester works for? Sean knows them?'

'Yeah, that's who she was working for. It was Katz.'

Conspiracy, spreading through my mind like a disease. 'You don't think Mark knew about this?'

'I don't think so. But who knows, I mean, Mark is... Mark.'

'*Fuck!*' The exclamation exploded out of me with such velocity that Noel started. 'He doesn't know! He was in

Chicago looking for Seven because of a Russian tip-off. Mark doesn't know this. Like, he *can't* fucking know.'

'Fuck me, he is human after all.' He blinked and picked gunk out of his eyes. 'We need to do something about this, but it's just... It's fucked. I don't want to get into a thing with that lot.'

'No...' I nodded. 'But you *need* to come into work if we're gonna deal with this, because we're not gonna be able to keep on otherwise.'

'I'm not gonna be much fucking use.'

'You'll be there. Put in some face-time for Edie, that's what matters right now. I don't even care if you're drinking, turn up hammered for all I care. Just fucking turn up. We should call Nic as well.'

He looked around, at the walls surrounding us, and I knew what he was thinking. He was thinking about escaping too. But, in the absence of a solution, he shrugged.

'If it'll make everyone leave me the fuck alone,' he said, when no escape hatch swung open.

I took that as a small victory, and clapped him on the knee. 'Good man. Right, let's get some coffee down you. If we have to waste a bitch, we're not gonna let Edie take our fucking place away, yeah?'

CHAPTER FORTY-FIVE

Daisy

I stopped just outside the tube station to roll and light a cigarette, and as I did so I felt Eli brush past me. Even though I didn't see him right away, something told me it was him. The air around him was corrosive.

The first thing he had said upon meeting me was, 'Who is this little piece?'

Little piece.

Not even a person, just a piece of one. All the while looking at me like I was a rodent he'd found in the cellar, cute until he broke its neck with his foot. I'd never trusted men who addressed women like that, and I wasn't about to start now just because he and Ronnie were bum-boys.

Forgetting my cigarette, I fell into step with him, lagging several feet behind until, apropos of nothing, he turned and met my eyes.

'You should have said hi,' he said.

'Well...'

It was deeply uncomfortable walking beside him. I kept veering away like one leg was longer than the other. Maybe he was his own force, throwing compasses out of whack.

It wouldn't surprise me to find out Eli had been walking the earth since the dawn of time.

'How are you finding it, being back?' I asked.

'You feel a lot bigger here.'

'I'd have thought given the size of most Americans you'd feel smaller.'

'I mean taller, in a way. Conquering the States takes size. Being back here makes you feel like a leviathan.' He reached out a hand, squinting at it as we walked. 'I feel like I could crush these buildings.'

'So... good then?'

He smiled. 'I could envision staying a while.'

'Well, as long as Ronnie needs you.'

'Maybe. What about you?'

'What?'

'You can't be staying here for ever. Shouldn't you be off to college? Sorry, uni? Or might you be looking at a more managerial role now?'

'Now what?'

'Now Ron's going it alone.'

'Noel's coming back, you know.' It was said with zero conviction, rolling a cigarette and pretending not to see the lighter he offered. 'He's just taking some time off for personal reasons.'

'That's not what I've heard.'

I took a long, aggravated drag. 'It's personal. So you wouldn't know.'

'Sometimes immersion can stop you from seeing the bigger picture.'

'There is no bigger picture, it's just Noel's private business.'

'It stops being private when it starts affecting your work.'

'Look, you know shit, *new boy*,' I snapped.

I dropped my cigarette, which was the only thing I registered until I realized he'd taken me by the throat and walked me sideways into an alleyway. He pinned me against a wall and there were no beads of sweat on his face and no dilation of his pupils. He was that fucking close and that fucking calm.

I couldn't breathe.

'I know about you,' he hissed. 'And you should stay out of my *fucking* way.'

I tried to twist out of his grasp but it was like being pinioned by metal. There was no give. A whisper of oxygen reached my lungs but I couldn't speak, couldn't move, couldn't do anything...

'Or I will *end* you.'

He took his hand away from my throat but didn't step back.

Coughing, I kept my back flat to the wall. Looking sideways towards the main road I could see an ocean of people choosing not to see.

'Ron will kill you for this,' I managed to say, with a weak rasping voice.

'He doesn't give a shit about you. You may have got the mistaken impression that you've accumulated some influence in his absence. But you're nothing. I wouldn't even remember doing away with you.'

I could have passed out, thrown up, started crying, but I held it all back, just about.

He took a step back, as suddenly as he'd attacked, and straightened my denim jacket for me.

We stood there looking at each other, and then he held out a hand, indicating for me to precede him out of the alleyway.

I refused to move.

He smoothed back his hair and left.

As soon as he was out of sight I exhaled, and a wave of tears came out with it.

'Oh fuck... Fuck.'

I leant against the wall with my hands over my eyes, taking deep breaths. My entire self felt violated, as if he had tried to suck out my soul through his hands. I forgot sometimes that I wasn't impervious. I'd been surrounded by men like this for so long, it had stopped occurring to me that any of them could do me harm.

Did Edie know what this guy was capable of? Did Ronnie, really?

I had a vague idea. It seemed stupid at first, but I took out my phone, angrily brushing the tears away, and composed a text to Mark. Before sending it, I hesitated, and then sent it to Nic as well.

Leaving the alleyway, I started rolling myself another cigarette and dropped tobacco all over the pavement.

Eli was long gone.

CHAPTER FORTY-SIX

Ronnie

I could tell she was thinking about throwing a plate at my head, but she couldn't with the kids in the house. It had been a while since someone had looked at me with that much venom. Only someone who really loved you was able to achieve that special brand of hate and disappointment.

'If you've got something to say,' I said, calmly. 'Then right before the school run probably isn't the best time.'

A beat, where she listened for the kids' whereabouts, confirming they were upstairs. 'You have the nerve to tell me, after *weeks* of nothing, that you don't want to talk about something right now?'

'There's no need to be dramatic, I was just busy.' I circled the table, away from her.

'Ronnie, *he's still here.*'

'I know, that fact hasn't *escaped* me. But where do you want him to go?'

'Anywhere!'

'Well, that's just not practical.'

'About as practical as getting off the plane with him, giving me *no* warning.'

'To state the obvious, Rach, you'd have said no.'

'That's not an excuse! Can you even hear yourself?'

We both took a moment to glance at the ceiling, to check our voices weren't carrying.

'I couldn't just abandon him.'

'So you keep saying, but apparently abandoning us when it suits you is fine.'

She didn't know it, but she landed that blow. It knocked the fucking wind out of me.

'You weren't *abandoned*—'

'Tell that to *them*. I had to make so many excuses for you!' She put both hands flat on the table, staring downwards for a long time.

Upstairs, Ryan was shouting something at his sister through the bathroom door.

'Either he goes or we do,' she said.

'Don't be ridiculous.' I walked out of the kitchen.

'No, I'm serious! The entire time we've been together it's been me who's had to change *everything*. You've never had to compromise—'

'Because I'm the one out there fucking *making* it, trying to sort this shit out, putting myself on the fucking line, to keep you guys living your lives of fucking leisure. You had nothing to say about this when the money was coming in, Rach. Nothing. *You?* Having to make a compromise? You never spared a thought for where our money came from.'

'I think about it all the time.'

'But you don't, do you?' I sneered, sitting on the arm of our sofa with my arms folded and feeling like the lowest piece of shit. 'You don't care about where the money comes from until it inconveniences you, not until *one* person, aside from you, needs a fucking handout—'

She slapped me. I'd wondered when that was coming.

I didn't even bother to unfold my arms.

Another pause, to hear Ryan move from hallway to bathroom and Chantal walk from bathroom to bedroom and shut the door.

There was something more vicious about the arguments where neither of you could raise your voices, where everything was spat out in whispers and hisses.

'I'm leaving,' she said.

I shrugged. 'You were looking for an excuse anyway.'

'No really, I'm leaving, if you think I'm such a charity case.'

I stood up and walked out, scrawling a smile across my face for the kids. 'You'll be back.'

When she was gone I went into the garden and sat cross-legged on the patio table, bathing in silence. I didn't think I'd felt a real sense of space since I'd been back. There was nowhere to get lost in, within this network of boxes and people to which I'd tied myself. I wanted to take my life by its edges and stretch it beyond recognition, until I could fall into the emptiness between responsibilities.

At the end of the lawn I could see a squirrel hanging upside down trying to get into the array of bird feeders Rachel insisted on putting out. I'd wanted to teach Ryan how to shoot an airgun by practising on the squirrels, but she said it would be inhumane.

I had abandoned them. I'd abandoned everyone, and I'd stopped feeling bad about it.

Without that regret, there was no longer anyone I felt compelled to care about. It was a calming realization; the definition of fucking *Zen*. I no longer felt guilty for not caring about the

Russians, my indifference to Noel's endless problems, Daisy, the neglect of family, of work...

The clouds parted and the sun came out.

I lay on my back smoking.

Maybe it was because he hadn't been home last night, but as soon as my phone started ringing, I knew it was about Eamonn. That's why it took me so long to answer it.

'Is this Mr O'Connell?'

'Yep.'

'This is Brixton police station: we're going to need you to come and pick up your brother.'

'You what?'

'He was brought in last night with two charges of assault, drunk and disorderly and assaulting a police officer. He's sobered up now but we didn't want to put him out onto the street without a lift home, he's...'

'An arsehole?'

'Well... difficult.'

'I need to be at work but I can pick him up on the way. Do I have to pay any bail?'

'No, there's no need. You'll need to make sure he attends his court hearing but that's it. We don't think the other guys involved will be keen on pressing charges.'

'Well, *great*. I'll be there soon.'

'Thank you, sir.'

I hung up, knowing that I didn't have the slightest intention of going to pick Eamonn up from a police station, finished my cigarette and fell asleep in the gentle sunlight for a spell.

CHAPTER FORTY-SEVEN

Daisy

I was surprised when he said he'd come over to Mark's place. He also didn't find it weird that I was living there. Maybe he and Mark had discussed me at some point, in some stilted manly way.

Even more surprising that he'd agreed to a morning visit, before I went to work.

I sat on the edge of the sofa, hugging my knees and watching the minutes open and shut on my phone.

I hadn't slept.

Every time I thought about Eli I forgot more of what he looked like. My brain was repressing his features. As I was falling asleep he kept leaping into my head, with more of his face missing and elongated limbs. If I had my way I'd cover him in petrol and light the fucker up like an abandoned car.

When the buzzer sounded I let him up without even checking who it was, delaying actually seeing him until the very last second.

A knock.

I thought I might throw up on him, but I forced myself to go and answer it.

Nic looked at me and said, 'Hi.'

And I realized he wasn't even fucking nervous.

I didn't know whether to shake hands or hug or what so I just pulled a ridiculous face and went and sat down again. He could have at least had the grace to seem uncomfortable, but he was at work. This was a work meeting, just as I'd fucking described it.

'You said you had something to tell me about Seven?' he said, remaining standing like a cunt.

'You can at least sit down.'

He did, but only a courtesy lean against a chest of drawers. 'Have you really?'

'Really what?'

'Really got something to tell me about Seven?' He said it with this pained tone of voice, like he had uncovered something embarrassing.

It was hard to keep myself under control in face of such arrogance. 'What, you think this is an excuse to see you?'

He shrugged.

He'd cut his hair, I noticed, and grown his stubble out. But there was always something about Nic that was going to remain stunted and teen-like. Sometimes I thought the only reason he'd become a professional killer in the first place was because he was so woeful at dealing with people. Must have been crushing for him to realize that what he did was just another form of customer service.

'Seven's working for this guy called Roman Katz,' I said. 'Heard of him?'

He came forwards and sat facing me on Mark's coffee table. He put down his man-bag and frowned. 'Katz?'

'Yeah. Me and Noel have both seen her.'

'No,' he said. 'Katz, really?'

'Yeah. There's this guy called Sean...' I trailed off. 'I haven't told Mark about it yet.'

A beat, then Nic shook his head. 'No, don't do that.'

'Don't tell him?'

'No. Mark's still in Chicago, he...' Clarity came over his face. 'He was given a tip-off that she was there.'

'From...'

'Katz. He never said it was Katz but it *was* Katz. Who else knows about this?'

'Only Noel and Ronnie but Ronnie's not really around and Noel's just...' I made a vague gesture to indicate another kind of absence.

'Not Edie?'

'We weren't sure what she'd do. Or if she'd even give a toss, y'know.'

'No, you're right.' I could see his mind whirring with info. 'Don't tell anyone else. *Especially* not Mark.'

'I might have... already said to him that I knew something.'

'Just say you were mistaken. He can't know.'

I glanced around the flat. It wouldn't surprise me if Mark had cameras or bugs in here somewhere. In my mind he almost became omniscient at times, able to see through walls and read minds.

'Really, you think Mark can't handle it? I know he's fucking the guy but...'

'I just think you should keep it to yourself for a bit. The more people know, the more space we have to fuck this up.'

It was strange hearing him say the word 'we'.

After a short silence staring at the floor, he looked at me again.

'I know you always said she wouldn't leave London,'

he continued. 'We should have listened to you. I... Yeah, we should have listened to you.'

Nice of him to remember. It was as close to an apology as I was going to get.

'She probably wants to get caught,' I said. 'I know it sounds a bit Psychology 101 but she's not... evil. She's kinda old-fashioned. If you guys came after her for revenge I think she'd actually respect that.'

'She'd still kill any one of us to save her own skin though.'

'Oh yeah. Obvs. She'll feel guilty but she's not stupid.'

'What's she still doing for Katz then?' he mused out loud. 'They'd have just killed her unless she's doing something worthwhile for them and she's only this tiny little girl.'

I raised my eyebrows. 'And you can't think of anything worthwhile a girl might be doing?'

He smiled a little, which was infuriating. 'Come on.'

'Come on, what?'

'Come on.'

'Come on, *what?*'

'It's just unusual, that's all.'

I glared at him until any trace of mirth left his features.

'Forgot about *that* look,' he said quietly, making me redden. 'OK, leave this with me for now. I'll need to speak to Noel and decide what to do about Mark. I can't see him taking this very well.'

His left leg had started jigging up and down.

'Speaking of evil,' I said, to quickly fill the silence, 'have you met Eli?'

'The guy who came back with Ron?'

'Yeah.'

'Not really. In passing.'

'What did you think of him?'

He shrugged. 'You can't make many assumptions about a guy from "Hi".'

'Except you do, all the time.' I grinned. 'You're so fucking judgey, Nic.'

'Judgey McJudgerson, I know.'

He snorted and I started laughing.

I stopped before he did, knowing I wouldn't be able to stand it if he lapsed into silence first. 'Seriously though, this guy is fucked *up*. I don't know why he's here but he's hella bad news, Nic. If you're going to see Noel then please, just fucking humour me, and take a look at him.'

'Are you sure you don't like him because you're also really fucking judgey?'

'Never said I wasn't, eh. But I've got the worst feeling about him. The *worst*. Even thinking about him makes me go all...' I shuddered. 'He's after something.'

'What, money?'

'No, I actually don't think it's that, it's... He's like the sorta guy who would randomly push someone in front of a train on the underground. Not because he planned it but because it would spring into his head that he'd find it funny.'

'That's a very specific vibe to get from someone.'

He picked up his man-bag, leg still twitching. It was restless either as a sign of anxiety or a sign of calm. If he was particularly relaxed in bed he used to rub his feet together and think it was imperceptible. It wasn't. It was one of the loudest and most irritating things a person could do in a silent and darkened room.

Nic must have picked up on the unwelcome invasion of emotion, and stood up.

'Well,' he said, 'you have to admit, those types of people are the ones who keep life interesting.'

I suddenly felt I was about to cry.

Before he left there was a moment, a moment where he paused and I thought he was going to apologize for everything. But he didn't. He looked down at me without words and then he left.

I took some MDMA on the way to work because if I didn't I was gonna spend the whole day crying. But it didn't help; I could feel it as soon as I hit the fresh air. It wasn't going to bring me up, it was gonna do that thing where any jolt, any pang of emotion, was going to be converted straight into anxiety. It went straight to my heart beat rather than to my head.

The first person I saw upon entering the club was Ronnie's little brother, sat in one of the sofa booths eating a bowl of cereal alone.

He waved as I walked in.

My eyes were like rabbit holes. 'What are you doing here? Don't you have a job or something?'

'No, not so much.' A nervous laugh.

I stared at him from behind the bar. I didn't even know where he'd got the fucking Cheerios from. 'Well... if I make you a coffee maybe you can go find one?'

I took the excuse to turn and fiddle with the coffee machine, taking deep breaths.

The clink of a spoon against china.

'Thanks. Just let me know if I'm getting in your way, OK.'

Maybe it was the MDMA making me soft, but I said, 'You're not getting in my way, it's fine. Why are you here so early?'

'Just getting a vibe off Rachel that she doesn't want me around the house so much. Thought I'd come eat here.'

'Maybe Ronnie should stick up for you.'

'It's not like I don't deserve it. I *am* a bit of an asshole. Eli's the only guy who doesn't seem to mind.'

'Like, I don't know what you were in prison for so I don't know what you *can* do, but have you thought about what job you want to do now? Must be weird to be able to think about that again. Is there still a part of you that thinks about being an astronaut and stuff?'

'A bit. Well, the same other stuff I wanted to do when I was young anyway.'

I blinked, hard.

He gestured at me. 'Did you wanna own a nightclub then?'

'What?'

'This is what you must be into, right. Why else would you be in here working like sixteen hours a day unless that was what you wanted to do?'

I'd never given it much thought. 'Um, I don't know. It's a job.'

'Ron said you were like Edie's deputy now.'

'He said that?' My eyes narrowed, unease spreading through my veins. 'Why would you tell me what Ronnie was saying about anything?'

'Because you seem all right, and Ron gets super weird about anyone he thinks is gonna take his stuff. Believe me. I know.'

To avoid any scrutiny, I remembered Eamonn's coffee and made it while trying not to shake, frown, or give any other indication that I'd made sense of what he'd said. It had never seriously occurred to me that Ronnie or Noel could see me as a threat. But maybe Seven had caused them to be a little more suspicious around small young women.

When I crossed the club to give Eamonn his coffee he smiled at me, and I realized he had a black eye and a slightly swollen lip.

He looked like Ronnie, if Ronnie was capable of looking self-deprecating. The one aspect of his personality that had always been missing – as I pointed out to Noel all the time – was any ability to take the piss out of himself. Ronnie went through life with the seriousness of a martyr.

I remembered once, in a club, I'd heard someone say to his mates that Ronnie was 'Too Goodfellas to function'. At first I thought Ronnie hadn't heard the comment. Several minutes later, without a word, he picked up his beer bottle and launched himself at the offender's throat. We ended up running from the police and hiding in someone's front garden until five in the morning.

'I'm sorry,' he said. 'I still don't know how to act around girls, you know.'

'It's fine. You're fine.'

'Thanks, man.' He raised his coffee.

'Can't Ronnie just give you a job? He gave me a job mostly coz of my boyfriend and I was just some nobody. You're his brother, that has to count for something.'

'You only count to Ron when you're useful. I think sometimes he has that Top Trumps vision, y'know, where he looks at someone and just sees this little block of stats.'

I sat opposite him, feeling on the verge of a panic attack. My arms were hot and I could see a rash springing up. That Mandy was whack.

Eamonn stared into his cereal with a remarkable level of desolation.

CHAPTER FORTY-EIGHT

Ronnie

'I don't wanna be harsh, Dad, but he's zero fucking use to anybody. My kids have a higher combined net worth than him and even underage they're *still* more likely to get a fucking job. I'd sooner Ryan come with me on a drop than—'

'Better there than here. The US is a lot more unforgiving, you know that.'

The smell of Thai spices wafted into my study from the kitchen and I shut the door. Downstairs I could hear Ryan and Chantal talking about some kid stuff, something school-related, and Rachel offering advice.

She was still here, because of course she was.

'Noel is no longer useful to you either, you know. You've been saying yourself.'

'That's different. He's my friend and I know he's capable because he's proved it in the past. Eamonn, not so much.' I sat back in my swivel chair opposite my father's face, flickering on Skype. 'He's already getting himself punched in the face. Rachel doesn't want him around—'

'And you're going to let a woman tell you how to conduct yourself with your own family.'

He'd count it as a victory if I hinted at the truth about the state of my marriage right now, so I sniffed and said, 'Rachel *is* my family, and I agree with her.'

'You can't be the only person in London with a spare room.'

'No, but do you have any idea what prices are like here?'

'More than you know, kid.'

'What the fuck is that meant to mean?'

'Don't you *dare* be insolent.'

As we looked at each other, I realized I felt nothing. Not even fear. Not love, certainly.

'You need to deal with Noel,' he said, with a stony expression. 'Whether you like it or not, you need to think about your future without your friend. He'll hold you back.'

'I'm not going to fire my partner just because he's gone through a shit time. We've all made fucking bad decisions.'

'If he was your subordinate you wouldn't even hesitate.'

'Maybe not, but he's not my fucking subordinate. And he wouldn't stand for it, it would be a fucking betrayal and we've had enough of those, from *actual* subordinates.' I opened my desk drawers to see if I had any baccy or gum, but there was nothing. 'Anyway, fuck this, you're not even here, you have no idea how I run my affairs.'

'You know what you have to do, and you have Eli to help you. So listen to him. Don't make yourself trouble you don't need. That's all I have to say.'

If he wasn't my father I'd feel like he was threatening me.

'Well thanks, Dad, it's been real nice talking to you. Give my love to Mum.'

I slammed the laptop shut.

I wondered why it had taken me so long to shut the laptop on him.

My phone started vibrating on the desk and I picked it up, thinking it had to be my father again.

But it was...

'Fuck me, I didn't expect to see you calling!'

Luiz laughed, and the sound reverberated around the inside of the speaker. 'You sound surprised I am still alive!'

'Where the fuck *are* you?'

'I am back in St Louis but leaving soon. I have been back a while now. Sorry. I am sorry I left...'

'No, don't be. He was your friend, you had to go with him. Where is Cathal now?'

'Fuck knows, he disappeared. He left me a note but I don't know if it was him who leave it or... I just came home.'

'So no word from him?'

'No.'

I shook my head. 'I never did work out if he was just crazy or whether there was anything to all that stuff he was working on.'

'Turning things into gold, eh?'

'Yeah.' I snorted. 'I actually almost believed him when he gave me back this spoon.'

'What?'

'I gave him a spoon and just before he left he said he'd turned it into gold. I've never tested it or anything, I don't really know how you'd do that, but I wanted to believe there was something to it.'

'Maybe there is. You know he did the same for me once, with a... I think it was something I stole from a party. He gave it back after a few weeks and it was flat and covered in marks. They were gold but... it is just a colour. So I forgot about it for a while until I met someone who could test the content. It was not entirely gold. But mostly gold.' He paused. 'I never mentioned it to him.'

I didn't know what to say to that.

'Did you find your man?' Luiz asked.

'Trent? Well... No, no we didn't. We might have done. We thought we had.. But it wasn't him.'

'He gone? You give up?'

'Probably.'

'Why?'

'We reached a dead end.' It crossed my mind then, for the first time since being back, that Melissa de Ehrmann lived in London. 'And Eli hasn't mentioned it since. Weird, it almost seems like none of the stuff in LA and Staten Island even happened.'

I wondered if Eli had paid her a visit. She had been on his list, after all, even if the list had just been a veiled attempt at pursuing his own obsession with chaos.

'What went on?'

'It was just... fucked. I don't even know.'

'I'm sorry I wasn't there, man.'

'Well it's good to hear from you, Luiz. Where are you off to now?'

'It's time to move on from St Louis. You don't need people in London, do you?'

I laughed. 'You know what, at any other time I'd take you up on that but I've got way too many fucking people in London right now. Give it a few months, but visit anytime.'

'I might drive up to Santa Cruz, chill for a while. I'm glad you and Eli are OK.'

Eamonn had arrived. I heard the front door and the volume of the voices downstairs increase a few octaves.

'Thanks, Luiz. You too. Gimme a call when you get to Santa Cruz, I could do with a fucking holiday. Maybe I'll come join you.'

'Look me up, man. Keep in touch.'

'Bye, Luiz.'

I put the phone down.

Opening my desk drawers again, I shoved aside a load of random crap – receipts, bags of the things – and found the mangled spoon where I'd unceremoniously shoved it. Picking it up, maybe it did look more golden than before. I held it close to my eyes and tried to believe. I really wanted to fucking believe.

The dead guys in the kitchen had been real.

The Ormus capsules had been real. Eli's ear had healed miraculously.

Cathal was gone now, of his own accord or not, but he had been real.

Trent was gone, and I wasn't sure if he'd existed.

I put the spoon down and stared at it for a while.

'Ron, dinner yo! Eli's here!'

Even through a closed door his voice grated on me.

My phone vibrated and it was a text from Noel, and that grated on me too.

Luiz's voice had been welcome, even in this alien surrounding. It took me back to something familiar.

I picked up the spoon again and put it in my pocket. I almost didn't want to get someone to test it; it was nicer to pretend. It was better to believe I could show my kids something a human had transformed into gold.

Later, when I asked Eli about Melissa over dinner he went very quiet, and started talking to Rachel about the political situation in Burma. I didn't try asking again. He'd either murdered her or he hadn't. I supposed it was none of my business.

CHAPTER FORTY-NINE

Daisy

Edie was in the office. I knew because it was the first fucking day since what felt like the dawn of time that Noel had decided to spend the morning there, and he'd texted me almost immediately.

I arrived about an hour later, around ten, with last night's make-up still gluing my eyes together.

Only Edie was there, making herself a coffee.

'Hey, where's Noel?'

'Morning to you too. He said he had to go out for... something. I think he just doesn't like to have the boss under his feet. You want anything?' She gestured at the machine. 'I'll get out of your way, I have some stuff to go over upstairs.'

'Are you selling?'

As I'd been rehearsing it in my head, I'd added a preamble to try and drag some information out of her by stealth. But standing in front of her now, it seemed childish. She'd appreciate a direct question more than being interrogated by an amateur.

'Let's talk about this upstairs, shall we?'

My heart started beating uncomfortably fast. I felt safe

stood with the bar between us. Any closer and I thought I might have a panic attack.

'Yeah, sure,' I said.

I followed her upstairs, eyeing the bar and wondering if I could get away with downing a shot of anything on the way. But I left it.

When Edie was here, the office was as far from the minimalist boy-space as you could get. There were photos on the desk for a start. BBC 6 Music was playing. A couple of coats and jackets were strewn over the sofa and the backs of chairs like decorative throws.

'So did Noel put you up to this?' she asked. 'Ronnie?'

'Neither actually.'

'But they know.'

'No, I don't think so. But then they haven't been around so... maybe it wouldn't be as apparent to them.'

'I haven't said yes, you know.'

'Yeah...' I sat down slowly, while she remained standing. 'But then instead of saying no and laughing it off you've called me up to your office and started quizzing me about which guy knows what.'

'True.' She half-smiled. 'There's a reason Ronnie's come back from the US with new muscle. You must have noticed, you're not stupid.'

'Eli's a fucking psycho and Ronnie's following suit like it's infectious.'

'You think?'

'He doesn't even talk about his kids any more. You never used to be able to shut him up about them. Now I wish he'd just say something to make me think he's the same guy.' I paused. 'You have kids too, right? Could anything make you stop caring about them?'

'Kid.' That was all she said, correcting me. 'Look, you don't have to worry about this. Your job is secure.'

I swallowed. 'I think I might have to worry. In fact, I think you should be worried because you don't seem to get how bat-shit Eli is. If Ron has brought him back then he must be prepared to put people in the fucking ground, that's all I'm saying.'

'I know.'

'And?' I spread my hands, feeling like I could scream. 'I don't see any fucking muscle here!'

'I don't need muscle. I'm not scared of Eli and the new owner will take care of everything.'

'And who are they?'

'This can never leave this room.'

'*Obvs*. Who is it?'

'Why should I tell you?'

'Because I hate Eli and anyone who's going to get him out of the picture is fine by me.'

'So you don't have any loyalty to Noel or Ronnie?' She stared at me, tapping one of her nails against the desk.

'Well... as long as Noel doesn't get hurt.'

She seemed pained by the idea. 'I like Noel. I've known these boys for years, you think I don't feel affection for them? But they're both off the goddamn rails. Noel's... Noel just needs help. And Ronnie's dangerous. You know he is. You think he wouldn't kill you to make his position more secure?'

'I didn't think so before.'

'We're women, Daisy. We need to protect ourselves. You know we're more likely to be killed by a man than anything else on the planet? You know what kills men most?'

'I don't know, *sharks*?'

'Heart disease.' She sipped her coffee and grimaced. 'Christ, that coffee machine is awful.'

'Who's the new owner?' I asked again.

'His name is Paul O'Connell.'

I hesitated. 'O'Connell. So... Ronnie's...'

'Father.'

'Does Eli know?'

Edie nodded. 'He's known from the start. The reason Ronnie took so long coming back was because Eli was keeping him busy. Eli's not here for Ronnie, he's here for Paul.'

I wasn't sure I bought it, but she sounded so sure.

'So you're banking on Ronnie not wanting to start anything with his own father. That's fucking harsh, but I kinda like it.'

'Paul's flying here tomorrow.'

'Does his brother know? Eamonn?'

'No. As far as I can tell he's irrelevant anyway.'

I felt a pang of something like guilt and wasn't sure why.

'So where are you going to go?' I asked.

'Probably to Manchester; I have places up there and they've been making more money anyhow.' Another sip of coffee. 'You know, if you wanted to come up, start afresh, send me a message.'

'I'll think about it.'

'Well, you'll have to give two months' notice either way.'

'What makes you think Ronnie won't just kill us both?'

'Because he knows there's not enough fatherly love in his family to keep him alive if that was the case.' She smiled her fluorescent perfect smile. 'That's what I was counting on. Paul O'Connell would do anything for a good deal.'

'Was all this your idea?'

A glimmer of pride. 'Yes.'

'So, this thing with Seven—'

'I couldn't give a shit about *Seven*.'

Anything else I was going to say was held back. Telling

her about Katz would only throw another snake into the pit. I'd keep it between me and Nic, for now. Regardless of what Ronnie or Noel wanted, it was bigger than their grievances.

'I need to go... work.' I stood up, hoping it looked purposeful. 'Thanks for filling me in.'

I needed coffee.

Out in the corridor I shook my arms out, taking deep breaths as I went downstairs—

And straight into Eli.

I stopped, dead.

'Morning,' he said, with a nod.

Oddly, he stopped as well.

I was on the higher step, but it didn't make much difference. He still matched my height.

'Just opening up,' I said, arms folded. 'Edie's upstairs.'

'Oh, is she.' He smirked a little. 'Great. You know if the machine's on downstairs I could really do with a—'

I shoved past him and it was like scraping against cold stone. 'Go to hell.'

CHAPTER FIFTY

Ronnie

What was the expected demeanour of someone after they brutally murdered their ex-wife? I supposed it would inflict a kind of sadness alongside the bravado. But Eli didn't really do sadness. Either way, I wanted to know. I had to know if the names on that list had meant anything. I had to meet the voice on the phone.

I asked Nic to track down an address for me and it took him less than nine hours to get back to me by text.

That boy was always worth his fee. I had no idea what kind of fucked-up computer system he and Mark had access to, but it always came good.

Rachel asked, 'Are you home tonight?'

'No, I'm working.'

'Of course.'

She didn't even turn it into a discussion, having lost any shred of interest in what I was doing with my time. This wasn't something we'd experienced before. Apathy was a step down from anger, I knew this. It was much worse to have stopped caring rather than feel the need to fight. Fight meant hope, hope for change, for something better. Without that we had nothing.

I looked at my car keys on the coffee table, thought, *Am I really going to do this? Am I going to overstep this mark?*

I picked up the keys and left the house without any further planning, other than to type Melissa's address into my satnav. Every night here had been so quiet, a post-apocalyptic amount of traffic in the road as if everyone knew something I didn't and had already fled the population centres.

Turning the radio on, I couldn't find any reception. I hit it a couple of times, but nothing.

End times.

It took me twenty-five minutes to reach Melissa's road, near Finsbury Park. I downed the window to get a better look at the house numbers, and heard live guitar on the wind, some gig, the murmur of several thousand people slurring and cheering in unison.

'You have reached your destination.'

I looked for a place to pull over and there wasn't one, so I rounded a corner and left my car at the foot of someone else's driveway. I was only planning to look through one of the windows, see a body and then go home. That's the only thing I could do. Just leave the body there and go home.

There were lights on in the house, maybe upstairs. I could see them through the glass.

I leaned away to eye the window to my immediate right, but saw nothing, so I knocked.

I looked the white terraced house up and down. It'd be hard to access the back windows on a street like this. It would probably involve leaping the fences of a dozen gardens. But I had to know. *There had to be a body.*

The door opened, on a chain, and Melissa de Ehrmann asked, 'Yes?'

I stared at her.

Say something.

Definitely her.

'I'm Ronnie,' I said, showing my hands and staying a good four feet away. 'Ronnie O'Connell.'

She was either a fantastic actress, or my name meant absolutely nothing to her.

'We spoke on the phone.'

'I think you might have the wrong house? Who are you looking for?'

'Melissa...' It definitely *was* her. 'It is you, right?'

'How do you know my name?'

'Melissa de Ehrmann?'

'Yes?'

This time she sounded concerned.

'We spoke on the phone, *loads*. You don't remember?'

She glanced back into the house.

'We spoke about Trent!' I couldn't help but raise my voice. 'Trent Byrne, you were telling me about his niece and how he tried to sue God before she died and...'

It was as if I was speaking Mandarin.

'You really don't know what I'm talking about, do you?'

She shook her head, a little uneasy now. 'I haven't heard anything from Trent for years. Last I heard he was teaching. Are you a friend of his?'

I must have been looking at her like a crazy person, but I couldn't help it. It was so far from the exchange I'd been envisioning. I didn't understand the genuine lack of recognition.

'No, I'm not a friend of his, we were looking for him. He disappeared, years ago. You said—'

'Trent lives in... Lincolnshire.'

'What? But he can't. He got fired in St Louis and... Wait, he lives in *Lincolnshire*?'

The thing in the tunnel.
The thing lying at my feet.
The thing, clawing with sharp faecal hands.
The face in my beam of light.

I frowned at her, put my hand in my pocket and pulled out my phone, as if showing her our method of communication would suddenly jog her memory.

'We talked on the phone.'

Hard eyes. 'I promise you, we didn't. Look, my boyfriend is upstairs—'

'No, you misunderstand me, I don't want any trouble.' I waved a hand, ran it through my hair, trying to find some answer in her face. It was definitely *her* face, her hair, the same voice... 'Did Eli come to see you? Did he put you up to this?'

A pause.

The road, impossibly silent.

Nothing crossed her face. Nothing.

That was why she had married Eli, I realized. They shared that blankness of expression. She didn't want to answer the question, so she didn't.

'I think you should go,' she said.

'No, I will. I...'

I was already backing away before she shut the door on me.

Walking back to the car, I stopped in the middle of the pavement.

No fucking way.

I turned back towards the house, not entirely sure what I wanted to do. The front door didn't look strong, but then none of them were really. If they had the conviction, pretty much anyone could kick a door in. Any *man* anyway. Four walls weren't going to mean a damn thing to someone who wanted to end you.

Without checking if anyone was watching – because let them fucking watch – I braced myself against the wall either side of me and donkey-kicked the thing – *once, twice* – damn near off its hinges. It swung open like it was welcoming an old friend, like this was my house. In a way it was, now.

A scream. 'What are you *doing*!'

Assessing the layout in a second – living room to my left – I saw her stand there, staring at me, and then disappear.

I sprinted into the kitchen after her...

She was tearing a knife from the magnetic rail on the wall...

And I grabbed her around the waist, pinning her arms.

'Drop it!' I snapped.

She kicked and thrashed, barely making a noise, barely making a dent.

'Drop it!'

And she did, eventually. It clattered down next to my feet.

I carried her through to the living room and dumped her on the sofa. She writhed, like a cat, as I turned her over and pinned her there. As the thought crossed my mind – *the thought* – I could rape her and no one would even fucking know, she started laughing, throat heaving under my grip, laughing right in my face.

'What *the fuck* is going on here?'

And as quickly as it had appeared, *the* thought disappeared. Because she was too much like Eli.

She kept laughing.

'Who's Trent?' I shouted, pinning her harder, until she began to choke. 'Tell me where Trent is!'

She went quiet and still, for long enough to make me loosen my hold enough for her to say, 'Which one?'

'Which *what*?'

'Which *question* do you want me to answer?' She started laughing again.

'Shut up!' I slapped her, not hard, but enough to stop the hysterics.

'Or answer your questions? I can't do both.'

'Who's Trent Byrne?'

'He's exactly who you think he is.'

'No. Is he the guy we were following around the fucking *States*?'

She looked up at me, sullen. 'Maybe. Is he the guy you found in Staten Island? No, he's not.'

'You know about Staten Island? So you and Eli have talked.' I frowned. 'Are you still married?'

'Not technically.'

'But…'

'It didn't make much difference to us either way.'

It didn't seem to bother her, conducting this conversation from beneath my knees.

'Did you call me? It *was* you who I was talking to? The things you told me about Trent, they were true?'

'They were true.'

I didn't understand. I didn't even know which questions to ask.

I settled for, 'Aren't you afraid Eli's going to kill you?'

'No more than anyone else should be.' A tiny smile. 'Actually, less so. I don't think anyone else understands him. He knows that. In another life we might have been two halves of the same person.'

'I'd have thought Eli would jump at the chance to kill himself without killing… himself.'

'Maybe. But he finds himself too fascinating. Looking at

me is the only time he can observe himself in action.' A slight roll of the eyes. 'He told me that once. I don't psychoanalyse my husband for sport.'

Feeling that I'd probably spent enough time on top of her, I stood up and let her straighten herself. We sat side by side on the sofa. I took the moment of calm to observe the house. There was something very young about it. Nothing in frames but all leaning and tacked, arranged like stuffed toys on all the surfaces. There were also books everywhere, overspilling onto the floor at the edges of the room.

'How did you and Eli end up married?' I asked.

'I was never shocked by anything he said.' She fluffed her hair. 'He likes to say things to shock people or to scare them, and I just never found it impressive. I always used to say something worse. I think he used that to try and convince himself that I was maybe as insane as he was, but I'm just good with words.'

'So you married him, even though you knew he was insane.'

'Had to be better than marrying someone who wasn't. What a boring life. You're married.'

'What?'

She nodded at my wedding ring.

I looked at it as if I'd never seen it before. 'Yeah.'

'And?'

'Well, Rachel's not insane, no. It isn't what I go for in a woman.'

'More's the pity.'

'I didn't really give it that much thought. I just kinda... Well, my parents always said I should get married to someone who would be a good parent. That was it. You and Eli never had children?'

'*God* no.'

I wasn't prepared for the disgust in her voice; not from a female.

'Have you seen Eli since we've been back?'

She shook her head.

'Does Trent really live in Lincolnshire?'

'Honestly, he could do. He could be anywhere. I just wanted to see if it would make you stay on Eli's crazy train.' When I glanced at her she had also glanced at me, and she smirked. 'You really killed Tom though, didn't you. And Cam.'

'Tom seemed like a prick anyway.'

'No, he... He was just shallow.' She took a deep breath. 'Look, Eli likes to misdirect people, keep them off balance. Think about what he might have wanted to keep you distracted from, and you'll work him out.'

I slicked my hair away from my face. I was almost there. Something – a thought – had almost fallen into place, but it needed one more nudge.

She made a run for it.

'It' was the knife still lying on the floor where it had fallen.

I grabbed her by the back of the neck and slammed her head into the coffee table. The amount of blood left painted against the sharp edge, when she sank to the floor, was definitely enough to be fatal. I wasn't sure she'd be getting back up.

The sudden shot of adrenalin had caused me to start shaking, but my breathing was steady.

There was a mirror on the wall opposite.

I met my own eyes and slicked back my hair again. My edges were harder, more defined, almost glowing with divine intervention.

The front door was still open but I closed it on my way out, leaving behind the body I'd been looking for.

CHAPTER FIFTY-ONE

I could see Eamonn out of the corner of my eye as I helped Chantal finish her maths homework. We hadn't spoken since I'd refused to pick him up from jail.

'So b is equal to...' I gave her a gentle nudge with my shoulder. 'Come on, take your head out of your hands, this isn't torture.'

'I don't *care* what b is.'

I leant my elbow on the dining table and sighed. 'Y'know what, darling, you're right. No one cares what b is. But life is kinda this game where you have to pretend to like things and as long as you pretend to like things and be really good at them, you'll win. That's how you win.'

A replica of my own eyes looked up at me. 'What do you win?'

'Nothing that great, to be honest. Why don't you go to your room, play PlayStation or something, we've had enough of this.' I shut her book for her and kissed her on the forehead.

Eamonn was in the kitchen, on his phone. I could see him through a slit in the door. I had my eye on him as Chantal took the other door out, into the living room and upstairs.

I sat and watched him, through the slit in the door.

Rachel was out for the evening, Ryan was at a sleepover and we were alone.

He took his eyes off his phone for a second. 'I know I'm not staying, Ron.'

'We can't talk about this here,' I said, standing up and barging through the slit to open up the back door. 'Outside.'

He stepped into the hall to grab his hoodie and followed me into the garden. It wasn't as big as my parents' and the trampoline was also smaller.

'Isn't it weird you never got a pet?' Eamonn said, hoisting himself onto the table and resting his feet on one of the benches, facing the house. 'Like, don't your kids want a dog or something?'

I started rolling a cigarette. Even out in the garden I felt starved of fresh air. 'I always said as soon as they can both keep plants alive they're allowed to have a hamster, and if they can keep the hamster alive they can have a cat, and if they can keep that alive they can have a dog. So far they haven't got past the plant.'

'Yeah, but plants are moody little shits.'

I smiled thinly.

'I know you're gonna ask me to go,' he said.

'Eamonn—'

'No, it's fine. It's obvious, I've actually been looking for a new place this week.'

'Find anything?'

'I got some viewings. I need a guarantor though.'

'I can guarantor you, that's fine.'

'Cheers, bro.'

'Not as if anyone else is going to do it. I'm not a total arsehole.' I handed him the cigarette I'd just rolled. 'If you wanted, I was thinking you could run a couple of errands for me over the next few days.'

I felt the energy between us change.

'Don't get too excited,' I said, rolling my eyes. 'You fuck up *once*, you're out.'

'All right, man, don't get too emotional about it, you'll make me cry.'

I looked at him for a long time, with shadows cast across his face, and tried to feel something, tried to feel something, tried to feel... Nothing. I reached into the depths and found nothing. Not even a memory of a feeling.

'Well, Dad has been suggesting it for a while and...' I shrugged.

'Oh *thanks*. Good to know you and Dad sit there talking about me like I'm some fucking baby.'

I rolled my own cigarette and started shivering. 'Get over it, man.'

'I suppose Eli's in on it too.'

'In on *what*?'

'These parent–teacher meetings you got going on.'

I shut my eyes for a while and then looked up at the black sky. 'You know, if you come out here and look up for long enough you can see bats flying from tree to tree. Have you ever even seen a bat before?'

'Course I haven't. There isn't really much nature in jail.'

How sad, I thought, but without actually feeling sad.

I wondered if I could get Eamonn to follow Katz around, or that Sean guy who worked for him. It would probably get him killed, but at least it would be a useful death. But the truth was, I couldn't even trust him with that; I couldn't trust him to get a packet of wine gums from the corner shop without drama.

The doorbell rang weakly from across the garden and I made a laborious show of getting up.

Eamonn flounced away instead. 'I'll get it.'

I thought about Melissa de Ehrmann, mostly because I knew the ring of the doorbell would be Eli. It had been so surprisingly easy to kill her, if I had indeed killed her. It was as if she'd already been hovering at the edge of mortality. I'd killed a few people and some clung on, even if their fingers were the only parts of them left with which to cling. Others just sidestepped out of life like it had always been on the verge.

Eli emerged into the garden looking amused. 'It's hardly summer here, Ronnie. Why are you outside?'

I shrugged again. 'Where's Eamonn?'

'Inside.' He glanced back at the warmth of the kitchen but then came and joined me.

'Do you miss driving through the crazy mid-states?' I asked, with an exhale of smoke.

'I miss it being warm.' He took the seat that Eamonn had vacated, on the table with his feet on the bench.

'But do you miss it?'

'A bit. You?'

'I do actually. I thought it was hell when I was there but it was... Dunno, I find myself thinking about it a lot. It was simpler.' I made a vague wave towards the house. 'Now this all feels like hell.'

Maybe it was a mistake to look at his face, but I swear I saw something like triumph fall across it.

'I've always thought that hell, if it does exist, would look a lot more like heaven than you'd think. It wouldn't really be hell if it couldn't fool you into thinking it was your home for a while.' A long drag. 'Your father is buying your club.'

I looked up and thought I saw a bat flicker across the slightly lighter shade of black.

I didn't hear him at first.

It took a second, or two, and then…

'What did you just say?'

'Your father is buying your club. Edie is selling up.'

'You fucking what?'

'Me fucking nothing. I just thought I should tell you, this is happening.'

My mouth had fallen open, making a mockery of the shock I felt. 'No.'

Eli nodded.

'He can't be.'

He just nodded again.

'How do you know this?'

'He told me. It's been on the agenda for a while. Edie's selling up and she contacted Paul because… well, she knew who he was. They're both American, they both come from the same coast and they have you in common. She got in contact and the rest is history.'

I didn't want to admit how obvious it seemed now. What would fuck me over most? What would turn me into a lesser threat better than my own fucking father?

'What do mean "history"?' I said.

'I mean—'

'When did he tell you?'

'Months ago.' As if it was nothing, he just tossed the two words aside.

Misdirection.

'So you *knew* about this, the whole time we were out there looking for— *Fuck.*' And my cigarette burnt my fingers. I dropped it and stood up. 'Was the whole thing some fucking distraction to keep me out of his way while he bought my life from under me? Fucking *answer* me!'

I grabbed him by the back of the neck and dragged him off the table.

He regained his footing but didn't look perturbed. 'Ron, listen—'

I punched him and his body snapped downwards, blood jetting from his bottom lip. He pulled a face that said *Yeah, ok*.

'Ron, listen,' he said, again. 'I'm telling you now because I think we both want the same thing.'

He spat a mouthful of blood to the side.

'And what's that? Tell me why I shouldn't just fucking kill you where you stand. *Please*. I'm fucking *dying* to hear why.'

But it wasn't him I wanted to kill, it was Dad. It made so much sense now. What a masterstroke from Edie, the lying cunt that she was. I almost had to admire her for it. Not Eli though; Eli might as well have put a gun to his own head.

'Because I can help you take revenge,' he said. 'You know I can.'

I raised my fist and, for once, he retreated.

'Ron!' he snapped. 'You know I can. We're alike, you and me. Fuck, we're the *same*. We could *end* this, we could do it tonight if we wanted.'

'Is he *here*? Is he in the fucking country?'

'No. He's flying in tomorrow.' In a remarkable show of courage, he took my arm. 'Think about it. Really, think about it. We could make an arrival for him he'll never forget.'

I didn't want to kill him any less, but there was something about the look in his eyes that I had faith in. I think it might have been utter madness; sadism that could rival mine.

'We want the same things,' he repeated. 'Think about it. Just think.'

'You sold me out. You helped him sell me out.'

'But I'm selling *him* out now. I'm telling *you* now. I couldn't have told you before, you'd have got yourself killed before you had a chance to return home.' He spread his hands. 'If you want to kill me, then kill me. But you know I can help you.'

I stared, fists clenching and unclenching.

My club.

It was like the world had ended, for a moment.

Eli's eyes were dancing with some insane glee, fixed on me with his startling lack of allegiance.

'Did Eamonn know?' I asked.

'Truthfully' – as if that word made a shred of difference – 'I don't know.'

It didn't matter, I was surprised to note.

I realized Eli's hand was still on my arm, and he didn't take it away.

He smiled. 'Come on. Come on, let's fuck them. Let's burn it to the ground.'

'I killed your wife,' I said, intrigued to see if it would alter his state at all.

Hand still on my arm. 'What?'

'I think I killed your *ex*-wife. Melissa.'

He cast his eyes upwards and said, 'I think I just saw a bat. I don't think I've seen one since I was young.'

'Did you hear what I said? I'm not joking.'

And then he started laughing, as if I'd told the most brilliant joke.

CHAPTER FIFTY-TWO

Daisy

He turned over in his sleep and dragged some of the cover off me, leaving my foot exposed. Without thinking, almost without waking up, I shifted towards him to regain the warmth and he put an arm around me in the darkness.

'I don't even like fishing,' he muttered.

Blinking awake.

I hadn't realized the fucking weirdo talked in his sleep.

'What?' I said, on the off chance that he was awake.

'Fuck fishing. It's wank.'

I started laughing but tried to keep it silent. Looking over at the clock on his bedside table, I saw it was nearing four in the morning. I'd only been asleep for an hour or so, but it felt substantial.

Last night's mascara was hurting my eyes so I sat up and found myself looking down at Noel thinking, *Well this is awkward.* One moment you're just over someone's house for a rant about someone you both hate while Edie was running the Underground for the night, and the next you're saying something utterly ridiculous like 'Hey, if the fucking offer still stands...'

I slid out of bed and put on my underwear to walk to the bathroom, wincing. It was like the muscles around my vagina were cramping. I was surprised Noel still had it in him, given that he'd lived almost exclusively on alcohol and Doritos for the last three months.

I paused.

Exactly how unattractive would it be to be caught straddling a bag of frozen peas in the kitchen at two in the morning?

Too unattractive, I decided, and carried on to the bathroom.

He didn't have any face wipes, because he was a man. So I washed my face instead.

Seeing myself in his mirror now, it was the only time in my life I remembered thinking that I looked older. Still pale, still baby-faced, but there was something there that appeared capable of making a decision now.

I couldn't work out if it was something I'd cultivated myself, or if it was something Edie had put there.

Was she the sort of woman I wanted to be?

Would she stay and work under a man she didn't know? Or would she strike out alone?

I wiped a combination of water and foundation off my face, rinsed it again and buried my face in Noel's only towel. It smelt of him and brought to mind the memory of me biting the skin between his neck and his shoulder barely two hours before, which made me think of Nic, which made me want to get out of there ...

Maybe I could get away with sneaking out while he was still asleep. He probably wouldn't mind. It was just sex after all.

I gave my hair a shake, dressed, checked the clock and then slipped out of his flat to go back to the Underground to oversee closedown. Mostly so that I wouldn't be there when Noel woke up.

★

The fire alarm was going off. I heard it from outside. At least I thought it was the fire alarm... It might have been the security box malfunctioning again.

There was no one outside, none of the girls or bar staff. Not Edie.

It was raining gently.

I went and stood in the front doorway, and I couldn't hear much else from inside. For some reason, survival instinct maybe, I backed out of there and walked around the building to use the staff entrance.

Where was everybody?

Moving through the dressing rooms, I could see that the girls had long gone. No one had stuck around for an after-work drink. I stopped just shy of the door leading out to the bar, and waited. The fire alarm stopped, abruptly. In its absence I could hear banging upstairs, men's voices.

No one in the bar though. I slipped out, looked for the gun we had stashed behind the high-top glasses and checked it had bullets. There were three.

The banging again. Like someone was kicking a door in.

Someone was robbing the place. But if that were the case, why not make off with the cash float? I turned the key in the till and held the drawer closed to stop it springing open. All the money was there, so it wasn't money they were after.

Keeping myself low, I crept along the bar and past the stage to the door to the stairwell. I leant against it just enough to make it open an inch.

One of the voices was Ronnie's.

The other voice was Eli's.

There was a bang, then a shout – a woman – a gunshot.

It was so fucking loud I fell backwards away from the door, straight onto my arse. As I fell there was another shot, and screaming that sounded like...

Edie.

The door had shut. I couldn't be sure they hadn't heard it, so I ran back to the dressing rooms. I could hear activity behind me, the sound of footsteps down stairs, conversation. Light-headed with panic, I hid in the Disabled toilet and locked the door, then unlocked it, then locked it again.

Would it catch their attention if it was engaged?

'Fuck fuck *fuck*.'

I left it unlocked and fell into a crouch, wedged between the toilet and the wall. It was pitch black. I knelt there, too afraid to turn on the light and too afraid to sit in darkness.

They must have come to kill Edie. They'd kill me too.

I put my ear to the door.

Their voices sounded distant, like they were on the club floor.

I reached up, feeling for the light, and pulled the cord.

Too late, I thought of the emergency pull we'd had installed. The emergency pull I'd just triggered.

'*Oh no, shit!*' I cowered, waiting for the alarm to sound.

But the light had come on. The emergency pull was on the other side of the room.

I clapped my hand over my mouth but I knew they would have heard the cry.

As I heard the door to the dressing rooms slam open, I locked the door.

'Daisy? Is that you?'

Tears sprang to my eyes. I couldn't reply. If I didn't say anything they might leave. If I pretended I wasn't there, maybe that would make it true.

One of them tried the door. The handle clicked and caught.

'Daisy? If you come out we won't hurt you.'

'Bull*shit*!'

There was a blast that made my head ring as one of them tried to shoot a bullet through the door, but it held firm. I covered my ears, then remembered the gun in my hand and pointed it upwards, firing a shot at the ceiling.

They went quiet.

'Yeah, I've got a fucking gun!' I was glad they weren't able to see I was crying. 'I'll fucking kill both of you if you try to come in here!'

I felt for my phone in my coat pocket – *Missed Call* from Edie – and dialled 999, putting it on speakerphone.

'*And* I called the police!' I yelled.

The handle jerked again and I shrank away.

'Daisy, open the fucking door!'

Then, much quieter, from Eli this time, 'Daisy… open the door.'

My skin crawled. I felt like I could choke on this fear.

I heard Eli say, 'Look, Edie called the police too. We need to go.'

They paused.

I couldn't breathe.

Could I shoot Ronnie? I thought.

Definitely. Fucking definitely.

I didn't hear anything more from either of them. I put the phone to my ear and managed to whisper the club's address to emergency services, who kept asking for my name over and over again, but otherwise I just waited.

I watched the minutes go by on my phone, ten… fifteen minutes, and then I moved.

I only moved because I could smell smoke.

The fire alarm started blaring again.

The gun was becoming heavy. I unlocked the door, hesitated for a second and then bolted out of the dressing rooms – black smoke billowing across the ceiling – to the back door. It was locked. I tried it again but there was no give. They'd locked me in.

I ran back to the club floor and the smoke was overpowering. I lowered myself until I was hunched over, but the whole place was ablaze. I didn't stand a fucking chance of getting to the main entrance.

Shutting my eyes, opening them, trying not to shut them again, I felt my way over to the bar and climbed over the top of it. I hit the floor on the other side and gulped some air before getting to my feet.

My eyes were streaming. I was still gripping the gun.

Using the bar as a guide, pressing my hip against it, I managed to get near the stage.

It was so fucking hot. I could see the flames from the booths dancing behind my scrunched up eyelids.

I left the bar and pressed my shoulder to the wall on my right, sinking closer and closer to the ground, and managed to find the stairwell. It was still dense, but the air was clear enough in here for me to start heaving for breath.

When I tried to kick open the fire exit it wouldn't budge, as if it had been jammed from outside.

'*No!*' I kicked it harder, rubbing my stinging eyes. '*Fuck!*'

I knew they had left too easily. Now they had sealed me into the burning building and I had given them the time to do it.

Kicking the door for a final time, I gave up and ran up the stairs. The handle had been shot off Edie's office door. I knew they weren't still here, but I held the gun out anyway, supporting it with my other hand, how Nic had always shown me.

I edged into the doorway, blinking sweat out of eyes.

'Edie?'

Pointless.

She was dead, partially hidden by her desk.

I leant against the doorframe. The alarm was doing my head in. I was glad I couldn't see all of her; just her legs. A chair had been overturned. A picture of Ronnie's kids was on the floor, smashed. Bullet holes in the far wall.

It seemed cruel to leave her, but there was no other option.

'Sorry,' I muttered. 'I'm sorry.'

I ran to the end of the corridor and barged out of the other fire escape. It was open. They had forgotten the upstairs exit.

Outside, the misty rain was soothing.

I made my way down the spiral stairs into the alleyway out the back. I could hear sirens, though fuck-load of use they'd be now.

I leant against the wall of the building next door, watching the main road but not venturing out until I saw...

'Nic!'

It looked like him.

It *was* him.

'Nic, over here!'

Blue and red lights across his face. He stopped in the middle of the road, which was being cordoned off, and searched for my voice. When he found me with his eyes, he jogged over.

'Daisy, stay there!'

He was wearing a suit, as he always did when he was playing the role of police officer. He did this by contacting whichever legit officer he was paying-off, who then vouched for him at any crime scene he needed access to.

My first thought was that he looked tired, shaken, handsome. My second was that it was absolutely fucking irrelevant.

I said, 'She's dead. She tried to call me but she's dead. They killed her, she's dead.'

'I know. She called me. She was barricaded in her office.'

He noticed the gun in my hand and took it from me, glancing about before tucking it into the back of his jeans. Then he took me firmly by the arm and led me across the road, away from the Underground, underneath the barriers blocking the street off and around the nearest corner.

'Are you OK?' he asked.

'It was Ronnie.'

'I know.'

'And Eli. They shot her, I heard it. She's dead, she's fucking dead.' I was finding it hard to focus. 'I hid and they chased me but then they tried to lock me in… Ronnie's gone insane, he's fucking lost it, he—'

'When they question you, Daisy, you can't mention that you had a gun or you might be a suspect, OK?'

But Edie was dead. It was all I could think. She was dead and it was so soon after I'd last spoken to her. It didn't seem possible.

'Daisy, you *can't* mention you had a gun or you might be a suspect.'

I didn't quite hear him the first time and he had to repeat himself, giving me a little shake.

'Yes, yeah, I've got it. I didn't have a gun.'

'Are you OK?' he asked again.

'I'm fine, I think.' I looked down at myself. 'I think.'

My throat hurt and I was drenched in sweat. But there was no lasting damage.

'Have you called Noel?' I asked. 'He doesn't know!'

'I called him just after Edie called me, he's on his way.'

'You didn't see Ronnie or Eli when you arrived?'

He shook his head. 'Long gone. They must have chucked some petrol around or something. The place has really gone up.'

I couldn't un-see those dead legs in the office. I thought I was going to throw up and I pressed my palms to my forehead.

'It's OK, they're not going to hurt you,' Nic said.

I glared at him. I wasn't going to say it but I finally did.

'I hate you. I fucking *hate* you.'

'Yeah. I get that.'

And he let go of my shoulders.

Nic had told me once, during a particularly candid discussion of his job, that you always discovered who a person really was when they were about to die. I wondered what sort of person Edie had been.

Statistically, we were more likely to be killed by men than anything else, I thought.

I wondered whether that had crossed her mind.

It didn't take long for Noel to arrive, and the first thing he asked Nic was, 'Can I see it?'

'What?'

'Can I see my club?'

Like it was on the mortuary table.

Nic, in an uncharacteristic show of sincerity, grasped Noel's shoulder. 'Not right now. But give me a while and just sit tight. It's safer for you to stay behind the cordons. I'll call you over when we're... well, *they're*... ready for you to make some statements. But you need to tell me *everything* you know about where Ronnie might be now, or Eli.'

'Ron...' Noel said. 'Fuck. Have the police sent anyone to his house?'

'Not yet, as he's not an official suspect. He won't be there anyway. Can you think of anywhere else he'd go?'

'No, I... No, I've got no fucking clue.' Noel fixed his eyes on me and said, almost accusingly, 'Did you know about this when you left?'

On the spot, I stammered, 'I only came back to close down, I didn't know until I got here. I didn't know.'

Noel didn't say anything. I couldn't imagine what it must have been like for him, coming to terms with this kind of loss; of his best friend and his livelihood in one night. I would have reached out to him but I was too conscious of Nic looking between us.

His gaze moved from me to Noel, and then back to me. I wondered if he could somehow tell that something had happened. But no emotional reaction had crossed his face.

He said, again, 'You're safest here, for the time being.'

For the time being.

'Thanks, Nic,' Noel said, staring in the direction of the Underground, just out of our sight behind the other buildings. 'Let me know when I can see it.'

'Just hang tight.'

Nic ducked below the cordon and walked off.

There was nothing either of us could say, so I took Noel's hand and squeezed a little, because it seemed like the appropriate thing to do. I looked up at the buildings shielding the cremation of our home, as the strobing of the sirens wordlessly struck us over and over again.

CHAPTER FIFTY-THREE

Ronnie

I took him out to Serpentine Lake in the early hours of the morning, where this fictitious pick-up was taking place. We could sit by the water and smoke some weed, I'd said, selling Eamonn the idea; hang out properly and talk, brother to brother. I felt bad for what I'd said earlier.

That's what I said.

And I kept thinking about a line from *Aliens* for some reason, on a loop.

I got a bad feeling about this drop.

Eamonn didn't have a bad feeling about this drop, even after being shaken awake by myself and Eli, both wild-eyed and smelling of gasoline. But then Eamonn so rarely had a bad feeling about anything. Life was just a big sign saying *Free hugs!* to him; an unmanned lemonade stand, a pie left to cool by an open window.

'You all right, bro? You're quiet.'

'Yeah, disco.'

I got a bad feeling about this drop.

We both left the car and walked towards the water, across grass. I was wearing trainers for the first time in my life.

The air was clear and the ground was dry. Even the water was silent. I could see people dotted around, here and there, but it was a Monday night; by far the best evening to attempt to leave the house without bumping into anyone.

Even in the smallest ways, it seemed like Eli had planned this perfectly.

Eamonn was carrying a briefcase with nothing in it because, in his naive way, that's what he thought being a gangster entailed. I knew he wouldn't question it.

'You know, I was beginning to think you'd given up on me, man,' he said. 'Even tonight, earlier. You looked at me like a real piece of shit. Made me feel real low.'

We walked, side by side.

'I can't pretend the thought hadn't occurred to me,' I said, certain I could still smell the scent of Edie's death clinging to my nostrils. 'But I couldn't do that. It'd make me too much like Dad.'

'I was even talking to Daisy the other morning about a room-share.'

'The two of you would probably get along, so long as you didn't try it on with her.'

'Yeah, I bet she'd kick the shit outta me.'

The lake came into view.

It must have been a while since Eamonn had seen a vast expanse of water up close. Flying over the ocean didn't really count.

He bounded to the water's edge, grasped the railings and inhaled. 'Sweet.'

'It's quiet here,' I said.

'Who's this guy we're meeting?'

'Katz,' I said, because it was the first name that came to mind. 'He's this Russian guy we occasionally do business with. I've been running a lot of stock through him recently.'

It was as if I was just making up words.

I leant against the railings next to him and Eamonn was nodding along like he understood everything I was saying.

'In jail we were encouraged to be religious,' he mused, eyes half shut and enjoying the bitter breeze. 'I meant to tell you, coz I thought you'd find it interesting what with your Catholic stuff. It was kinda the only way we were allowed to do anything. The more religious you were the more you were allowed to talk to people, read, work, do stuff. If you didn't buy into this idea of God it was like there was something wrong with you. I think some guys even got years off their sentences because being into Christianity counted as "good behaviour". Isn't that weird?'

'I find it weirder that you're not,' I said, my entire body tingling.

'Na, I think it was you that put me off it.' He grinned at me. 'For real. Some of the stuff you said growing up... You were already so fucking *scared* of everything.'

'You thought I was scared?'

'Yeah. That's why you ran away and got married and had kids and went to church all the time. You did all that safe stuff.'

'I guess I did.'

'But then I went to jail and... fucked everything up.' He hung over the railings, searching for his reflection. 'Maybe it's better to be scared.'

'It makes you more careful.'

'Maybe.'

I took a few paces back, mimicking someone who might have been taking in the scenery. In my mind, I couldn't get enough of the expression on Edie's face as she'd known she was going to die. It filled me with purpose, with conviction.

I was doing the right thing.

'Eh, so when's this guy arriving?' Eamonn asked.

I shot him through the back of the head, caught his weight
as he fell and tipped him over the railings. The silencer hissed,
there was a dull thwack when he hit the surface of the lake,
but other than that there was no sound.

Deaths like these were the most convincing argument for
atheism. If we did have a soul, it shouldn't be able to leave
the world that quietly, leaving the body behind for garbage.
Especially not Eamonn's soul, which had never been able to
enter or exit a room without causing a commotion.

For about fifteen minutes I waited there, for hell or the
afterlife or the ferryman to spit Eamonn back out, bending my
ears with a stream of reproach and complaints. But wherever
he'd gone, I realized, he was staying there. No argument was
forthcoming.

> Therefore we are buried with him by baptism into death: that
> like as Christ was raised up from the dead by the glory of the
> Father, even so we also should walk in newness of life.

Damned as we were, shouldn't we try and save the few souls
we could?

I had no interest in a better place, anyway. Not now. It wasn't
for people like me and Eli.

With heavy footfalls, I turned and walked back to the car,
putting the gun inside my coat.

I opened the boot, took out my bag and shut it.

There was a flash of headlights and I walked towards them.

I circled the other car, slung my bag into the back, and got
into the passenger seat beside Eli.

I expected him to say something, a knee-jerk expression

of condolence perhaps, but there was nothing. He had seen this arrangement coming for months. I wondered if somehow we'd telepathically decided on it in the moments we'd sat in silence, looking in different directions while sitting in the wasteland off Interstate 15, fantasizing that all the things tethering us to society didn't exist.

He'd sat down on the ground.

I'd repressed a laugh.

And that had been the moment we'd decided.

It was only in hindsight that I was able to recognize it.

Eli started the engine.

I rubbed my eyes and face, and started fiddling with the radio.

'Driver picks the music,' Eli said, reversing out of the space.

For a moment the crackle of the static through his speakers sounded like the clapping of an audience, scattered rapturous applause. The voices from the stations were a singular dissenting protest trying to fight their way through and be heard. Then they were cut off entirely, when Eli slid a new CD into the player.

Headlights shone onto the foliage, grass and trees, then the streetlights hit us and we were bathed in gold.

END